KU-876-164

RUNNING RINGS

Also by John McLaren

Press Send
7th Sense
Black Cabs

RUNNING RINGS

by

John McLaren

POCKET
BOOKS

LONDON · SYDNEY · NEW YORK · TOKYO · SINGAPORE · TORONTO

First published in Great Britain by
Simon & Schuster UK Ltd, 2001
The edition first published by Pocket Books, 2002
An imprint of Simon & Schuster UK Ltd
A Viacom company

Copyright © John McLaren, 2001

This book is copyright under the Berne Convention
No reproduction without permission
® and © 1997 Simon & Schuster Inc. All rights reserved
Pocket Books & Design is a registered trademark of
Simon & Schuster Inc.

The right of John McLaren to be identified as author of this work
has been asserted by him in accordance with sections 77 and 78
of the Copyright, Designs and Patents Act, 1988.

1 3 5 7 9 10 8 6 4 2

Simon & Schuster UK Ltd
Africa House
64–78 Kingsway
London WC2B 6AH

www.simonsays.co.uk

Simon & Schuster Australia
Sydney

A CIP catalogue record for this book is available from the
British Library

ISBN 0–7434–1524–8

This book is a work of fiction. Names, characters, places and
incidents are either a product of the author's imagination or are
used fictitiously. Any resemblance to actual people living or dead,
events or locales is entirely coincidental.

Typeset in Palatino by Palimpsest Book Production Limited,
Polmont, Stirlingshire
Printed and bound in Great Britain by
Cox & Wyman Ltd, Reading, Berkshire

whenever I may find her

Acknowledgements

I am greatly indebted to Ian Chapman, Martin Fletcher, Suzanne Baboneau, James Kellow, Glen Saville and Rochelle Venables, and just as much to Jonathan Lloyd, Nick Marston and Robert Bookman. Another key contributor was Peter Fox, who isn't a writer yet, but should be very soon.

Karen Mistry, Miriam Mulcahy, Chris Owen, Emily Stonor and Sally Yap all went far out of their way to help.

A special vote of thanks goes to all associated with Talay Sawan – the loveliest house in the world to write a book – especially Rupert Nicholl and Bee Suwannakul, and also: Krieng Chucharoun, Top Petchai, Aey Plodboot, Nok Plodboot, Tanin Saeton and Anan Udompol.

Many good friends gave their time, their wisdom and their kindness. They include:

Neville Abraham, Peter Barnes, Anthony Branley, Hanna Brightman, Carl Brown, Hilary Browne-Wilkinson, Peter Buckley, Richard Caseby, Jean and Tony Charters, Luisa and David Charters, Edward Chorlton, Andy Embury, Lorne Forsyth, Clement Freud, Paul Graham, Nick Grant-Thorold, Darren Henley, Clive Hilton, David Howe, John Jay, Freya Jonas, Tracy Long, Dena and Gordon McCallum, Margaret McLaren, Emma Sergeant, Anne and Tony Smith, Fleur Strong, Tony Thompson, Lynne Townley, Nigel Williams, Peter Yao.

1

At least it wasn't red. The blue Ferrari flung itself into view seconds after Rupert first caught the snap crackle pop of its exhaust echoing down the Fulham Road. Sod's law decreed there was a space slap bang outside the Brasserie, so that all the pavement brunchers would get full benefit of the spectacle. The car surged past them, braked sharply, and reversed smartly towards the kerb. Rupert's fervent prayer that the driver would balls up the parking went unanswered.

A stocky, friendly-looking man in his early thirties emerged from the car, pressed the zapper to lock it, and grinned broadly as he walked to their table.

'Hi, Rupes, sorry to be late. Hello, Prim.' He bent to kiss her cheek. 'Hey, you've cut your lovely hair.'

She smiled shyly. 'I didn't think I looked enough like a lawyer.'

'Well, it's a pity, but it looks great anyway.'

Rupert brushed one hand through his own floppy gold mane.

'Peter, we were getting hungry, so we already ordered.'

'Okay, give me one second and I'll catch you up.' He glanced at the menu and waved, successfully, for a waiter. 'I'll have the Eggs Benedict, a fresh orange juice, and a filter coffee.' The waiter trotted off. 'So, Rupes, how *are* you? How's the new job at Orbia?'

1

'It's not really new any more. I've been there ten months.'

'Ten months? Christ, time flies. Anyway, you did absolutely the right thing leaving McKinsey. Everyone says working there is as much fun as rowing on a Roman galley. Orbia may still be a management consultancy, but I imagine in a smaller firm they let you have more of a life.'

Rupert's mouth tightened faintly. 'It's not all that different. As a matter of fact, Orbia makes more money per head than McKinsey, which would hardly be the case if we all knocked off at five. Anyway, I thought *you* were the real workaholic. That's what the papers always say.'

'Oh, I just tell them that to keep our shareholders happy. They love to read that my nose is surgically attached to the grindstone.'

'How are things going at *Timbookedtoo*?'

'Not at all bad, actually.' Peter paused while the food was set down before them. 'As you know, like most internet companies, we had a terrible couple of years and our share price got totally trashed. We're back up over four pounds now, and the analysts finally seem to believe that a dotcom *can* be profitable. Bookings for holidays, restaurants and concerts are going through the roof everywhere. We're in twenty-six countries now, and soon we'll be celebrating getting our millionth customer. We're making good money in the UK, Germany and France, and our Tokyo outfit is going like the Bullet Train. So I'm not complaining.'

Peter cut off a large chunk of Benedict and began chewing it happily. Primrose used her fork to indicate the Ferrari.

'Looks to me like you haven't got a lot to complain about. How long have you had that beast?'

Peter grinned shyly, trying not to look too excited about his new toy.

'Three weeks. I'm still getting used to it. You have to take care going over sleeping policemen or you'll rip the whole underside off. But it goes like a bat out of hell.'

Rupert shot a glance at Primrose.

'Peter, as I said in my e-mail, there's something I'd like to discuss. Do you remember, just before I left McKinsey, I showed you a business plan?'

'Some sort of e-commerce play, wasn't it? Whatever happened to that?'

'Market conditions were lousy. I couldn't get it financed.'

'Sorry to hear that. I saw some really amazing plans round that time, and none of them raised a cent.'

'Do you think things are easier now?'

'A little. There's money around for the right ideas with the right management teams. It's no cakewalk, though. There's still a lot of scepticism about the whole sector. Thinking of dusting that idea off, are you?'

'No. I've got another one – something much sexier. A new way of compressing full motion video over the internet. We'll have a more cost-effective solution than anything else that's out there. We've called the company *Invid*. It could be huge.'

'Great. So . . . what can I do to help?'

'We've been going round the venture capitalists, but we're in a classic *Catch* 22. They all say that unless we can get the technology verified by a potential customer, they won't come in. We thought that – assuming you like the idea, of course – *Timbookedtoo* could come in as a corporate investor.'

'Frankly, Rupert, we get tons of approaches like that and we usually pass on them. What's so special about your plan?'

'We'll harness existing technologies, but bolt them together in a particularly smart way. That will reduce the cost and the risk, and make us much faster to market.'

'Who exactly do you mean by "we"? Are you part of this, Prim?'

Rupert answered for her. 'No. She's only here because we're off to my parents' straight after this. I've been working on this for over six months with a pal at Booz Allen. There are two techies pencilled in, who are ready to jump ship just as soon as we get the money. They're top people. What I want to suggest, Peter, is that I take you through the business plan. I've got one right here.'

Rupert fished in a black attaché case and pulled out two copies. He sat forward. 'If we start on page one with the executive summary . . .'

Peter listened patiently till the end.

'So you're looking for five million pounds, right? How much are you expecting from the corporate investor?'

'Two to three million.'

'You know I want to help, but I'm afraid that's out of the question for us. Our shareholders would be furious if we put that sort of cash into a start-up. Sometimes we do agree to endorse a product in return for shares.'

Rupert shook his head agitatedly. 'That won't do it.'

'Then I'm sorry.'

'What about you personally?'

Peter took his time over a sip of coffee. 'Me personally what?'

'Investing. One million, or even half, coming from you would be a powerful statement.'

Peter was cornered. He'd guessed that the brunch would be about this. Several of their mutual friends had warned him that Rupert was doing the rounds with his rattling-can. They had been fairly close friends at Cambridge – that was reason enough to hear Rupert out and show interest, but not to lose lots of money on what sounded like a no-hoper. He shook his head slowly.

'I'd like to, Rupes, really I would, but all my money's tied up in *Timbookedtoo*.'

'I thought the lock-up period was long over. You're free to sell now, aren't you? Your stake must be worth, what, two hundred million?'

'Something like that. But whenever a founder starts selling, everyone else rushes for the door. It sends the wrong signal to the market.'

'You seem to be able to find money when you want to.' Rupert's eyes flicked towards the Ferrari.

'I borrowed from the bank to buy that.'

It was time for Rupert's last roll of the dice. It stuck in his craw, having to go for the emotional appeal. The truth was that the techies they'd lined up had stopped believing that the cash could be raised, and were rapidly losing interest. If he couldn't get the money soon, his dream of riches would be over. Again.

'Look, Peter. You know there were lots of times I

helped you out. When you were getting *Timbookedtoo* going, whose flat did you live in for three months?'

Peter nodded. 'Yours, Rupert, and I was and still am grateful. I hope you haven't forgotten that you had the chance to join. You refused, remember? Said we wouldn't last till our first Christmas. If you had joined, you'd be worth over fifty million on paper.'

'What's done is done. I'm talking *now*. You know very well that you could save our project by raising your little finger. Your bank would let you borrow any amount. What I want to know, Peter, is will you do it?'

The two men caught each other's gaze and held it. Primrose squirmed. She was only there because Rupert sensed that Peter liked her; he thought that her presence might smooth the way to his wallet. Primrose wasn't crazy about being used in that way, and had tried to wriggle out of it. But Rupert had begged and cajoled, and knowing how much *Invid* meant to him after the ignominy of being pushed out of McKinsey, she didn't have the heart to refuse him.

Peter finally answered. 'You've got to realise how the market has changed. When I got my company going six years ago, anyone with a half-decent idea and a half-pound of chutzpah could raise money. It was a positive advantage to have no experience. Now it's back to the past. The companies that get financed and succeed are the ones with great management teams. Don't get me wrong. You have a strong CV – banker, MBA, consultant. But the track records of bankers and consultants when they try to become entrepreneurs isn't great. In your place, I'd want to be the prime mover in pulling it all together, but aim to bring in someone with

6

real management experience to head it up. If you did that, of course I'd be happy to take another look.'

Rupert stuck out his jaw contemptuously. 'And that's your last word?'

Peter nodded curtly. This was quite a stunt to pull in front of Primrose, making him look like a hard-hearted cheapskate. He glanced at his watch. 'I really have to go.' He pulled out a credit card.

Rupert shook his head fiercely. 'Don't worry, Peter. I wouldn't want you wasting your precious money.'

Peter's eyes flashed. He nearly said something, but bit his tongue and stood up.

'Primrose, nice to see you again. Rupert, good luck. I hope you get the money.'

Rupert stared into the middle distance. Peter squeezed Primrose's hand and got up and left. They sat in silence until the Ferrari exploded back into life, executed a neat three-point turn, and roared away from them.

Rupert glared after it. 'Can you *believe* that? After all I did for him! What a selfish, arrogant tosser.'

Primrose kept quiet. Rupert turned towards her. 'And you didn't help, banging on about his penis extension.'

She replied quietly, 'I was just trying to make him happy, that's all.'

'Yeah – worked a treat, didn't it?'

*

Even in high summer, faint mists form over the Channel at night, making ghostly the sudden towering appearance of the big ships that surge down this maritime motorway.

Equipped with only the most ancient navigational

equipment, the knackered old hulk of a coaster pressed half-blindly on through the gloom. On the poorly illuminated little bridge, three men huddled together, peering at the chart. They had only the roughest idea of where they were. There was nothing for it but to head nearer in to try to pick up some bearings. The coaster swung round to starboard.

Soon lights began to appear in the distance. One of the three, a man in his early fifties who passed for a skipper, looked through the binoculars and checked the chart one more time. He straightened the course, keeping two or three miles from land as they chugged further west. Ten minutes later the mobile phone lying beside him rang with an incongruous Bach tune.

'Just west of Sandwich, we reckon . . . Ten, fifteen minutes . . . Okay.' He put down the phone and altered course once again, veering back inshore.

Just outside Dover, two men sat in a Mitsubishi Shogun off-roader. They'd driven around for an hour or more, sent this way and that by the guiding voice on the mobile phone. Now, as instructed, they were parked in a lay-by on the A20.

The phone rang again. The man in the passenger seat answered, listened, and put it down again without a word. In a voice like a concrete mixer, he repeated the instruction. 'St Margaret's Bay.' The driver checked his mirrors carefully, started the engine and pulled out.

A tall, well-built man stepped out of the phone box near Bromley and got back into the BMW parked across the road. In the thin yellow light of the street lamps, he could see a figure approaching. At two in the morning there should have been no one about. A black youth in trainers and woolly hat ambled up, half-glanced at the car, and pulled open the door of the phone box. With the press of a button, the man let his window down and called out to him.

'It don't work.'

The youth swung round. He hadn't realised there was anyone in the car. He looked across, recovered his cool, and went on in.

The man was quickly out of the car and across the street. He wrenched the door open.

'I said, it's out of order.'

'Fuck you, man. It's working okay.'

'I said, it's *bust*. Now piss off and find another one.'

The boy shrugged and loped off, swearing defiantly once he was a safe distance away. The man checked his watch, pulled out a handful of coins, and dialled a number. He spoke with rasping urgency.

'You got to St Margaret's Bay? . . . Okay, carry on through the village and take the road down to the sea. There's a pub on the right. Wait outside it. I'll call again, five minutes.'

He pressed the button to make another call, this time to the boat.

'You near now? . . . Okay, aim further in towards the bay, and get everything ready. Wait till I call one more time before you go in. When you get within about fifty yards, flash the torch five times. They'll do the same with the car lights. Otherwise don't land.'

The Mitsubishi made its way quietly down the steep

9

road to the deserted shore, then to the west end of the bay, where it parked facing out to sea, right in front of the darkened pub. Both men lit up.

They had a hell of a job getting the inflatable down the side of the coaster without tipping it over. All three men were sweating and swearing. After several abortive attempts they got it right, and a skinny guy slithered gingerly over the side, and lent a hand to his much burlier companion who almost capsized the thing as he jumped down into it. Once they were safely aboard, the skipper began passing down plastic-wrapped parcels, and the others stowed them carefully in the bottom of the bobbing craft. Last of all, the skipper handed down the mobile. Casting off, they opened the throttle and headed in towards land.

Now in the moonlight they could easily make out the mass of the headland keeping St Margaret's at arm's length from Dover. The skinny man checked the torch, shining it down against his hand, then flashed it slowly five times. Seconds later they got the blessed answering lights.

The passenger threw his half-smoked cigarette out the window onto the ground.

'Okay, let's get it done.'

The driver started the engine, pulled out of the car park, and eased the lumbering vehicle down over some slippery rocks to the edge of the shingly beach. They watched as the little boat, buzzing like a hornet, cut through the waves. As soon as it beached, they ran the last yards to the water's edge.

Seconds after they had been handed the first few parcels, round the headland came two whining cutters, searing searchlights rearing up from their bows. All four men froze. Then there was another noise, the sound of vehicles screaming down the cliff road to the beach.

The driver was the first to react. He dropped the parcel he was holding and raced back towards the Mitsubishi. The passenger tried to follow, but slipped and crashed down hard on the shingle. The driver glanced back, then up at where three sets of head-lights were now bouncing fast towards him. He jumped into the car, getting it started just as the Land Rovers screeched to a halt, fanned out in front of him, barring the only path out. His only hope was to scatter them or ram a way through. He thumped it into gear.

The men in the inflatable had shoved it back into the water, swung the tiller frantically round, and revved the engine until the nose lifted and it roared back out to sea. In less than a minute the white glare of the cutters' spotlights were almost on them. Both men were using the last precious moments of darkness to jettison the cargo. The big guy yelled out: 'The *phone*. Sling it.'

At that moment it rang, scarcely audibly above the noise of the surf and the whining engine. He screamed again. 'Fuckin' aim it. *Now*.'

It was still ringing as it hit the water.

They threw out more parcels, but there were still a dozen or more remaining when the cutters came up on either side, all but trapping them. A loudhailer assaulted their eardrums.

'Cut the engine.'

The big man, dazzled in the lights, waved a hand in surrender. Under his breath he growled, 'Get ready.' Then he pulled the throttle wide open again, and gained them a few crucial yards. They got the last parcels overboard before they were caught up again. The hailer ordered them to put their hands in the air.

From one of the boats two divers flopped overboard, carrying a battery of powerful underwater lights. They re-emerged two minutes later and held three dripping packages aloft.

The captives were taken on board one of the cutters, and the inflatable was tied behind it, while the other sped off after the disappearing coaster. Even with the old tub's pensionable engines whipped to their geriatric max, the skipper didn't have a hope in hell of outrunning them.

Keeping well away from the road, the passenger had hobbled his way to the side of the pub and started up the steepest section of cliff. Somehow he climbed up sixty feet before daring to look back down to where the Mitsubishi had glanced off the wing of one Land Rover, smashed into a second, and flipped right over. Now they were swinging a light up towards the cliff, yelling and pointing, and running over in his direction. He looked up above him. It was only another fifty feet to the top. Then he heard barking. He scrambled another eight or ten feet, only to slither back five.

His knee gave way and the dog was on him.

* * *

The man in the phone box tried both numbers time and time again. Fuck, fuck, *fuck*. He banged the handset violently back on the machine, pushed the door open and ran over to the car. Then he went in the box again.

Thank God he hadn't broken it. He dialled one last number, said a few words, got back in his car and drove off.

2

At three minutes past seven in the morning, two squad cars pulled up outside *The Gables* in Tinker's Lane, Chislehurst. Detective Chief Inspector Chris Owen of the National Crime Squad walked over to the video intercom at the side of the sturdy wrought-iron gates. He glanced at the extra-high fences that ran all round the property and wondered, not for the first time, how Hill had ever got permission from the council to erect them.

He stubbed his finger on the pad a second time. Two German shepherds appeared as if in answer and stood just inside the gate, howling furiously. A voice came through the crackle.

'What you want?'

'It's me, Ronnie – Chris Owen. Open up.'

'Fuck off. Come back at a decent time.'

'Open up, Ronnie, we've got a warrant.'

'I don't give a monkey's. Come back at nine o'clock. Ten, better still.'

'Open up, I said.'

'Shit. What a load of . . .'

The gates whirred slowly open. The cars drove up the gravel drive to the elaborate porch of the mock-Tudor mansion. By the time they got to the front door, they found it ajar. Owen pushed it open and went inside.

Ronnie Hill, his great barrel of a torso wrapped in a monogrammed dressing gown, was making coffee in the kitchen.

'Hello, Ronnie.'

Hill didn't look up. 'White, two sugars, right?' Owen nodded. 'The rest of your lot ain't gettin' none.'

Owen walked over and picked up the mug. 'Sorry to bother you at such an unsocial hour, Ronnie. I imagine you were expecting us, and I didn't want to keep you waiting.'

'Why's that then?'

'Don't you keep in touch with your sons, then? Thought you lot were thick as thieves.'

'My family affairs are my own business.'

'They're mine too.'

'Chris, it's seven o'clock on fuckin' Sunday. If you got somethin' to say, say it. If not, tell your animals to do their jobs and get out of my 'ouse. Only one thing . . .'

'What's that, Ronnie?'

'I don't want them botherin' Susie. She's asleep, and she'll give me grief all day long if you wake 'er.'

Owen smiled. 'I'll think about it . . . Did you hear we picked Dan up a few hours ago?'

Hill topped up his mug. 'Did you, now? Why was that, then?'

'You lot had a big one going down last night, didn't you? But in case you haven't heard, some fellas you might be acquainted with got themselves locked up in the Tower of London. Nearby, anyway, at Customs House. Know it, do you, Ron? Lower Thames Street. Lovely building. Georgian, I believe.'

'I prefer Tudor.'

'Of course. Yes, from the amount of gear they threw overboard, it must have been two, three hundred kilos. Mix of synths and charlie, probably, but we're guessing it was mainly charlie. That's a *lot* of cocaine. At twenty-five grand a kilo wholesale, that's worth how much? Five million? Street value twenty mill? I'd say whoever owned that lot must be well pissed off this morning.'

Ronnie ran his fingers calmly through his few strands of steel-grey hair. 'So, tell me, Chris. Where'd this go down, then, this coup you're on about?'

'St Margaret's Bay, round the corner from Dover. Pretty spot.'

'You're not sayin' Dan was down there, are you? Last night Dan was with me at Parmigiano's in Bromley. Lee, too.'

'Right old family gathering, eh? What about your daughter? Wasn't she there too?'

'I told you before, Chris, don't you talk about 'er. Ever.'

'Okay, okay. Anyway, you may have been safely tucked up in bed with Susie by the time the fairy carriage turned into a pumpkin, but your boy Dan got a case of insomnia. Went for a bit of a wander. Didn't get home till nearly three.'

'That against the law these days?'

'Got a bit lonely, we reckon. Felt the urge to chat to a few friends, over the phone. Except it seems his mobile wasn't working, and his phone at home must've been out of order too, 'cause we think he was using a call box.' Owen held out his mug for Ronnie to refill it. 'Doing a spot of the old marshalling, p'raps.'

'And are we talkin' about any phone box in particular?' Ronnie was trying not to sound too interested. Owen laughed.

'Don't fret, Ronnie, I'll tell you the score. To be honest, we didn't have a clue. Could've been any phone box within fifty miles of here. But Dan got a bit unlucky. The boys on the boat slung their phone over the side all right, and we all know that divers would never find something that small. As it happens though, the driver on your beach party had a bit of an accident. Bumped his four-by-four up against a couple of Customs vehicles. Hurt his head, and you know what? He didn't have time to get rid of his phone. So we woke up some nice people at the telephone companies and they helped us out.'

'Did they now?' Ronnie knew what was coming next.

'And you know what they found? The beach party's phone got about ten incoming calls from a phone box in Chesterfield Road. That's only, what? Two miles from where Dan lives.'

'So what? Could've been anybody.'

'That's true. But why should "anybody", after making about thirty calls to two mobiles with distinctly dodgy origins, end up making one more call at two twenty-two to a land line registered to a Mr Ronnie Hill?'

'Not the faintest.'

'So you don't recall the phone ringing in the middle of the night? You or Susie must have answered it in your sleep, because someone did so. Anyone else staying here at the moment, Ron?'

'Oh, yeah, there was a call in the middle of the night. Wrong number, it was.'

17

'The call lasted fifty-three seconds. That's a long time for a wrong number.'

'Gave 'im a right volley, didn't I? Wakin' people up at that time. So that all you got, Chris? 'Cause that ain't fuck all, and you know it.'

'We'll get more, don't you worry your pretty head, Ron.'

'All bluff and bollocks.' Ronnie kept a brave face, but he knew they were in trouble this time. If Dan had got it right, there should be no one on the boat or the beach party who knew him. Like always, it had been done using enough middlemen to break the link. The ones who'd been caught were just lowlife mules paid to collect the gear in Rotterdam or on the beach over here and drop it off somewhere safe. That was the beginning and end of their involvement and knowledge. You could never be sure, though. The Old Bill might tell the lowlifes that Dan was involved and persuade them to fit him up in return for a year off their sentences.

There was no point in delaying any more. He always took care to keep nothing at the house. Might as well let the bastards get on with it. With a contemptuous wave of the hand, he gestured to them to begin.

'If they break anything or make a mess it's down to you, Owen.' He jabbed a hard sausage of a finger in the policeman's chest. 'And don't go disturbin' Susie. Oh, and one last thing. Let me see that warrant.'

Owen spoke to a sergeant, who produced it. Hill was looking only for the date and time. Nine p.m. on Saturday night. They hadn't wanted to take a chance on not being able to rouse a magistrate to sign it. Shit, that meant they knew everything in advance. So why hadn't they just followed Dan and picked him up when he left the phone box? Probably because they didn't want to risk him clocking them and calling the whole thing off. Ronnie threw the warrant down on the kitchen table, and without another word took the remains of his coffee out to the sun lounge.

*

The previous afternoon, the aftershocks of the Brasserie encounter had rumbled on in Rupert and Primrose's conversation until they reached the M4. Then, having decided not to put the roof of his Mercedes SLK up for the motorway, they'd ridden in silence, enjoying the warm August sun. Once at Rupert's parents' house in Hampshire, there had been no more chance to be alone until bedtime.

By then they were both utterly pooped. They'd both had wretched weeks. Primrose, who worked for a large City law firm, was involved in a big Continental merger, and Rupert was manacled to a cost-cutting exercise for a telecoms company, Telesys. Apart from being tired, Primrose was upset that Rupert hadn't said sorry, and even if he'd wanted to fool around, she wouldn't have responded immediately. As it was, he kissed her good night, rolled his six foot three frame away from her, and within minutes was snoring.

On Sunday they got up late and sat around downstairs reading the papers. Rupert's father, who'd been chairman of a big City bank, felt strongly that being retired was no excuse for being ill-informed, and always insisted that lunch wait until the Radio 4 news was over. His reaction to the news was equally consistent.

Anything short of the assassination of a head of state meant that 'nothing was happening'. Today's bulletin – new worries about BSE, drought in East Africa, and a drugs bust for the customs near Dover – prompted the usual comment.

After lunch, Rupert took Primrose for a walk. They settled down in the corner of a field, under the shade of a splendidly gnarled oak, and Rupert lay with his head in her lap. Realising that she was acting cool after his flare-up on Saturday, he apologised fulsomely and begged her passionately to forgive him. Before long, Primrose was won round and started stroking his hair.

She just wished that he was like this more often. It was hard to keep up with, let alone match, moods which swung from tender to uncaring, and comments which flipped from the kind to the devastating. At times, like now, he loved to be mothered, while at others he accused her of suffocating him. Sometimes she was unequal to the struggle to compensate for the impact of the loveless childhood that he always said was the key to his psyche. During the year they'd been together, Primrose had walked out on him more than once, resisting for days on end the fusillade of phone calls, flowers, and uninvited appearances. In the end, though, he always got her back, through his charm, his extraordinary persistence, but most of all because she couldn't stop herself responding to his neediness.

It had taken time for her to perceive that part of his character. To most people, Rupert Henley came across as utterly confident and self-assured. At the supper party where they'd met, he'd held the whole table in his grip, cleverer, faster, more amusing than the rest. Right under the noses of two other interested parties, he'd smoothly extracted her e-mail address, made a point of committing it to memory, and had proceeded to bombard her with jokes and cute little questions until she tripped gaily out on their first date. After that the real siege started. Primrose had known other lovers before, but emotionally had stayed safely within her own strong stone walls. This time her battlements crumbled, and she'd fallen headlong in love.

The air was so warm that Primrose grew drowsy, and they dozed blissfully for half an hour before a wasp interrupted Rupert's dreams. He flapped a hand at it, looked at his watch and shook Primrose. He knew his mother would be upset if they got back late for tea.

*

'Where did you go?'

'Only over by Markham Farm. It was lovely. One or two trees were beginning to turn. It was so warm, we lay down in a field and fell asleep.'

Primrose had volunteered to help Rupert's mother make sandwiches and cut cake. Although they'd met five or six times, they hadn't yet got beyond early skirmishes.

'You probably don't get enough rest during the week. You work too hard, Primrose.'

'No more than Rupert.'

'It's different for men. They have to get on. I know girls these days take their careers more seriously but, after all, they can opt out any time they like. Men don't have that choice.'

Primrose decided to let this go and hoped that the subject would change naturally. Mrs Henley, however, wasn't one to give up that easily.

'What does your mother have to say about it?'

'I don't see very much of her.'

'Oh, I'd forgotten. She lives abroad, you said?'

'Gran Canaria. She never comes to England, and I only get out there once or twice a year.'

'That must be hard for her. You, too, I suppose. How old were you when they split up?'

'I was about thirteen when they separated, and fifteen by the time the divorce went through.'

'And neither of them remarried? Once bitten, twice shy, probably . . . You went to St Mary's in Ascot, didn't you? Did your mother go there too?'

'No, Mummy wasn't Catholic then. She converted before they got married. I can't remember where she went to school. My memory's dreadful these days . . . Shall I take the cake through?'

'Give me just one more minute to warm the pot and we'll do it together. I was going to ask you something. It's restaurants your father's in, isn't it?'

'That's one of the things his company does.'

'I hear the restaurant down the road isn't doing too well. You remember – that place we all went to for lunch the last time you came. It would be such a pity if it closed. I don't suppose your father would be interested in buying it?'

'I'll ask him.'

'If he wanted to take a look, you could bring him here afterwards. We'd love to meet him.'

'That's very nice of you, Mrs Henley, and I'll certainly

22

pass that on. He's so busy, I don't see much of him myself.'

'So it seems. Even Rupert hasn't met him yet, has he?'

'I've tried once or twice, but it's never worked out. I must try again.'

'You know, I think that *would* be a good idea. Quite odd, really, to be together for a year and never meet the parents once . . . Now, let's see. I think we have everything. Why don't you take that tray, and I'll take this.'

*

It wasn't until past four that they had their council of war. Ronnie's younger son, Lee, came in his black Porsche, and Jack Price, Ronnie's half-brother, turned up soon afterwards. Jack was a one-off, a former middleweight boxer who, after the bell tolled for the last time, found he had a surprisingly good head for figures and kept a sharp eye on the firm's accounts. If the auditors ever thought about querying the firm's accounting policies, one look from Jack was usually enough to discourage them. They didn't know that more recently a bad road accident had robbed him of much of his strength. It had also taken away his wife and his much-loved only child. All he had left was the firm.

Susie brought through a gold-plated cafetière of coffee and left the three of them to get on with it. Ronnie opened proceedings.

'Weasel's been down there – thinks they'll charge Dan tomorrow.'

The firm's trusted solicitor was Colin Weizler. For

donkey's years no one had called him anything but Weasel.

Lee looked shocked. 'Dan'll get bail, though, won't 'e?'

Ronnie shook his head. 'Weasel says no. They'll go for remand.'

It was Jack Price's turn. 'What about the others? The beach party and the fellas in the boat?'

'They're all lookin' at ten to fifteen. We got to assume that each and every one will sell their own mothers to get anything off that.'

Jack nodded agreement. 'Ron, we need a better idea of what them geezers are sayin'. What about gettin' Weasel to find briefs for 'em? Don't suppose they can afford their own, and we wouldn't want them to take Legal Aid, would we? They need the right sort of advice.'

Ronnie considered. 'Okay, Jack. Get them briefed up. But make sure no one finds out who's payin'.'

Lee pressed his slicked black hair back in the jasmine leather recliner. 'What I wanna know is who grassed us up. I'll fuckin' kill the bastard.'

Ronnie didn't waste his breath replying. What would happen if they found the scum was a given. He moved the conversation on.

'We put down five 'undred grand up front, with three million to pay once we sold the shit. I better go over to Rotterdam in a few days and straighten things out with Fat Boy Dutch. I reckon 'e'll forgive us one million, and give us credit on most of the rest till the next time. We'll need to give 'im some cash, though. Three 'undred, maybe.'

Jack nodded. 'It's the second lot of 'is gear we've lost

24

this year. You don't reckon Fat Boy'll think we're takin' the piss, do you, Ron?'

'It'll be all over the papers tomorrow. I'll take a few cuttings and a copy of the charge sheet if they've done Dan by then. When Fat Boy sees our own flesh and blood got nicked, 'e'll know we're straight up. I can't fuckin' believe the run of luck we've 'ad recently, losing that other gear, problems with fags, the bust-up with them Turks . . .'

Jack nodded. 'Not to mention our little load of Bengalis. Lost another two 'undred large ones on that, we did. Ronnie, you do know we're not in great shape, don't you? Three 'undred grand will just about wipe out our petty cash.'

The phone rang. Ronnie ignored the cordless phone on the table next to him and walked over to a regular handset. Radio waves were too easy to intercept. When he came back over, he looked even more troubled.

'It was Weasel again. Says the Filth's over the moon. Got word from the Dutch police. They've found the geezer what sold Dan the old tub. Next thing they'll be trying to trace that inflatable. Lee, where did Dan get it?'

'I dunno.'

'Then go there tomorrow and ask 'im. Jack, see what you can sort out short term on the money side. I'll drop round and see Maureen. After that miscarriage, it'll devastate 'er if Dan gets a long stretch. What is she? Thirty-five, thirty-six? She could be fifty by the time 'e gets out. And the boys. Six and eight. Don't bear thinkin' about.'

They ended the meeting and the visitors walked out

to their cars. Ronnie saw them off. Lee spun his back wheels, scattering gravel. Jack moved off more sedately, then braked and reversed a few yards. As his Cadillac's window whirred down, he called out to the host.

'Ron . . . Did you tell Rose?'

3

On Monday Rupert went into Orbia's grand offices in Mayfair, which were stuffed to the gunwales with bright young men and women, paramedics on constant standby to minister to sick companies.

For decades now, hiring management consultants had been company bosses' most comfortable option. Costs too high? Get the consultants in to reduce them. Sales flagging? Ask consultants to suggest new types of products. Corporate hierarchy too complex? Have the consultants cut a few layers out. The great thing was that the very act of employing consultants seemed like a bold executive decision itself, and the more they cost, the bolder the decision. The consultants would arrive in comfortingly large numbers, so willing, so industrious, so confident that their advice would be right. And, even if the advice was actually lousy, it would take years for that to show up, and by then a host of other factors could be blamed for the disappointment. Whenever it was time for the sackcloth and ashes to be handed out to the management, it seemed there were never enough spare sets to go round the consultants.

At least with cost-cutting exercises, the results were instantly measurable. Rupert and his team had been camped out at Telesys's headquarters near Reading for weeks. Today they were all back at their own office for a periodic engagement review meeting. Fraser Morrison, the partner on this account, was due to meet the company's Chief Executive, and needed to be updated on where the team had got to. The project had reached a critical stage. After three months of intensive work, beginning with a diagnostic analysis, followed by a study of the specific issues that this kicked up, the team of fourteen were entering a final phase to design the cost-cutting strategy. This was a rich piece of work – mountains of man-hours, which at their charge-out rates of five thousand a day for a partner, three thousand for project manager, fifteen hundred for a consultant, and one thousand for an analyst, would add up to a very juicy invoice.

However, this might be no more than a lucrative start to a really major killing. If the client hired Orbia not only to frame the strategy, but to assist in implementing the cost-cutting programme, the exercise could last for years, with billings that would run to millions. It was Fraser Morrison who had secured this client, having run across its boss at a technology conference, and he was anxious that things should go smoothly. However, he'd been unable to devote a lot of his own time to it, which meant relying very heavily on the project manager, Rupert Henley.

The fact that Rupert had failed to make the grade at McKinsey didn't bother Morrison unduly. Orbia had made a habit of recruiting rejects from the top-tier consultancy companies like McKinsey, Booz Allen, and Bain, and found that they usually did a pretty good job. Having worked for one of them himself, he knew that in those firms once an individual slipped by over a year on the relentless promotion wheel, recovery was nearly impossible. Denied work on the glossier projects, even their successes could seem trivial, and getting personal motivation going again was fearfully hard.

There was no reason why Henley should lack that now. When he'd joined Orbia, he'd been given a strong steer that, if he worked well, a partnership would be his at the end of this year. The firm had thirty-four partners scattered over eight offices across Europe, and continuing expansion and retirements meant that in most years four or five lucky people could be invited to join this exclusive club. Henley was handily placed to be among the chosen ones, and a strong performance on the Telesys project would be a big factor. Even so, it was no slam dunk. Two people in the Munich office had come on strongly in the past months, and one woman in Stockholm would be hard to refuse. Paris, too, had its candidates, not to mention the inevitable bunch of bright-eyed hard triers in the Mayfair headquarters.

The team filed into the conference room and took up their seats. Nine men, five women, with age ranges from twenty-three – a pre-MBA associate – to Rupert Henley at thirty-five. Fraser Morrison came in last, exchanged a few words with one or two individuals, and swept to the middle of the table.

'Okay, Rupert, let's hear it.'

'Thanks, Fraser. Let's begin with an update on what we've accomplished since our last review. We've spent most of the month with the client team drilling down to Telesys's core manufacturing processes, and that's gone well. In terms of greater outsourcing possibilities, we've captured most of the low-hanging fruit, and we're now onto the shorter strokes. We're well through our industry benchmarking, which should help us establish the ideal profile. The main achievement has been getting far greater transparency on the current cost structure.'

'Have the middle management of Telesys co-operated with that?'

'We're still meeting some resistance there. The last few years have taken them by surprise. Essentially, they used to *own* the market, and now they don't. There's a new paradigm developing in their industry, which will demand more innovation, more proprietary solutions. They're poor at responding to this, so we're tailoring a toolkit to help them. Top management have already bought into it, but it may take longer to get acceptance lower down.'

'I'd better raise that with the CEO. What news on the business process redesign?'

Everyone else in the business adored abbreviations and acronyms. Fraser Morrison preferred rolling the whole, perfectly-formed phrases around his mouth. His slow Scottish burr imbued them all with rich meaning. Henley thought it absurdly pompous. He preferred the normal short game and didn't mind showing it.

'The BPR is coming along well, and I think that the client accepts the need for a leaner, more nimble structure.'

'Specifically?'

'We should be able to downsize administrative and management functions by over twenty per cent. The task force on their side now sees eye to eye with us.'

'And I'm confident you're making sure that their

own individual prospects are being handled . . . sensitively?'

'Naturally. Any one of them who proposes eliminating their own post will be reclassified into a surviving job before any cull is announced.'

'So overall relations with the client are satisfactory?'

'Yes. Generally speaking, we're in good shape.'

'Very good. Let's move on to the financials. What's the current projection for improvement on their return on capital employed?'

There he goes again, thought Rupert.

'The ROCE should rise by at least four per cent, assuming that . . .'

The session went on for another three hours. Fraser felt he could go to his meeting in confident mood. Rupert seemed to be doing a good job. There was only one thing Fraser wasn't too sure of, and it was more a matter of style than of substance. In review meetings, more confident project managers would make a point of bringing subordinates in, getting them to present parts of the report, or field the partner's questions. It made them feel more valued, and gave the partner a better sense of the mood of the team. Rupert Henley's approach was the opposite: he always hogged the limelight. Did he just like the sound of his voice, or was he too insecure to spread the credit around? It made Fraser slightly uneasy.

*

When Primrose heard, she thought she would retch. She ran straight to the loo and bolted the cubicle door. On Sunday night, she hadn't gone back to her own place, and had kept her mobile switched off. In her Monday-morning rush, she hadn't checked either phone for messages until she had got to the office.

In recent years she'd gradually been lulled, and no longer felt that dreadful anxiety rush whenever the news mentioned an armed robbery or a drugs bust. Though he never went into detail, her dad always assured her that these days they operated so carefully, and kept so far away from getting their own hands dirty, they were all but immune. He himself hadn't been in trouble since he got out in time for her twenty-first birthday, seven years ago. Dan's stretch in his early twenties now felt like some half-forgotten youthful rite of passage, and although Lee had recently served a few months, it was for something quite minor.

She sat on the toilet seat, terrified. She was scared for Dan and his family, and almost as scared for herself. The fear of being found out had haunted her as long as she could remember, and still played centre-stage in most of her dreams. At Durham University, she had never let any boy get beyond a vague, snoggy friendship, and even later she would not risk spending the night with a man, fearful that some careless sleeping whisper would betray her. Her boyfriends had always been kicked out late at night, drowsily, resentfully. Rupert had been the first to refuse and get away with it. For the first few months with him, she had fought against tiredness, forcing herself to stay awake until he was safely asleep.

What would happen if it came out now that she was from a criminal family? Even if Linklaters couldn't give her the sack, her position might soon be untenable. How could she bear the shame of it, among colleagues, among clients? She'd have no choice but to leave. And what about her friends, from St Mary's, from Durham, and ever since – all those who had accepted her carefully crafted carapace, which in the beginning had protected but later imprisoned her, and now might be blasted to pieces.

How could she have known at thirteen where that first fatal lie would lead her? How, once a fiction was invented, it would build up an insatiable hunger for care and maintenance. Or how hard it would be to file away and remember your very own lies.

As childhood gave way to maturity, she had finally learned to stem the tide of creativity, but had tamed that beast to discover another monster – the questions which lay in wait at suppers and drinks, at lunches and house parties. Questions about family. About what they did, where they lived, where they had gone to school, even tell-tale things like their names? To make matters worse, enquiries from strangers often had to be answered in front of older acquaintances. Would the story always be word-perfect? Would some of the listeners detect little inconsistencies, and wonder? Had some of them worked out the hideous truth long ago, and never told her? She desperately hoped it was not true. And there was no way on earth to find out, without giving the whole wretched game away.

She looked at her watch. She'd better get back. She went by way of the coffee machine and pressed for a double espresso. Her stomach was in such a knot, she could hardly swallow it. She thought of Dan's boys. Those poor darlings. They worshipped their dad. By the time he was free, they would be close to their twenties. In the meantime, they would learn, as she'd had to do, the strange mixture of horror and excitement at visiting him in prison, the look in their father's eyes when he was led away again, the unfathomable, inexplicable moods of their mother, and the depression that would seize her after they'd been there. Maureen was so pretty, so full of bubbly life that she seemed more like a girl in her twenties than a mum in her mid-thirties. Would she grow bitter and resentful, as the last embers of her looks got no more response than lewd whispers in pubs?

If she stayed with him at all, that was. The theory that villains' women stuck by them, voluntarily or otherwise, was a thing of the past. Their own mum hadn't stuck it out, had she? And she was of the generation that was supposed to, if those myths were to be believed. Not that Primrose blamed her, with three kids to bring up, and a burgeoning drink problem to boot. Hardly an easy brood, either. She hadn't been much trouble herself, she hoped, but though Dan was kind-hearted he was always in bother, and as for Lee . . . The little bastard would have made any mother's life a misery. As long as there was someone to clout him it was all right, but when their dad went inside, that vicious streak was given free rein. Dan would sort him out from time to time, but Dan spent most of his teenage time out with his mates, and was rarely there to witness – let alone stop – Lee's kicking, punching, threatening. Smashing his mother's favourite things out of badness. Torturing, then killing the cat. This time, when Primrose got the message and called her dad back, she instinctively prayed it was Lee and not Dan who'd been caught. She simply couldn't stop herself.

Slowly she walked back to her desk and pretended to work on the draft sale and purchase contract that gaped from the screen. How bad would this get? Were the others in jeopardy, too? On the phone her dad had only given her the bare bones. He promised to come up to town that evening to tell her more. In the meantime, she should do nothing, he said.

*

Ronnie Hill stepped into the bar of the Meridien Hotel in Piccadilly and took a good look around. One or two other drinkers glanced up, and quickly averted their gaze. Even when he was trying to act discreet, an air of menace followed him like a shadow.

He ordered a vodka tonic, and settled down in a corner as far away from other tables as possible. He'd got there early to have time to work out how to best handle this. Although the hard facts couldn't be kept from Primrose, he didn't want to rattle her more than necessary. So it was important that he didn't look rattled himself.

This couldn't have happened at a worse time. He found it hard to admit it to himself, let alone anyone else, but his confidence had taken a few knocks recently. He felt he was losing his touch in the business, and he had other worries as well. For so many years, taking no exercise and drinking a lot of brandy had never seemed to matter. He'd always been strong as a horse, and never got ill. Suddenly, a few months ago the problems had started. He got out of puff going up the stairs, and had aches in his back, knees, everywhere. Having long ignored Susie's pleas, he'd finally been persuaded to go for a general check-up, and it didn't go well. His blood pressure and cholesterol were lousy, and the doctor issued all sorts of warnings. Much as Ronnie tried to shrug all this off, it was gnawing at him, siphoning off a lot of his pleasure in life. Before the weekend, he'd felt underpinned by the knowledge that if his powers faded or anything worse happened, Dan could take over. Losing him would kick that crutch right away.

He looked up to see Primrose walking elegantly down the stairs. Her wavy black hair, willowy figure, long legs, and big dark eyes made every man in the bar stop and watch. She came over, kissed him and sat down.

'Hello, Dad. Sorry to be late. Work's busier than ever.'

'Don't worry, love, I understand. You're a credit to me, and your mother. A bloody sight bigger credit than either of us deserve. Still like your job as much as ever?'

'Apart from the hours, I love it.'

'Well, you know if you ever want to change tack, there'll always be a place for you advisin' the firm.'

They both smiled. It was an oft-repeated conversation, their own private bit of banter. He knew perfectly well she'd never do it. Ronnie was prouder than hell of his daughter, and as the years went by, ever gladder that she'd steered well clear of the business.

'Tell me, Dad, how bad is it?'

'Too early to tell, love. There's this copper called

Owen from the National Crime Squad. He's been gunning for us for ages now, trying to find something to put on us. Feels like a family friend, he bothers me so often. This latest bit of business was somethin' between 'im and the Customs. We was totally grassed up, but I ain't got no idea whether it was the Law or the Customs that got the word first. Or who the grass is. *Yet*.'

Primrose reduced her voice to a whisper. 'But was Dan, you know, *involved* in this Dover thing?'

Ronnie said nothing. That was answer enough.

'How much do the police have on him?' No one else in the family ever called them 'the police', and when Primrose was little, they had been 'the Old Bill' to her, like everyone else. Now she felt odd calling them that, as if she was mimicking her own family.

'Quite a lot, probably, or they wouldn't have gone for the charge right away.'

'And he's been remanded in custody?'

'Yeah. Weasel tried to get bail. No joy at all.'

'What about you, Lee and Jack?'

'I don't think they got nothin' on us.'

'What'll you do without Dan, Dad? I know that Jack's a big help, but it's Dan you depend on.'

'I know, love, I know. No choice but to give Lee more say, I suppose. It's what 'e's always been after. Maybe the responsibility'll be the makin' of 'im – cool that temper a bit.'

Primrose kept her thoughts to herself. As far as she was concerned, Lee was a lost cause. She took his hand. 'Poor old Dad.'

'Couldn't've come at a worse time, as it 'appens. Business has been awful recently.'

'Couldn't you ease off for a while?' She knew what the answer would be before she'd finished the question.

'And make all them other bastards think we've gone out of business? No way. Plus, we can't stop right now. We got a cash-flow problem.'

'What about the clubs and restaurants? Can't you milk them more?'

Ronnie's eyes flashed with irritation. 'Rose, you *know* none of 'em makes any money. They're not *meant* to. You're missin' the point altogether.'

'Okay, Dad, sorry. I was just trying to help.'

'I know, I know. We got no option but to struggle on.'

He paused and took a sip. Primrose sneaked a sideways look at him, trying to work out whether she could dare ask now. It was a really bad moment. But if she didn't, Rupert wouldn't forgive her. She decided to go for it.

'Dad . . .'

He knew that voice. 'What?'

'You know Rupert?'

'You told me the name. You know I never get to meet your friends. That's okay. I understand why you're protective of us, really I do, treasure.'

He patted her hand sympathetically. It was a bridge he'd crossed long ago, the price he found too late that he'd paid by sending her to boarding school. Sending her away from all she knew and transforming her into something else. He couldn't stop it hurting a little, though. The world might have strong opinions about him and his like. As for himself, he was proud of what he'd built, the family success, the respect the family got in their own community.

'Dad, I've never been ashamed of you, or any of the rest of the family as people. Or where we all come from. It's what you *do* that I have a problem with.'

'Anyway, what about this Rupert?'

'Well, I know the timing is all wrong, but I'd like to introduce him to you.'

'*What*?' Ronnie was so surprised his tinted glasses almost fell off. 'Why?'

Primrose hesitated, unsure how to say it. She decided to opt for the unvarnished truth.

'One of the reasons I've never brought any boy home before is it wasn't serious. I've always known that if it ever *did* get serious, sooner or later it's something I'd have to do.'

Ronnie looked down at his drink, miffed in spite of himself. 'That's big of you.'

'I'm sorry, Dad, I don't mean to offend you . . . it's not easy.'

Suddenly he swung round and looked her straight in the eye. 'You got yourself engaged and not told your dad?'

Primrose smiled and shook her head. 'No, no, nothing like that. But I do like him, and we've been together for a year. I've met his parents a few times, and he's finding it very odd that he hasn't met you.'

'You told 'im your mother and me split up?'

'Course I have.'

'And that your mother's only friend these days is a bottle of vodka?'

39

'Not that. Not yet, anyway. Thing is, Dad, Rupert's always on about it, and yesterday even his mother had a go at me. I'm beginning to think that it'll only become more of an issue with his whole family, and then get harder and harder to do.'

'So?'

'So I've made up my mind and now I want to get it over with as soon as I can.'

'Ta *very* much.'

'I didn't mean it like that.'

'What if this Rupert don't approve . . . of you comin' from workin'-class stock?'

'It's a chance I'm going to have to take.'

'And the family business?'

'That's different. I'm sure if I told him everything right away, he'd run a mile. But can't I open up with him a little at a time? This is already a big step I'm taking. Hill's a common enough name. Even if he sees anything in the papers about Dan or the firm, there's no reason to make a connection. Maybe later, I'll tell him the rest.'

Ronnie patted her arm again. 'Okay, what d'you want me to do?'

'Meet us for lunch on Saturday or Sunday. Keep mum about the real family business. I've told him you own restaurants and so on. Stick to that.'

'I won't let you down, princess. Make it Sunday. Come down to us. Susie'll knock up some roast beef and I'll open a decent bottle.'

'Dad, does Susie *have* to be there? Can't we keep it just the three of us?'

'For better or worse, Susie's my girlfriend. I can 'ardly

give 'er a fiver and tell 'er to go out and enjoy 'erself, can I now?'

'Course not. Sorry, Dad, I shouldn't have said that. Will you forgive me?'

4

It was past nine by the time Primrose got away from the Meridien. She and Rupert had agreed that they might meet up for supper. She tried his mobile, but it was switched off.

As sometimes happened when things didn't go perfectly to plan, Rupert rather lost interest, and he had made sure he wasn't contactable. There was a bar in Beauchamp Place where he quite liked hanging out on his own. It had a couple of pretty waitresses, and often as not, some equally picturesque customers. In any case he had to go through the most recent draft of the *Invid* business plan, and it was as good a place as any to do it.

The bar was quieter than usual. He chatted to one of the waitresses for a while, and when she finally went off to serve a new customer, he pulled the document out of his briefcase. After a page or two, he found it hard to concentrate. Peter Nicholl had been their last proper hope, and now they were clutching at family straws. Rupert's younger brother, a successful and increasingly fashionable architect, was notoriously tight-fisted and simply not worth asking. His sister had recently got hitched to a ludicrously overpaid banker and she was too nervous to twist his arm so soon. Last weekend, while Prim was helping his mother make tea, Rupert had chatted in the garden with his father and, after offering lavish praise for the climbing roses, had made the pitch. His father had kept right on with his secateurs, muttering something about the inadequacies of his pension plans, the incomprehensible failure of his financial advisers to foresee the stock market's lousy performance, and the additional strain which his daughter's wedding had imposed. Only after Rupert pleaded did he relent to the tune of a miserly fifty thousand.

His friend at Booz Allen had done little better and, even with a few shares that were spoken for by some well-heeled friends, total commitments had only reached a hundred and sixty thousand. That would pay the bills for three to four months, far too little to develop the product sufficiently to convince doubting Thomases, and not nearly enough to tempt the techies away from the warm security of their current jobs.

If *Invid* collapsed, it would be another defeat, another little nail in the coffin of his reputation. Ever since he could remember, Rupert had sensed his father's unspoken disappointment in him. At his failure to get a First at Cambridge, his lack of any real athletic prowess, and his less than stellar few years in banking. Even reinventing himself with his MBA had brought no more than muted approval, and later his father's network had proved too developed to conceal for long the reality of how he had fared at McKinsey. How this contrasted with his parents' ecstatic reaction to the welter of press articles about his younger brother or the successes of his sister's high-flying husband, who was earning millions compared with Rupert's paltry £120,000. To his white-hot irritation he was being typecast as the loser in the family.

It was little different when he was compared with his contemporaries. A hideous number of them seemed to be powering ahead, whether in the media, business, technology, or even government. One of his Cambridge contemporaries was already a junior minister, for God's sake, and three or four of his Marlborough classmates had their own successful companies. It seemed that the world Rupert inhabited was awash with stock options, flotations, and newspaper profiles. Since they'd all passed into their thirties, some of them had begun to amass ritzy possessions: the shockingly large Holland Park villas, the second houses in Tuscany, the Porsches, the yachts. It seemed to Rupert that all their trinkets were arrayed in front of him like a glamorously dressed window at Harrods. And there he was, standing outside in the cold and the rain, his nose pressed hard against the pane.

There was only one other hope left for *Invid*, and a long shot at that. Although Prim was reticent on the subject, it seemed like her dad owned quite a few restaurants. That suggested he was worth a few quid. Whether he would countenance a hi-tech punt, who could tell? But unless he was an unusually hard-hearted father, his only daughter ought to be able to wheedle something out of him. If, for example, he would chuck in half a million, then together with what they already had, there would *just* be enough to get them out of the starting blocks.

Rupert had been on at her for some time about getting to meet the man. That had made it easier to turn up the heat on Sunday night with a well-judged air of terminal sadness, and an expertly aimed dart suggesting he was close to drawing his own conclusion about her lack of seriousness in the relationship. She hadn't actually agreed to anything, but when he detected some softening, he added carrot to stick by switching the subject adroitly to accommodation. Instead of moving into the place she'd just bought in Shepherd's Bush, why not rent that out, and move in with him in Kennington? If this relationship had legs, after all, it might be the natural next step. Again Primrose said little, but her eyes provided their own answer. Instinctively he felt it was time for the kill, and abruptly relapsed back into sad resignation until she officially agreed to think about it. And not only to think about it, but to arrange a meeting with her father sooner rather than later.

Rupert hardly knew himself whether he was serious about Primrose. At thirty-five, he was beginning to get spasms of interest in settling down. Most of his friends had married, and he sometimes felt strangely left out when they started discussing nannies, nursery schools, and Volvos. At the beginning he'd been excited by Primrose's heady combination of looks, sweet, lively personality, and potentially high earning power. After a few months, though, his passion began to wane. That regularly happened to him in relationships, especially if the girl became overly keen. The sex with her had got duller as well. For his taste, Prim was too proper, too much the virgin, too little the whore. Like most management consultants, he spent half his life feeling knackered, and unless there was spice, it was easy to lose interest in the bed part altogether.

45

The truth was that Prim was a curate's egg of a woman. She was good to have around if you were feeling down; with her kindness, her sympathy, she would caress and cuddle your blues away. But when you were on a high, that was the last thing you felt like. She didn't seem to know when to turn down the TLC. Where did that leave her on balance? Was she wife material? It depended a lot on what her family were like. If they weren't sufficiently well bred and heeled, obviously she would rule herself out. If they passed muster on those fronts, maybe, maybe not. He could do worse.

He knew that, with his moods and his flashes of temper, he risked driving her away. So far, whenever she'd flounced out, she'd come back. Probably she always would; she seemed besotted by him. And if he ever pushed her too far, would it really matter, as long as there was someone at least as attractive waiting in the wings?

He drained his second Becks and put the *Invid* paper back in his case. He just wasn't in the mood tonight. He'd spent so much time and effort on it, and so far had damn-all to show for it. He was risking taking his eye off the ball at Orbia, and the less well *Invid* went, the more important his day job became. If getting passed over at McKinsey had been humiliating, failing to make partner at Orbia would be nothing short of disaster. Imagine what his father would say if he was passed over again!

Much as it rankled, he had tried to take to heart the things which had held him back at McKinsey. His annual appraisals there always had the same mix: high scores on application, creativity, and analytical skills; low scores on junior staff management and relationships with clients. Frankly, he reckoned that it was all balls. He knew very well why one or two junior colleagues had rated him poorly. They'd hated him for insisting on getting things right if that meant being a tough taskmaster or assuming more of the burden himself. As far as he was concerned, in the long term it was better for their careers, and certainly better for the firm, than exposing their deficiencies to the harsh gaze of clients. Not that you could expect much gratitude in the short term.

It was a similar story with clients. He had always enjoyed good relations with top management, and made a point of cultivating them. Further down the food chain he tended to get along less easily. Many of them were lazy, obstructive, or plain thick, and ever since childhood, he had been known for his reluctance to suffer fools gladly. Privately, he saw that as more of a virtue than a vice. However, not everyone agreed, and at Orbia he'd resolved to trim his sails accordingly. Until he made partner, anyway.

The decision all turned on Telesys. As long as they looked likely to get the implementation assignment, his promotion should be in the bag, for Orbia would surely never jeopardise the whole thing by risking losing him. It was the uncertainty that was the killer, with the better part of three months to wait. He needed to get someone to mark his card. Although nothing would be official until all the partners gathered together in conclave, surely Fraser Morrison, fresh from his session tomorrow with the CEO of Telesys, would have a pretty good idea. If not, perhaps it was worth hinting that he was being courted by another consultancy. That might be enough to extract a bit more from the windbag Jock, and perhaps tip the balance.

The clock at the back of the bar struck eleven. Time to call Prim and see if she'd delivered.

*

It was on the stroke of eleven that Lee Hill, his girlfriend Michelle, and the rest of his retinue marched past the queue and the bouncers and trotted down the stairs to the deeply fashionable Pacific Bar off Wardour Street.

Tommy, Jack Price's lantern-jawed, twenty-five-year-old nephew, had been deputed to collect Michelle first and then assemble the rest of the gang – three men in their early twenties, all related one way or another to the Hills, and all peas from one bulging pod. They did have names – Mark, Dave and Keith – but the family always called them 'the toe-rags'. It was not far off the truth: they were there to do Lee's dirty work and clean up after him. They in turn liked being around him – for the money, the glamour, the lifestyle and the licence for violence.

That evening they had met first for a quick snort at Lee's place in Docklands. Along with his new Porsche turbo, his flat was his pride and joy. It was covered in black leather and chromium, had electric-powered everything, a kidney-shaped bath with marble surround and, best of all, a broad balcony with a vista from Canary Wharf to the City. He often had parties there, and liked to invite his glitzier friends – celebrity boxers, Chelsea players past and present, and occasionally minor rock stars.

Lee liked to be out every night, and saw no reason to change his habits just because of the business with Dan. With any luck the fella would get off lightly. It was dumb of their dad to depend on him so much anyway. Dan might not be stupid, but he wasn't exactly Brain of Britain either. The very idea that the old man rated Dan above himself was ridiculous. Lee had a bit of a temper, it was true, and Ronnie didn't like that. Always said a short fuse was bad for business. Lee saw it different. Standing up for yourself mattered. It got you respect. All right, Dan was a big guy and could hand it out if he had to, but he was too reluctant, and people took advantage. Maybe Dan doing some time would be good for the family in the long run. It'd give the old man a chance to see what others were made of. For a start, Lee would put his foot down and insist on joining that outing to Rotterdam.

As the six of them marched into the noisy bar, space magically opened up in front of them and one of them got in a bottle of bubbly. Lee drank a silent toast to himself and gave Michelle a big wet kiss. She was looking lovely tonight, he thought, in her off-the-shoulder silver top and her short red skirt. He felt like giving her one then and there.

The first bottle emptied, and then another. It was always hard to hear yourself think in this place, and it didn't help that they were standing next to a bunch of braying Hooray Henrys, probably City bankers celebrating some big deal. Lee looked across at them once or twice.

With a little squeeze and a peck, Michelle went off towards the powder room, having to push past the bankers as she went. Lee watched her go. One of them blocked her way for a moment before letting her pass. Then he made some comment to his mates and they burst out laughing.

Tommy said something to Lee, but he wasn't listening. He was waiting.

Finally Michelle emerged, looking slightly flushed. She looked around, but had no choice but to run the same gauntlet. The dickhead had been keeping an eye open too. As she went by, he put out his hand to slow her, bent down slightly and whispered in her ear. For a second she hesitated, then smiled, shook her head and brushed past him.

When she rejoined the group, she tried to thread her arm back through Lee's, but he pushed her roughly away.

'What's the matter, Lee?'

'Fancy 'im, do you? Want 'im to shag you, do you?'

'Oh please, Lee, *don't*.'

''Cause I bet the wanker wants to shag you. See?' He spun her round. 'The fucker's lookin' at you again. Right, let's find out.'

He dragged her over towards the still guffawing bankers, followed closely by Tommy and the toe-rags. As Lee got closer he fixed his stare on the main miscreant. Suddenly the guy looked like he might wet himself.

'Fancy 'er, do you?'

The poor guy didn't know what to say. His suddenly joyless friends were examining the floor.

50

'Look, I'm terribly sorry if I've caused you offence in some way. Utterly unintentional, I do assure you. We were just celebrating something, and maybe we got a little carried away. Look, can we make a small gesture? How about letting us buy you a bottle of champagne?'

Lee's face relaxed into a broad smile. The man looked mightily relieved, and trotted off. Michelle stopped sobbing, sniffed, and pressed Lee's arm affectionately.

When the bottle was presented, Lee took it, examined the label, and nodded his acknowledgment to the buyer.

'Dom Perignon. Very nice.' Then he upturned it and poured the contents all over him.

Around them, everyone stopped and watched. Michelle had an idea of what was coming next. She was right. Lee swung round on her.

'You. I want more respect from you.'

She closed her eyes as his great scything hand smashed into her cheek. Lee turned to the toe-rags and flicked a thumb in the direction of the champagne victim.

'Take 'im outside. Give 'im a slap.'

The bravest of the bankers had a go, holding on to his drenched friend, who was now shaking uncontrollably. 'Come on now, he *has* apologised.'

'You wanna go too?'

He shook his head. Lee indicated the door. Urine began to dribble from the trouser leg of the victim. One of Lee's men screwed up his face in disgust.

'Fuckin 'ell, 'e's pissed 'isself.'

Lee laughed. 'Don't forget to wipe your shoes afterwards, chaps.'

5

Rupert had e-mailed him more than once, and it wasn't until Wednesday morning that Fraser got back to him. He wandered into Rupert's little glass box and closed the door.

'Sorry, Rupert. Up to my eyes yesterday.'

'How did it go with the head of Telesys?'

'Pretty well, overall.'

'Did he mention the implementation project?'

'No. I'd hoped that he might pre-empt the decision and confirm right away that we're going to get it. I did cast a fly by talking about planning our future resources. Sadly, he didn't rise to the bait.'

Rupert was nervous. Was this the whole story, or was Fraser holding something back? Had anyone at Telesys made some snide criticism of him?

'Did it seem like the team on their side were happy?'

'Oh yes, yes. I'm sure there's nothing to worry about. Would've been nice to know it was in the bag, that's all.'

Rupert couldn't have agreed more. Maybe this wasn't the perfect moment to drop that hint about another job offer, after all. But he did need to know where he stood.

'Fraser, there's something else I'd like to ask. I know my formal appraisal isn't until November, but I'd really appreciate some sense of how I'm doing. When I joined, Paul O'Neill assured me that if I made a good start, I would make partner this year. Ever since then I've been flat out on Telesys, and haven't had a chance to show my paces more generally. Naturally, I'd like to feel that I won't be held back on account of that.'

Fraser nodded thoughtfully, trying to work out how to play this. If he was too downbeat, Henley would go straight back to his desk and phone headhunters. Though far from a star, he would have no problem landing a job elsewhere. Losing him right now would make Orbia look ragged and would probably seal the fate of the implementation project. On the other hand, he had to stop short of an indication that could be thrown back in his face. It would be unwise to build too clear a link with landing the extra Telesys work. The best thing would be to broaden the issue, so there was always an out.

'First of all, let me reassure you that I know where you're coming from. In your position, I'd want the same . . .'

Get on with it, thought Rupert.

'. . . so it's a perfectly legitimate thing to be thinking about. Equally, you must understand that I can't say anything definite. It's a matter for all the partners. What I think I can do is give you some sense of how you might be viewed.'

He stopped to watch Rupert's face. It was twitching with impatience.

'. . . As far as I'm concerned personally, I wouldn't look for more than a continuation of the good work you've been doing. If we get the implementation assignment, in my eyes you'd be home and dry, and even if we don't, you'd be in with a strong shout.'

'Sounds to me like there's a "but" heading this way.'

Fraser smiled. 'Only a small one. Naturally, in a partnership of thirty-four individuals, there's a wide range of views, and some of my partners feel that winning business is as important as executing business . . .'

Rupert went to interrupt. Fraser raised a hand.

'Oh, you don't have to tell me, Rupert. I know you've hardly had time to draw breath, let alone think about bringing in business, so of course it's unfair. All I'm saying is that I can imagine some of the partners – a minority probably – thinking that after you've finished the current phase of Telesys, you should be freed up a bit, and given a chance to operate on a broader canvas.'

'You mean, be held back another year?'

'Conceivably. Merely to be given a chance to show you can do it. As you know, Rupert, our style here at Orbia is basically the same as McKinsey, Bain and Booz. Theoretically, we never pitch for business, both because it looks cheap and so we can always claim to give utterly independent advice. The reality is different, of course, or no consultancy would ever get any work. So we hang out where the decision-makers hang out – at industrial conferences, at economic forums, and on the grander arts and charitable boards – and, hey presto, we get clients. We don't ever call it marketing, but that's what it is. Maybe you would enjoy doing that for a few months.'

Rupert was beginning to look thoroughly irritated. Fraser realised he wasn't getting the tone right.

'I don't want to over-emphasise this. As long as your overall appraisal is good, you can afford to relax. And naturally I'll go into bat for you myself.'

The conversation tailed off after a few more minutes. The moment that Fraser left his room, Rupert picked up the phone to a headhunter and asked about getting an immediate partnership somewhere smaller. However, the man painted so gloomy a picture of life in the little leagues that Rupert got too depressed to act on it immediately. Maybe he'd leave it till after Sunday, and see first how he got on in Chislehurst – wherever that was.

*

As the week wore on, Dan wasn't short of visitors. Weasel, of course, had been there several times, as had Ronnie. Maureen had dumped the boys on her sister and had been in there as much as they'd let her. Lee had shown up early in the week to ask about the inflatable, but on Friday while Ronnie and Jack were across in Holland, he'd thought he'd better put in another appearance.

Neither Lee nor his dad had told Dan what a screaming row they'd had at *The Gables* over that trip to Holland, Lee ranting and raving, the veins on his temples bulging fit to burst when he was denied permission to join them. Despite extreme provocation, at first Ronnie had kept his cool, believing that they had enough problems at present without any more family squabbles. Then Lee picked up a much-loved red cut-glass decanter from the sideboard and flung it at the fireplace, shattering it in smithereens, and Ronnie erupted, force-feeding Lee with a double helping of home truths. Jack Price hadn't seen Ronnie lose his rag so completely for a long time, and had forgotten what it was like to witness this force of nature unleashed. He almost felt sorry for Lee trying to stand in its way.

For Ronnie, the decision to keep Lee away from Rotterdam wasn't a hard one. However much he might now need to lean on his younger son, the first priority was to sort out things with Fat Boy Dutch, to agree a sensible settlement and, above all, to make sure that there would be no interruption to the service or drop in the quality. Fat Boy's own private factory – a genuine pharmaceutical manufacturing plant – had a sideline in making synthetics like ecstasy and speed. He was also a dependable source of cocaine from Colombia, and with the equipment he owned, could run better tests on the charlie than most. After patchy experiences elsewhere, for some time now the Hills had crammed all their eggs in Fat Boy's basket. This wasn't the time to piss him off. He was a bit of a headcase himself, Fat Boy, and all it would take was one stupid comment from Lee to set him off. And that, right now, they didn't need.

It wasn't as if there was nothing else to take care of. Apart from getting straightened out financially and doing whatever they could for Dan, there was the burning issue of who'd grassed them up. After he'd calmed down, Ronnie reminded Lee that he should be worrying most about that. Until they found out who had done it, none of their operations were safe.

Lee reached Belmarsh Prison at ten, made a few cheeky comments to the screws on the way in, and ten minutes later was in a small, square room at one end of a wide table. Remand prisoners were allowed full privacy only with their lawyers. The rest of the time they had to put up with a screw sitting in the corner, either straining his ears or dozing off, depending on how he felt at the time. Either way, any questions had to be coded.

Dan came in, nodded to Lee and sat down. Lee started them off.

'Okay?'

Dan nodded.

'Want a cig?'

'You forgotten? I've given 'em up. Promised Maureen.'

'Food shit as ever?'

'Course.'

'Screws?' Lee looked pointedly at the corner.

'Usual bunch of arse'oles. Specially 'im.'

They both laughed.

'Might need someone to 'elp with the garden. Plant a few flowers, dig some veg, mow the lawn, that sort of thing. Any ideas?'

Dan twigged that he was asking about grasses. He shook his head. Lee pressed on.

'Any foreign fellas spring to mind?'

Dan shook his head again. Fat Boy had no reason to stitch them up. It didn't make sense.

'What about any of the chaps?'

Chaps could have been anyone. It was a term they used all the time to mean their own sort. In this case, Dan understood perfectly well that Lee meant the others who'd been nicked at Dover. Could any of them have been dumb enough to let something slip to some mate?

'Don't think so.'

'What about the little fella?'

During Lee's last visit, Dan had found a way to tell him who had supplied that inflatable – a geezer out of Whitstable, known to them all. A little fella called Jimmy, a petty thief and an unhealthy old bag of skin and bones who owned a scruffy old boat-repair shed there. Dan shook his head.

'The little fella wouldn't know one end of a mower from another.'

Lee got Dan's drift. Jimmy had got hold of the boat for them, that was all. He knew nothing of their plans for it, though he might have guessed.

'Fella could've 'ad other things on his mind.'

Dan scratched his chin. He saw Lee's meaning. If the Old Bill had given the little runt a pull on something else, he might have traded this for a let-off. Jimmy had kept the inflatable safe for them for two weeks. If he'd been picked up around then and given the game away, the Law could have stuck one of those microchip things on it. Then the Old Bill and the Customs could have sat back with their arms crossed, nice mugs of tea in front of them, and watched on a screen as the little dot went over to Holland towed by a car, was loaded onto the tub, and chugged nice and slow back across, giving the bastards plenty of time to follow it round the coast and arrange a welcome-home party. And the little fella himself would be in the clear, wouldn't he? Supplying boats wasn't illegal.

Dan scratched his chin and nodded. 'Could be.'

'Then maybe I'll 'ave a word with 'im.'

'Better ask the old man first.'

That concluded their business, and they moved

smoothly on to football, the horses, and Saturday night's heavyweight bout in Vegas. Dan had kept one watchful eye on the screw. Unless the guy was a hell of an actor, he hadn't taken anything in.

*

On his way out, Lee bumped into Primrose. They greeted each other coolly, and she went in. She had been dreading the moment. It all brought back hideous childhood memories of visiting her dad, seeing him caged and diminished. She'd have given anything never to see the inside of one of these places again. She couldn't abandon Dan, though. Hard case that he was, Dan had always been good to her when they were kids.

They sat for an hour, saying not too much, smiling a little. Like always, he asked when she was taking tea with the Queen. All of the family except Ronnie took the piss out of her accent, but in Dan's case there was never any malice in it. Eventually she stood up and left, promising to come back the next week, and fled into the open air. She headed straight to the Ritz where dear Uncle Frank would give her lunch.

*

He was there early, sitting in the lobby, as immaculately dressed as ever, with his carefully groomed silver hair, and his air of quiet authority. Who could have guessed, looking at him or hearing his cultured voice that, like Ronnie Hill, he was a product of Beaufoy School for Boys in Lambeth, rather than Eton and Balliol?

Frank wasn't her uncle really. He and Ronnie had known each other since Frank had moved to Kennington at the age of nine. His parents had been killed in an air raid a few years before, and after being shunted round sundry relations, he was settled there with his granny. This formidable, steel-haired widow-woman was determined that the boy would get on in life. In spite of his protests and the mockery of his peers, she bullied him into passing enough school exams to get into accountancy, and refused to allow him to adopt the local South London brogue, at least in her hearing. He had good reason to be grateful for her obduracy, and his accountant's qualification and classless tones later proved a launchpad for a successful business career.

Despite their marked difference in speech and academic aptitude, when they met as young boys, Frank and Ronnie quickly became best friends, and had stayed that way ever since. Nowadays Frank lived in Gerrards Cross, none too handy for Chislehurst, and didn't see as much of Ronnie. Not that it mattered. It wasn't one of those friendships that need constant tending.

Years back, what Frank had done for Primrose was amazing. When everything became too much for her mother, and Ronnie, at Her Majesty's Pleasure, decided that boarding school was the only answer for Primrose, a vulnerable, unhappy thirteen year old, it had been Frank who had found a proper Catholic school and, declaring himself as her legal guardian and finessing her parental provenance, persuaded the nuns to take Primrose in, oiling the wheels with a hefty donation to the convent building fund.

When she arrived at St Mary's, Primrose was so overawed she hardly opened her mouth. When she did, she was mimicked by girls who didn't look like her, think like her, speak like her, or act like her. She was isolated and friendless, and she was clutching at straws so desperately that when some of the girls, slightly smitten by the elegant man who came there in his Aston Martin, jumped to the conclusion that he was her father, she didn't disabuse them.

Primrose had never ceased to be special for Frank. He and his wife hadn't been able to have kids, and she became like a surrogate daughter for him. They spoke on the phone almost daily, and the highlight of his month was when they met for lunch. He smiled happily as she approached, took both of her hands in his, and gave her a kiss on the cheek.

'I swear you look more lovely every time I see you.'

'You're not half bad yourself, Uncle Frank. If you weren't married to Molly, I could quite fancy you.'

'Shall we go through then, my dear?'

Primrose smiled and slipped an arm through his. It was a lovely day and he'd booked a table out on the terrace.

'So, Rose, how is he bearing up?'

'Dan's Dan. Never one to be gloomy. He *is* very worried, though. Dad thinks that the police would never have charged him if they weren't confident it would stick. If he's convicted, the judge might make an example of him. You know, organised crime, gangland family, that sort of stuff and hand down twenty years.'

'Does your dad have any idea who was . . . indiscreet?'

'I don't think so. He probably wouldn't tell me anyway. You know the way he likes to keep me at arm's length, to protect me. Doesn't it bother you, Frank, knowing what they get up to?'

'To tell the truth, I don't dwell on it very much.'

'Yes, I suppose we all have our way of coping with it. Odd isn't it, though? The way someone like you can grow up in the very same street as my dad and turn out so different.'

'Takes all sorts.'

'That's true. So how's the property business? Booming?'

'I just signed a big new deal.'

'That's wonderful. Congratulations. Oh, wow, doesn't this look good?'

They paused to settle into their starter. Frank took a mouthful and sighed with contentment.

'Now, Rose, tell me . . . What you were saying on the phone yesterday about Rupert. You're really going through with it?'

'It's all set up for Sunday. Dad's having us over for lunch. I feel so bad – I said the most horrible thing. I was worried that Susie might be the peroxide-bleached straw that broke the camel's back, and asked Dad if we could meet without her. The moment I'd said it, I regretted it.'

'So she will be there?'

'Yes. She's going to cook. Which is kind of her, since she finds it so hard.'

'I know what you mean. Susie could show King Alfred a thing or two . . . Tell me, how much does Rupert know about your background?'

'Nothing yet. The truth is, I keep putting it off.'

'For what it's worth, Rose, my advice is not to worry

too much. If Rupert's half the man I hope he is, he won't judge a book by the cover. Your father's a decent man. Not in the eyes of the law, perhaps, but I've known plenty of pillars of society who I wouldn't trust a tenth as much. And I'll tell you something else. If Rupert does look down his nose, or even *thinks* of dropping you on account of your family, he's not the one for you, and you should think good riddance . . . Having said that, I imagine that your dad's not planning to be overzealous in describing how he made his money?'

'God, no. He's promised to stick firmly to restaurants.'

'I think that's probably wise. Even the most open-minded young man might need time to get accustomed to the idea of being married to the . . . you-know-what.'

Primrose tisked. 'No one's thinking about marriage, Uncle Frank.' The soft twinkling in her eyes was telling a different story. 'I suppose we have talked about moving in together, though.'

'You have now, have you? Where? In this new place of yours in Shepherd's Bush?'

'No. Rupert has his own house he bought last year. Did I never tell you where it is? You'd never guess – Methley Street.'

'Off Cleaver Square – two streets away from where your dad and I grew up? Do they have indoor toilets yet? Very fashionable, I'm told, nowadays. How much did he pay?'

'Seven hundred and forty. Mind you, he has a huge mortgage on it.'

'At the time we lived there we were all tenants, but

when your family moved away in 1970 you could buy any house in Kennington for less than three thousand.'

'Amazing. Anyway, Rupert's talking about me moving in with him there and letting my place out.'

'Is he? . . . Aah, here we are. How I adore Dover sole. Yes, off the bone for me, please. How about you, my dear?'

6

As they approached *The Gables*, Primrose called ahead on the mobile, so the gates were already open and the dogs were making their usual fuss. Rupert looked alarmed. Primrose smiled.

'Don't worry, they don't really bite. Not often anyway.'

As they got out of the car, Ronnie came down the steps, a broad smile on his face.

'Hello, my darlin', 'ow about a nice kiss? . . . You must be Rupert. I'm Ronnie. Now, come on inside. Susie's makin' us a champagne cocktail. That suit you, Rupert?'

'That'd be very nice, um, Ronnie.'

They walked inside.

'Susie, Susie! Where are you? *Susie, love*?' Ronnie was blessed with powerful lungs. 'Oh, there you are.'

'Sorry, sweetie, I was just powderin' my nose.' As she walked towards them, she was still adjusting her hair. 'You must be Rupert. Pleased to meet you.'

Ronnie smiled proudly at her. 'You got them cocktails made, love?'

'I put 'em out in the sun lounge. Thought it'd be nicer there.'

Ronnie and Susie led the way. Primrose gave Rupert's hand a squeeze as they walked. They all found seats, and Susie passed round the gold-plated tray.

Ronnie raised his glass. 'Cheers.'

'Your good health. Thank you, both of you.'

Rupert made a point of showing interest in everything about the area, the house, the potted plants, and the garden. Ronnie answered his questions, with Susie constantly chipping in. No more than half-listening, Rupert sipped the sickly sweet drink, and drank in the situation. What a comical couple. Prim's father, with his crimson trousers, the belt with the oversize buckle, his big yellow shirt unbuttoned halfway to the waist and on the middle finger of his left hand a hideous jaw-breaker of a sovereign ring. And *her*, a riot of designer labels, with her overdone make-up, her tits almost popping out of the Versace-emblazoned top, and a skirt so short you couldn't help watching out for the flash of white knickers every time she crossed or uncrossed her legs.

Rupert kept saying the right things, and made a few little jokes which, once Ronnie had explained them, Susie found hilarious. After she'd mixed herself a second cocktail, she ventured to explain to Rupert that he was very nice indeed, not at all stuck-up like she'd expected. And it was very nice to meet a real Rupert, 'cause she'd always liked Rupert Bear when she was a kid, and didn't know they existed in real life.

Rupert smiled indulgently and asked more thoughtful questions, nodding with evident fascination at every joint answer. Primrose's initial terror began to ebb away and she relaxed enough to volunteer to go to the kitchen with Susie to get the lunch ready. Leaving Rupert alone with her father wasn't such a frightening prospect any more. She wasn't even as bothered as she might have been when, as they left the men behind, Susie whispered much too loudly, 'Never 'eard you call Ronnie "Daddy" before.'

'So, mainly restaurants you're in, is that right, Ronnie?'
  'Yeah.'
  'Anywhere I might have been?'
  'Doubt it. You're always welcome, though. As my guest, course.'
  'Thank you. It's absolutely amazing how the restaurant scene has changed in England, isn't it? Twenty years ago you could hardly get a decent bite. Now we're spoilt for choice. London's the restaurant capital of the world, some people say. Certainly in the same league as New York, San Francisco, Paris, Sydney, Hong Kong.'
  'Could be, could be.' Ronnie had been to Paris. Not to the others.
  'Tough business, I imagine, all the same. Fierce competition. And it must be hard to stop the staff pilfering.'
  'Never 'ad a problem with that.'
  'And is it only restaurants you're in?'
  'Mainly. We got a few night clubs, and a sports club too, plus a sideline in mobile-phone shops.'
  'So that gives you a bit more of a spread.' And hopefully enough cash flow to provide lots of loot for interesting investment opportunities.
  'True. And what's your line of country, Rupert? Rose said you're some kind of adviser to big companies. That right?'
  'Mmmm. I'm something called a "management consultant" and yes, we do advise companies. They're

mainly big ones, but not all. As long as they can afford the fees, we're not too fussy.' He smiled. He was trying hard to sound friendly, approachable.

'Pricey, are they, your fees?'

'Outrageous.'

'Like 'ow much?'

'It varies. What we do is sell time, like accountants and lawyers.'

'And plumbers and electricians.'

'Yes, absolutely. The difference is, if a plumber comes round and it's only a blocked sink, he unblocks it, charges you for one hour and he's gone. Whereas consultants have made an art-form out of selling time in big blocks. Even if we have a pretty good idea of what a client should be doing, it would never do to tell him right away. First we design a process that takes literally thousands of hours. Then at the end we give him the same answer anyway.'

'Is it always like that?'

'I'm exaggerating, of course, but quite often it *is* rather like that.'

'So, what sort of advice is it you give, eh? Must be worth *somethin'*, I suppose, or people wouldn't keep on payin'. They can't all be mugs.'

'Consultancies vary quite a lot. Some concentrate on process, like introducing new IT systems. Then there's firms like the one I started with, McKinsey, which mainly do strategy. You know – what markets a company should be in, what structure it should have, how it can make more money – that sort of thing.'

'And the firm you're with now – what's it called?'

'Orbia. We're a medium-sized firm, but just as good

as McKinsey. It's a bit of a hybrid: equally balanced between strategy and process.'

'What I don't understand, Rupert, is why can't these clients do this for themselves, eh? I mean, surely they understand their own business better than someone like you. No offence intended.'

'Of course, that's usually true. Not always, though. Sometimes they get so close, they can't see the wood for the trees. At other times, they don't have the resources to do all that analytical work themselves. Then there are situations which require a different perspective – the lateral approach . . .'

'What's that?'

'Lateral? You know, sideways. Away from normal channelled thinking.' Rupert could see he was losing Ronnie here. 'And, of course, the top man at the client often knows exactly what conclusion *he* wants, but it suits him for it to have an outside seal of approval.'

'And when you say it's pricey, 'ow much we talkin' about?'

'Hard to say.'

'Go on, give me some idea. Just to satisfy my curiosity.'

'Let me think. On a minimum assignment of, say, three months . . . not less than five hundred thousand.'

Ronnie laughed in astonishment. 'Five 'undred grand, for a bit of advice that you could probably work out for yourself, if you could be bothered? Nice work if you can get it, eh?'

'I'm with you there, Ronnie. Don't forget, though, a lot of our clients who take that advice end up saving far more than that.'

'All the same, money for old rope, if you ask me.'

Rupert couldn't be bothered to argue the toss. Plus, he needed to get onto the other matter before they were dragged away to lunch.

'I agree. So much so, in fact, that I'm thinking seriously about moving out of consultancy myself. Perhaps Primrose told you?'

'No, don't think she did. Won't be easy to find another job that pays as well, I imagine.'

'That's true in terms of salary.'

'As opposed to?'

'Capital gain. The profit when you sell shares. That's where you can make real money. Take high technology, for example. Get the right idea and a company can be worth hundreds of millions in only two or three years.'

'Amazin'. Even more money for old rope.'

'Absolutely. Anyway, that's what I'm thinking of doing. I've got together with a few friends – really clever people – and we're pretty sure we've come up with the best idea for how to have full motion video over the internet. Most current ways are still very clunky. Slow, awkward, jumpy. Others can give a decent image – *if* you have a very fast computer *and* a good connection. Our way should overcome both of those problems at a very competitive price.'

'Lucky you, eh? Rose didn't say anythin' about you bein' a future billionaire.'

Rupert smiled modestly. 'I'm glad to hear it. I'd hate it if she went round shouting about this from the rooftops. It's still a bit hush-hush, actually. We wouldn't want the competition to find out too soon, would we?'

'So when does this thing go on sale?'

'Well, we have to build it first. For the time being, it's only on paper. However, we *have* had it verified – checked – by lots of highly qualified people. Definitely looks like a winner. All we have to do is raise a small amount of capital, and work like billy-o for a year.'

'And this small amount is . . . ?'

'Surprisingly little.'

Rupert was finding it hard to assess Ronnie. He didn't want to under-ask, and then find out that the man wouldn't care whether it was a hundred thousand or five million. He glanced around at the house. Usually you could have a pretty good idea of someone's net worth from the value of their house. If it had been Central London, or Hampshire, or Gloucestershire, he would have known to the nearest hundred thousand what this would fetch. Not that there were many houses like this in Hampshire, thank God. But in Kent? He had no idea. One million, two? It was no help. It would have to be a shot in the dark.

'We believe that it could take as little as two or three million . . .' He watched. It looked like he'd overshot. Better take it down a notch. 'In fact, our most recent calculations show we could maybe get away with one million – which would be great, of course. Who wants to sell more shares than they need to?'

A hint of a smile played round Ronnie's lips. He had an inkling of what was coming. Seemed like Rose's fella was a little bit lively.

'Yeah, Rupert, and since this thing of yours is such a dead cert, you'll be able to raise all the money you need, just like that.'

'No doubt about it. Only thing is, though, what sources of money are the best? We could take the normal sort of finance for hi-tech start-ups. That's called "venture capital". There are two snags with it, though. One is they interfere an awful lot, insisting on having board seats, and generally getting in the way. The other is that, astonishingly, they're often not interested in such small investments.'

'So where do you go, then, to get money?'

'Normally, with a project of about our size, you'd go to individuals who like to have a bit of a punt, and aren't afraid to back their own judgement.'

'Like family, d'you mean?'

'Could be, could be. My father, for instance, is so confident about it, he wanted to do the whole million himself. I wouldn't let him. Indeed, I cut him back to fifty grand. He was furious. No, I want to spread this around a bit more. My dad's rich enough as it is. He'd be insufferable if he had more.' Rupert paused to make sure he was wearing the right, confidently conspiratorial smile. 'No, the most we'd want any one investor to have is maybe half a million. For that he'd get about five per cent of the company.'

'Very reasonable, I'm sure.'

This was the big moment. Rupert felt his throat going dry. 'In fact, since you've been so kind inviting me down today, I was going to ask whether you'd like to take a look at the business-plan yourself?'

'When it comes to things like the internet, Rupert, I don't know my arse from my elbow.' .

'That's all right. Plenty of our other investors are in the same boat. They *do* know it's a big opportunity, that's all. There's no obligation, of course. Shall I pop a copy in the post? Just for your reference.'

'Okay, if you want to. I doubt it's my cup of tea, but I'll take a look.'

'I'll get a copy to you then. You should get it on Tuesday. Come to think of it, it'd be a pity if you liked the look of it and missed the boat, so why don't I send it down tomorrow by courier?'

'Whatever suits you. That sounds like Susie. Shall we go in?'

'Of course.' They both stood up. 'Ronnie, one last thing.'

'What's that?'

'Since Primrose hasn't mentioned my plans to you yet, would you mind keeping our little conversation between the two of us?'

'Course, Rupert, course. I don't believe in mixin' business and women either. Now, you must be ravenous. I 'ope you like your roast beef well done. Susie's family call 'er Cinders, and not without reason.'

*

Back in Rupert's place in Kennington, Primrose made them some tea, while Rupert threw open a few windows to relieve the stuffiness.

'So?'

'So what?'

'Don't play hard to get. What did you think of him?'

'I thought he was . . .' He held it for a moment, to tantalise her all the more. Then he grinned. 'Utterly charming. I really liked him.'

'D'you mean it? Really?' Her eyes were dancing now.

'Yes, I do. Susie's all right too. Not a great cook, but she has nice tits.'

Primrose jumped onto his lap, nearly spilling his tea.

'Watch out, watch out . . .' It was real annoyance which showed in his eyes and voice for a second. Then he got hold of himself again, and it was gone as soon as it came, replaced by that warm, loving smile.

'And you don't mind that my father's not, you know, smart, educated, middle-class?'

'Makes no difference at all. What did you take me for? Some awful Sloaney snob?'

'No, of course not. It was a big deal for me, all the same. Since the age of thirteen, I haven't known who I am or where I fit in . . . Oh, Rupes, I can hardly believe it. I feel such a weight falling off my shoulders.'

Rupert smiled again, that same nice, kind, reassuring smile. It was exactly what she wanted. Excitedly, she jumped up off his lap.

'Tell you what. You know that champagne I brought the other night? It's in the fridge. Let's open it now, to celebrate.'

'Celebrate what?'

'Me outing myself to you. Come on.'

'It's only a quarter past five.'

'Who cares? I'll get it now . . . Is that your mobile?'

'Sounds like it. You fetch some glasses while I answer it.'

Rupert rummaged around, following the sound. He glanced at the little screen to see who it was. His parents' number. He pressed the green button and walked smartly through to the bedroom.

'Hi, Mummy.'

'So?'

'So what?'

'How was he, of course?'

'NQOTD. NBALBC.'

'I know the first part. "Not quite our type, darling", isn't it? What's the second one.'

'Stands for "Not by a long bloody chalk". I just made it up.'

'Oh, I'm so sad for you, darling. Does that mean I have to stop thinking about buying a new hat? How disappointing. And I did like Primrose so much. Poor child. Have you told her yet?'

'Don't be daft, Mother, we only got back twenty minutes ago.'

'Well, I hope you'll be as kind to her as you can in the circumstances. All the same, you mustn't lead her up the garden path. After all, she'll soon be thirty. Oh dear, what a shame. What was their house like?'

'I can't tell you now, she might come in here any moment.'

'Call me tomorrow. I'm simply *dying* to hear more.'

'Okay. I must go.'

'Bye, darling . . . oh, Rupert?'

'What *is* it, Mother?'

'Penny de Montfort came for lunch today, and brought some photos of Lucy. She looked totally different from the way she used to. Lost all that puppy fat, by the look of it. Anyway, she's broken off her engagement with that Charters boy, and, as the estate agents would say, is "unexpectedly back on the market".'

'What's that to do with me?'

'Just thought I'd mention it, that's all. They are an *awfully* nice family.'

'That's her coming. Got to go.'

Primrose knocked gently and opened the bedroom door. 'You coming? The champagne's getting warm.'

'Course. That was my mother. She sends her love.'

'That's nice of her.'

They went through to the sitting room and clinked glasses. After a while Rupert noticed that Primrose had gone quiet again, and was looking out of the window pensively.

'What is it, Prim? Everything's all right now, isn't it?'

'There's one other thing. It's my biggest secret of all.'

'What?'

'If I tell you, you must promise *never* to tell anyone.'

'I promise.'

'When I was sent to boarding school I did the most awful thing. Dad was always so busy. He has this friend called Frank who lived near the school, and used to come and take me out.'

'So?'

'I was sort of embarrassed that my own father never came, so when the other girls assumed that Frank was my dad, I let them believe it. And of course, then I had to keep it up. They all remember him and still ask after him. The long and short of it is that my schoolfriends – like Emily, Alina, Sophie and Tash – all think my father's called Frank Hill, and instead of being chunky and bald, he's tall and slim with lots of lovely silver hair.'

'O what a tangled web we weave, when first we practise to deceive!'

'Not quite my favourite quote.'

'I can imagine. Okay, your secret's safe with me. No Ronnies, no bald pates. Now, enough of your mysteries. Is there anything on TV tonight, or shall we rent a vid?'

7

Jack, Lee and Tommy were summoned to *The Gables* an hour after Rupert and Primrose had left. Weasel was there too, asked to cool his heels in the library, in the company of its many leather-bound, mail-order classics, their handsomely illustrated pages uniformly undisturbed. Ronnie and Jack had only got back from Rotterdam the night before, and it was a while since they'd all spoken. Wherever possible they were avoiding the phone altogether, or using it only for the most basic or cryptic messages.

Holland hadn't gone well. They'd met with Fat Boy on Friday. He'd asked for time to think things over, so they'd stayed on for another chat over lunch on Saturday. Jack did the report.

'It wasn't good. Fat Boy's forgiven us a bit, but we still owe five 'undred grand and we won't get no more supply till the dust settles on this last lot. Ronnie put the pressure on, but 'e wouldn't budge.'

Ronnie added his own commentary. 'Basically, till we can show 'em we've found out who grassed us up, they don't wanna know. Fat Boy's too worried the same'll 'appen again. It ain't only losin' the gear 'e's frettin' about, either. Now the Old Bill's got 'old of that Dutch witness, Fat Boy's wettin' 'isself. Thinks our grass could lead the Dutch Law to 'is own operation. Can't say I blame 'im.'

Lee disagreed. 'Bollocks. What's that old tub got to do with Fat Boy's factory, eh? Tell me that. If you ask me, 'e's takin' the piss. We've been doin' business with 'im for fuckin' *years*. What right 'as Fat Boy got to drop us the moment one little thing goes wrong? If I'd been there, I'd've sorted 'im out, I tell you.'

Tommy looked at Lee admiringly. He'd never heard him stand up to the guv'nor like this before. Ronnie looked less impressed.

'That's one of the reasons I never took you, so shut the fuck up, Lee. We got no choice but to do what 'e wants. All we got to do is find that grass, and that's what I told you to concentrate on while we was away. You find anythin' out?'

Lee, who'd been smarting a second before, smiled smugly. 'Got it worked out, ain't we? Dan and me, that is.'

Ronnie looked puzzled. 'Dan and you what?'

'Well, it was more Dan than me. What Dan reckons is it was that little shite Jimmy, the one what got the inflatable for us.'

'Why?'

'Think about it. Jimmy kept that thing for two fuckin' weeks before Dan picked it up. If 'e grassed on us around then, it would've been easy as pie for the Filth to put one of them tracker devices on it. Up till now, we didn't 'ave Jimmy fingered for a grass, but when you think about it, 'e's the logical one.'

'And Dan figured this out?'

'Yeah.'

'So why didn't 'e tell me or Jack or Weasel, eh?'

'Because two 'eads are smarter than one, that's why. It took a conversation with me.'

Lee knew very well how provocative he was being. He needed to earn back, with interest, the respect he'd lost in Tommy's eyes when he was shouted down a few moments ago. He glanced sideways to check if he had. Tommy sniffed appreciatively.

Ronnie considered. 'Okay, Jack, you better go and 'ave a word with Jimmy.'

Lee started forward in his chair. 'Why should fuckin' Jack get to do it? What's wrong with me, eh? It was *my* idea – mine and Dan's, anyway.'

Ronnie knew he had a point, and if he didn't give his son something to do, he'd go stir crazy.

'Okay, okay. You do it. Only don't fuck up. And I want proof. If 'e done it, bring 'im 'ere.'

'Sure.' Lee was pleased with himself. He looked gloatingly in Jack's direction. 'I'll take Tommy along too.'

Ronnie shrugged. He wasn't bothered either way. Tommy was so pig thick, he made Lee look like Einstein, and he seemed to worship the ground Lee walked on. Mind you, if you told Tommy a bottle of Milk of Magnesia was a god, he'd probably start worshipping that too. Ronnie had better things to think about.

'Jack, if we go quiet for a while, we'll 'ave to make ends meet in other ways. If the restaurants and clubs ain't required to recycle cash for the next few months, we'll need to take a closer look at them.'

'You're tellin' me. If you put their laundry services aside, they cost us over four 'undred grand a month.'

'I know. Can't they make a profit, like what other restaurants do?'

'We've never thought about that before. Never needed to. I'll ask around and see if anyone knows 'ow.'

'Gettin' some more payin' customers wouldn't be a bad start. Whatever we do, let's do it fast. Get new chefs, advertise, raise the prices – I dunno. I don't know fuck all about restaurants.'

'Me neither.'

'Well, find someone who does. If you can't, let me know. I got an idea.'

'What's that?'

'Never mind. I wanna think a bit more about it . . . Right, let's get back on to Dan's case and see what Weasel's got to say. Lee, go and get 'im.'

Lee gestured to Tommy with his thumb and sent him scurrying off instead. Ronnie thought about yelling at Lee, but decided against it.

*

Once they'd found which boozer he was in, Lee and Tommy sat outside in the Vectra they'd borrowed. Whitstable could be rough in places, and Lee didn't like leaving the Porsche unattended at night. There were other reasons too why it wouldn't have made sense to use it.

If it had been Saturday, Jimmy would have propped up the bar until the last minute. As it was, all his mates had buggered off home by nine-thirty, so he bored the publican for another half hour before wandering out into the warm night.

They waited to make sure he was definitely on his own, then started the car and cruised up alongside him. As he heard the car stop, Jimmy turned towards them.

Lee's window was already open.

'Hello, Jimmy.'

Jimmy had to look carefully before he recognised him. 'Oh it's you.' Jimmy wasn't sure he liked any of the Hills. Specially not this one.

'How're you keepin', Jimmy?'

'Mustn't grumble. Sorry to 'ear about your brother.'

'Yeah, Dan's not too thrilled 'isself . . . Can we give you a lift anywhere?'

Jimmy looked nervous. Whatever this was about, he knew he didn't like it. After he heard that Dan Hill had got nicked, he'd been half-expecting to hear from the Old Bill. Even the Filth were easier to handle than psychopaths like Lee.

He glanced back at the pub, to see if he could make a run for it. It was fifty yards away. He'd never manage it. Lee had read his mind.

'Don't even think of it. Get in.'

Lee reached behind him and swung a rear door open. Jimmy was still considering his options. Right now he didn't have many. Better see what this was about, and worry what he could do about it later. He got in.

'What you want with me, anyway? I ain't done nothin'.'

Lee turned round and looked at him. 'Course you ain't. We want a little favour, that's all.'

'What sort of favour?'

'A boat. We want another boat.'

'What kind of boat?'

'Don't matter too much. Inflatable, maybe. Anything with an engine.'

'Okay, I'll fix it. When for?'

'Tonight.'

'*Tonight?*'

'Yeah. What you got in your yard?'

'There's an old wooden dinghy with an outboard. If I were you I wouldn't want to use it for any cross-Channel stuff, though.'

'What about closer to land? Could it take us from 'ere to Deal, for instance?'

'Should be all right.'

'Good. I'd like a test drive. Can you take us out for a turn?'

'What, *now*? You can take it yourselves. Money back if you don't like it.'

'No, we want you to come with us. Tommy and me ain't very good at this sailin' lark, are we, Tom? We'd feel a lot safer if you was there too, know what I mean?'

Jimmy liked this even less, but what could he do about it? Lee was probably carrying, and even if he wasn't, he would have his trademark Stanley knife with him. Riling him would be fatal.

'Okay, okay.'

They drove down to the little yard. Jimmy had to clear things away, rig up a navigation light, top up the petrol, and hook the boat to a trailer to carry it down to the waterline. It took the better part of half an hour. They'd checked that he had no mobile on him, and Tommy watched like a hawk in case he tried to make a break for it or call on the land line. They wouldn't even let him go to the bog, in case he was thinking of doing a runner out the back window. Lee told him to piss right in front of them if he needed to.

Jimmy eased the trailer down over the pebbles and

the sand and floated it off into the water. They all jumped in. Jimmy started the outboard.

'So – where d'you want to go? You're not serious about Deal, are you? It'll take fuckin' hours.'

'Nah. Just wanna see that it's seaworthy, that's all. It's lucky there's a full moon. Take it a few miles out and we'll come back for a nightcap.'

They motored down the estuary, then out into the Channel proper. Three times Jimmy asked if that was far enough, and three times he was told to shut up and go a bit further.

'Is *this* far enough then?' The waves were getting higher, and Jimmy had no wish to prolong this one moment longer than necessary.

Lee looked back at the distant lights. 'Okay, this'll do.'

'Good. Can we go back now?'

'In a minute. We'll 'ave a little chat first.'

Oh fuck, this was what Jimmy was dreading. He feathered the throttle. 'About what?'

'Tell you what, you don't look very comfortable there. Why don't you go up the sharp end, give yourself more space? Tommy can steer.'

'I'm fine where I am.'

'Do it.'

Gingerly, Jimmy stepped past the other two as the boat rocked crazily. Tommy moved back and took hold of the tiller. Lee stayed in the middle, and turned to face the little man.

'Right. What you been sayin' to the Old Bill?'

'I ain't *seen* the Old Bill for months, let alone talked to 'em.'

'Bollocks. You've opened your big mouth, we know you 'ave.'

'You're fuckin' mad. I ain't done nothin' of the sort.'

'Yes, you 'ave. You fuckin' grassed up our Dan.'

A bigger wave swept them yards sideways. Lee decided to get on with it.

'Admit it, you grassin' bastard.'

'Go to 'ell.' Jimmy was terrified, but defiance was all that was left for him now. Even in a position as dire as this, he knew full well where admitting something he hadn't done would lead.

'If you won't admit it, I'll fuckin' *make* ya.'

From his jacket pocket Lee pulled out his Stanley knife, and began nudging closer to the terrified man. Jimmy's voice grew more falsetto.

'You keep that thing away from me.'

He pushed himself as far back in the prow as he dared. Lee came nearer and scythed the air with the knife, taking care not to touch him.

'I'll cut the words out of your mouth, if I 'ave to.'

He tried to grab Jimmy's arm. Jimmy swayed out of reach, but now had nowhere to go as the knife was brandished ever nearer his face. All he could do was shove himself backwards and up until he was virtually standing. Lee clambered to his feet too, his knees half bent, one hand holding onto the side for balance, and stumbled forward.

Jimmy swung a wild, weak fist and missed, the motion upsetting the boat even more. Tommy yelled out at them to take it easy. Lee lunged forward, caught hold of Jimmy's collar and yanked him towards him.

'Admit it, you turd.'

Instinctively, Jimmy thrust himself further backwards, trying to get away. Without warning, Lee suddenly let go his grip, and Jimmy, his arms semaphoring wildly, toppled into the water.

Lee swung his head round towards Tommy. 'Where's 'e gone?' He pointed. 'Quick, quick – over there.'

All in a fluster, Tommy swung the tiller round and revved the engine. Lee urged him on.

'Faster, *faster*.'

Tommy was lost in confusion. 'Why the fuck are we goin' this way? Jimmy fell in back there.'

'Bollocks. I can see him, straight ahead – *there*. No, I'm wrong. Try a bit further.'

'I tell you, 'e's back that way. If we don't pick 'im up quick, 'e'll drown.'

'Fuckin' shut up and keep lookin'.' They roared on another hundred yards. Lee looked left and right. 'Can't see 'im nowhere. Maybe you was right, Tom. I s'pose we should go back and look again. Nah, no point, really. The silly little sod must be drowned by now. What did 'e go and do that for, eh?'

''Cause you was wavin' a fuckin' Stanley knife in 'is face, that's why.'

'What you talkin' about, Tommy? I ain't got no Stanley knife on me.' He held out his hands, then pulled out the fabric of his jacket pockets. 'Look.' He'd dropped it silently overboard while Tommy was preoccupied with steering the boat. 'Anyway, main thing is now we know who our grass was.'

'What you on about?'

'The little fella confessed. Said 'e done it. You 'eard 'im.'

'No, I didn't. With the noise from the engine and the waves, I couldn't catch a bleedin' word.'

'Then you and me got a problem, Tommy. All we wanted to do was to find out if the runt done it, and then drag 'im along to see the guv'nor. Now 'e's gone and drowned 'isself, we can't do that, can we?'

'S'pose not.'

'And that don't only put me in the shit. It puts *you* there too. Unless, of course, we can say that Jimmy confessed loud and clear, and then got so scared 'e threw 'isself overboard, and tried to swim away for all 'e was worth. You still sure you didn't catch nothin'?'

'Maybe I did a bit, after all. It's startin' to come back now.'

'Then I'm sure you recall that, before we could fish 'im back out, this great big wave came out of nowhere, and carried the little fella under.'

'Oh yeah.'

'And though we searched for ages, we couldn't see 'im nowhere, so in the end we 'ad to give up.'

'Yeah.'

'Okay, that's settled. Jesus, Tommy, for a moment there I thought I was goin' to lose *you* overboard as well. Two in one night would be careless, eh?'

Tommy managed a nervous laugh.

'Now let's get back. It may be summer, but Jesus, it's brass monkeys out 'ere.'

8

On Monday morning Fraser Morrison whistled cheerfully as he walked along Mount Street to Orbia. Inside,
the building was thoroughly modern, but the tall Port-
land stone façade, decorated solely with a nicely worn
brass plate, projected precisely the right blend of solid-
ity, discretion, and prestige. Life was good for Fraser
these days. He had a chic French wife, two kids so
cute you could eat them, and work was going very
satisfactorily. As he entered his fortieth year, he often
reflected that, if life really begins at forty, then life might
get very good indeed.

He'd started his consulting career with Booz Allen,
and had duly made partner right on cue at thirty-three.
Getting that far hadn't been effortless, but when he
raised his eyes to the very top of the hill, he saw that
he'd only reached base camp. It would be years before
he could consider an attempt on the summit. Too many
people stood in his way – clever people, older people,
people who were at least as adept at politics as him.
And none of them would step aside to smooth his path.
He would never be truly rich or be made managing
partner – for all the theoretical internationalism – that
always fell to an American. For all his conservative
dress, and his studiedly unflamboyant manner, Fraser
Morrison was hungry. Hungry, but not greedy. He could

accept failing to achieve power and riches: he would be perfectly satisfied with either.

Having concluded that the odds of that were too long at Booz, he'd looked around for a faster, smaller steed. Smaller meant less prestigious, naturally. A worthwhile trade-off, though, for Orbia at the time had only twenty-odd partners, compared with nearly five hundred at Booz Allen, and over six hundred at McKinsey. And it wasn't only a smaller absolute number. He did his homework carefully and calculated that there was no sure-fire successor in line for when Paul O'Neill hung up his boots at sixty. O'Neill had been fifty-two at the time, and now had only two and a bit years left. If Paul had retired before now, Fraser Morrison would have been seen as too callow to be a contender. As it was, he'd used the years wisely, establishing a strong record in winning new business, and making a point of cultivating other partners both in London and on the Continent. He was confident that he had positioned himself handily without seriously alienating anyone.

Well, not quite anyone. One was unavoidable. Alistair Haslam, at forty-four, was the nearest thing there had been to an heir apparent and, although at first friendly to Fraser, he changed his tune sharply when he saw the challenge the Scot was mounting. Paul O'Neill watched this developing, considered whether to be seen to be grooming either of them, and decided against it. After all, the decision was ultimately for the partners as a whole, even if his voice would be particularly influential. Sending a strong signal too early would mortally offend the unfavoured candidate and his supporters, might trigger internal warfare, and would certainly extend the lame-duck period of his own rule.

Unfortunately, his decision not to take a decision didn't work to plan. He'd hoped that the two would merely continue to compete in a genteel, positive way, struggling fiercely to land more and bigger fish for all of the partners to feast on. Not that either stopped doing that. It was just that, so late in the bout, both fighters were looking not for points, but for knock-outs. And that was extremely destabilising.

Contrary to O'Neill's expectations, it was the normally unpugnacious Alistair Haslam who swung the first haymaker. Having long assumed that the crown was his for the taking, Alistair had adopted a laid-back, statesmanlike style, expecting greatness to be thrust upon him. He felt insulted by the apparent willingness of the partners to entertain a wider contest, and disgusted by Fraser's patent politicking. The man was behaving like a prime ministerial candidate on the stump. Well, if he wanted to treat this like a general election, so be it. Those were usually won by whoever seized the high ground of the 'big idea', and Alistair suspected that there was only one sure way to win the partners' hearts and minds. Make the buggers rich.

He had swung this punch a couple of months back, when he, O'Neill and Morrison were having one of the regular lunches that they held as the three top dogs in the firm. His big idea was to convert the partnership into a company and float it on the stock market. Paul O'Neill went apoplectic, railing against the perils of public accountability, and fulminating about one generation of partners cashing in on the goodwill and patrimony that had been built up by many.

If Fraser Morrison had weighed in against it straight away, it might have been killed off there and then. Fraser was a wily fox, though, and instinctively felt that this could be a mistake. If the partners got to hear of it – and Haslam would arrange that they did – they might be annoyed at the summary dismissal of an idea which, whatever its demerits, would enrich them all personally on a magnificent scale. And if it were to happen, he as one of the leading partners, could expect to benefit disproportionately. It therefore quite suited him for this proposal to get an airing, but in a such a way that, if it proved impracticable or unpalatable, he could distance himself from it. Equally, if it looked like the notion had legs, he could credibly claim to have been an early supporter.

So while O'Neill kept on ranting, Fraser held his peace, and declined Paul's invitation to speak directly against it or oppose Haslam's suggestion that they appoint an investment bank to examine the practicalities. Instead Fraser improvised a tactical master-stroke, proposing that Goldman Sachs was the natural bank to choose. Not many years before, they had been through precisely the same process themselves, and had lived with the accusations of greed and doom merchants' catastrophic predictions. What he didn't add was that one of his closest pals worked there. Still glowing with having won the first skirmish, Haslam quickly agreed.

In the face of a united front, O'Neill was obliged to go along with all this, insisting only that, until the way ahead was clearer, the proposal should be discussed on a need-to-know basis, and as far as he was concerned only the three of them had a need to know.

Things got underway quickly, and soon the bankers indicated that a flotation was eminently achievable. Orbia had an excellent track record of growing both profits and revenues, and there had been no recent glitches that might complicate or scupper it. They reckoned that the company would be valued by the market at around four hundred million pounds.

Haslam was delighted. Fraser, for his part, had thrown himself into the project with enough gusto to be confident that he could claim half of the credit. The problem was, half might not be enough. He talked the situation over carefully with David, his pal at Goldman. David was always creative, and came up with something special. In order to wrong-foot Alistair, Fraser made sure he made no mention of it before today's meeting of the three of them.

Naturally, Paul O'Neill took the chair. 'So, what news this week, Alistair?'

'All looking good as far as I'm aware. Goldman believe there will be strong retail interest for the shares in France and Germany as well as the UK. We've pencilled in the fourth of February as the day trading begins. However, if we're to keep to that, we need to start pushing buttons no later than mid October.'

O'Neill's face clouded. He wasn't, generally speaking, more averse than the next man to having his personal coffers filled. He was already privately wealthy, however, and had other priorities, such as the knighthood which he felt he richly deserved for all the pro bono work he had arranged for the firm to take on.

According to his Whitehall sources, things were now developing very nicely and he could begin to look forward to good news, if not in the New Year's honours, then by the official birthday next June. The last thing he needed in the near future was a spate of 'fat cat' articles, pillorying him in the press.

'Is there really need for such haste? What do you think, Fraser?'

'Basically, I'm with Alistair, Paul. Sooner or later, we'll have to bite the bullet. I should perhaps mention another idea that David from Goldman came up with.'

Haslam looked alarmed. 'What?'

'I had dinner with him last night. Purely social, I thought, otherwise I would've invited you along too, Alistair.'

The other man looked coldly at him.

'David had been thinking the whole thing through again, I discovered. As you know, he thinks that we can ride out any turbulence on the greed issue, though he concedes it could be rather bumpy for a while. What he's *more* concerned about is liquidity. Goldman's own float was enormous, of course, and the turnover in the stock is more than enough to absorb occasional bouts of selling by staff, as long as it's properly handled. What he says he's worried about is that if any partners in a much smaller stock like Orbia were to sell any shares, the price would be hit disproportionately. It would be seen as a vote of no confidence, and the share price might crash. On the other hand, it would be seriously demotivating for our people if on paper they were worth lots of money, but in practice couldn't realise a penny.'

Haslam's fists were clenching and unclenching under the table. None of this was new. Morrison and he had made a tacit agreement not to flag this to Paul since it would clearly provide ammunition to block it. His irritation showed in his voice.

'Get on with it, Fraser. What's David's brilliant alternative?'

'To sell the company.'

O'Neill's eyes popped halfway out of his skull. *Sell Orbia?* We can't do that! Independence is our whole ethos. It's central to everything we believe in! It's the reason our clients come to us. It's the key to the outstanding quality of our work. If we sold out to one of the bigger consultancies—'

'David's not suggesting that.'

'. . . Or a bank, or a . . .' Since the accountants had migrated out of this field, he couldn't think of any other sort of buyer.

Haslam, his voice chilly with resentment, asked more directly, 'Who, then?'

'A software company.'

'Any one in particular?'

'Synapsis.'

O'Neill knew the name. Haslam knew a little more.

'They're a relational database company, aren't they? Based somewhere near San Francisco. What on earth would they want with Orbia?'

'I've no idea. I didn't ask, and David didn't volunteer. He was already going out on a limb telling me this much. What he *did* say is Synapsis has lots of cash, and it's burning a hole in their pocket. He thinks they'd be very seriously interested. After all, two hardware and systems companies, Hewlett Packard and Cisco, have got keen on consulting, so why not Synapsis?'

'Whatever their reasoning, I can't see for a moment why you think this is better than floating and, as Paul says, it means losing our independence completely.'

'True, I can't deny that. However, David reckons that Synapsis would understand the need to give us free rein, and they have the financial firepower if we want to expand more ambitiously. There are other advantages, too. Any transaction could be negotiated entirely privately, and only announced when it had been signed. No deal, no announcement. Whereas, as we know from recent years, if you announce a flotation and have to pull it because the market turns sour, you suffer major embarrassment. Added to which, the process is cheaper and quicker. If we started in earnest, we could get a deal done by Christmas. Then there's the liquidity point. David says Synapsis would be happy to pay cash. All the partners would achieve total financial security for the rest of their lives.'

'Then they'd all leave, wouldn't they?' Haslam was reduced now to scoring smaller points.

'I'm sure that Synapsis would want to secure all key staff by including us all in their group stock-option plan. David says it's very generous. By the way, I asked him for his take on the greed issue.' Fraser looked at Paul to see how he'd react. 'His view, perhaps surprisingly, is that the perception would be much better. First, the sale of a company tends to get covered in the press only for a day or two, compared with a float which runs for weeks. Second, as long as we handled the PR properly, he believes that allying with a group like Synapsis could be perceived as a very astute move. He thought that the partners – and as managing partner, Paul would be fronting this, of course – would come up smelling of roses. Anyway, it's just another idea to throw in the hopper. I promised David I'd pass it on. You tell me if you think it's worth pursuing.'

As Alistair sat in grim silence, Paul nodded approvingly.

'I think it sounds well worth investigating. Interesting . . . hmm. Very interesting.'

9

'Can I speak to Mr Henley, please?'

'Who's calling?'

'Ronnie 'ill.'

'Thank you, I'll put you through, Mr Hill.'

'Hello?'

'Rupert?'

'Ronnie. How good to hear from you. I can't tell you what a good time we had on Sunday. And I really enjoyed meeting Susie – she's delightful. You must both come over for supper at my place.'

'That'd be very nice.'

There was a brief pause.

'So, Ronnie, I take it you got the business plan?'

'Yeah, the messenger brought it yesterday afternoon.'

'What did you think?'

'Interestin', as far as I can judge. Which isn't a lot.'

'But do you think you might be interested enough to have a modest pop at it?'

'Tell you what, Rupert, I was turnin' over in me mind what we talked about, and I wondered if I could come and see you some time.'

Rupert wasn't sure how to read this. The fact that Ronnie wanted to meet up again had to be positive. On the other hand, he hadn't come right out and said he would do it. Most likely he hadn't done any start-up investing on anything like this before, and had some basic questions that he was too embarrassed to ask over the phone.

'Of course, that would be very good. When would suit you?'

'You got any time this afternoon?'

'This afternoon . . .' Good – he *must* be keen. '. . . I'm supposed to be leaving here at lunchtime to go out to Reading. I could put it off till tomorrow. How about three o'clock?'

'Three's fine. What's your office address?'

'Tell you what, rather than meet here, why don't we get together at the Dorchester?'

'Okay. Whatever suits you.'

'See you in the lobby there then. Bye.'

*

When Primrose got out of the lift at lunchtime and walked through the lobby, she almost bumped right into Peter Nicholl.

'Good God, what are you doing here?'

'Hello, Prim. Didn't you know? We've just changed our lawyers from Ashursts to you lot.'

'Have you? How awful of me not knowing. I never find time to read internal e-mails.'

'Don't worry. We only appointed Linklaters three weeks ago, and you are rather a large firm. How are you anyway? – apart from looking more gorgeous than ever?'

'Liar. I look a fright. I'm overworked, of course, but otherwise fine.'

'Where are you off to?'

'I was due to have lunch with a girlfriend, but she blew me out, so I thought I'd get a sandwich and eat it beside the fountain in the Barbican.'

'Mind if I come along?'

'Okay then, if you'd like.'

They walked along to the end of Silk Street, bought tuna sandwiches and Diet Cokes, and made their way through the Barbican maze. Sitting down on uncomfortable metal chairs, they unwrapped the food.

'I still feel embarrassed not knowing. You must've thought it was rude of me not to mention it when we had brunch.'

'Not at all. In fact, I almost said something myself, then thought better of it.'

'Why on earth?'

'I didn't want Rupert getting the wrong idea.'

'*What* wrong idea? I've no idea what you're talking about, Peter.'

'I mean my reasons for choosing Linklaters. I didn't want him thinking it was because you work there.'

'Why should he think that, or care?'

'It's probably me being silly, or over-cautious. After you and I met that time before at the Youngs', I heard that Rupert was going round saying I'd been hitting on you.'

'That's ridiculous. You weren't hitting on me, we were just talking. About Tibet, wasn't it?'

'And Mongolia. And maybe I did monopolise you a tiny bit. Anyway, I didn't want to risk causing any more problems, or upsetting Rupert any more . . . Has he had any joy elsewhere?'

'Not much. It's getting to crunch time. He doesn't

know this, but I'm wondering about selling the flat I've just bought and putting that money in.'

'Are you sure that's wise?'

'I know what you think. I do believe in Rupert, though, and he's so sure it'll work.'

'Prim, I really think you should consider carefully before you do that. I know you probably don't want to hear this, and if you pass it on to Rupert it will be the end of what little friendship he and I have left.'

'Don't worry. Whatever you say I won't mention.'

'Then, let me tell you, Prim, that venture's a dog. There are tons of companies trying to do the same thing. Most of them are in the States, and a lot of them are much further down the track, and have far greater technical and financial resources.'

'He's tried *so* hard, though. It will be a real body blow if this falls through.'

'He can always look out for the next thing. Presumably he'll be promoted to partner soon, and that'll give him a boost.'

'I hope so. Anyway, how are you? What did you get up to this weekend?'

'I was up with my parents in Sunderland.'

'I thought I detected the odd Northern vowel, but I wouldn't have placed you as a Geordie. *And* I spent three years in the north-east, at Durham University.'

'I sandpapered the rougher edges of it while I was at Cambridge. When I arrived there, I felt so uncouth compared with all the smooth public school Southerners. When I met girls of your sort, Prim, I got so tongue-tied I could hardly get a word out. Not that they had any interest in the likes of me anyway, being not only a peasant, but a short-arsed peasant at that.'

Primrose giggled. 'You're not short.'

'Yes, I am. I come up to about Rupert's chin.'

'What are you? Five ten?'

'Five eight. Almost. My accent hasn't gone away altogether – it's hibernating. As soon as I get up there, it comes back, as thick as a chip butty.'

*

They sat, side by side, on one of the chintzy benches directly behind the lobby in the Dorchester. Seeing Ronnie's great bulk daintily perched, looking as out of place as a gorilla at court, Rupert wished he'd thought of somewhere less public. The smartly clad waiter brought tea and served them.

'So, Ronnie, tell me. I'm sure you've got lots of questions, and I hope I've got most of the answers. Needless to say, if you want to meet my main business partner or the other guys we're thinking of bringing in, that can be arranged.'

'Rupert, I'll be straight with you. I couldn't understand very much of it. Too much technical jargon for me . . . Not only that. This ain't the cleverest time for me to get stuck into new ventures. I got other problems what need takin' care of. So, if I did think of an investment, it couldn't be right away.'

Rupert couldn't work this out. If the man wasn't able to move, why rush up to town to see him so soon? He decided to keep a friendly look on his face until he heard the reason.

'When would you be thinking of?'

'Quite soon, possibly. Depends 'ow quick I can solve these other problems. In fact, there was a little proposition I wanted to put to *you*.'

'A . . . proposition?'

'Yeah, a business proposition. Tell me, Rupert, d'you do any moonlightin'?'

'Moonlighting?'

'You know, doin' some of that consultancy stuff, but in your spare time, not through your company.'

Ah, so that was it. Wanted some work done at a knock-down rate? Well, balls to that.

'I'm afraid that at Orbia we have rather strict rules about that sort of thing.'

'I thought you was plannin' on leavin'.'

'True, but until such time as I do, I must behave properly. My reputation would be totally ruined if anyone ever found out that I'd been . . . moonlighting. It's not only the risk of being found out; I don't think I could live with it myself. One has to have ethics.'

Ronnie nodded slowly. 'Well, I respect that, Rupert, I respect that. It's a pity, though, 'cause I thought we could scratch each other's back nicely. My business needs a bit of a rethink, some of that lateral thought you was on about. You see, if you made a new strategy for us, I could pay you part of the money up front, and that'd give you some of the cash you need to get started.'

Basically it was still outrageous. It proved that his first impressions of the man had been right on target.

'How much were you thinking of?'

'Well, there's got to be somethin' in it for everyone, right? You said on Sunday that Orbia won't take on a new customer unless they get 'alf a million from them.'

'At least.'

'And if I thought that'd be money well spent, I could just march in the front door, couldn't I?'

Oh yeah, thought Rupert. I'd love to see the reaction if you tried.

'Frankly, I don't 'ave 'alf a mill lyin' around at the moment. But if I could get the work done for, say, a third of that, it might make sense all round. That way you'd get a decent wedge, and I'd get a bit of a discount.'

'How much would you be willing to pay up front?'

'Fifty grand.'

Rupert sank back in his chair. As he had thought, outrageous.

'Sorry, Ronnie, it's kind of you to think of me, but this doesn't work for me. To get *Invid* underway, I need much more.'

'I thought you said it was a red 'ot deal?' Ronnie had to fight back a smile. He'd been right. The geezer was bluffing. Nice stunt to pull on your girlfriend's dad first time you meet him.

Rupert cursed himself for dropping his guard. Even if this vile creature didn't matter any more, Rupert didn't like looking silly.

'Perhaps I didn't express myself very clearly. It *is* a hot deal. All I meant was that if I were for one moment willing to *countenance* doing something so morally questionable, I certainly wouldn't do it unless my potential personal client was willing and able to make a major commitment to my project.'

Ronnie nodded again. 'Well, I would've liked to do more. You caught me at a bad time, that's all. I 'ope at least I didn't offend you with my little proposition.'

'No, no.'

'Well, I'd better be gettin' back to Chislehurst. Goodbye, Rupert. Thanks for seein' me.'

Ronnie paid, and they shook hands and left. Rupert walked back to the office. As soon as he got there, one of his colleagues, another hopeful for partner status, dashed in and closed the glass door.

'Guess what I heard.'

'No idea.'

'There's a rumour that there are so many candidates from abroad this year, they might not elect anyone based here to the partnership.'

'That's absurd. Why should they do that?'

'No idea. Perhaps because last year it was only London people who made it and they have to even things up. Or maybe they think none of us is ready. If it's true, I'm out of here, I tell you. I think I'll try and do a bit more digging. Fancy a drink after work?'

'No, I've got plans. Do let me know if you hear more, though. I'll do the same.'

The colleague left. Rupert swung round on his swivel chair. Rumours were always circulating in consulting firms when promotions were close. If this was true, though, it was scary. It would mean that his hard slog on Telesys wouldn't be enough. They would still have an out. As Fraser Morrison had said, proof of potential for winning business would become critical. What the hell could he do about that in a couple of months?

Unless . . .

When Ronnie got back home to Chislehurst, Jack Price was waiting for him.

'You 'eard the radio news? Body's been washed up near Sandwich. They ain't identified 'im yet. All the same, they say the Old Bill's treatin' it as suspicious.'

'Fuck. That stupid pair of bastards.'

Lee and Tommy had come round first thing on Monday and told the tale. Ronnie had blown his stack altogether. If Jimmy had grassed them up, what they needed to do next was to put the frighteners on him big time so that no prosecutor would get him to testify in court that he'd supplied Dan with that boat. He could be sorted out for keeps once that was over. Him dying like that would only make the Law more determined to get them all, and might guarantee Dan a very long time away from his family.

If Lee had been on his own, Ronnie wouldn't have believed him. Since he was a child, he'd always been a right little liar, and many was the time Ronnie had given him a hiding on the strength of it. Tommy was different, too stupid to invent a tale like that, and too loyal to the family to back up Lee's lies on something so important. It probably meant it was true.

But how bleeding dumb, taking Jimmy out to sea in a boat like that in the dark. The fella's body wouldn't be a pretty sight after the better part of two days in the water. Lee had sworn that he hadn't laid a finger on him. Just as well, because the pathologist would find any bruises or cuts. Lee had been full of himself for getting a result, and kept insisting that they'd get respect for finding the grass fast and dealing with him. Ronnie was less sure. Knowing how Lee would've handled it, there was always a chance that Jimmy had said whatever Lee wanted. It wasn't something that Fat Boy Dutch would swallow too easily unless Ronnie staked his own word on it. That he would have to do. It would always niggle, though, not knowing for absolute sure.

Jack wasn't too happy either. 'If the Old Bill didn't mark Jimmy down before as the geezer what got Dan the boat, they fuckin' well will now.'

'I know, Jack. I should never 'ave let Lee take care of it.'

'Don't blame yourself, Ron. You got to give the boy a chance to prove hisself. If you don't, one day you'll pay for it.'

10

On Wednesday and Thursday Rupert had no choice but to go out to Reading, so it was Friday before he managed another meeting with Fraser Morrison. Fraser was very pushed, and only accepted in the belief that it was something about Telesys. Rupert concocted a question on that front before switching.

'There's something else I need to ask you. Do you have five more minutes?'

Fraser was irritated, keen to get on. He made a point of looking at his watch. 'Only five.'

'That's all I need. Remember our internal group strategy meeting back in June? Alistair Haslam was saying we should get more into the leisure sector – hotels, gaming, et cetera.'

'I remember.'

'Well, I've run across a company in that sector. Not quite the same niches, but not far removed. Sports clubs, restaurants, night clubs.'

'Are they publicly traded?'

'No, they're privately held. Although . . .' he was busking it already '. . . a stock-market listing is one of the issues they want to look at. The Chief Executive has taken a bit of a shine to me. He was thinking of appointing Booz Allen or Bain. If we wanted to go for it, though, I'm pretty sure we could get the work.'

'How much work are we talking about?' Fraser meant how big are the fees.

'The company isn't enormous, and I don't suppose they've used consultants before. If we proposed a big, intensive exercise costing a million or so, we might scare them off. It might be smarter to suggest around fifty thousand a month for three months, and then ratchet it up later when they see the value we're generating.' Rupert paused. Fraser looked very uninterested. 'Now, I realise that in itself this is a pretty marginal piece of business. However, if it's a sector where we're trying to build up a contacts base and a track record, surely there could be a strategic dimension.'

'Strategic dimensions are all very well, but the practice is stretched to breaking point at the moment. I can't see you persuading any partner to devote any real time to something like this.'

'That's okay, I think. We'd need to have a partner on it for form's sake, of course. However, I believe I could handle it myself with only the minimum supervision.'

'Won't the client be upset by that?'

'This guy's unusual. Bit of a rough diamond, frankly. Could've been a heavyweight boxer, from the look of him. He said he'd want me to be in charge personally.'

'Can you spare the time yourself? What about Telesys?'

'That would remain my priority, naturally. But I am getting freed up a little more than before, and you said the other day that I need to start thinking about getting new clients. I followed your advice to the letter.'

Morrison rubbed his chin. He'd deliberately introduced the issue of winning business to provide a let-out if they turned Rupert down for promotion. The guy was smart, trying to close off the opening. This was a tricky one. If he blocked this, Rupert might justifiably throw a fit. And, after all, it wouldn't be that hard to come up with some other reason not to promote him, if it came to that.

'Have you already spoken to any partner about this? Is there anyone you have in mind?'

Rupert had the tactics perfectly worked out.

'Not yet. Since it was Alistair Haslam who first took an interest in the leisure sector, maybe he'd want to keep control of any initiative there.'

'Hmmm . . .' As an individual piece of business, this was way too small to matter. However, if it came to be seen as a precursor to something bigger, it might prove more significant. Why throw any bone in Haslam's direction if he didn't have to?

'Alistair is very busy at the moment, and I don't think he's the type to sit back and give the project manager a free hand, particularly as it's a sector he wants to get more personal experience of. I rather think he'd suggest waiting for something meatier to come along. No, I'm not sure that's the smartest move. I suppose, since I was the one who gave you the advice in the first place, I should help you myself. On the clear understanding that the call on my time would be minimal.'

Rupert beamed. Perfect. He'd taken the bait. 'Absolutely. I wouldn't need much of a team either. A couple of junior associates, that's all.'

'Sounds very thin. Are you sure?'

'Quite.'

'Very well. I'm happy in principle to sign the engagement letter. I'm assuming, though, that you'll do all the normal client checks first?'

'Of course.'

'And I suppose I'd better meet them. Can you arrange to bring in the CEO, and whoever else from his top management team?' Rupert nodded. 'What's the company called, by the way?'

Bugger. Rupert had forgotten to think of that. He improvised. 'Interleisure.'

'One word or two?'

'One.'

Rupert got up and left Fraser's office, and walked back to his own with a sense of some satisfaction. Thank God he hadn't gone right ahead and finished with Primrose.

*

Even once the body of the drowned man was identified, it took until Friday afternoon before it got on the radar screen of the National Crime Squad. The Kent police were becoming increasingly mystified and perplexed by it. At first it looked like one of the drowning accidents they had to deal with all the time. Someone swept out to sea by a freak wave when walking by the coast. Or a suicide. Maybe he'd jumped from a cliff, or taken a boat out to sea and scuttled it.

However, the more they pieced together, the less it added up. The deceased, Jimmy Smith, was known to the Whitstable police, and about as petty a villain as you could find. He'd spent both Saturday and Sunday nights in his regular pub, and according to the licensee had been in a cheery mood. They'd spoken now to the lad who helped him out in his dilapidated little boat-shed. The lad said that when he got in on Monday, there was no sign of Jimmy, but things had definitely been moved around over the weekend. The little trailer was outside, down by the water, and a wooden dinghy was missing.

A charred hulk, which might well have been the same boat, had been found less than a mile away. It had been doused with petrol and torched, eradicating any evidence. As for the boat-shed itself, apart from those of the lad and the dead man, there *were* lots of different fingerprints, but that was normal when there were boats in for repair and hundreds of bits of metal, fibreglass and wood lying around. Unluckily, the items which the lad said had been moved showed fresh prints only from the deceased.

It was looking increasingly like murder, and something for the NCS to take a look at. When the Kent police report reached DCI Chris Owen, he reacted fast. Could this be the link with the inflatable at St Margaret's that he'd been looking for? The inflatable was a common type, and it hadn't been new. He'd traced the shop that first ordered it from the makers – a chandlery in Shaldon in Devon – and their credit-card records had got Owen as far as the original buyers. They had kept it for one season, and flogged it through an ad in a shop window. They couldn't remember much about the man who'd bought it, and there the scent had evaporated.

But now this. The murder of a man who repaired and dealt in boats. Most likely taken out to sea and chucked overboard to drown. The fittest of men and strongest of swimmers would have stood little chance of making it back to the shore or surviving long enough to be picked up by some passing craft. This one stood none. Fifty-six, and in lousy health according to his GP. Fully clothed, and with three or four pints of beer inside him, he would've been dead in five minutes.

Was this the man who'd supplied the inflatable, and had the Hills killed him in case the police tracked him down? If so, it reconfirmed his views of them. Sometimes when you chatted with Ronnie Hill, you could get lulled into believing that he had a half-decent side to him. This showed that this impression was wrong. The likes of the Hills would shoot their own granny for a fiver. They should be locked up and the key dumped far out to sea, like they'd done with the boatman. Oh, what he'd give to put the whole evil lot behind bars. This was fast becoming a personal crusade.

*

Ronnie had been out for most of Friday, and Rupert didn't manage to get through to him until seven forty-five, not long before he had to meet Primrose at Chez Gérard. He was amused how surprised Ronnie had been. However, once the man had got over the shock, he didn't seem as deeply grateful as Rupert had anticipated. Rupert was rather put out. To be taken on as a client of Orbia put Ronnie's two-bit outfit in very select company. After some hesitation, and after asking some questions, he had accepted. He'd agreed to see Rupert one more time privately, and then to go in to Orbia to meet Fraser Morrison and the team at the back end of next week. Rather to Rupert's annoyance, he had insisted that they now tell Primrose. After all, it was totally above board, with no more thought of moonlighting or backhanders, so what had they got to hide? Ronnie said he didn't want her involved in any way, but he didn't want to deceive her needlessly. Rupert agreed, and promised to tell her himself that very evening. In return, he got Ronnie to go along with keeping quiet about the whole *Invid* episode, especially as that no longer figured in the arrangements.

And they left it like that. Ronnie thanked him politely. Rupert, still mildly miffed, got in the car and drove to the South Bank.

'Sorry to be late. Couldn't find anywhere to park.'

'Don't worry, I've only just made it myself. Lovely to see you. Can we order right away? I don't feel like a starter. I just want the onglet.'

They did that, and got a bottle of Chenas and some water. Rupert smiled. 'Guess who I was talking to before coming here?'

'No idea.'

'Your dad.'

'My dad? Why on earth?'

'He's going to be Orbia's newest client.'

'Rupert, what *are* you talking about?' Rupert noticed a slight shadow pass across her face.

'I thought you'd be pleased. He wants advice – on how to improve the performance of his restaurants and so on. He wants me to do it, and I talked Fraser Morrison into giving him the mother and father of deals.'

Primrose was wary. 'I don't understand. When did this come up – between the two of you, I mean?'

'We talked about it a bit on Sunday. Then he phoned me a couple of days later.'

'And why didn't you tell me?'

'We agreed to keep it a secret until we saw what sort of deal I could negotiate. We both thought it would be a nice surprise for you.'

'Well, it's certainly a surprise.' Not necessarily a nice one, she was thinking. It was good that Rupert and her father had hit it off well, but if Rupert got too close to his business, wouldn't he smell a rat sooner or later? She didn't know much about those outlets, just suspected that the accounts must look pretty unusual. Was there anything she could do to stop this?

'Is it okay for you to be taking on new clients, when you could be leaving Orbia soon to launch *Invid*?'

'Frankly, Prim, it doesn't look like we can raise any money anywhere. In the last few days, I've pretty much concluded that I have to put it on ice, and concentrate on getting that partnership.'

Although Peter Nicholl's views had dampened her optimism, Primrose still had half a mind to take the big risk. This tipped her over the edge.

'I've been thinking about your funding. There could be a way I could find you the better part of three hundred thousand.'

'Oh yeah?' Rupert looked sceptical. He cut a slice of steak and chewed it. 'Like what?'

'Remember we chatted about the possibility that, instead of moving into my new flat, I let it out and move in with you . . .'

Rupert kept on chewing. 'Go on.'

'If we were moving in together anyway, then that flat

114

of mine would only be a financial investment. And if so, I could look at other investments. Like *Invid*. What I'm saying, Rupes, is that I love you and believe in you, and I'd be willing to sell that flat again right away, and invest both my deposit and anything I can borrow.'

'No way.'

Primrose had anticipated a very different reaction. She felt rather hurt. 'Why not? I thought you'd be happy.'

In any other circumstances he would have been, and only a few weeks ago, he'd have leapt at this offer. Not any more, not with what he'd found out about her. It would send altogether the wrong signal to let her move in and if he was unable to pay her back, he'd be horribly trapped. He might not be able to get her out for ages without trashing his reputation terminally among their mutual friends. Now that he'd agreed to take on her father as a client, it wouldn't make sense to end the relationship until the partner decision was taken. After that, if he and Prim split up, and Ronnie took his business away in a huff, who cared? There was also another factor at work. *Invid* was increasingly looking hopeless. Two more American companies had announced competing products in the last two weeks. Without heavy-duty funding they had no chance, and the amount Primrose could scratch together simply wasn't enough to make a real difference or to be worth such a compromise in his private life. He looked her right in the eye.

'What do you take me for, Prim? The type who'd grab all his girlfriend's capital, her only security, and put it at risk?'

'You wouldn't be *grabbing* it; I'm offering it willingly. I know what I'm doing, Rupert.'

He looked down at the table and shook his head, signalling utter incomprehension at her insensitivity.

'I can't believe that you think I would do that. I feel very hurt.'

She reached out and tried to touch his hand. He pulled it away.

'Rupert, I'm so sorry. I just wanted to help, that's all.'

'Well, I'm sure you meant well. It shows, though, doesn't it, that our minds work in totally different ways.' Rupert had spotted that he could turn this conversation to advantage. While he had every right to be in high dudgeon, and she had good reason to be in dejected submission, it was the perfect moment to knock on the head *any* notion of living together. 'At times we're on completely different wave-lengths. You know, Prim, since you've raised the whole issue of accommodation, I think it's something we need to think very carefully about.'

'What d'you mean?'

'I'm as committed as you are to making this work, but given that we don't always see eye to eye, maybe the very worst thing we could do for our relationship is to force it at this stage into the hothouse environment of living together. Instead of bringing us closer together, it might blow us apart. We've only been together for one year; we don't know each other that well yet. Perhaps I was allowing my enthusiasm and my love for you to get the better of common sense. On more mature reflection, perhaps we should put that off for the time being. I don't mean that we rule out doing it later. If all's going well between us, it would be a natural step. I just don't think we're ready for it yet.'

'*I* am.' Her eyes were brimming with tears.

'Well, maybe it's me, then. This has no connection with how often we'll see each other . . . Prim, people are looking. You're taking this the wrong way. I still love you very much indeed.'

He took her hand. She didn't withdraw it, but got no comfort from it, and couldn't stop a stray tear escaping. Rupert smiled encouragingly.

'Now come on, Prim, they have a great chocolate mousse here.'

11

Ronnie Hill knew he'd get a bollocking. Susie warned
him on Friday night when he told her what he'd been
up to. Worst of all, he knew he deserved it. Rose was
his little baby, and by common consent was one of the
kindest, gentlest, most warm-hearted girls around, but
when she was roused, you had to watch out. To say big
Ronnie Hill, the guv'nor himself, was terrified would
have been to exaggerate. Plain bloody scared was nearer
the mark. The waiting made it harder when he knew
it was coming. He wanted to call her and get it over
with, but didn't want to risk calling in case Rupert was
with her.

What he didn't know was that Primrose had left
Rupert's place early on Saturday morning and gone for
a long walk by the river to clear her mind. She refused to
hide from herself her grave disappointment about last
night's conversation. It wasn't that she was counting
any chickens about getting married. She wasn't at all
sure she was ready for that herself. However, she was
committed enough to want to feel that they would give
this relationship their best shot. His earlier talk about
living together had seemed like a sign that his feelings
were deepening too and that things were moving in
the right direction. After last night she found it much
harder to fathom where she stood.

On the brighter side, she had to admit that recent events had also thrown up some good points about Rupert. His willingness not only to accept her father in a social context, but to introduce him to Orbia and work with him on his business was, frankly, astonishing. It spoke volumes about him. And, much as she wished that he'd decided otherwise, his principled refusal to take her money was rather chivalrous. Perhaps he had greater strength of character than she'd realised, and was worth persevering with, even if the road together might be rocky.

However, if only for pride's sake, she'd never be the one to raise living together again. Why not speed up moving into her new flat? She'd held off until things were sorted out with Rupert. Now that the die was cast, maybe she should look for a flatmate. She didn't particularly fancy living on her own, and the extra income would come in handy. The second bedroom wasn't enormous and didn't get a lot of natural light, but it did have its own bathroom, and the agent was sure it would fetch three hundred pounds a week.

Most of the furniture had already been delivered, but she had to buy lots of other stuff like cutlery, bedding, lamps and ornaments. Peter Jones and the Conran shop ought to be able to take care of the lot. Before she went there, she had to speak with her father. She wasn't looking forward to this conversation, but needed to have it. She was glad that she hadn't called him as soon as she was told. Then she might have got up on her high horse in a big way. She did feel let down that he hadn't consulted her, but it was a pretty minor betrayal, and in the cool light of morning, she realised that her dad might have meant well. Perhaps he'd offered the work to Rupert as a kindly gesture of support for their relationship, without thinking through the risks. He only deserved a bit of a bollocking.

She smiled at herself as she pulled out her mobile. 'That you, Dad? I need a word with you.'

'Oh, 'ello, treasure. I was just goin' to call you myself.'

She could hear the nervousness in his voice. There he was, a fifty-eight-year-old man, weighing something like seventeen stone, terrorised like a naughty boy waiting outside the headmistress's study. She couldn't help it. She burst out laughing.

'You're terrified, aren't you?'

'I've been shittin' meself all mornin'.'

'Bloody right, too. You're in the doghouse.'

'Sorry, love. I know I should've asked you first.'

'Course you should've. Why didn't you, Dad?'

'I don't rightly know. We really do need some 'elp. With Dan out of action, looks like we got to take the above-board part of the business a bit more serious than before. And it occurred to me that, if we need one of them consultants to advise us, it'd be a friendly thought to offer the work to Rupert. I didn't stop to think, I admit it. If you want, you can come down to Chislehurst and give me a good clump.'

Primrose laughed. 'I can't be bothered. Tell Susie to do it for me . . . Dad, seriously. You do know why I'm worried about it, don't you?'

'Course I do, princess. Don't worry, I won't breathe a word.'

'What if he finds out in some other way?'

'Why should 'e? This is a kosher business, with

proper accounts, and so on. Jack's a smart fella, you know that.'

'Dad, do please take care. Rupert's been amazing, accepting me – despite everything. I'd hate to lose him over this.'

'You won't. Not on my account, anyway.'

'Okay then, I'll let you off.'

*

Chris Owen spent the weekend with his family. Since he'd joined the National Crime Squad, it was rare that his private life went uninterrupted, and he made the best of it, fulfilling a long-standing promise to take them to the seaside at Eastbourne. He and his wife were only too well aware that, at twelve and fourteen, the kids would soon grow bored or embarrassed going on trips with their parents, and they wanted to do their best to enjoy the good days while they lasted.

Not that they saw much of them that day. The children were far more interested in amusement arcades than the sea itself, so Chris and Sally gave them some money, fixed a rendezvous time and place, and left them enthralled, while they themselves took a stroll hand-in-hand down the front.

They'd met in the force eighteen years before, and Sally had struggled on past their firstborn, only surrendering when the second came along. She had no difficulty in keeping up to date, though, since coppers and coppers' wives formed the backbone of what social life they had. It made it all the more easy for her to take a lively interest in Chris's work.

'I can't believe how unlucky you were with that man from Holland.'

'Yeah. If we'd realised how nervous he was, we'd have given him more time to acclimatise. The description he originally gave the Dutch police was spot on. That's why we were so confident.'

'In the end he picked Dan Hill out, didn't he?'

'Yes, but not at the first attempt. The clot picked out *three* possibles. By the time his recollection got clearer, the damage had been done. He's willing to testify if we want it, but it's not much use to us now.'

'Did the other two look much like Hill?'

'In build and age, yes. Tall, broad, tough-looking. Other than that, not really. If we'd used eight-stone weaklings with glasses and goatee beards, Hill's lawyer might've had something to say.'

'What's Dan Hill like? Apart from being a villain, I mean.'

'Tell the truth, he's not the worst of that bunch. Hard as nails and strong as a bear, but not truly evil. Uses violence – or the threat of it – like they all do, but doesn't get carried away. Thinks of it as a tool of the trade, like a plumber uses a spanner. Doesn't do drugs himself, as far as we can work out, has a nice wife, two kids. Come to think of it, Dan is about the nearest thing I can imagine to a nine-to-five villain. The opposite of his brother, Lee. Now there's a piece of work.'

'Nasty with it?'

'They don't get any nastier. He's always been able to terrify people, not so much on account of being a hard man himself, but because everyone knows he's one of the Hills, and that, if they cross him, they might have to answer to Ronnie or Dan.'

'Does he play a big part in the business?'

'As far as we can work out, not very much up till now. Ronnie depends mainly on his own half-brother, Jack Price, and Dan of course. Indeed, what we're hoping is that, if we can put Dan away for a good long stretch, we'll rip the heart out of the Hill operation. Ronnie's getting on a bit – fifty-seven, fifty-eight. Made a good dishonest living from crime. Big house in Chislehurst and a villa in Marbella. He came from good villain stock himself. His dad was a well-known crook, so Ronnie was pretty much born with a sawn-off shotgun in his hand. Until a few days ago, he was probably planning to hand the reins over to Dan eventually, so they could keep the dynasty going for another generation.'

'So does Lee step into Dan's shoes?'

'Maybe. Jack Price was a tough guy too once, but nowadays he's more of a book-keeper than a thug. The problem with Lee is he's too hot-tempered. Sooner or later he'll fall out with someone in a big way, and that'll be that. Plus, he's not very bright. Ronnie's a shrewd old fox. I can't see him trusting Lee like he does Dan.'

'So what can Ronnie do? Change his plans and stay active till Dan gets out?'

'I doubt it. If we get that conviction, Ronnie will be seventy by then.'

'*Will* you get your conviction?'

'It's looking a little shakier than I'd like. We're still appealing for witnesses who might have seen Dan using that public phone box in Chesterfield Road. And I still live in hope that we can find some way to link the

123

inflatable to that boatyard in Whitstable. If we do, we should have strong circumstantial evidence that it was the Hills who drowned the boatyard owner, Jimmy Smith, and burnt that boat. That might've been their fatal mistake. Unlike Ronnie to do something so dumb, to be honest. Good news for us, though. We might be able to pin murder or conspiracy to murder on the lot of them. Crimes like that go to show you should never forget what you're dealing with. Cold-blooded killers when they need to be.'

Sally was worried about this case. Chris was on secondment to the NCS from the Kent Constabulary. If a high-profile case like this collapsed, it could mean no promotion for him when he went back.

'Chris, to be devil's advocate, if you *don't* find an eyewitness for the phone box, and you can't prove a link with the boatyard . . . what have you got left in your locker?'

'We've still got five villains who were caught red-handed, and who'll go down for up to fifteen years. One of them's bound to turn Queen's Evidence.'

'They haven't yet, have they?'

'No, but it's early days.'

'But what if they simply don't know? The Hills are experienced, sophisticated criminals. Surely the name of their game is to keep everything at arm's length, to break the connection at each stage, to make sure that every man involved knows as little as possible about where the gear comes from or will go, and who controls it at any moment? In other words, to be prepared for exactly this situation?'

'I accept that. And that's what they're all saying so

far. The ones who sailed the boat over from Holland were told which quay to find it at, and that it was all pre-loaded. The beach party claim that they were going to be told where to take it once it was safely in the Mitsubishi, but I don't believe them. Some of them must have worked for the Hills before, must have recognised a voice, or seen some pattern in the way it was set up which could help us nail them.'

'You can't be sure, though?'

'No, I bloody well can't. Christ, Sal, you're worse than the Crown Prosecution Service.'

'Sorry, sorry. Just trying to help.'

'I know. And I'm sorry to get shirty. You're right, and I'm worried. I thought by now we'd be home and dry, and we're still out and wet.'

'And no chance of hearing again from your informant?'

'Doubt it.'

'You think he's close to the Hills, though?'

'Must be, to tell us where and when they were landing, and put Dan's name up.'

'But he didn't say where the boat was coming from?'

'No. And he only called us at five p.m. Either he only found out at the last minute, or didn't want us mounting surveillance on the coaster when it was still berthed in Holland. If he had, the Dutch police could have nabbed whoever brought the gear to the boat, and they might've been able to trace the source of supply.'

'And you've got no idea who the informant was? Not even a guess?'

'The incoming call was recorded routinely, but our

voice experts haven't got anything from it. The informant deliberately chose a public phone in a noisy pub
to help mask his voice. Probably used some other
device – maybe as simple as the old handkerchief over
the mouthpiece. Other than male between the ages of
twenty and forty, probably London-born, their guess is
as good as yours. We've tried to work out a list of possibles, and got nowhere. Ruling out the Hills themselves
and Jack Price, who's family too, the only other obvious
candidates are the lowlifes who run errands for them. It
doesn't add up, though. Like all gangs these days, the
Hills must work on a need-to-know basis, and those
lowlifes will be kept in the dark. It's more likely that
someone else with a grudge overheard something, and
decided to stitch them up. That could be *anyone.*'

'Where was the pub he called from?'

'Wapping – the Nelson. Come on, Sal, that's enough
shop for the moment. I thought I was supposed to be
getting a day off. Shall we see what our own lowlifes
have got up to?'

126

12

Rupert used whatever scraps of time he and his young team could muster over the next few days in preparation for Thursday's first formal session on the Interleisure project. He met Ronnie privately late on Wednesday to alert him to his unilateral adoption of that name, to explain how the team would be configured, to fill him in on the role of Fraser Morrison, and to suggest very firmly that they draw a veil over the personal nature of their relationship. Fortunately, Rupert kept work and private life well separated, and even when Primrose left messages for him at Orbia, she used only her first name. There was no reason why anyone should make a connection.

For his part, Fraser was so frantically busy he only had time to skim through the materials the team had prepared, and sit with them for a paltry fifteen minutes before the clients arrived on the dot of ten. He paid no more attention to the client engagement letter that Rupert stuck under his nose and he scribbled his signature.

As they filed in, Ronnie, Jack, and Lee, it was clear that punctuality wasn't the only thing about them which was sharp. They were all dressed in their Sunday best, Ronnie's imposing bulk enclosed in a tailored blue suit and a gleaming white shirt adorned with silver dice cufflinks, offset by a brightly striped silk tie pierced with a gold pin. Jack's approach was essentially similar, but he favoured a tangerine tie. Lee had chosen a light houndstooth with a distinctly Italian accent.

Rupert quickly took care of the introductions on the Orbia side, while Ronnie reciprocated for 'Interleisure'. When Rupert took his first eyeful of Primrose's brother, he felt sweet relief that he had not considered dealing on her without doing the necessary family due diligence. Imagine how all his friends would react if they'd turned up to his wedding and been introduced to *that*.

Fraser took up a central position and began right away. He wanted to be out of this room in ten minutes flat.

'Well, a warm welcome to Orbia, and let me say how delighted we are that you have decided to retain us. I think that Rupert has already given you some information on the nature and breadth of our practice, and he'll be running through more of that later, so I won't waste your time on it. The team is small by our normal standards, but this is because the first stage of this project will be essentially diagnostic, trying to work out what is currently holding Interleisure back. You should think of the team as the tip of a very large iceberg. As the project moves on to specific problem solving, I'd expect to see it grow, and if you decide to use us for any larger-scale implementation work, you'll meet many more of our storm-troopers. We also have a powerful research group which is available to our teams and, as for myself, although I won't be actively involved on a day-to-day basis, I can assure you that I will be monitoring progress very closely. Rupert will be reporting to me every week, and I will be devoting a lot of my mind-space to it. Above all, Mr Hill, you should feel free to call me or come and see me any time.'

Ronnie nodded. Fraser smiled.

'Now a few general words about how we operate. Orbia is essentially a hypothesis-led consultancy . . .'

Ronnie felt Lee's body twitch into question-asking mode, and put out a hand to silence him. Ronnie had no idea either, but he didn't want them to embarrass themselves and Rupert so early on.

'By that I mean our teams take a look at a problem, and try intuitively to guess the most likely answer. Then they set about gathering information and test this hypothesis. If it withstands the test, all well and good. However, if we find evidence which contradicts the hypothesis, we go back to the beginning and start again. That means being willing to change tack with great speed and agility . . .'

Lee had lost interest. Ronnie was hoping that Jack was understanding some of this, and Jack was praying to God that Ronnie wouldn't ask him.

Fraser clasped his hands together. 'Any questions so far? Everything clear?'

All three nodded.

'The final thing I want to mention is the kind of materials we use. We don't believe in long papers. They only serve to obfuscate issues, as I'm sure you'd agree . . .'

More nodding.

'. . . So we prefer presentations in slide form. You'll find that these are often surprisingly short. One of our core beliefs is that words should be used clearly and sparingly. We use something we call MECE – mutually exclusive, collectively exhaustive. In essence, it means that our written thoughts should cover the subject without omission and without overlap. We also use what we call "logic trees", and have always found that strong arguments usually come in threes.'

As he was finishing that thought, he lowered his left arm below the polished surface of the long table, and discreetly pushed back his left cuff with his right hand. Pausing for breath, he simultaneously glanced down at his watch. Twelve minutes past ten. Time to be on his way.

'That's no more than a brief thumbnail sketch, and I'm sure you want to get into the meat of the subject. So why don't I leave you there, and let you get on? Before I do so, let me say what an exciting project this is. We at Orbia are completely committed to it, and I'm confident that we will add significant value.'

He stood up, shook hands solemnly with all three, and swept out the door. Rupert moved to his vacated seat and one of his two younger colleagues shuffled closer to fill the gap.

'Now then. Coffee, tea?'

They chose. The most junior from the team poured the drinks into the porcelain cups and handed them around.

'Okay, let's get to work. I'm glad to say we haven't been idle over the last three days and we've been able to gather a fair amount of information, especially on the restaurant side. It looks to us that, put simply, there are a few basic drivers in this business. One is critical mass in purchasing. The cost of food, beverages, and sundry supplies falls dramatically when you reach a certain level. A second one is systems. With all the employment and health and safety legislation that's around now, you need a clear set of procedures, which is more cost-effective to implement across a number of outlets. The same applies to IT systems, like POS – point of sale – terminals. These are invaluable as an information source, so you can monitor precisely what's being consumed. Not only that, they can be configured to automatically re-order items before stocks are exhausted . . .'

Rupert stopped for a moment to see if there was any reaction so far. Apparently not.

'Branding and marketing are, of course, closely inter-related. It makes very little sense to have a high mar-keting spend promoting a single restaurant, when you could spread the same expenditure over several outlets. These, we know, are very obvious points to anyone in the business, and consultants always run the risk of trying to teach grannies to suck eggs. So please regard these as no more than markers for our own understanding. Now, let's switch to specifics. Within Interleisure's restaurant division, exactly how many outlets are there, Ronnie?'

'Five.'

'And how many brands?'

'Five.'

'O-*kay*. In the leisure operation?'

131

'One sports club.'

'Of course. But you have a wider range of . . . social clubs?'

'You mean the night clubs? Three.'

'And recently you've diversified into telecoms, I think.'

'Two shops.'

'Right. So there's five, six, nine . . . eleven operations in total. And group turnover is about how much?'

Ronnie asked Jack to comment.

'It varies a lot from month to month.'

'For example, how much was it last month, and how much the month before?'

Jack looked through the numbers in the small ledger book he always carried.

'The last month I got figures for is July. We did one point four million. June was two million.'

'And what would you guess August would be? So we have a three-month perspective.'

'Two 'undred grand.'

Rupert looked astonished. 'Two hundred thousand? That's an incredible drop.'

Ronnie weighed in. 'August was 'orrible.'

Rupert was casting around for an explanation. He'd never known a business with swings like this.

'Is it a seasonal thing, perhaps? A lot of people away on holiday?'

Ronnie nodded again. 'Yeah, that's it, seasonal.'

'But overall, is the business profitable? I presume we're looking at an annual turnover of, what – twenty odd million?'

Jack confirmed that the figure was not far off.

'So what's your pre-tax profit? Shall I hazard a guess

from the wider statistics we've collected? Two million, maybe?'

Ronnie and Jack shook their heads in unison. Jack spoke up.

'Less, much less. Not more than fifty grand.'

Rupert looked slightly queasy. The team were by now all aware that they'd been drafted onto a project that wasn't up there in the size and prestige stakes. However, he didn't want them thinking it was a complete turkey.

'But Ronnie, you do see the potential to get to the sort of profitability I mentioned, don't you?'

'That's why we're 'ere, Rupert, that's why we're 'ere.'

*

By that same Thursday, Primrose was feeling much better about life. Rupert had spent a lot of Sunday, plus Monday evening, reassuring her in the sweetest way. He'd bought flowers and chocolates, and even cooked stir-fry vegetables for her. Just as important, she'd actually moved into her new flat.

The flat was on two levels, the ground floor and the first, and though there was a decidedly weird woman living upstairs, Primrose had the marvellous advantage of owning the garden. At present it was more of a rubbish dump than a garden, and she would have to devote most of the coming weekends to sorting it out. She doubted that Rupert would lend much of a hand. Perhaps her flatmate would turn out to have green fingers.

There was some news on that front too. Almost all of

Primrose's closer friends were already set up, whether in places they owned, with settled flatmates, or with boyfriends or husbands. Her best friend from school, Emily, was in the market, but concluded reluctantly that a commute from Shepherd's Bush to Canary Wharf was too much of a good thing. By Wednesday, Primrose had almost decided to resort to a small ad in *Time Out* when Emily rang back to ask if Primrose had thought of Georgina Parham.

Georgina Parham had been in their year at St Mary's, and had been an automatic choice for the in-set, for which neither Primrose nor Emily had ever been faintly considered. Georgina was the most beautiful girl in the class, tall with deep chestnut hair, emerald eyes, and a voice which had been husky even back then. Her father was a minor aristo who was seriously loaded, and Primrose remembered Georgina being given some outrageous sports car on her seventeenth birthday. Primrose hadn't seen hide nor hair of her since school. All she could really recall was the girl's cool, dry, effortless superiority, which made Primrose feel effortlessly inferior, and even had the nuns in a bit of a spin.

She needed to be brought up to date by the better informed Emily. After studying History of Art at the Sorbonne, Georgina had joined Christie's, and had worked for them in Paris, then New York. She was now coming back to London, and needed accommodation pro tem while she worked out whether to settle back here or move on to other parts. The story was that, after breaking many hearts in France, she had finally met her match in New York, where a successful and absurdly good-looking attorney had persuaded her to fall for him, and then abruptly thrown her over for a newer model. It was thought that her departure from New York was not unconnected both with the emotional upset and the all too socially visible manner of his rejection.

Primrose hummed and hawed. She wasn't at all sure about Georgina. On the other hand, taking in a complete stranger would be risky too. Better the devil you knew, maybe, and it would only be for a short while anyway. Decided, she called the Christie's number, got through, and invited Georgina to come round for a glass of champagne some time. Georgina said she would come that very evening.

'Primrose, how absolutely *wonderful* to see you again. Why, we haven't seen each other since about nineteen ninety . . .'

'Since school.' Primrose couldn't be bothered to beat about the bush.

'Is it really that long? And, my, how you've changed. Quite the beautiful swan.'

'From the ugly duckling?'

'Don't be silly, you know what I meant. You do look marvellous, though.'

'So do you, but that's hardly a surprise. Champagne?'

'Thank you.' Georgina waited patiently while Primrose wrestled with the wire retainer on the bottle. They clinked and sipped. 'Now, do tell me everything. I'm dying to catch up. You're a lawyer, I hear.'

'Yes, that's right. With a firm called Linklaters.'

'I don't know any law firms, I'm afraid, apart from the one Daddy uses. And they are incompetent idiots. Lost my poor father millions through some wrong clause or other. Infuriating. Still, that's another story . . . So you enjoy it, do you? Doing whatever lawyers do.'

'Yes, I do.' Georgina had only been there five minutes and was already making Primrose feel like she was the one being interviewed.

'Well, that's good, isn't it?'

'What about you, Georgina? How are Christie's treating you?'

'I got rather bored in New York after a while, dealing with all those appalling wealthy Americans. It's rather nice to be home, especially when the weather's like this. I'm sure the first autumn storm will knock the enthusiasm out of me though, and I'll get itchy feet again. Boyfriend?'

Primrose was so taken aback, some champagne went down the wrong way.

'Sorry. Yes. He's called Rupert Henley.'

'What does he do?'

'He's a management consultant.'

'Age?'

Jesus Christ. 'Thirty-five.'

'Have you been together long?'

'Oh, a year or so. How about you, Georgina?'

'No one. I'm a lonely old maid.'

'What about when you were in New York?'

'The Eurotrash you meet there are frightful, and the Americans are even worse. I did have the odd fling while I was there, but I didn't bring any of them back in my hand luggage . . . Now, can I look round my new home? I'm terribly excited. The flat looks so wonderfully *mignon*.'

Primrose hardly knew what to say. She wasn't at all

136

sure she wanted the woman, and as far as she was concerned, nothing was decided yet. Had Georgina misunderstood, or was she presuming?

'Well, as you see, this is the sitting room. And through here's the kitchen. All the appliances are new.'

'Good.'

'Apart from the loo through there, that's pretty much all there is on this floor. Then we go up the stairs. This is the second bedroom, here.'

Georgina stepped in and spun round, taking it all in. 'Hmmm. Just as well I'm tidy, isn't it?'

She threw open the doors of the fitted wardrobe. 'Not what you'd call capacious. Still . . .'

'And you have a bathroom to yourself, across the corridor . . . here.'

'Mm-hmm.'

'And that's it, basically.'

'Is that your bedroom through there? Can I take a peek?'

'Of course. After you.'

Georgina pushed the door open. 'Oh, that *is* nice . . . and I see you have your bathroom *en-suite*.' She uttered the phrase in a manicured accent. 'I don't suppose . . .'

'You don't suppose what, Georgina?'

'Oh nothing. Nothing at all. Just a thought . . . Now I suppose we'd better talk cash. I'm rather hard up at the moment, I have to warn you. Needless to say, Christie's pay me a pittance, and after losing all that money because of that ridiculous lawyer, Daddy's becoming incredibly tiresome about helping me out.'

'Didn't you have some sort of trust of your own?'

'How terribly clever of you to remember a little thing

like that. Yes, I do. Problem is, it's all tied up in long-term thingies that I don't understand, *and* I already dipped into it once or twice earlier this year. The trustees have become quite mingy. The bottom line, as they say in New York, is that I'm broke.'

'The agent I talked to said that it should be about three hundred.'

'A month?'

Primrose couldn't stop herself bursting out laughing. 'No, a *week*. This isn't the Salvation Army, you know.'

'Three hundred a week, in an area like *this*? Well, clearly I'm way out of touch with London prices.'

'Yes, you are, aren't you?'

'But that *does* at least include electricity, gas, water, and so on?'

'No, we'd share those.'

'So, actually, it's *more* than three hundred.'

'Georgina, it's pretty simple. I need help paying my mortgage. I think this rent is fair, but if you don't agree, or you can't afford it . . .'

'No, no. Don't get cross. I was only asking. I'll take it. Mind you . . .'

'Mind me *what*?'

'Thinking about it, if your agent said it should be three hundred, that would be before deduction of his commission, wouldn't it? And that commission would be, say, fifteen per cent, which is . . . forty-five pounds a week, *non*?'

'Georgina, I think—'

'Don't get me wrong. I don't mean to suggest you should give up *all* of that . . .'

'So what do you propose?'

138

'That we split it – right down the middle. Three hundred, minus half of forty-five, how much is that? I never could do mental arithmetic . . . about two hundred and seventy-five, give or take the odd penny?'

Primrose sighed. 'All right, Georgina.'

'And we'll have such fun together, won't we? Just like the old days.'

13

Paul O'Neill was travelling the next week, so it wasn't until the following Monday that the triumvirate were able to meet. The Goldman team had presented to Fraser and Alistair in the meantime. Fraser took the lead in reporting.

'Basically, Paul, it's good news. What they're saying is that we could do either. We're still on track for the flotation if we want to go that route. Equally, following some soundings that their San Francisco office have taken, they seem comfortable that Synapsis have a serious interest.'

'Could they move quickly?'

'Looks like it could be done in a couple of months.'

'And the likely valuation they'd put on us?'

'Much the same as flotation. Between three-fifty and four-fifty million.'

'Well, you've both had time to think about this. Where do you come out, Fraser?'

'For all the reasons we've discussed before, I'm for Synapsis. If it doesn't fly, we could always look for another buyer or float later next year.'

'Alistair?'

'I'm still against selling out. This is a great company with a great future. The moment we lose our independence, it'll get harder to attract and retain good people, and the same will go for clients. As you know, we're now close to the point of no return on gearing up for the February float. I recommend the precise opposite approach: that we go hell for leather for that, and if it comes off the rails, we consider selling to Synapsis.'

The casting vote was clearly with Paul. He got up and walked round the room.

'Alistair, I have to say that, overall, I'm with Fraser. A sale to Synapsis would be quicker, cleaner, altogether less complicated.'

Alistair looked defeated. Fraser couldn't stop himself looking a touch triumphant. Paul continued.

'However, if we as a management team appointed consultants, I'm sure they would be telling us not to put too many eggs in one basket, and never to go into a negotiation without an alternative. If we mothballed our flotation plans and entered an exclusive process with Synapsis, that's the mistake we'd be making.'

Fraser interjected. 'But, Paul, surely you can't be suggesting running the two processes in parallel? Think of the cost.'

'Fraser, if Synapsis *do* buy us for around four hundred million, I think it will have been worth spending a couple of million on an insurance policy. Do you disagree?'

A tiny smile had returned to Alistair's face. Fraser's, by contrast, was looking far from sunny.

'No, perhaps not. But have you thought this through? For expenditure of that order, we'd have to consult the wider partnership.'

'It might surprise you that I *have* thought it through. I did little else, in fact, while I was spending so much

141

time on planes last week. And the more I thought about it, the more uncomfortable I began to feel about how close we three have come to taking a decision without consulting them.'

Fraser didn't like the way this was going at all. 'That's not true, Paul. All we've been doing is exploring options. We've always known that in the final analysis the partnership as a whole would have to sanction it.'

'Unfortunately, that phrase "the final analysis" rather gives the game away. I suspect that many of our partners might feel that they should have been involved at a much earlier stage. I think we must, without further ado, call a meeting of the partners, and see what they think.'

Alistair felt very much happier. 'I absolutely agree, Paul. However, think of all the partners' commitments, and the need to get as many as possible here from the overseas offices. If we called such a major meeting at too short notice, we'd get the whole firm wondering what was going on. They might think we had some frightful crisis.'

Paul consulted his diary. 'Today's the seventeenth of September. Remind me, Alistair, when is the last date by which we would have to appoint accountants, lawyers, et cetera?'

'The absolute latest would be Monday the fifteenth of October.'

'Okay, let's hold it the weekend immediately before then. That will minimise the disruption to everyone's schedule. If we do it here in the offices, we'll get all the other staff wondering, and public places like hotels make me nervous . . . I tell you what, we'll do it at West Point.'

West Point wasn't the American military academy, it was Paul's country house in a picturesque, remote part of Dorset. Paul was enormously proud of it, and loved to have opportunities to show it off.

'Pam can get some caterers in. We won't be able to put many people up, but, though we are in the middle of nowhere, there are some charming hotels not far away.'

*

If Peter Nicholl and his staff ever had such a thing as a quiet day, this was it. Not that you'd have realised. The *Timbookedtoo* office in Farringdon was like bedlam as usual, with the electric crackle of a still young, exciting company which had ridden out the storms of a bumpy early stock-market career, and had now graduated to greater self-confidence. As on any other day, the hundreds of staff sat at their workstations, some answering technical queries, some updating pages on the site, others on the phone to hotel groups or airlines, negotiating and renegotiating terms.

They were quieter than usual because most of them had hangovers. They'd had a bash the previous evening to celebrate getting their millionth paying customer. A million was a lot. A lot of flights, of hotels, of restaurants, of theatres, concerts, and exhibitions. If only ten per cent of those got in the habit of using the service regularly – say three times a year – they would be in great shape.

The other thing they'd celebrated was agreeing the last of three acquisitions, mopping up some minor competition in Sweden and Spain. Linklaters had done a good job for them, and the deals had been signed in double-quick time. Those being out of the way, there should be no further distractions for a while, and Peter Nicholl and his top team would be free to get on with running the business.

As he sat at his unimposing desk in a corner of the huge room, Peter reflected that he quite liked distractions. Their systems were now so developed that the company almost ran itself. It was so different from the early days when he and his fellow founders rushed around like mad things, bootstrapping everything, bouncing from one calamity to another as computers crashed, unhappy customers yelled, and airlines had to be bludgeoned into doing business with them.

Peter had loved it, for the adrenalin, for the intense team-spirit, for the feeling of doing something groundbreaking. And also because the company became a sort of surrogate social life. Several of his closest friends, as well as some less close ones, had joined the company, which meant that his professional and private life had fused into one, especially with the crazy hours they'd worked back then.

Now the madness had abated a little, and the socialising which was part and parcel of it faded too. They were a few years older, many married, most in relationships, and they all wanted a private life. Peter could understand that, even if his own life hadn't followed the same pattern. Everyone said he was married to the company, and it was true it was still his passion and obsession.

He was amused at how it had altered things socially in another sense. Challenged vertically and regionally, he'd been of zero interest for the other sex at Cambridge, and got through the whole three years without much more than the odd fumbly snog. For a while there was a girl back in Sunderland who'd been in the year below him at school. For the first few terms she'd called and written, and when he visited home they'd enjoyed the odd frolic when her mother was out. After that, her interest had weakened, and eventually she'd fallen for a travelling salesman from Doncaster, who was older and married, but could afford to take her to smart restaurants in Newcastle, and who to an eighteen year old must have seemed sophisticated beyond belief.

After Cambridge Peter had worked in a humdrum travel job for a while, then taken himself off to do an MBA at Wharton School in Philadelphia, which romantically was as barren as Cambridge. What a turnaround it was when the publicity machine first started to crank. Suddenly, girls who previously wouldn't have given him the time of day cornered him at parties and hung on his every word. Some wanted share tips, some wanted discounts, some wanted glamorous travel, all sooner or later wanted husbands. And although as a short-arse with a strange accent and a doubtful complexion he most definitely was not from the right gene pool, a net worth of two hundred million changed the equation dramatically. In Darwinian terms, he had gone from the bottom to the top of the heap.

For a while, Peter was like a kid in a candy store. The very idea that he could go up to a gorgeous girl at a party, and invite her out with a ninety per cent chance of success was remarkable. So for a while he had the odd fling. He couldn't let himself go, though, and risk getting emotionally involved, knowing that it was only his money which was attracting them. And that, if fortune should ever whisk away that money, he wouldn't see any of those women for dust.

So in the end, he more or less gave it up. He lived very simply, having bought a cosy but tiny garret in Culford Gardens at the back of Sloane Square. The Ferrari was his only true indulgence, together with a lock-up garage which he'd rented to go with it. He knew that everyone thought it was flash, or no more than a crumpet-catcher, which in the circumstances was ironic. Actually, Peter had bought it because he loved it. Loved its shape, its sound, adored driving it, and would have washed it himself, if he could have done that unobserved.

Sometimes he wondered if he would stay single for ever. Maybe all the best girls were already taken. Girls like Primrose Hill, for example. He hadn't known her before Rupert introduced them, but a beautiful creature like that, with a lovely personality, doubtless came from some frightfully smart family who propelled her into society as a deb. Peter doubted that she'd ever had a day without a boyfriend since she was sixteen. And of course she was with someone like Rupert – vastly good-looking, a million feet tall, oozing that insouciant arrogance that women always seemed to fall for, and perfectly turned out on every occasion, right down to his manicured hands and the inevitable signet ring with his family crest.

He realised he'd been in a reverie for over ten minutes, and looked down at his notepad. What a strange thing to do! Quite unconsciously, he'd doodled the word 'Primrose' about fifty times.

*

Over at Orbia, Rupert and his team were making good progress, enough for a further session with Interleisure. On this occasion, both Jack and Lee were busy with other things, so Ronnie went alone. Rupert let rip.

'Okay, Ronnie, this is still essentially desk-work. We haven't been out in the field yet, and we want to do that next week, visiting both your own sites and those of some of your competitors. However, as Fraser Morrison said at our kick-off session, we're a hypothesis-led consultancy, and we wanted to let you know what our first cut at a hypothesis looks like.'

'Okay. I'm all ears, Rupert.'

'As we see things, it's all about critical mass. Although the sports club and the two mobile telephone shops may be nice small businesses, we don't see that they make sense unless you're willing to throw far more resources into them. You have neither the purchasing power on the phone side, nor enough expertise on the sporting side.'

'So what you recommend?'

'Well, of course, we're not recommending *anything* at the moment. This is merely a glimpse into our thought-process. However, if our intuition proves correct after more investigation, we'd probably recommend selling them, and ploughing the proceeds into other areas.'

Ronnie looked unconvinced. 'I'm not sure we would want to do that, Rupert. We want to improve 'em, of course, make 'em more profitable, but gettin' shot of 'em altogether, I'm not sure.'

This response made Rupert a little testy. Why appoint

consultants with supercharged brains if you were only going to bat away what they suggested? He dug his nails into his palms and silently counted to ten. This was not the time to bring this to a head.

'I hear you, Ronnie, but all I ask is that you keep an open mind while we check that hypothesis out.'

'Okay. What about the night clubs?'

'Those sort of clubs are by their nature rather individual places, and we suspect that economies of scale are limited. The main thing you're buying is alcohol, and there you rapidly reach a competitive purchasing power. In simple language, you wouldn't get much cheaper prices for drink even if you doubled the number of clubs. So what we'll be concentrating on there will be cost control and your own pricing policy. It should be easy to squeeze another ten to fifteen per cent on the margin.'

'Fair enough. That leaves the restaurants.'

'Now *that's* where we think you have a big opportunity. Although there's far tougher competition in that sector than in the past, restaurant groups do make decent money. And it *is* fundamentally a great business to be in, with none of the problems that most small businesses have of being reliant on a few big customers who always pay late. That's the good part, Ronnie.'

'So, what's the bad?'

'Frankly, you're all over the place. Not only geographically, either. Look at your brands. What a mixture. You've got a French brasserie called *The Legless Frog*, an Italian called *Pasta La Vista*, the Tex-Mex *Spic and Span*, a Chinese called *Cool Coolie*, and a sushi bar *Raw and Order*.'

'What's wrong with that? I like them names. Thought most of 'em up meself.'

'There's nothing wrong with them, as far as they go. Some might think them a touch corny, perhaps. Would you yourself go to a restaurant with any of those names if you were on a hot date?'

'Tell the truth, Rupert, it's been a few years since I been on one.'

'Maybe that's the problem. You're only appealing to an older clientèle . . . Anyway, that's not our main point. We believe your restaurant strategy needs a complete overhaul. We think you should take a fresh look at whether your existing sites have the right locations. If they all do, fine. If any don't, you shouldn't hesitate to close them. After we do our site visits, we'll have some input on that ourselves. Whatever sites you're then left with should be consolidated into a single style of cooking and a single brand.'

'Which one d'you think's best?'

'None of them, to be honest. We don't see that any of the existing names has the right up-market feel.'

'So what do we do? Think up another?'

'Probably not. Inventing the right brand is hard in any business, and getting it established is even harder. We've taken a look at what's out there. Recent transactions have been done at very low values, reflecting a general drop in confidence about what direction the economy's headed. Our preliminary view is that you should look to acquire another restaurant company, both for its brand and its sites, and then plan a serious national roll-out.'

14

Primrose was trying to get her house in order while dodging from airport to airport documenting yet another tricky transnational merger. Particularly vexingly, she had been made to give up a whole weekend, cancelling various plans with Rupert, and work for four straight days at her client's Turin headquarters. When she got home on Monday evening, she found that Georgina had spread her possessions liberally round the flat. Predictably, the mantelpiece was filled to overflowing with a wide range of glossy invitations, all inscribed to *The Hon. Georgina Parham*. When Primrose crawled in, exhaustedly dumping her suit carrier, her square black lawyer's briefcase, and her company IBM laptop, she saw Georgina sitting there in a tracksuit, nursing a gin and tonic, her slippered feet up on Primrose's new Chinese lacquer table. Georgina looked up from her *Vogue*.

'Well, there you are. Welcome home. You look knackered.'

'God, I am. What a journey. We sat on the tarmac for two hours while Alitalia advertised for a pilot.'

'Brutal.'

'I think I need one of those too.' She went in to the kitchen, helped herself to a gin and tonic, carried it through and sat down. 'So, how are you, Georgina? How's work been?'

'Fine, fine. Rather too much socialising. Too many tedious dinner parties. That's why I'm so glad to have a night off tonight. Shall we order something in?'

'I won't be able to join you tonight, I'm afraid. I'm having supper with Rupert. Haven't seen him for days.'

'Oh, that's nice. Where are you going?'

'He's booked somewhere near here.'

'So is he coming to collect you?'

'Yes, that's the plan. I'd better jump in the bath, if you don't mind.'

'Not at all. In fact, I might do the same. So relaxing. And I do feel such a slob dressed like this.'

When Primrose made it back into the sitting room, Georgina was there, feet up as before, and reading the same magazine, but dressed very differently, her hair looking irritatingly fantastic, and in Manolo Blahnik stilettos.

The doorbell went. Primrose walked smartly across to the machine and pressed the button to let him in. When Rupert came through the door, she hugged him.

'It's so good to see you.'

He smiled, gave her a little kiss, and pulled a bottle of champagne from behind his back.

'Oh, *Rupes*, you shouldn't have.' She took it from him and led him by the hand. 'This is Georgina.'

Georgina slowly put down her magazine and looked up. 'Hello.'

'Hi . . . Hey, Prim, the place looks great. Shall I open the bottle? How about you, Georgina? Fancy a drop?'

Georgina looked down at her half-empty glass. 'I'm on gin and tonic. Oh, what the hell. Why not?'

Rupert poured three glasses. Georgina looked at him carefully as he sat down.

'Primrose tells me you're a management consultant. You must be terribly clever.'

Rupert laughed. 'Not at all. We're just like teachers: those who can, do. Those who can't, consult.'

Georgina smiled. 'They're not really the same, though, are they? I hear that consultants are terribly well paid. Teachers get nothing, rather like people who work in the art world. That's what I do, by the way.'

'Yes, I heard from Primrose.'

'Oh dear, what else did she tell you? Did she say I was an absolute nightmare? Primrose is such a doll to put up with me. Aren't you, darling?' Georgina acknowledged Primrose's smile and turned her gaze quickly back on Rupert. 'Do you like modern art?'

'Absolutely. Everything from Jackson Pollock to Damien Hirst. I go to the Tate Modern all the time.'

Primrose looked down at her watch. 'Rupes, we should really make a move.'

'Sure.' Rupert quaffed the rest of his champagne. 'Where are you off out to, Georgina? Somewhere fun, I hope.'

'No, I'm going to see if they do deliveries here.'

'Why not come with us?'

'Oh no, I couldn't possibly.'

Primrose got up and stepped over to where Rupert remained resolutely seated. 'Darling, Georgina was telling me that she *wants* a night in. Don't twist her arm.'

Georgina smiled back at Primrose. 'Oh, it's not that. In other circumstances, I'd have loved to come with you. But I know you two haven't seen each other for a few days, and I'm sure you've got so much catching up to do.'

Rupert laughed. 'Not really. We talk on the phone every day. I have to admit that I don't think I've got anything particularly earth-shattering to say. Have you, Prim?'

There wasn't much Primrose could do except shake her head.

'Okay, that settles it. I'll call the restaurant and tell them, and let's be on our way.'

'Don't you want to see my room first?'

'Can't I see it later? If I'm invited back afterwards, that is.'

And he turned and smiled at Georgina.

*

Over the next few days, the team at Orbia did a lot of field studies at Interleisure outlets. Ronnie got a call asking him to come back in with his colleagues. When they got there, they were surprised when Rupert came into the meeting room unaccompanied. Ronnie greeted him cheerily.

'Morning, Rupert. Where's the foot soldiers? Been out for a night on the tiles at one of our clubs, and not made it in?'

'No, I can assure you they were in bright and early.'

'So, what's goin' on?'

'Sit down, please. The fact is, Ronnie, having visited all your premises, asked a few questions of your staff, and waded through the figures Jack provided, I'm left with more questions than answers. I thought it might

153

be better for us to discuss this privately and not in front of the team.'

Ronnie considered. What had the clever little bastard found out? Oh well, there was no backing down now. Might as well hear the worst.

'Okay, Rupert, shoot.'

'Well, for one thing, the swings of income that we touched on before don't seem to be seasonal at all. Over the last two years there have been sharp monthly dips in a February, in an October, and in a December, as well as some of the summer months. We checked against other restaurant groups, and there is no pattern which correlates with this. Odder still, both the peaks and troughs appear to be broadly consistent across the whole group, despite the fact that there is no connection that we can identify between phone shops and night clubs.'

Ronnie exchanged looks with Jack. It looked like they'd been too free with the info. He did his best to hide his concern.

'Is that it?'

'No, there's more. We're none of us gourmets exactly, but we do eat out a lot, and we all agreed that the food was third-rate. There were hardly any customers either, which suggests that our view is widely shared. And yet, when we refer back to Jack's books, it appears that some of these outlets are taking more money in the best months than leading West End restaurants. Very bizarre. Finally, the way all the businesses are run seems incredibly old-fashioned. From the statistics we gathered, bills at most top restaurant groups – the ones which set the industry benchmarks – are now paid over eighty per cent using credit cards. We know that, as in any retail business, there's a cost associated with accepting credit cards, but there are many more pluses, including appealing to the business user, encouraging incremental spend, and acting as a barrier to theft by staff.'

'We agree, Rupert. That's why we accept cards everywhere we operate. Right, Jack?'

'Course,' chimed in Jack.

Rupert wasn't put off that easily.

'Yes, we know you do. But the statistics for actual usage are less than five per cent. That's ridiculous. We tried to get an explanation from staff, and frankly there was nothing that made any sense. Some said you couldn't force customers to use them, which is no more true of your outlets than anyone else's, and others said that management didn't like paying the commission. If that's the real reason, it's unbelievably short-sighted. Ronnie, I'm not exaggerating when I say that this is the worst-run business I've ever seen. It's as if you don't *want* it to work.'

Getting no clear reaction, he was beginning to run out of steam. 'Unless you're willing to take root and branch action, you might as well sell the whole lot for what little you could get. Mind you, I don't know who'd buy it. In its current form, the only use for the outlets I can imagine is to launder cash for crooks.'

All three on the other side of the table went very still. Rupert saw their reaction and put his hands out in apology.

'Hey, it was just a joke. I didn't mean to . . .'

Ronnie stopped him with a glance. 'Rupert, I think

it's best if we go now. Send the invoice for the work you done so far, and let's leave it at that.'

Rupert's mind was spinning. Oh fuck, what had he done, saying something so stupid? Obviously, he'd insulted them grievously. And if it *was* true, that was far worse.

The three men stood up and started filing out. Rupert sat there, paralysed. As the meeting-room door closed behind them, the enormity of the situation began to dawn on him. He would have to go to Fraser Morrison and tell him what had happened. That would be the absolute end of his partnership chances. He might even be fired for skimping on client checks. Oh shit, what could he do?

He got up and dashed from the room. The lift wouldn't come and he hurtled down the stairs. Out in the street, he looked left and right. There they were, getting into a Merc. He took to his heels, and just managed to intercept the car as Ronnie's driver started to pull away from the kerb.

Ronnie opened the rear window.

'Ronnie, I'm *really* sorry for what I said.'

The older man nodded coldly. Rupert had no idea what to do or say next.

'I should never have . . . And please don't get me wrong. If it *is* true, it's not something I'd be judgmental about or anything . . .'

Still Ronnie stayed silent.

'In fact, if you'd felt able to level with me, maybe I could've helped in some way with that business too.'

'What the fuck you on about?'

'As you know, Orbia is—'

Ronnie cut in sarcastically. 'An 'ypothesis-led consultancy.' He'd looked the word up in the dictionary after that first meeting.

'Precisely. Well, let me try another hypothesis. If what I just blurted out is true – and I assure you that until that moment, it hadn't crossed my mind – it follows that what we've been looking at is only a part of your business activities, and a peripheral part at that. Is it conceivable that, however experienced you might be, you could do with advice on your core business too?'

'I've no idea what you're on about.'

'What I'm on about, Ronnie, is that I've never seen a business yet that wouldn't benefit from consultancy, and there's no reason why yours should be any different. I know nothing about crime, okay? But I bet you invest time, effort, and money. You take some calculated risks and try to protect the downside. And in the end, there are winners and some losers. Where's the difference from any other business?'

Ronnie's expression was still coldly aggressive.

'Let me get this straight. Assumin' – and me, Jack and Lee are as much 'ypothesis-led as the next man – assumin' for a moment that what you said was true, are you tellin' us that you'd simply march into your boss's office and say, "Guess what, the project's changed, and now we're workin' for a bunch of villains"?'

'No, that's not what I'm saying.'

'Then you've lost me altogether. What *are* you sayin'?'

'That as far as the rest of my team members are concerned, the project would go ahead as before. I'll tell them that we had a full and frank exchange, that you're committed to making major improvements to the restaurants.'

'What about you?'

'For me, things would be different. You'd have to open up to me, and I'd see what I could suggest by way of improvements.'

'Why would you wanna do that?'

Rupert felt he was getting somewhere, and his brain began kicking back in.

'First, because it'd be exciting, a new challenge. Believe me, consulting can be pretty bloody dull. Can you imagine being sentenced to six months' hard labour on non-woven fabrics, or life insurance? This would be different, a thrill.'

'And that's it? All for kicks, eh?'

Rupert hesitated, then decided on the spur of the moment to go for broke. 'No, I'd want to have some upside too.'

'What's that mean?'

'The price you were quoted by Orbia was only for the clubs, restaurants, and so on. That'll continue as before. You wouldn't expect to get a whole lot of additional value without paying a little more, though, would you?'

'And 'ow'd you explain that one to Morrison?'

'I wouldn't. Remember you once asked if I'd moonlight for you? I said no then, but I've just changed my mind.'

Ronnie was calculating too. His instinct told him to walk away from all this. But what if Rupert called Rose right away and told her the lot? He decided to play for time.

'For the sake of argument, what would we be talkin' about, per day, or whatever?'

'I'm not sure. How about a share of any profits I help generate?'

'How big a share?'

'I don't know. I'm sure we can work something out. Won't you at least think about it? Whatever your decision, I give you my word of honour that I'll never mention this to anyone, including Primrose.'

'You'd better not, or I'll cut your balls off. As to your proposition, I'll be in touch.'

The dark-tinted window whirred up and the car moved off, leaving him standing there on the pavement.

15

Rupert couldn't go right back to work so he walked over to Hyde Park for a breath of fresh air. He found it hard to think straight. What a fool he'd been for not seeing it before. Look at them, for God's sake! It should've been obvious. On the other hand, people like him didn't run across professional criminals every day of the week. You didn't expect to discover that your nice, well-educated, solicitor girlfriend came from the mob. Was it possible that they'd all kept this from her, that Prim didn't know what her own family were up to? No. Unless Prim was an idiot, which she certainly wasn't, she would have worked it all out. She must know the whole story, and be keeping quiet about it.

He could see why she wouldn't want to yell it from the rooftops. All the same, to introduce her boyfriend to them, to let him start consulting for them, and not tell him . . . What a little minx. That put things in a very different light. He had always seen Primrose as essentially kind-hearted, decent and straightforward. Maybe he'd got her wrong. Maybe beneath this smooth, gentle surface she was cunning, deceitful, manipulative. He'd have to take more care what he said in front of her.

And what now? The chances they would open up to a total stranger were slim. Although they'd been rumbled, it didn't mean much. The police must have lots of information about them already. The only hope was if they needed help badly. Now that he understood the primary purpose of the retail outlets, that August downturn suggested that they must have had serious setbacks in the core business. They might be in real trouble.

If they wanted him, that would solve his Fraser problem in the short term, but he might be jumping from the frying pan into a far hotter fire. That wouldn't make sense unless he was very well paid. How much might he get? Assuming that, say, one third of the takings at the outlets were legitimate, then in a normal year turnover from the core business should be twelve to fifteen million. There would be costs, obviously, like payments to suppliers, guns, black cars, sunglasses, and so on. As a wild stab, maybe they would have a gross margin of forty per cent and a net profit of around two to three million. Not bad if there were only a handful of them. Now, assuming they were experiencing a cyclical downturn, and right now profits were almost nil, and that with a mixture of natural recovery plus his input they could get that up to five million. For him, anything less than a million wouldn't be worth all the risks, so that meant he'd somehow have to negotiate a twenty per cent share. Was there any way they would live with that?

They'd never tell him the truth about the takings, would they? What he might have to do was drip-feed advice, rather than supply it all in one great splurge, so they'd have to keep him sweet till the end. The more he thought about it, the more he needed that hold over them, or he'd be like a deer going into the lion's den.

These were hard, ruthless people. If he crossed them, they wouldn't need guns or knives. Ronnie or Lee would snap him like a dry autumn twig. He would have to be very, very careful.

And what about being caught? Could any amount of money be worth it? If the risk was, say, ten per cent, then no way. What if it was only one per cent, though? After all, any time he drove after drinking one glass too many he was probably running a worse chance of causing an accident and ending up in jail. And think of the ninety-nine per cent chance that he got away with it. If you compared that million with ordinary taxed income, it was the equivalent of twelve times his current salary. It would propel him immediately into a totally different bracket. That might be worth a one per cent risk. And surely there were precautions he could take. As long as he gave no written advice, and said nothing on a phone that could be compromising, he could deny everything.

Rupert's mind turned back to Prim. If he went along with this, would it increase the pressure on him to stay with her? He'd have to take care that they got no clue that he was planning to drop her. Ronnie's parting words about cutting his balls off sounded like a threat he might carry out. Once the work was over though, as long as he handled it civilly, they could hardly object. And Prim wasn't the vindictive sort. If he said that he'd just fallen out of love, she'd accept that.

God, he was feeling shaky. Part of him wished that he hadn't panicked and run after them, had just taken his medicine with Fraser and been done with it. Another part was still wanting to survive to fight another day.

It wasn't in his hands now anyway. How long would Ronnie take to get back to him? Until he heard, he'd have to dodge both Fraser and the Interleisure team. Better go down to Reading to see how Telesys was getting along.

*

Ronnie returned to Chislehurst in a gloomy mood. After the meeting they'd talked in the car, of course. Lee wanted nothing to do with it. Jack was nervous. Ronnie was still negative, but before deciding, he wanted another opinion. Susie was always worth listening to.

He sat her down and told her what had happened. When she heard what Rupert had suggested, her eyes opened wide.

'Rupert said *that*? Fuck me. So much for those famous business ethics. Sounds to me like our Rupert is less of an ethics boy than I'm an ethics girl.' She flung herself back in the chair and kicked her legs delightedly in the air.

Ronnie didn't grant her even a token smile. 'This is serious, woman.'

'Sorry, Ron. So, what *are* you goin' to do?'

'If it wasn't for Rose, we'd walk away, no question. But when you add her to this mess, frankly, Susie, we're screwed either way. If we go on with it, I've got to keep 'er in the dark. If we suddenly stop, she'll smell a rat.'

'It's all your fault. Daft you was, daft and cocky to think Rupert wouldn't twig.'

'I know.'

'The way I see it, Ron, it's split milk. Rupert's found

out that Rose's family are villains. That's the thing she was afraid of most. If 'e chucks Rose now, it's your fault.'

'Thanks a lot.'

'It's the truth. So in a way, it don't make no difference to Rose whether you stop now or go on. In fact, it might be better for 'er if you *do* carry on. You stop right now, and 'e'll ditch Rose, sure as eggs are eggs. If you carry on, 'e might get used to the idea, you never know. Apart from that, Ron, it depends what the fella can do for you.'

'Not a lot, prob'ly. Can't imagine gettin' a consultant's advice on the best way to smuggle a job-lot of Bangladeshis through Dover.'

'You don't know, do you? Face facts, Ron. You've got one son in the boob, another who's an evil little sod, and not that bright either. Then there's Jack who's seen better days, and you can't get up the stairs without wheezin' like a pair of bellows. Not exactly the A-team, is it?'

'We've just 'ad a run of bad luck, that's all. Things'll get better.'

'I'm sure they will, Ron, but if I was in your position, I'd take any 'elp I could get. Rupert's a clever bugger, you said that yourself. Don't look a gift 'orse in the mouth.'

'It's not a gift. Our little friend wants a share of any profits.'

'Fair enough, in't it? Anyway, whatever deal you agree with Rupert, you and Jack could squirrel away some of the profits before you divvy it up, couldn't you?'

'That's what Jack said.'

'Then I'd agree to what Rupert asks for. What else did Jack say?'

'That if we go ahead we'll 'ave to keep a tight look at 'im. That Rupert prob'ly ain't realised that if 'e gets involved with the firm, 'e can't just resign at a fortnight's notice, and 'e might cut up rough when 'e finds out.'

'You can cross that bridge when you come to it, can't you? I'd still stick with 'im.'

'And not tell Rose?'

'Don't breathe a word. If she finds out, she'll stop it.'

'All right, doll. I'll call Rupert right away, before 'e changes 'is mind.'

*

Rupert took the call on his mobile, left Telesys's offices as soon as possible, and was back home by five. He felt both exhilarated and very scared. Ronnie had wanted to reconvene right away. Rupert argued that it would look fishy for him to have another session without the rest of the Orbia team, so instead they settled on having dinner the next day in the private room at *The Legless Frog* near Waterloo. Tomorrow he'd be genuinely swamped during the day, so tonight was his only chance to do some background research. The bugger was that he had agreed to see Prim again, who was then back off to Italy for a few days, and he didn't think it would be wise to blow her out. That gave him only a couple of hours.

It wasn't long before his search engine started kicking off some useful stuff. The gem was the site of the NCIS, the National Criminal Intelligence Service. He scrolled through page after page. Christ, if most industries had a source like this, consulting would be a lot easier. This would give him some good raw data, and an idea of the size of the market. It would also stop him looking too green. Wow, there were even prices for every type of drugs. Weird. How come cocaine fetched twice the price in Sheffield than it did in Nottingham? Or that heroin retailed for £120 a gram in Belfast compared with £45 in Manchester? Anomalies like these were the stuff of consultants' wet dreams. Lots of low-hanging fruit here. He clicked on print and his laser printer whirred into life.

Two hours later he was done. Then he had another idea. He rummaged around until he found the small tin box where he kept spare keys. There it was, a spare set for his house. Up till now he'd never offered a set to Prim. Before last night, he wouldn't have been desperately excited if she'd given him keys for her new place. After meeting her new flatmate, though, it was easier than before to imagine occasionally jumping in the Merc and flogging over there through the dreadful traffic.

He glanced at his watch. Mmm. Even if Georgina was going out, she might still be at the flat now, and he knew that Prim was trapped at the office on a conference call with New York. He dialled the number. Good, there was an answer.

'Hello.'

'That you, Prim?'

'No, it's Georgina. Is that Rupert? I'm afraid she's not back yet. By the way, thank you for dinner last night. It was *so* kind of you to let me come along. I felt guilty all day. I knew I shouldn't have. But it was terribly good fun. You have such a wicked sense of humour.'

'I . . . we really enjoyed it. Georgina, I'm sure you're going out tonight.'

'Yes, I am. But is there anything I can do before I go? Leave a message for Primrose or anything?'

'What time are you leaving?'

'I'm being picked up in half an hour. Why?'

'I thought I might come round and give Prim a surprise. I wondered if you could let me in. The prob is, it's raining, which always makes the traffic even viler than usual, and even if I jump in the car right now, I don't think I'd make it by seven thirty. More like quarter to eight.'

Rupert couldn't resist a slight smile. If he was any reader of women, after the way she was delicately flirting with him last night, she'd make very sure her date had waited.

'I'm really sorry. We're going to a play, you see. Can't be late. Definitely next time, though. Come to think of it, Rupert, there's one thing I was going to mention to Primrose, but since I may not see her tonight, maybe you would. I'm going to a gallery opening on Thursday. A rather entertaining young Colombian who paints the wildest things. I thought it might amuse the two of you, if you've nothing else on.'

'That's a pity. Prim's away again – back to Italy till Friday.'

'Of *course* she is. She did say – quite slipped my mind. Well, just in case her plans change, or yours for that matter, it's from six to eight at a gallery called Long and Ryle, in John Islip Street, near the back of the old Tate.'

'I may be tied up too, but if anything changes, I'll see if I can stop by for a few minutes.'

'That'd be nice. Well, I'd better jump into a shower. Bye, Rupert. See you soon, I hope.'

'Me too, Georgina.'

16

They settled down in the cosy, gaudily decorated little room at the back of *The Legless Frog*. Rupert was on edge, and had taken a double whisky before leaving the house to ward off any panic attack as he entered the lion's den for the first time. Ronnie ordered a bottle of vintage champagne to launch the next stage of their collaboration.

He and Jack were all smiles. They'd talked long and hard about how to handle this, and concluded that, however much it went against the grain, they had no choice but to open up properly. Otherwise, Rupert would quickly realise that they were again holding back. In many ways, the deeper he got in, the better. When he was up to his neck, it would be easier to trust him.

Rupert tried smiling at Lee, but got only a sullen grimace in return. Rupert guessed that he had opposed this and had been outvoted. He knew from some of his mistakes with clients that it was dangerous to ignore a disaffected underling. More often than not, they had a way of undermining your efforts unless you made a big effort to turn them round. He made a mental note to have a go at that.

'Cheers.' Ronnie banged his oversize glass against Rupert's, spilling some. ''Ere's to profits.'

Rupert smiled warmly back. 'To profits. Now tell me, Ronnie – and Jack and Lee – now that I've committed, what have I let myself in for? I've been doing some research . . .'

They all laughed. Consultants' habits clearly died hard.

'. . . I know that the total UK market in your chosen business is around fifty billion, which, according to my guesstimate, gives you a market share of about nought point nought nought three per cent.'

Lee looked mystified, but on standby to take offence. Rupert flashed a quick smile.

'Now in my language, that means plenty of room for growth. What I've done is to try to segment the market into categories that make sense to me. In Group One I've put anything involving moving products around, like drug importation and distribution, tobacco and alcohol contraband, unofficial immigration, and anything to do with cars. Group Two I see as the brainy stuff. That's mainly the borrowing of intellectual property, manufacturing alternative currency, and being creative with VAT, excise, income tax and credit cards. Group Three is what before now I would have thought of as *proper* crime – robberies, theft, burglary, maybe kidnapping, and Group Four is the naughty stuff – ladies of the night, exotic videos and so on. Now, what I want to know is which of the groups are you mainly active in?'

Ronnie took the lead. 'Let me see. We do pretty much the lot in your first group. Group Two, that was what you call the clever stuff, wasn't it? VAT, tax, and excise obviously. Apart from that, not really. We never got into credit cards. Printin' money ain't our game neither. Very technical these days. Intellectual property? Nah.'

'But you do rather more in the third group?'

Ronnie took up the narrative again. 'Less than you'd think. Goin' across the pavement's a risky business these days.'

'What's "going across the pavement"?'

'Robbin' somewhere, like a bank. There's too many cameras everywhere, and though we got shooters, so do the Old Bill. Not only that, sometimes they fuckin' well use 'em.'

Jack helped Rupert understand. 'Proper villains don't do bank robberies no more. Once you go in, you only got thirty or sixty seconds to get out of the place. Grab what you can over the counter, that's all. It's only junkies and other scum what do it. As for burglaries, that was always a no-no with us. Unless it was a big country 'ouse or whatever, which was different. Kidnaps are a mug's game too, most of the time.'

Ronnie agreed enthusiastically. 'You wouldn't believe the staff you need to run a good kidnap. Amazin'. And the pay-off's always a problem. So, no, not the third group either. As for the last one, we ain't pimps, and we'd never get involved with that porn stuff. Specially not that nonce stuff with kids. Disgustin' it is. They ought to bring back 'angin' for them lot.'

'So, to sum up, basically it's drugs, fags and booze, a bit of helping people who're on the move, and a sideline in tax fraud.'

'Yeah, that's about it.'

'Well, that sounds admirably focused. So, what's been going wrong?'

'Not a lot. For years we done well. It's only recent that the old wheels 'ave come off the wagon. We lost a bunch of Bengalis and a load of gear in the same week. Then, a few weeks ago, we 'ad a real bad one. Grassed up, we was. The whole bunch was picked up as they beached. Not only that, the grass put my older son, Dan's name up, so 'e got nicked too.'

'Will he be convicted?'

'I dunno. The Old Bill were very cocky at first, then they made a balls-up of an identity parade. I talked to our brief today, and 'e reckons the odds are seventy to thirty against. If Dan does go down, 'e'll get a fifteen stretch minimum, which means out in around ten.'

'That's terrible. Does he have children?'

'Two boys.'

'Poor them. And the loss – temporary, I hope – of Dan: how much does that weaken your, er, management structure?'

'Leaves a big gap.'

Lee was looking very unhappy, but was saying nothing.

'So, in fact, how many of you *are* there in the company? How does it all work? I mean, these valuable cargoes – it must require a lot of manpower to take care of purchasing, importation, and distribution.'

'That's where things ain't the same as ordinary companies. We do the buyin' ourselves, and the general arrangements. Beyond that, as much as possible, we keep it at arm's length. The geezers 'andling the gear don't know who controls it. The distribution we take care of before the stuff arrives. It's all sold in advance, and the customers are told where and when to collect it.'

'Actually, Ronnie, it's not so different from other businesses as you think. More and more companies are outsourcing activities. In their case, usually because it's more cost-effective. In yours, presumably because if any of them gets caught, they can't inform.'

'Correct.'

'So what happened in Dan's case? Did you manage to track down the guy who grassed?'

There was a silence for a moment, and something hardened in Ronnie's face. Jack looked away. Lee jumped in.

'That scum won't grass no one no more.'

There was a cold glint in his eye as he said it, and Rupert felt a wave of fear sweep through his system. Still Ronnie and Jack said nothing. Rupert was sharply aware that, whatever the reason, he'd trodden on a corn, and resolved not to go anywhere near there again. To his relief the food arrived, a cue for a general return to conviviality. Rupert was still wary though, and had decided to stop trying to lead the conversation. After a while Ronnie filled the gap.

'So, Rupert. Now you know a bit about our business, anythin' strike you right away where you might give us some new ideas?'

Rupert shook his head. 'That's not the way I work, Ronnie. I'll be approaching this like any other assignment. The information I pulled together for tonight was only so I had some background knowledge, and didn't have to waste your time with ludicrously elementary questions. Over the next few days I want to do a lot

173

more research. I might make some pretext to visit the NCIS, and some of these other police bodies so I get a better feel for how they operate. Then I want to spend a serious amount of time with you guys to get more up to speed on the strategic and tactical side. I'll need to figure out what the capital requirements of the business are, and what the return looks like, how detection rates vary according to product type, and so on.'

'Sounds like that could take quite a while.'

'Give me ten days, and I'll be ready to present the findings from this diagnostic stage. Not only that, I should be able to give you my first cut on what you – we – should be implementing.'

'Not just an 'ypothesis then?'

They all chortled. Rupert joined in.

'Gentlemen, may I propose a toast? To hypotheses and profits.'

Glasses were banged together. Ronnie pressed a hidden buzzer. The waiter appeared, and at one word from his boss produced a bottle of XO brandy. It looked like it was bonding time, and Rupert decided to pick up that vibe.

'The one thing that you can't get from websites is a feel for how it all comes together. I mean, how do professionals communicate with each other? Are there pubs in the East End that you all go to, to pass on the word about what's happening?'

All three of them smiled.

'That Bethnal Green stuff? Nah, Rupert, you won't find one face what lives in Bethnal Green, Hoxton, or any of them places. Know why? 'Cause they're all piss 'oles. Maybe their mums and dads lived there, but not them. They're all out in Kent where we are, or in Surrey, Essex, Buckinghamshire. Smart places, nice places. 'Cause they got the money and they ain't stupid.'

'What's a "face"?'

'A face is a somebody. Somebody that gets recognised, gets respect, gets treated right.'

'I suppose *you're* all faces.'

'Course.' Ronnie looked offended at the very idea that they might not be. 'Anyway, we don't meet up much with villains. Apart from phones and computers, the biggest risk in our business nowadays is other villains. Course, it weren't like that in the old days . . .'

Lee rolled his eyes. He couldn't stand it when the old man started that sentimental shit.

'When I was young, there used to be somethin' called the Monday Club. It wasn't a place – more of an 'ypothesis that we enjoyed gettin' ratted on Mondays. At around eleven in the mornin', the chaps would get together at their favourite local. If you was 'oldin' – if you was in the money – you'd stick a score in the whip . . .' he saw Rupert looking puzzled. 'A score's twenty quid. You better learn some of this stuff. One's a nicker, two's a bottle, three's a carpet, four's a ruof, five's a ching, seven's a neves. It goes on and on. Ten's a cockle, twenty-five's a pony, fifty's a bull's eye, five undred's a monkey. I ain't got time to tell you the lot. Can't think why we use 'em. Load of old bollocks, when you think of it, grown men talkin' like that. Anyway, we'd 'ave a few drinks till around three o'clock when the boozers closed, then all jump in our motors and go to a drinker in the West End. The main ones we used were the A & R Club in Charing Cross Road and the Tin Pan Alley in Denmark Street. The chaps would come from all over the place, from North London, South London, and the East End, of course. You'd go upstairs, knock on the door, and the fella on the door would let you in. Outside, you'd 'ardly 'ear a sound, but inside it'd be mobbed alive.'

'Did you do business in there?'

'A bit, maybe, not a lot even then. If you 'ad somethin' goin' down, and you needed a bit of 'elp, you might tell some fella that you needed to meet up, but that was about the length of it.'

'Was there any rough stuff in there?'

'There weren't no biffin' or bashin' allowed. It was the doorman's job to stop that. If 'e knew there was bad blood between any of the chaps, it was down to 'im to stop the second lot comin' in. Didn't always get it right. There was one drinker, that one in Endell Street – remember, Jack?'

'The Gothic Club.'

'That's it, the Gothic. One day I was in there and the doorman's made an 'orrible mistake. There was somethin' goin' on between two fellas, and 'e should've known it. One of 'em slit the other's throat right in front of us all.'

'What happened?'

'That club was levelled. The doorman 'ad to go on the missin' list.'

'I meant what happened with the body? Did the police come?'

'Don't recall. Don't suppose so. Taken care of, it would've been . . . Anyway, them days are all gone.'

'Hallelujah.' Lee's patience had run out. Rupert smiled in his direction, but was careful not to look like he was agreeing with Lee's sentiment.

'So no more Monday club?'

'Oh, there's still a few of the older fellas who get together in a boozer of a Monday lunchtime. Not the same at all, though. Wouldn't bother meself . . . Well, it's gettin' late. What say we leave it there for tonight, Rupert? You give us a call whenever you want to get together again.'

'Okay, Ronnie. Hey, thanks. You too, Lee and Jack. It's been a great evening.'

Jack smiled. 'What you think of the food? Third-rate?'

'No, it was fine, just fine.' It was time for a gesture to Lee. 'Hey, Lee. When we were doing our research, we went to your night clubs, but it'd be much more fun to go with you sometime. Any chance?'

For the first time that evening, Lee looked faintly pleased. 'You name it, Rupert.'

'Great, I'll be in touch. Okay, 'bye everyone. Oh, d'you think they could call me a cab?'

Ronnie nodded to the waiter, who whistled up a Mercedes.

17

The second time Chris Owen went to bed that Wednesday night he was exhausted but in a good frame of mind. Until very recently things had been gloomy. They were painfully close to being forced to conclude that either the five they'd caught at the St Margaret's bust were exceptionally loyal, or more likely, they had been kept behind firewalls and genuinely had no idea who they were working for.

Progress had been slow on the inflatable too. The good part was that the lad at the boatyard had remembered a boat like that being in the yard not long before the bust. What he had no idea of was where it had come from or where it had gone. As far as he could recall – and he wasn't the brightest thing on two legs – it had arrived and departed when he wasn't about. It looked like the trail had gone cold, with no means of linking the boatyard with that inflatable.

Then, on Friday, a gratifying combination of a lot of old-fashioned policing and some useful co-operation with the Devon and Cornwall region of the NCS had borne fruit. The apparently impossible had been achieved, and they had found that the inflatable had been sold at an auction in Bristol in July. It had been bought by a dealer in London, who in turn had sold it for cash. The dealer didn't recall much about what the buyer looked like. He responded with no more than a shrug to a photo of Jimmy Smith, though the age, height and build were a match. Fortunately he was a bit of a car buff, and recalled that the car the buyer used to tow his trailer was a blue Mondeo, a '94 or '95, he reckoned. Jimmy's blue Mondeo was actually '97, but that was close enough.

When you added this to what had happened to Jimmy, it was obvious to any reasonable man that the Hills had taken him out. Chris reckoned that any scientist would put the statistical probability at ninety-nine per cent or higher. Sadly, as he knew all too well, ninety-nine per cent didn't always count as 'beyond reasonable doubt' for the courts, who would demand more explicit proof. And that he didn't have yet. But at least he was satisfied that he knew for sure what had happened.

Anyway, he might not need to depend on the boat link. After he'd gone to bed the first time that night, he'd been woken at midnight to be told of a king-size dollop of luck. A late-night patrol had been sent to a phone box in Beckenham town centre following a tip-off that someone was robbing a phone box.

He was a black lad, seventeen, from Bromley. He denied everything at first, but when they put a bit of pressure on, he admitted he'd been at this racket for a while. It looked a totally standard nick, when to their surprise, he suddenly announced that he wanted to do a deal.

They'd chuckled at that to begin with. What did he have to trade with? When they heard, they stopped chuckling, and called up the NCS. Chris Owen was woken, heard and immediately went round. The lad said that, like everyone who lived locally, he'd heard the appeal for witnesses who'd been near the call-box in Chesterfield Road that August night. When they asked why he hadn't come forward sooner like a good citizen, the lad laughed in their faces.

Chris's initial scepticism vanished when he asked for a description of the white man. It was very, very close. And the exchange of words he'd had with the man rang true. But when the youth was told he'd be wanted to do an identity parade, he went all cagey. Owen withdrew for a few minutes. The duty officer told him that they couldn't hold him longer than the morning over something so petty. Chris knew that this golden opportunity might turn to sand if he didn't grasp it fast. Before long the boy would work out that testifying against the likes of Dan Hill wasn't the greatest career move, and taking the mild rap for the phone boxes might be smarter. It was now or never, and three a.m. wasn't the ideal time to consult one of his NCS superior officers. He bit the bullet, and had another word with the duty officer. The man wasn't thrilled at erasing the record of the black boy's arrest but the whole Kent force wanted to see the Hills put away. After doing the identity parade, the boy would be let go, without so much as a warning, as long as he agreed to testify.

*

There was the gallery, Long & Ryle. Rupert could see from the street that the party was still in full swing, so much so that, despite the dank evening, guests had spilled out onto the pavement. He nudged past them, grabbed a glass of red wine and a catalogue and went in.

No sign of Georgina. A friend from the old days at Lazards came up and said hello. Rupert wasn't particularly thrilled about bumping into him, but was glad enough of some company to help while away another few minutes.

By twenty past eight, the party was thinning out. It was a definite no show. Pretty fucking cheeky to ask him along and not turn up herself, unless she'd already come and gone. He decided to find out and went in search of someone who might know, and found Sarah Long, the dishy co-owner, who assured him that Georgina hadn't put in an appearance. Bitch.

There was nothing else for it. He went home, called Prim in her hotel in Turin, and by ten-thirty was curled up asleep.

The loud ringing tone almost gave him a heart attack.
    'Hello?'
    'Rupert, is that you? God, I haven't woken you, have I? It's only ten to eleven.'
    'Georgina? No, no.'
    'I'm *so* sorry. I rang Sarah to apologise for not making it, and she told me you were there. Will you forgive me? I got terribly caught up in something.'
    'I know the feeling. Don't worry, I had a good time.'
    'I still feel dreadful. I tell you what . . . are you really still up?'
    'Course I am.'
    'And not too tired?'
    He was knackered. 'Not at all.'

'Why not come and join me, then? I'll buy you a glass of champagne to make up.'

'Where are you?'

'Home House. D'you know it?'

'Yeah, yeah. It's that newish club in . . .'

'Portman Square. I'm in the bar on the first floor, with some rather fun friends. You might like them. Do hurry.'

He put the phone down, marvelling at what a soft touch he was, had a shower and ten minutes later was in his car.

'Hi.' He raised one hand in greeting to Georgina's group.

'Rupert, how fantastic. Everyone, this is Rupert Henley. Rupert, this is Sebastian, who is a terribly famous interior designer, or if he's not yet, he will be soon. That's Hermione, who dances for the Royal Ballet. Next to her is Christophe, who's something very important in the French government, don't ask me what, and this is Cynthia. Cynthia has just published her first novel. Now, let's get you a glass. Again, I am *so* sorry.'

Rupert smiled and sat down. He chatted for a while to the novelist, who wasn't very pretty, and mouthed a few words across the group at the dancer, who was. After a while, there was a move to go clubbing. Rupert would cheerfully have gone along, but Georgina announced that she wasn't keen, Hermione agreed with her, and a party of three men and a dog wasn't Rupert's idea of fun. So the three keen ones left, Hermione decided to head for bed, and Georgina and Rupert were left alone.

'So, at last I have you in my clutches.' She grinned seductively. 'Now there's one thing I've been dying to ask you.'

'Fire away.'

'Tell me, when are you going to do the decent thing and marry that sweet girl?'

Rupert spluttered. 'I've no idea. We haven't even talked about it. It's only been a year.'

'Well, in my opinion a year should be plenty. Indeed, if you don't know in six months, you probably never will.'

'How about you? When are *you* going to get married?'

'Next year.'

'Oh wow, congratulations. You didn't say anything the other night, you coy little devil. Who's the lucky man?'

'I haven't chosen yet. But I think women should be married before thirty.'

'So, let me get this right. You'll just pick? From how many contenders?'

'I don't know.'

'What if nobody asks you?'

'They will.'

'Jesus, you're confident.'

'No, realistic. Do you find me attractive, Rupert?'

'Very.'

'I'm relieved to hear that. But it would be false modesty for me to claim that yours is a minority opinion. If I were penniless, good looks might not be enough. As it happens, I have quite a lot of money in my own right, and in due course I'll inherit a large chunk more.

Plus a nice house or two. And I come from what I think is generally regarded as a good family. Overall, not a bad package, I'd say. It's not arrogance, it's the truth.'

'So you'll just line a bunch of us up against a wall, pull out your love gun, pick the likeliest lad, and fire?'

'Something like that, but who said anything about you?'

'By "us", I meant guys.'

'Good, because Prim should have wrestled you to the floor by then.'

'We'll see.'

She looked at her watch. 'Rupert, dear, I hate to say this but I think it's close to my witching hour.'

'Can I offer you a lift? The car's outside.'

'That would be very nice. But you mustn't even think of coming in. However tempting it might be, that would be disastrous.' And she held a long finger out, and ran the point of it slowly against the underside of his chin.

'Don't worry, Georgina. I wouldn't risk it either, especially when you're in a slinky number like that. In case I forget later, we should sort one thing out. Are we going to tell Prim that we met, or not?'

'I don't mind either way, so whatever you think, Rupert, whatever you think.'

18

Primrose had been away so much that she'd hardly had a chance to visit Dan. She tried to make up for it by going both at the weekend and on the following Tuesday. He was looking in great shape physically, with little to do but pump iron. Even through his clothes she could see that his body, always powerful, was beginning to look like the side of a house.

His mood wasn't equally good. From what she'd heard from her dad when they met for lunch on Saturday, he'd been buoyant until this latest identity parade. The police weren't obliged to tell Weasel who the witness was, or what he was meant to have witnessed. And unlike the case of the Dutchman, when they'd told him in the hope that it would pressure Dan into confessing, this time they had given nothing away. However, they *were* required to invite Weasel to be present at the parade, and when he later described the black youth, it didn't take Dan long to make the connection with the argument at the phone box, and to concede that in the light from the box the lad might have had a fair old gander at him.

Dan couldn't talk about it to Primrose in front of the screw, of course, but she'd heard from her dad that at the parade the lad had picked him out, no problem. Ronnie had told her that Weasel was worrying away at the problem, but it didn't look good. Before that, it had seemed that this part of the story was okay. Admittedly, they had the record of a call being made from that box to *The Gables*, but that could have been anyone. Provided Ronnie stuck to his story about it being a wrong number, there wasn't much they could do about it. This changed all that.

Dan tried to be jokey, but Primrose could see he was bleeding within. The boys had got over the novelty of visiting prison and now didn't like coming, or created if they did. Maureen's mum, who'd come down to help for a while, had gone back to Glasgow to look after her drunkard of a second husband, leaving Maureen in a terrible state, munching handfuls of pills. The rest of the family were all doing what they could – including Primrose, who'd agreed to go and stay with them the next weekend. But it was only sticking-plaster stuff. If Dan got sent down for a long stretch . . . it didn't bear thinking about.

Good old Frank had been to see him too. He wasn't nearly as close to Dan or Lee as he was to Primrose, and it was good of him to make the effort. Naturally enough, the subject dominated the next of their lunches that Thursday at the Ritz.

They'd reached the coffee, still talking about Dan, when Primrose noticed a man of late middle age making his way across the room to them. He smiled to her as he approached, but directed his attention to the other side of the table.

'Hello, Frank.'

Frank had been looking in the other direction and

186

hadn't seen the man coming. He swung round, and it took half a second for his eyes to open wide in recognition.

'Brendan. How *good* to see you. How are you? Here, come and join us.'

The man beamed back, but shook his head. 'I won't, thank you very much, Frank. I don't want to interrupt. Couldn't leave without paying my respects, that's all.'

'Well, at least let me introduce you. Brendan Walsh, meet Primrose Hill.'

'Ronnie's girl?'

Primrose nodded and smiled. The man took her hand and clasped it between his.

'We've met before, young lady, when you were about eight or nine. My, didn't you grow up lovely?'

Primrose kept smiling. Finally the man released her hand.

'How's everything, Frank?'

'Oh, can't complain. Still putting up the odd shack here and there. How's the transport business?'

'Very good, Frank, thank you for asking. Moved into hotels now, as well. Got a particularly nice one in Cornwall. If ever you and Molly would welcome a break there, please let me know. You'd be my guests, of course. Stay a month, if you like. Anyway, I must be moving on. Very nice to meet you, Primrose. Frank, please give my best regards to Molly.'

They said goodbye, and as soon as he was safely out of earshot, Primrose asked about him.

'Brendan was once in the same line of business as your dad. Got out when it all turned to drugs. Since then he's made a lot of money for himself in road haulage.'

'And is he totally legit these days? Doesn't haulage have the reputation of being a pretty rough business?'

Frank took a sip of coffee. 'As far as I know, Brendan upholds the law of the land nowadays. That's not to say that his previous experience goes entirely to waste, though.'

Primrose giggled. 'You are amazing, you know, Uncle Frank. Whenever I'm with you and you run across any of Dad's friends, they all seem to remember you so fondly, and show you such *respect*.'

'Well, I respect them too.'

'I know you do. Listen, I'm afraid I'm going to have to run soon.'

'Of course you must. Before you dash, what news on the Rupert front?'

'I've been abroad so much recently I've scarcely seen him. I told you on the phone about him not wanting to live together, didn't I?'

Frank nodded.

'Well, at least he was keen for us to have keys to each other's places, so we've done that. I don't pry about the work he does for Dad, but they both say they're getting on well.'

'And what about the flatmate from hell?'

'Oh, she's not that bad. Mind you, d'you know what she did the other evening? Asked me how much my mortgage is, which I answered honestly.'

'What cheek.'

'You wait till you hear the rest of it. What she'd worked out was that her rent was more than half of the mortgage payment, which it is, ignoring my deposit. Her argument was that, since she was paying more than half, it was only fair that she should have the bigger bedroom.'

'You're *joking*! I hope you told her what to do with herself.'

'For once I did. I think she was quite surprised.'

*

The great day arrived. Rupert had taken the precaution of sending his Interleisure team out on some wild-goose chase doing field research on sports clubs, and accordingly he deemed it safe to use a meeting room at Orbia.

The trio arrived in a state of genuine anticipation. Even Lee's sourness had gone. Since their dinner, Rupert had been out on the town twice with Lee, Tommy, Michelle and the toe-rags, and had buttered them all up a treat. Lee had basked in the praise and the attention, and whereas previously he had been scathing about Rupert behind his back, now he was completely turned around.

Rupert poured the coffee himself, then sat down. 'Right.'

Lee grinned. 'Get on with it, Rupes, the suspense is killin' us.'

'Okay, here's my take on where you are. There really are no issues about market share. The ethnic groups look after their own patches. The Triads do Chinese immigration, prostitution, protection, and drugs, but only for their own people. The same largely goes for the sub-continentals. The Yardies mainly shoot each other. The Turks control heroin, but that's not a market sector you bother with. Within your core competence of transporting cocaine, amphetamines and ecstasy, the basic position is that if you can get the gear, you can sell it. This is reflected in prices, which have been stable to strong for the last year . . .'

The three said nothing. So far, so not very interesting.

'What the key issues therefore become are your return on capital, the risk profile you choose to adopt and, perhaps most important, your fundamental mission statement.'

A question was coming, but he waved it away.

'No, if you don't mind, Ronnie, I'd like to come back to the mission statement later on. Let's concentrate first on your return on capital, and take a typical case, maybe the one which went wrong recently. That was a mixed consignment of synthetics and cocaine, I know, but to keep it simple, let's say it was just two hundred kilos of coke. Now you sell that wholesale at about £25,000 a kilo, and you pay, what, twelve, fifteen?'

Jack nodded. 'Nearer fifteen.'

'Okay, so that's a cost to you of three million, right?'

'But we only pay around a quarter of that down, and the rest when we've flogged the shit.'

'Yes, I know, Jack, that'll be part of the calculation. As will an estimate of the other costs of bringing it in – boats, lorries, whatever. Now, assuming an interval of two weeks from making the down payment to getting the cash yourself . . .'

'And don't forget, we can't give our supplier *any* old cash; we got to clean our own money up before we can use it.'

'Exactly. Which introduces another delay of, realistically, a month. Nonetheless, assuming all goes well, my back-of-an-envelope calculation for such an operation is that your ROCE – remember, that's return on capital employed – is between three and four hundred per cent. By any standards that's fantastic, and puts you way ahead of almost all other sectors. You'd have to have been in Silicon Valley in the nineties to beat it.'

The three turned to each other and grinned. Lee commented, 'Not bad, eh?'

Rupert, now in full flow, had stood up and was pacing around, with the air of a lecturing professor.

'Not bad at all. Don't break open the champagne just yet, though. Your operations don't always succeed, do they? I know you've had a run of bad luck recently, but typically, what proportion of consignments go wrong?'

They debated a while and Ronnie summed up.

'If we include accidental loss, gettin' busted, poor quality, the lot – I wanna say one in ten, but bein' the conservative fella I am, I'll call it one in five.'

'Okay. So, averaging it out, that brings the ROCE over a range of operations down to, say, two hundred and fifty per cent. Now, next point. What if you lose a member of senior management? Let's hope it won't happen to Dan, but again, since it's current, let's take that case. If he serves ten years, what will be the additional cost you'll have to bear supporting his family?'

That was another one for Ronnie. 'That could be one 'eck of a lot. Fifty grand? No, more to keep a woman like Maureen. Call it a round 'undred grand a year.'

'Right, so that's a total of a million over ten years,

which discounting back to a present value . . .' he tapped into the Hewlett Packard calculator that lay in front of him '. . . is around five hundred and sixty. That brings us down to two hundred and thirty per cent.'

He realised they were getting lost in the maths.

'Please don't worry about the detail of these calculations. All I'm trying to do is establish a ball park figure. Now, back to Dan. It's not only a matter of supporting his family. Dan is a highly trained, experienced manager. The cost of that training must be in the millions. However, while he's inside, he's a totally non-performing asset. What we have to look at is the opportunity cost. If Dan had worked on a lower-risk assignment, the return would've been lower, but so would the risk of him being caught. He would have been *far* more likely to be out there over the next ten years, earning. What I want to suggest is that we have to evolve some sort of weighting system under which we can assess risk against reward. And for reasons I'll come on to, I believe that drugs importation should be given a very high-risk quotient. Not only for the chance of being caught, but the length of sentence you receive. I propose, arbitrarily, that we give it a risk quotient of point five, meaning that we recalculate the ROCE by multiplying it by that number. That has the effect of halving the return, bringing it down to something only just north of a hundred per cent – still good, I grant you, but no longer intergalactic. By now, you're about on a par with the sexiest of conventional businesses, and those managers don't face the possibility of going to jail . . .'

Lee wasn't understanding a word of all this, but it

was his mate Rupert, and that was okay. Ronnie and Jack grasped the broad principle, if not the detailed numbers. They asked a couple of questions and then Rupert was cleared for take-off again.

'Staying with the issue of jail, it would be wrong of me not to point out that in any company if there are, say, ten members of top management, you can usually lose one or two without any serious disruption to the business. However, if you've only got three, as you have at present, losing anyone else could be catastrophic. I suspect you would lose critical mass altogether, and find it hard to function. If you were in any other business sector, I would certainly recommend taking out so-called "key man" insurance, but I imagine that in your case that may be tricky. And if you can't insure against it, I would argue that you need to adjust your risk profile downwards . . .'

They had some discussion. Lee didn't agree, and thought that, even with two, plus some junior staff, they could carry on much as before. Ronnie, however, thought there was something in this. Rupert was pleased, and felt it led him on nicely to the next section.

'Now we need to cover regulation. Nearly all large businesses have to cope with regulators. In the telecoms sector it's OFTEL, for newspapers it's the Press Complaints Commission, for *you* the regulators are the police and HM Customs – in particular, the National Crime Squad, and the investigation branch of the Customs. They're both big organisations: the NCS has nearly 1,500 officers, all on secondment from regional forces, and of the total Customs staff of 23,000, no less than 2,000 work on investigation. Going back to the NCS, they have two top rankings for professional criminals. The highest one, like getting an Oscar, is called a "core nominal", which means a major national or international criminal. The level below that is called "current nominal".'

Lee was fascinated. 'What are we, Rupes?'

'Core nominals.'

'Right on!' Lee punched the air.

'It's not as good as you think. That's why that copper – what was his name?'

'Chris Owen.'

'It's why he's on your case so much. Assume he spends one tenth of his time on you, add in the cost of all the investigation, back-up, input from the NCIS, et cetera -- not to mention interception operations – and I bet that, fully costed, tracking the Hills is costing the taxpayer over two hundred grand a year. They can't afford that for many gangs, and the ones they target in that way must be much more likely to fall foul of them than ones who stay out of that limelight. What I'd like to suggest is that you should regard it as a priority to drop first to current nominal status, and then get out of the rankings altogether.'

Lee looked horrified. 'That's like a football team *tryin'* to get relegated.'

Rupert was unfazed. 'Maybe, but don't you want to get left in peace and quiet? Anyway, don't worry, Lee, it won't happen overnight. Even if you changed tack completely, there would be a time lag of at least a year before they concluded you were no longer a serious threat. Still on the regulators, they've got a lot better organised in recent years, mainly thanks to two new organisations, the NCS and the National Criminal Intelligence Service, the NCIS. However, like all major armies, they're set up to fight certain types of wars and not others. They're fundamentally weak on computer crime and sophisticated fraud. The drugs arena is their main battleground, and I anticipate that intensifying. Now, you, Ronnie, might say that you concentrate on drugs because it's rich pickings and not too hard work.'

'Sounds about right to me.'

'And I say that your policy has two vital flaws. First, it's a "me too" approach, with no differentiation, no "unique selling proposition". Basically, you're identical to hundreds of other similar organisations. Businesses that think that way always fail sooner or later. Where's the innovation? Where's the cutting-edge technology that will keep you ahead of the pack?'

'What's the second?'

'The second is that the battle lines are drawn up with you facing the police's biggest guns. That's madness. You should be thinking and acting far more like a guerrilla army, using terrain where they can't marshal their big battalions, making hit and run attacks, engaging in battle at a time of *your* choosing, not theirs.'

Ronnie picked up a pencil and scratched his scalp. 'Rupert, are you seriously suggestin' that we stop dealin' in gear altogether? It's our main thing, for fuck's sake, it's what you'd call our core competence.'

'Yes, that's exactly what I may end up recommending. To explain why, let me get on to that matter I mentioned at the outset, a mission statement. All companies have them. Some are just silly slogans, while others really help staff focus on what's important. In the same way, I think you need to take a long, hard look at the fundamental reasons why you do what you do. So what are they? I know you enjoy the trappings, but is crime a lifestyle choice for you? Do you enjoy the thrill of the chase, of trying to beat the system? Does being who you are give you a position of respect in your community which matters to you? If the answer to any of these questions is yes, perhaps you should go on as before. Sooner or later you may end up in prison, but that goes with the territory. Maybe you can't be a "face" without living with those risks. If, on the other hand, what you want is to make money and *not* go to jail, you might adopt a very different approach. As you can imagine, however, the mission – the aim – would be very different.'

Rupert paused and looked around. He had them in the palm of his hand.

Ronnie broke the silence. 'So what's the answer? If we agree to change our whole approach, what would we 'ave to do?'

'I've thought about that very carefully, Ronnie, and this is what I think the plan should be. Design maybe three crimes, each innovative, each with a low-risk quotient, but a reasonable ROCE, each targeted at areas of weakness for the regulators. Each one should be different from the others. Commit each crime once, then never do it again. Don't allow the regulators to learn your tricks and ambush you next time. Taking the three together, aim to make a good sum of money, the equivalent of many years of regular operations. And then when you've done that, *stop*.'

'What d'you mean, stop?'

'Stop being criminals. Put your feet up and enjoy the money or, if you prefer, put it into *real* legitimate businesses. Never commit another crime beyond feeding a parking meter. You'll drive the Old Bill crazy. And provided the three jobs have gone well, you'll never, ever go to jail.'

Ronnie was impressed. 'What about these three jobs? Who'll invent them?'

'*We* will, together. We have leading criminal experts and, though I shouldn't say it, one of the country's top business brains. The best of both worlds. In fact, I already have the makings of one idea.'

Lee's eyes opened wide. 'What? Tell us.'

'Only when we've had some lunch. I don't know about you boys, but I'm starving.'

Ronnie looked at Jack and Lee. 'Gentlemen, I think Rupert deserves a small round of applause.'

They stood up and clapped furiously, and Rupert took a little bow.

19

With all the warm goodwill generated before lunch, whatever operation Rupert had proposed would probably have gone down as well as the gourmet sandwiches. As it was, his basic idea was welcomed on its own merits, and within half an hour, Ronnie, Jack, and Lee had contributed input from their side of the fence which buffed it up nicely.

And it was, indeed, the ideal début. The scheme was nicely balanced between the physical and the intellectual, or put more simply, criminal muscle and business know-how. They assessed each of the three elements in the operation and concluded that it had an admirably low-risk quotient. For Rupert, fearful of being ripped off, it had the additional advantage of transparency – there could be no dispute over how much they'd made. And, exhilarated as he was, he was acutely aware of the desirability of getting this whole surreal project completed as fast as possible. Stretching it out would not only lengthen the period of his personal exposure, it would inevitably increase the chances of something going wrong, of them losing interest and chasing some other rainbow, or of a dispute developing between them. As in many projects he'd worked on, momentum was key. His aim was to get all three operations done and dusted by Christmas, and the others went along with that too. It was excellent, therefore, that this first one could be implemented quickly. It would allow them to get a few points on the board, to show that the collaboration worked. He couldn't be expected to come up with all of the ideas unaided, and an early success would help prime the whole team's creative juices.

So, the concept accepted, they switched without delay to the details of implementation. Without mentioning any personal connection or motivation, Rupert explained that the boss of the target company was well known to disapprove vehemently of his staff using drugs, and that, although this had never been made public, he had fired several people who were discovered to be taking them. Having heard that the company's workforce was mainly young and very hard-working, Lee was sure that if they checked out the bars or clubs which the juniors migrated to after work, they would soon find someone who was either a user, or with a judicious blend of coaxing and alcohol, could be encouraged to experiment. Then all they'd need would be a tiny video camera secretly recording the process, and they'd be in business. He reckoned it would take two weeks, tops.

The part that Ronnie and Jack undertook was even simpler. As they'd said, there was no way they'd do a burglary themselves. It was beneath them in every sense. The proceeds from any one operation would be pathetically small once the items had been fenced. Plus the chance that you'd get identified, caught, or grassed up were disproportionately high. However, simply *arranging* for burglaries to occur was a different matter, provided they limited their involvement to passing on tips to scum, without demanding any cut or a pay-off. That could be done very discreetly through intermediaries, so discreetly that the scum would never know who their fairy godmothers were. In addition to that, Ronnie and Jack were charged with pulling together some funds that they had lying around in various accounts abroad, and standing by to transfer them when Rupert instructed.

That left Rupert. He also had two things to take care of. One was to do a few checks to find out which tax haven offered the best blend of efficiency and discretion and could recommend local brokers who dealt daily in decent volume on major stock markets, including London. He was duly put in touch with some people in Bermuda, arranged for an account to be opened, and told them to expect both funds and trading instructions in due course. The second thing was to refresh his own memory. It was many years since he'd worked in the City. He'd been able to explain the broad principle to Ronnie, Jack, and Lee. Now he needed to make sure he understood the detailed mechanics. He put in a call to his friend at Lazards.

'Hi, Toby, can you help me? Someone was asking me a technical question about share dealing, and I'm so out of date, I couldn't answer it. I promised to find out and get back to him. Would you mind?'

'Not at all. What's his question?'

'He wanted to understand how "selling short" actually works. Would you mind taking me through it step by step, to make sure I get the hang of it?'

'Right-oh. Well, in simple terms, selling short means selling shares you don't actually own. You do it because you have a hunch that the share price of the company in question will fall.'

'But I can't remember how you can do that.'

'Hold your horses, Rupes, give me a chance . . . Of course, when you agree to sell, you have to actually deliver that number of shares you've sold. What you do is to *borrow* those shares from some big bank that holds plenty of them. Then, assuming your hunch is right, the shares fall, and you buy the same number back in the market, and return them to the bank, pocketing the difference between the price you first sold at and the price you bought back at. For example, if you sold short a million shares of company X at, say, ten pounds, and then the share price fell to, say, nine, when you bought them back, you would stand to make a profit of one pound per share, a million quid in total.'

'What happens if your hunch is wrong, and the share price *rises* one pound?'

'Then you're a million in the red. Whatever price you have to pay, you have no choice: you have to return the shares to the bank.'

'Isn't there some risk for the bank? Surely if the shares fall, they're out a million too, even though they do get them back.'

'True, but that's not the point. All those big banks have huge holdings in most listed companies, which are true long-term holdings in their portfolios. Whether any one share rises or falls, it makes no difference to them, because in the short term they're not sellers. For them, lending stock to short sellers is just a way of making an extra turn on shares they hold anyway.'

'How much do they charge?'

'Can't remember exactly. Between one and two per cent of the value of the shares they're lending, I think. Of course, that depends on how long you need the stock for. A fortnight to one month is the norm, I believe.'

'So, if my friend wanted to sell something short, what would he have to do?'

'It's not an area where these big banks want to take any risk on the counter-party, so they only lend stock through something called "prime brokers". Your friend would have to get his regular stockbroker to open an account with one of them, and place a deposit.'

'How much?'

'You'd have to double check. Any idea of the value of the shares he wants to sell short?'

'No idea. How about if it were, say, two million quid?'

'Maybe half a million, then, something like that.'

'And these "prime brokers" – can you give me some names?'

'Not off-hand. Tell me your e-mail address and I'll find out and send some details through.'

Rupert was about to agree, when one of Ronnie's comments about IT risk came back to him.

'Actually, I've been having ridiculous difficulties with e-mails recently. Can't open them half the time, and anyway I'm going to be on the run most of today. Would you mind if I called you again later, and took the details down over the phone? . . . Thanks.'

*

'Is that Mr Owen?'

'Speaking.'

'Sorry to bother you at home, Mr Owen. It's Tony Stafford – groundsman at the cricket club.'

'Oh, *Tony*. Of course. Sorry, Tony, half the time I forget my own name.' Chris occasionally turned out for the local club's second eleven. 'Nice to hear from you, Tony. What can I do to help? Is it something to do with the annual dinner?'

'Nothing like that. It was Mr Evans who suggested I called you.'

Phil Evans was a sergeant from the local nick. He opened the batting for the Firsts and also bowled wicked seamers.

'What about?'

'You've met my son a few times, I believe.'

Yes, of course. The lad helped out his dad occasionally. Nice lad, eighteen, nineteen. Chris racked his brains for the name.

'Course . . . Ed, isn't it?'

'Ted.'

Same bloody difference. 'So what's up, Tony? Has Ted got himself in a spot of bother?'

'He's been in Bromley Infirmary since last night.'

'I'm sorry to hear that. Road accident?'

'No. He was in some club and accidentally spilled his drink over someone. This man and his friends marched Ted outside, beat him up, and cut his face horribly.'

'That's appalling. I presume the police have interviewed him?'

'Yes. The poor boy got himself to hospital in a mini-cab. I don't know how he made it. The nurses there called the police, who came and saw him. Then they

203

went down to the club after that, but no one would admit to having seen anything.'

'Was Ted able to identify them, or at least give good descriptions?'

'That's the problem – he won't tell the police anything. All he says to us is it'll be worse all round if he does. We think they could have threatened to do more to him if he informs.'

'So, what have the Bromley police said to you?'

'They saw Ted for the third time this afternoon, and called round here an hour ago, when we got back from the hospital ourselves. They said that, since there are no known witnesses to the assault, unless Ted can help them, there's nothing more they can do.'

'Sadly, that's often the case.'

'Beth and I can't leave it there. I gave Mr Evans a call a few minutes ago to ask him what else we could do. He said that there was a chance it was some gang called the Hills, who he says use that club a lot, might even own it. He said that you know more about them, and maybe wouldn't mind giving us some advice.'

'Tell me, Tony, Ted's cuts . . . did he say what sort of weapon was used?'

'Ted couldn't rightly remember. He was probably too shocked at the time. The doctor who did the stitching said it must have been something very sharp like a razor blade or a Stanley knife.'

'Mmm. I'd like to see Ted. I'll go first thing tomorrow and call you afterwards.'

*

'Hello, Ted, remember me?'

The boy raised himself up a few inches and nodded. His head was swathed in bandages, with just the hair, eyes and mouth peeping through. His eyes looked very frightened.

'Don't worry, Ted. I'm not here officially. Your dad called me to tell me, and I thought I'd come and see how you're doing. I just talked with the Sister. She said they're pleased with your progress. Sounds like you might need a few more operations, though, at one of the specialist hospitals. Amazing what they can do nowadays . . .'

The boy was watching him carefully.

'I understand how you feel, Ted. Villains like that often threaten to come after their victim again if he helps the police.' No reaction. 'Even if they don't, it's enough that the victim thinks that they might.' Still nothing. 'I bet you know who they were, don't you? Some of them, anyway. Come on, Ted, you can tell me. I'm here as a friend. Anything you say to me is strictly between us. It's up to you what you tell the police officially. I won't even break your confidence to your mum and dad, I promise. You *do* know them, don't you?'

The boy thought about it for a while, then slowly nodded.

'Thanks, Ted. You see, the thing is, I've got a pretty good idea myself who did it. I think it was Lee Hill and his scum friends.'

Almost imperceptible. A nod all the same.

'I thought so. Lee Hill is one of the nastiest, most evil pieces of filth I've ever had the misfortune to meet. He's done things like this often enough before, and he's only been convicted once. And that time, some witness got interfered with and he got off with six months. As I said, Ted, I do understand how you feel, but unless victims like you are willing to help the police, we'll never be able to put him where he belongs. Won't you reconsider?'

The lad shook his head.

'Is that your last word? Frankly, Ted, after this, what more harm can they do you?'

Ted looked straight at Chris, his eyes burning now. The words came out slowly painfully.

'They . . . said . . . they'd . . . get . . . my . . . mum . . . and . . . dad.' And tears flowed, tears both of fear and of anger.

Owen clenched his fists. That fucking little *shit*. He stood up, bade farewell and left. He went down to the car park and walked around for a few minutes, trying to calm himself. Oh, to hell with it, he didn't want to feel calm. He pulled out his mobile, checked the number in his book, and tapped it in.

'Hello?'

'Susie, it's Chris Owen. Can I have a word with Ronnie, please?'

'Wait a minute . . . Ron says 'e's busy. Can you call back in an hour?'

'No, I bloody well can't. Tell him I want a word *now*.'

'All right, all right, keep your 'air on.' She put the phone down. It took half a minute before Ronnie grabbed it.

'What right you got to speak to Susie like that?'

'Shut up, Ronnie, I'm not in a mood to take attitude from you.'

206

'Me neither.' Ronnie knew something was up, though. Chris Owen didn't usually come on like this. 'What's all this in aid of, anyway?'

'Like cricket, do you, Ronnie?'

'Not particularly.'

'Well, I do. I play for a local team. And right now I'm standing outside Bromley Infirmary. I've just been visiting the son of our groundsman.'

'And?'

'The "and" is that this lad, who's not twenty yet, will maybe never get a woman to look at him again for the rest of his life, and he'll find it hard even to get a decent job.'

'On account of what?' Ronnie already had a sneaking feeling.

'On account of the fact that the night before last, the nasty little piece of excrement you call a son slashed his face to ribbons with a Stanley knife.'

'What makes you think that?' Ronnie's voice was subdued.

'Cause he told me. Oh don't worry, Ronnie, the lad told me unofficially. He won't make a statement – you know why?'

'Why?'

'Because they said they'd get his old mum and dad.'

There was no comment from the other end.

'What, lost your tongue, have you, Ronnie? You got nothing to say?'

'Not to you, anyway.'

'Ronnie, you know I've been aiming to put the whole bad lot of you away. Up till now, though, it's been purely business. Now it's personal. I've got Dan, I hope, and I want you too, and Jack Price. But most of all I want that vicious little bastard. I want him, Ronnie, and I'm going to get him, I swear it. Whatever it takes. Goodbye. Have a nice day.'

Ronnie clicked the handset down once and lifted it up again. He dialled and stood there waiting till it was answered.

'Lee, get 'ere right away or I'll rip your bollocks right off. And bring the brainless wonder as well . . . Yes, I *do* fuckin' well mean Tommy.'

20

In the run-up to the big day at West Point, Fraser made very sure that Goldman Sachs kept Synapsis warm. Like Alistair, he also engaged in discreet lobbying among the partners, coming so close to telling the full story that most of them were already well in the picture as they headed for Dorset.

They converged at West Point on a damp morning. Crunching down the long, poplar-lined drive, they parked on the broad gravel semi-circle outside the fine Georgian brick house with its handsome honey-coloured stone portico.

Once they were all settled, Paul began proceedings with a rehearsal of the history of Orbia, comparing it with other global, regional, and national firms. Then he led them gently nearer the heart of the matter.

'What it boils down to is simple. Are we happy staying a respected but medium-sized firm, or do we want to take a big step forward? I have given a lot of thought to this, and reached the conclusion that if we do not move forward, we will inevitably move back. We either need to raise more capital to give us firepower to expand far faster, *or* we need to become part of a larger group that shares this ambition and can provide those resources. That's what we're here to discuss. I'm not proposing that we take any decisions today, but

I do want to try to get a strong flavour of what the partnership thinks. In preparation for this, I thought we needed to get some investment-banking input, so we retained Goldman Sachs to take a preliminary look at our options. I want to begin proceedings by asking Fraser and Alistair to report on what Goldman have advised.'

The two ran through it, each presenting their preferred approach and going on to field a wide range of questions which took the whole morning. After lunch Paul invited a general discussion, and one of the younger London partners immediately spoke up vociferously in favour of maintaining the status quo. Many nodded sympathetically as he spoke, and that led on to a lively debate about strategy, positioning, the image of the firm, and client and staff retention. However, sooner or later someone had to ask a different sort of question. It was Pierre from Paris.

'What I want to know, Paul, is: if we float or sell to Synapsis, who gets what?'

Paul knew this was minefield territory. He had decided in advance that, as far as possible, he would like to leave that subject for another day and a smaller group. It showed he took an optimistic view of human nature.

'So far we've been concentrating on the more fundamental issues. Naturally, if we decided to take this further, we would have to look at an equitable way of sorting things out.'

There was a dissatisfied rumble around the room. Pierre didn't need much encouragement to persevere.

'Forgive me, Paul, but that just won't do. If you want

a decision from us even in principle, we'll need to have some idea of what it means for us personally.'

There was a strong supporting murmur. Paul realised he'd have to give ground, but he was determined to yield no more than an inch at a time.

'Well, since the business is owned by the partners, we will be the principal beneficiaries.'

Pierre was never going to let him leave it there.

'Paul, we all know how the structure works. When you're elected to the partnership, you get the chance to buy a first tranche of shares at book value. You buy more every year, and when you leave or retire, you sell them again at book value. As long as the system stays as it is, it's fair for everyone, but now you're talking about a one-off event. There are people who've been partners for twenty years and are due to retire soon, who are no longer big earners for the firm, and would freely admit that they contribute less than the average partner of, say, five years' standing. But if the distribution were made pro rata according to the number of shares held at that instant in time, that older partner would stand to get four times the reward of the younger one. Surely that can't be your intention?'

Paul had no choice but to keep ducking and diving.

'Pierre, you've put your finger on a very important point. We'll have to find a methodology which reflects both the contribution that some more senior partners have made over many years *and* the current importance of some of our younger colleagues.'

'So, it definitely won't be pro rata, right?'

Damn. Another foot of ground was about to go. To make matters worse, he could see a few of the older guys getting ready to take up arms if he conceded too much.

'I don't want to get too far into that today, but I imagine that it might have to be more . . . sophisticated than pure pro rata.'

Everyone looked unhappy with that answer. Paul was glad to be distracted by a hand going up from Sandy, the very oldest partner, who took an emollient line on most things. Paul's relief was short-lived.

'Paul, I daresay that most of us will ultimately look at this from the point of view of what's in it for ourselves, and I'm no exception. As you all know, I'm due to retire at the end of this year. Assuming I've understood what Fraser and Alistair said correctly, if we sell to Synapsis it'll happen in November to December, whereas if we float, it won't be until February. As we all know, there's a vast gap between our book value, which is around fifty million, and the value we'll realise through either transaction. Now, if we sell in, say, November, I presume the three of us will receive our whack like everyone else – subject, of course, to whatever this "sophisticated" formula of yours is. What I want to know is, if instead we opt for the float, which therefore happens after we leave the partnership, are we forced to sell our shares at book value in the old way? Because if we are, firstly that would be absolutely bloody iniquitous, and, secondly, no prizes for guessing which I'll be voting for.'

Fraser smiled quietly. Alistair frowned. But it was Paul who had to field this swerving, scudding ball.

'It's a fair point, Sandy, and another thing we'll have to look at.'

'Why?' Tanya, one of the more aggressive women

partners spoke up. 'Nothing personal, Sandy, but fundamentally I don't see much difference between your situation and the guys who left last year. They would have almost as much right to feel aggrieved as you would have. Either way it's an accident of timing.'

Paul saw Sandy getting red in the face, and quickly said that treating all partners fairly would be paramount. Before anyone else could challenge what he meant, Paul moved smartly on to the question of what, if any, provision should be made for staff below partner level. Tanya continued her cuddly approach.

'I can see why they should be considered for stock options to incentivise them for their future performance, but I can't see any reason why they should expect to get anything else. We own the company, we bought the shares, we took the risk, both financial and legal. We'd be taking money right out of our own pockets.'

There were plenty of people in the room who were glad that someone had said that, if only to put a marker down. However, not so many wanted to go public with such a hard line. It was Alistair himself who put the contrary view.

'I hear you, Tanya, but if the company floats – or is sold – at a value of around four hundred million, and we pocket every last penny, the other staff, especially those at project-manager level, would be very unhappy indeed. At a minimum they would be demotivated, and they might leave. I know we're not getting into detail today, but I really do think we'll have to look at putting aside a certain proportion of the proceeds as a windfall bonus for the troops.'

There was more to-ing and fro-ing on it. The nearest

thing to a consensus was that there should be such a provision, but it should be modest – not more than five or ten million pounds in total. Paul thought that was about it for tricky topics, and was about to start summing up when another threatening hand shot up. It belonged to Eva from Stockholm.

'Paul, what does this mean for promotions? We always announce the new partners by the end of November, although they don't officially join until the first of January. What happens to them?'

Paul hadn't thought about that one. 'I don't know. I imagine they'll be included as beneficiaries, although at a modest level.'

Eva was one of the few who wasn't thinking about herself. But she *was* thinking about her office and the two candidates whom she was keen to support.

'But this means that the partnership election will be far more important than usual. Anyone who narrowly fails to be elected will miss out on a one-time bonanza. Whatever formula you use, if the better part of four hundred million pounds is distributed between thirty-odd partners, even the most junior will surely get a seven-figure sum. And anyone who's held back even for another year will get next to nothing.'

This set the room off again. Paul feared it was getting out of hand, and trying to quell things, simply chucked fuel on the fire.

'Well, maybe we might have to promote more people than usual. We normally elect four or five. As far as I know there are ten or eleven good candidates. Maybe, as a one-off gesture, we should consider electing them all.'

That was his most ill-judged remark of the day and prompted true uproar. Fraser Morrison, who had played the day quietly, judging it wiser to observe the mood rather than try to lead it, decided this was the moment to step in. Although the majority had supported Alistair's proposal of a pool for other staff, he suspected that secretly they grudged it. If the way to their hearts was via their pocketbooks, so be it.

'Paul, may I beg to differ? Firstly, I think that electing so many people would be strange. We would effectively be taking two years' worth in one, and that would distort the firm's whole structure. As is it, we're often short of good project managers, and if through promotion we lost not four or five, but ten or eleven, I don't know how we'd staff projects.'

There was a huge swell of support for his view. Paul was already looking abashed.

'And in any case, it wouldn't solve the problem, it would only pass it on. The individuals coming up after the next ten would feel just as much that they had missed out. So, forgive me, Paul, but I don't think we can do that. In fact, I think there's a strong case for doing the opposite.'

Paul looked astonished. 'You mean, promote no one?'

Fraser waited and watched. If enough had looked in favour of that he would have chanced his arm, but there were too many incredulous whispers to take the risk.

'No, not necessarily. But given all the problems of satisfying all the existing partners, I think there could be a strong case for restricting it to, say, two.'

From the general reaction it looked like he had judged it well. For those thinking only of their personal rake-off it was satisfactory: the dilution would be small. And for those more concerned with the promotion of their protégés, it left the door open to achieving it.

Alistair sensed that Fraser had scored some points, and was desperate to claw some back quickly.

'Excuse me, Fraser, this is all very well, but we know it's hard enough even in a normal year to persuade an unsuccessful candidate that he should hang around and not sugar off somewhere else. When they know what's on the line here, and that we're promoting fewer people than usual, tell me, what the hell can we say that will satisfy them?'

It was the first time that day that the two gladiators had locked in direct combat. It was Alistair's doing, and now Fraser had to kill off the challenge. The partners, well aware of the tensions between them, fell silent.

Fraser paused for dramatic effect. 'Alistair, I think you forget who we're dealing with.'

Alistair was genuinely thrown by the point. 'If you're talking about our project managers, they're all highly intelligent, analytical, driven people, who can detect flannel at a hundred paces. If you think you can pull the wool over their eyes, Fraser, I tell you, you're wrong.'

'And I say again, Alistair, you forget who we're dealing with. Not their intellect and ability, which I agree we should never underestimate. I'm talking about their psyche. They're consultants, for God's sake, and let's never forget that, like most consulting firms, the people we always try to hire are insecure overachievers who can be manipulated into working so hard for a quarter the pay that investment bankers get. When they were at school or university they always got the top marks, partly because they were clever, but mainly because they worked their balls off, knowing that they'd feel utterly naked unless they could cover themselves in certificates with large "A"s stamped all over them. *That's* who we're dealing with . . .'

He stopped and looked around. They were all staring at him. Of course this was how they ran the firm, keeping staff on their toes, desperate for approval, willing to embrace disappointment and stay as milk cows a little longer. Most of them had once been on the receiving end of this treatment in their time, and knew this was the only way the great money-making machine was maintained. It was a necessary evil. But no one had ever *said* it before. Fraser carried on.

'What I suggest is that, apart from the two we do promote, we simply tell the others they're not ready yet. They all have strengths and weaknesses; let this be the year of the weakness. Do the clients like them as much as they might? Are they creative enough? Is praise for them in their teams slightly muted? If we look hard enough, there will always be some insecurity somewhere.'

He stopped and took a glass of water. Alistair was aglow, sure that Fraser had blown it. He was wrong. They could see it was the only way.

There was a silence for a while, then Paul quietly suggested that Fraser was right, and moved to adopt his idea of two new partners only. No one objected. Then he moved back to the fundamental issue. The mood was different now, and nobody wanted any more fractious debate.

Paul called for a straight show of hands on the various

options. The supporters of the status quo had dwindled to a handful. The other two attracted roughly equal support. Paul avoided taking a tally, and proposed that they defer the decision till they were far further down the track. He concluded with a grave warning about the importance of keeping these matters entirely to themselves.

The long-case clock struck five.

'Well, I think we've all richly deserved a glass of champagne.'

21

Everything was in very good shape. Rupert was unaware of the humiliating roasting Lee and Tommy had received from Ronnie, but all too aware that Lee's mood was black. However, it hadn't stopped the two young men performing. Well within the projected time-span, they had found an inadequate mousy twenty-two-year-old who was so mortified at the thought of being fired, so terrified that the police might be called, that she would have agreed to anything. Twenty-four hours later she came back to the bar and tearfully handed over a handwritten page bearing dates and addresses. She was sent on her way with a warning ringing in her ears that if she *ever*, under any circumstances, admitted to anyone what she had done, they would find her and maim her.

The money that Ronnie and Jack had got together had been transferred from Switzerland to Bermuda, and from Bermuda to a London prime broker. Rupert had passed one last fretful night assailed by vivid dreams of police, courtrooms and jails, before taking the deepest of breaths and instructing the broker to implement a selling programme, phased over several days, so that by now they had built up a short position of two and half million shares, all sold at around four pounds fifty a share.

Now they had to wait for the hours of darkness.

*

The neighbours in the mews near the end of Sydney Street groaned as they heard an alarm going off for the nth time that year. It was Friday night and they'd just got to sleep after a long hard week. They were a nice couple, that architect and his wife, but it was high time they got a system that didn't go off all the time. To make matters worse, they were away on holiday in the Far East, and hadn't left a set of keys. Christ, how long would that thing go on ringing? If it didn't stop soon, they really *would* have to call the police.

Saturday night was a foul one, pouring with rain from dusk till dawn. That was fine for business: in this sort of weather fewer people walked their dogs in the wee small hours. Hampstead was such a good place to work; the street lamps had a warm, friendly glow that didn't shine too brightly. Let's see now. This shouldn't be too difficult . . . There . . . Ah, what a pretty kitchen. He had no reason to hurry tonight. How about a nice cup of tea first?

Sunday night. Oh look – lovely paintings of old ships. Handy sizes too, no longer than about fifteen by ten, most of them. What was this on the mantelpiece? Antique carriage clocks always found a ready market, and silver frames were almost as good as cash. If he knew his Holland Park, there should be jewellery upstairs in the bedroom. Amazing, the way people like this spent millions on a house, and couldn't be bothered to get a better alarm system than that. His seven-year-old kid could have disabled it.

Monday, Campden Hill. Tuesday, Kensington and Chelsea. Wednesday, Highgate, Lancaster Gate and Putney.

On Friday afternoon the call went in to the business editor of the *Sunday Times*, Rory Godson. When the caller wouldn't give a name, Rory nearly didn't take it. When he did, he was fascinated, but told the man from the payphone that, unless he identified himself or offered proof, they couldn't run it. The man gave some details, but still not his name, and the call ended without resolution.

Hmmm. A crank most likely, or someone with a grudge against the company. If it was true, though, it was a bombshell. He didn't want to set hares running without checking, and Sunday's business pages were all but put to bed. Rory summoned a junior reporter and told him to check a sample of them with local police. By six in the evening he had his answer. He'd tried five, and in each case the answer was yes. Jesus. Time for a word with John Witherow.

It took the editor fully ten seconds to make up his mind. It would be huge in the business section, of course, but, yes, it was a much bigger story than that. Maybe even the lead. He called in the head of the *Insight* team and they all agreed on a strategy. What they had to avoid was alerting the company so soon that they rushed an announcement and the story broke in the Saturday papers instead of the *Sunday Times*.

Plus, they couldn't be sure yet. All they had was a bunch of addresses that had been burgled. The *Insight* team should start by checking with their police sources whether all the houses on the list had been hit, and try to get an idea of the scale of the swag.

By nine-thirty they'd done that. Twelve out of twelve. The team met again. Okay, this was big. If there were no earthquakes, political sex scandals, or mass murders, this was their lead story. The tactics had to be thought through. They should be safe on the Saturdays now, but that still left the radio and TV. Plus they didn't want the other Sundays getting an early edition of their own paper on Saturday night and sharing their thunder.

That meant two things. First, they should leave it till the last possible moment before contacting *Timbookedtoo*. Late Saturday afternoon would be about right, giving the company enough time to check it, but too little to take counter measures. Second, they should consider running a filler in the first edition. The first edition had a print run of only 200,000, and any half-decent story would do. The real excitement and the lurid headlines would be held back for the mass second edition which would accompany coffee and boiled eggs up and down the land.

The whole *Sunday Times* team spent Saturday on tenterhooks, nervously checking every news agency item, every broadcast, terrified that their scoop would be purloined. By five p.m. there was nothing, and as agreed, Godson scrolled down his personal organiser containing the work, home, and mobile numbers for most of the business powers in the land, and dialled the mobile number.

'Hello?'

'It's Rory Godson. Is that you, Peter?'

'Oh hi, Rory. How are you?'

'Peter, something's come up. Something rather urgent. We've received information today that personal information on customers who've booked holidays with you is being leaked systematically to criminals, and that your clients' houses are being burgled while they're away.'

'Bullshit.' There had been a few tall tales about the company before, but this took the biscuit. 'Who told you this?'

'He wouldn't say, other than that he knew what was going on and wanted to blow the whistle.'

'I hope, Rory, that you wouldn't consider running garbage like that, on the basis of one wild, unsupported, anonymous allegation.'

'Of course not. But it may not be garbage. He gave us some sample addresses and we checked with police. They *have* been burgled. Now, it may be that none of them were your customers . . .'

'But we'd better check, I agree.' Hearing that burglaries had actually happened had changed things. Peter had a sinking feeling in his stomach. Pray God there was no connection with his company.

'Shall I e-mail you the addresses?'

'Yes, please do. It's Peter.N@Timbookedtoo.com.'

'Got it. Peter, as you can imagine, if there is anything in this, we'll have no choice but to run it tomorrow.'

'I understand. Just don't do anything till I've looked into it.'

'I won't, and if we're right, naturally we'll be willing to give you space for a right of reply.'

'Thanks.'

'And can I depend on you, in return, not to call anyone else?'

'Look, Rory, I'm still assuming that this is poppycock. If it's not, we'll have to do whatever we can to protect ourselves. Having said that, I appreciate you letting me know rather than running it speculatively, and I'll undertake not to initiate any contact with other media. If they call us, though, either because your informant has rung them too, or they've picked it up anywhere else, we'll have to respond.'

'Fair enough. Okay, will you call me later?'

'Yes. I'm not in the office now. It'll take me half an hour to get back there and another hour to check this out. It's pretty binary, isn't it? If they're not our customers, I can breathe again. If they *are*, we're fucked. Don't quote me.'

'I won't. But I think you're right.'

*

On Saturday night Rupert cancelled his long-standing plan to go with Primrose to *La Traviata* at the Opera House. He was like a cat on a hot tin roof and wouldn't have been able to sit still for five minutes. By eight-thirty he was already hanging round Piccadilly Circus waiting for the next day's papers to appear. He couldn't remember if it was nine or ten p.m. they went on sale.

It turned out to be a quarter past nine. Heart thumping, he shouldered his way past a couple of other customers, handed over the coins, and grabbed a copy

224

of the *Sunday Times*. He flung aside the main news section and pulled out the business pages. It wasn't there. Why hadn't they run the damn thing?

He was due to meet Lee in an hour to celebrate. *Shit*. There was bugger all he could do about it tonight. He would have to go to the bar, mollify Lee somehow, and try another paper tomorrow.

Lee was pissed off to begin with, but relaxed as he imbibed and as Rupert assured him that this was the most minor of hitches. They both got drunk, and Rupert didn't get home till four. Stupidly, he forgot to switch off his radio alarm, and it cut through his slumber at seven.

As he groped out to silence it, the lead story on the news penetrated his hazy consciousness. A second later he was bolt upright, and three minutes later, unwashed, unbrushed and unkempt, he had hotfooted it down to his local newsagents. He tore inside and looked at the fat pile of papers. There, on the top, on the very first page, was the most beautiful headline he'd seen in his life.

TIMBOOKEDTOO CAUGHT IN THE NET

To the astonishment of everyone around, he let out an ear-piercing *'Yippee!'* and, leaving a fiver by the till to beat the queue, he grabbed a copy and ran down the street jumping for joy.

*

Peter Nicholl had been up all Saturday night, and spent most of Sunday at Linklaters, where his lawyers, bankers and brokers tried desperately, hopelessly, to control the damage. Of course they had to prepare a general press release and a statement to be issued by the Stock Exchange. The brokers were sure they'd agree to the share price being suspended until the scale of the problem was better understood. It was now undeniable that everyone whose address had been leaked to the *Sunday Times* had been burgled during their holidays. What they couldn't establish immediately was whether this had been going on for a long time or was a purely recent phenomenon. In fact, unless they contacted every past customer and asked them, they couldn't know for sure. Now the story had broken, others might come out of the woodwork. Before that, any victims would have put it down to bad luck. Christ, what a mess.

The police, of course, were preparing to interview all *Timbookedtoo* staff, and wanted the human resources department to give contact details for former employees. They also needed to speak to the IT people to understand how hard it would be to crack the password system which governed access to customers' details. The system had been carefully designed, with security very much a consideration. Credit-card details, including billing addresses, were all done by customers on-line, and were fully encrypyted. But it was basically a travel company, for God's sake. Someone had to mail out the tickets, and tickets had dates on them. There would always be somewhere where the cyberworld bumped into the real world of paper, streets and postmen. They'd done what they could. It looked like it wasn't enough.

Another group who showed up at Linklaters were the company's non-executive directors. When they arrived, a board meeting was held immediately, with the lawyers on hand to offer advice. Later in the day, the non-executives held a further meeting alone. They were in no doubt that this was a major catastrophe, a public relations disaster, a body-blow from which the company might never fully recover. Heads would have to roll. Not theirs, of course. They couldn't have been expected to anticipate something like this. However, the head of IT should be fired summarily, and Peter Nicholl would have to resign. All very sad for the fellow. They liked him, and he had undoubtedly put all his energy and enthusiasm into it. Now they were suffering from his lack of real business experience. The only hope of rebuilding the company's reputation would be to get someone in with a solid track record in management. Somebody older.

And then there was the press. The dailies were naturally irritated that it wasn't *their* story, but this was too big to ignore. The journalists and the snaparazzi laid siege to *Timbookedtoo*'s Farringdon offices, and when someone there, in an attempt to dislodge them, said that top management were meeting elsewhere, they quickly worked out that it had to be at their bankers' or lawyers'. Before long, Linklaters' offices in Silk Street were surrounded. What they all wanted, of course, was an interview with Peter Nicholl, preferably accompanied by photographs of a sleepless, ashen face.

In the meantime, they were putting their stories together, drawing heavily on earlier interviews with him. The fact that Peter had never been one to be boastful or flashy didn't help him now. There was only one story to write. From hubris, move to nemesis, do not pass 'Go', do not collect £200. The Cambridge-educated dotcom multimillionaire who thought he walked on water.

The company's beleaguered PR girl was able to dodge their questions about what kind of car he drove – mainly because she had no idea. However, some neighbours in Culford Gardens had seen the blue beast. Was it a Ferrari, or a Porsche, perhaps? Who cared? Either would do. Digital photos of the latest models were pulled from the files in seconds. And what about that flat? Again, the neighbours helped fill them in. One even arranged for them to see the identical place next door. A modest sitting room, two bedrooms, a galley kitchen and a single bathroom, all tucked up under the eaves, with sloping ceilings. Didn't sound right at all. Luxury penthouse was more like it.

The top prize for creativity would go to the *Sun*. They were planning to run a help-line for victims of *Timbookedtoo*. They knew it was sure-fire. Burglaries often happened when people were on holiday, as everyone knew. With the hundreds of thousands who had booked through the company, statistically there were *bound* to be a number who'd suffered that fate. Now they could get their names in the paper, and be neatly positioned for whatever compensation package *Timbookedtoo* were forced to hand out. And the *Sun* would fearlessly champion their rights.

*

Primrose had been in the office most of Sunday herself, preparing some documents for a meeting in Paris the next day. The night before she hadn't felt like going to the opera herself, so she'd given the tickets away to a friend, and gone to bed early. On Sunday morning she'd neither seen the papers nor listened to the news, and it was well through the day before one of her colleagues excitedly told her about the swarms downstairs, incredulous that Primrose was unaware of the news.

Her heart went out to Peter. The poor guy. How he must be feeling. And if there were so many photographers here, there would probably be the same number outside his flat if they'd got the address. And it seemed they *always* got the address. She knew what a crisis atmosphere there would be in the meeting room, and certainly didn't want to intrude. However, she felt she had to do something, so she penned a brief note, stuck it in an envelope, and got one of the security guards to deliver it to him where they were gathered.

Leaving Silk Street around five, she went to Rupert's. He looked tired, but otherwise was in good spirits. She kissed him very tenderly, then as they sat curled up together, she pointed at the *Sunday Times* which lay on the floor.

'Isn't it terrible?'

Rupert nodded. 'Dreadful.'

'They're all at the office.'

'Which office?'

'Ours. Didn't I tell you? We recently became *Timbookedtoo*'s lawyers.'

'No, you didn't. Was that something to do with you?'

'Don't be daft. I knew nothing about it. I only found out a few weeks ago when I bumped into Peter in our lobby.'

Rupert sniffed, but decided to let it go. 'So are there lots of reporters hanging around?'

'Hundreds . . . Before I left I sent him a message. If it's like that at Linklaters, his flat will be besieged too.'

'Yeah. If I were him, I'd stay in a hotel.'

'I hadn't thought of that.'

'What d'you mean?'

'I said if he needed it, I was sure he could come here and stay with us.'

'You said *what*?' Rupert's eyes went wild.

'I'm sorry if it was the wrong thing to do, Rupes. I did it on the spur of the moment.'

'What happens if he arrives with thousands of journalists in tow? I don't want to get involved in this mess, for fuck's sake.'

'Okay, okay. I just wanted to help. If he rings I'll tell him.'

22

Rupert hadn't reckoned on the shares being suspended, and the delay cost him more sleepless nights. The news was still playing heavily in the press, and in the finance pages there were widely varying estimates of where the share price would settle when trading restarted.

Peter Nicholl didn't ring on Sunday night, and the first Rupert saw of him was the deliciously ignominious spectacle of him reading his statement of resignation on Monday night's news. He accepted total responsibility, and apologised abjectly to *Timbookedtoo*'s customers, shareholders, staff, board, and apparently anyone else he could think of.

By Thursday the company's new caretaker boss was able to issue a statement that their own investigation had shown that these had been relatively isolated incidents which had happened over a very short period and only in London. Therefore, the likely legal liability should fall well within their insurance provision. They had instituted changes to their systems to ensure that there could be no recurrence of this problem, and that customers could again book with confidence. The Stock Exchange agreed that trading in their shares could restart on Friday. In a further announcement, co-ordinated with police, it was said that one of their employees had been suspended and was helping police with enquiries.

The stupid bitch. If she had kept her nerve, no one would have found her. However, if the team had known the whole truth, they wouldn't have worried. When, along with all the other staff, the girl was questioned by police, she cratered, but her tearful attempts to describe the men who'd blackmailed her were feeble. The other boys and girls from the company who'd been in the same bar vaguely recalled her being chatted up by some guys, but had no recollection of what they looked like. Without any useful description, the police had no starting point. Was it the burglars themselves who'd blackmailed the girl, or was it some scum drug-dealer friends of theirs? The police checks with their regular informants produced nothing. In due course the girl would be charged with conspiring to steal with person or persons unknown, and she would plead very guilty. In a less high-profile case, she might get off with probation or community service, given her age and clean record. Not this time, especially since she'd admitted taking Class A drugs as part of the package. She was looking at two to three years.

Beyond that, it was looking hard for the police to do much. For all the brouhaha in the press, the reality was that in crime terms this boiled down to a dozen small-scale break-ins, the kind of thing that happened every day in the capital. They simply couldn't commit the resources, not when they had the war against organised crime to fight. The company's lawyers had pressed them to investigate whether this could be part of some wider scam. The problem was, there was no evidence of it at all. The perpetrators had been ingenious all right, but it really had been simple, opportunistic stuff. Most likely they were normal burglars who for once in their lives had come up with a smart idea. Not *that* smart, though. In total they'd got away with goods worth two hundred and eighty-five grand. Once they'd fenced it all, they'd be lucky to see more than a third of that. Hardly the big time. In fact, it barely crawled out of the petty-crime box.

*

Ronnie and Jack stayed down in Kent, but Rupert, who'd grown increasingly chummy with Lee and Tommy, went round to Lee's flat in Docklands for the start of trading on Friday morning. Rupert had instructed their broker to buy when the expected wave of selling came in, but to do it cautiously. There were good reasons not to be clumsy. It wasn't only to avoid drawing attention to themselves: if the market sentiment was encouragingly negative, they wouldn't want to buy so aggressively that they turned it.

They needn't have worried. As they clustered round Rupert's laptop, logged on to one of the internet brokerage sites, they watched *Timbookedtoo*'s share price open at 240, down from the previous close of 453, and go into freefall. 220, 210, 200, 180, 160. For a few minutes it seemed to stabilise at 150, then resumed the plunge down to 120.

Seeing this, Rupert feared that something had gone wrong. Could their broker in Bermuda have forgotten to set his alarm clock for an early start? Rupert put in a call. All was well. It was just that the volume of sell orders was even greater than anticipated. It seemed that the vast majority of private investors were stampeding out, and the normally more phlegmatic institutions were of the same mind. The word among their analysts was that, for some time at least, revenues at *Timbookedtoo* might dry up completely. The share price could be close to meltdown, and if they didn't get out now, they might not get another chance for a long while. The net result was that, of all the shares in the company not held by founders, something like two thirds were potentially for sale: forty or fifty million shares, compared with an average daily trading volume of less than one million. The few bargain-hunting buyers were hopelessly outnumbered, and any price bid was grabbed in a flash. By the time Rupert called, the broker had bought eight hundred thousand. He should be well past the million mark within the hour, and, even buying deliberately in relatively small lots, it looked liked the market could easily absorb their entire programme today.

Had they known, it would have amused them that even the big international bank from which they'd borrowed the stock had itself joined in the Gadarene rush and, like everyone else, was trying frantically to unload its holding at literally any price. The multi-coloured screens in the bank's vast trading floor were telling the same story. 110, 100, 90, 80, 70.

By two o'clock it was time for the champagne corks to start popping. The broker called through to say he'd bought two and a half million shares at prices ranging between 210 and 63, with an average of 110. Rupert flipped out his calculator. That, against their original selling price of about 450, meant a difference of three pounds forty a share. Times two and a half was ten point seven fucking million. Yo!

They all roared like lions, and stood up and did a jig. Lee got them out on the balcony, grabbed the champagne bottle and frothed it up Formula One fashion. Their clothes were a mess, but who gave a damn? They were all rich, and it was clean legal money. Now the good times could roll.

Rupert went to call Ronnie again. Lee was joyful enough to forget the scowl he'd recently adopted whenever his old man was mentioned, and agreed that they should invite him and Jack up to town for a knees-up.

When they heard the number, Ronnie and Jack needed no second bidding. Tonight should be a big one. Ideally, they needed a private room, but none of them wanted to go to one of their own places this time. Ronnie suggested an old stand-by, the Oak Room at the Meridien. The tables there were spaced far enough that, if they kept their voices down, they could talk freely. He was sure the maître d' would find room for them.

*

Primrose had changed her plans for that evening at the last minute. She and her best friend Emily had arranged to do something together. At five-thirty Peter Nicholl had called her, and when he found that, as expected, she had dinner plans, he begged her to find time to have a quick drink with him beforehand.

They met at seven in a wine bar in Covent Garden. Primrose was taken aback by how awful he looked. At first they sat up on stools at the counter, but everyone kept looking at Peter and nudging each other, and they knew that the people sitting next to them would be straining to listen in to the conversation. When a booth became free, they retreated away from the prying eyes and ears, and ordered a whole bottle.

'How are your parents taking it, Peter?'

'They're being great. Telling me that the world is full of idiots. My dad's not what you'd call bookish – in fact, he's probably only read about twenty books in his life – but he likes that old Rudyard Kipling chestnut about success and failure both being imposters, so I've had a lot of that this week.'

'Good for him.'

'Apart from that, they keep telling me to quit the rotten South and go back home. They're always saying I could buy a palace up there for the price of my tiny flat down here.'

'And will you? Go back there?'

'I've no idea. I'm stuck at the company for a few weeks yet. Although I've been pushed off the board, they insisted that I stay on as a consultant for a while to help clean up the mess.'

'How bad is it?'

'Pretty bad. This week bookings are down by eighty per cent in the UK. It should recover a bit, but it'll be ages before it gets back to where it was before.'

'What about the offices abroad?'

'They've all been hit, though not as much. Down twenty to thirty per cent. The story appeared in all their newspapers too.'

'I know your shares started trading again today, but I only saw the opening price.'

'It finished at forty-eight pence. Up, believe it or not, from a low of forty-four.'

'Christ, that's—'

'About ten per cent of our previous level. My famous paper fortune of two hundred million just became twenty.'

'I'm so sorry, Peter.'

'Frankly, that part doesn't bother me a lot. I live pretty simply.'

'And even if you didn't, most people could struggle by on twenty million.'

'I'll drink to that.'

They clinked.

'What will you do next? It's early days, I know, but is there anything you've always wanted to do?'

'Nothing, apart from building up *Timbookedtoo*. I suppose I'll have to think of something else. It doesn't really matter what I do, as long as no one has to depend on me getting it right. I don't know what I could do. I feel pretty lost at the moment.'

'Course you do, Peter. And you'll feel that way for a while. You've lost your baby, and you'll have to grieve for it. Grieving takes as long as it takes. You can't hurry it.'

He put his hands up to his face. 'I'm sorry.'

'Look, I understand how you feel, but you mustn't torture yourself. Peter . . .'

She tried to pull one hand away; when she realised it was hiding tears, she let go of it. His voice was cracking up as he went on. 'I feel so horribly responsible.'

Peter's face stayed buried in his hands. Primrose didn't know what to say. The poor guy was in a bad way. She decided to slip away from the booth for a while to give him a chance to sort himself out.

When she came back, he was blowing his nose.

'I'm really sorry, Prim. I didn't mean to embarrass you.'

'You didn't. Peter, forgive me for saying this, but you look a mess. And you also look like you haven't eaten all week.'

'As you can imagine, I haven't had a huge appetite.'

'They do food here. How about having a steak?'

'You said you had plans. You're probably seeing Rupert, aren't you?'

'He's busy – he's got some business dinner. I was going to see a friend called Emily.'

'You'd better go then. I don't want to ruin your evening.'

'I just called and cancelled. Tonight I think your need is greater than hers.'

'You sure? Thank you. God, I appreciate it. Prim, would you do me one other favour?'

'Anything.'

'I don't want you to lie or anything, but would you mind not giving Rupert a complete blow-by-blow account of, you know, everything this evening?'

Primrose reached out and squeezed his hand again. 'You have my word. And I won't lie to him, but if he assumes that I did see Emily and doesn't ask, I may leave it at that.'

*

When they all swaggered into the Oak Room at half past eight, Ronnie was warmly welcomed. They were shown to one of the best tables. When the waiter tried to take orders for drinks, Ronnie asked for the sommelier. He was determined not to stint on the wine, and told the happy man that he wanted the best for his guests, regardless of price. The sommelier immediately started them off with a magnum of Krug 1990, then dashed off to check that the white Montrachet '92 which he selected to go with the first course was at precisely 14 degrees. After much debate, Ronnie agreed to his suggestion of skipping red Burgundy, and opting instead for a comparison of great clarets.

Seeing the bored look on the faces of Lee and Tommy, Rupert proposed that it would be more fun to do it like the late stages of the FA Cup, and quickly invented some rules. By the fish course, it was game on. Cheval Blanc '82 eliminated Latour '86 in one of the quarter finals, setting up a clash in the semis against a Lafite, which sadly it lost. On the other side of the draw, Petrus had swept all opposition aside, including, surprisingly, Le Pin. The beef Wellington having by then been polished off, it was agreed that the final should be played over the cheese. It was to be a game of two halves, with each side allowed to substitute vintages three times. They were in injury time, and Petrus one goal ahead, when Lafite brought on two subs in quick succession, levelled the scoring with the '59 and, seconds before the final whistle, clinched the match with the '48.

They all enjoyed the match thoroughly. Tommy admitted that he didn't realise that wine tastings were such fun. Jack glowed in quiet contentment. Out of pure curiosity, Rupert asked the sommelier the running score for the wine so far. Looking mildly embarrassed, the man scribbled a calculation and showed it to him. £16,745 excluding service. Ronnie laughed like a drain.

Meanwhile Lee was becoming so boisterous that several other diners were muttering objections. If the waiters hadn't been in such delighted expectation of munificent tips, they might have been more moved to pass on the complaints. As it was, this merely encouraged other customers to pay up and leave, grumbling as they went, which suited the team fine. On any other occasion, Rupert would have been mortified to be seen with such a loud, uncouth group, flashing their money around in this parvenu way. Tonight, he didn't give a damn, couldn't get his head far away from the thought that as of today, due almost entirely to his own inspiration, he was personally worth over two million.

They had pudding with a bottle of Yquem, then sat contentedly back with fat cigars and glasses of Armagnac from the century before last. Ronnie looked around to make sure no waiter was within earshot, and patted Rupert's thigh.

'Well, Rupert, you certainly started us off with a bang. So, what's the next?'

Rupert relighted his Cohiba and took a long puff. 'Give me a break, Ronnie, I haven't got over this one yet.'

'I know, I know. All the same, if I know my Rupert, I bet that mind of yours is whirrin' already.'

Rupert shook his head. 'Sorry to disappoint you all, but I haven't a clue. Give me a few days and I'll come up with something.'

Ronnie nodded. 'Course, course. Know what I'd like to do? *Really* like to do?'

It was Lee who asked what.

'Go over the pavement.'

Lee looked dumbfounded. '*What*? Rob a bank? You gone off your rocker? What would we wanna do that for, eh?'

'For old time's sake. Just to see if it could be done. In some new way, I mean. I bet Rupert could think of somethin'.'

'Bollocks! Sorry, Rupes, I don't mean bollocks to you bein' able to do it, I mean bollocks to goin' over the pavement. Not what we're about, is it? We're about *clever* crime, in't we?'

Ronnie chuckled 'Don't worry, Lee lad, I ain't bein' too serious. Rupert knows that.'

Rupert smiled. 'Course I do, Ronnie. I was involved in a project about retail banking once, when I worked at my old firm, McKinsey. Most branches these days don't have much cash, do they? If I remember rightly it was typically two to four hundred grand, depending on the location and size.'

Jack nodded. 'That sounds about right, and it's assumin' you can clear out the place. You never get the time. Alarm goes off, and the Law's round in seconds. Mug's game.'

Rupert smiled at Jack and scratched his chin. 'Interesting though. It would be a fascinating intellectual challenge, trying to think of a way of re-engineering bank robbery, both to get enough loot and to make it safer.'

'Impossible,' Jack grunted. He, like Lee, wasn't going to be budged on this one.

Rupert was finding it fun to think about it. He knew

it was mainly the wine talking, and the high he was still on. But as the adrenalin began to subside, he almost had a feeling that *Timbookedtoo* had been *too* easy. The thought that you could take on the establishment – whether the business establishment or the police – and beat them hollow was glorious.

Jack carried on with his charge. 'You're the one what told us to bring down our risk quotient. Banks are way up there in the risk stakes.'

'Not necessarily. Remember what we said about how the police arrange themselves – head on at organised crime. But for all the reasons you say, organised crime isn't interested in bank robberies. So it can't be a priority for the police – to prevent it or to investigate it. We shouldn't dismiss it out of hand, that's all I'm saying.'

Ronnie smiled and stubbed his cigar out. 'Tell you what, Rupert. I'll give you a little incentive. If you can come up with a way for us to cross the pavement that nets us at least one mill, but keeps the old risk quotient down, I'll personally give you 'alf a mill from our share of today's little caper.'

Rupert held his hand out. 'You're on. And if I can't, the next dinner's on me.'

23

Surprisingly in the circumstances, Rupert had no more than a medium hangover. He woke near eleven-thirty and, with much stretching and baritone yawning, wandered through to brush his teeth. Still in T-shirt and boxer shorts, he went into the kitchen, made a coffee, and stared out at the leaden sky. It looked certain to rain. It wouldn't be a fun drive. He and Prim had to go that afternoon to Chipping Norton to stay with friends from his business-school days. God, it would be frustrating, bursting with his success, and unable to whisper a word about it, even to Prim. Come to think of it, he'd better call her and arrange when to leave.

To his annoyance, Prim said that both her nephews had flu, and that now their mother had gone down with it too. There was no one else to help. She had no choice but to pull out of the weekend and play nursemaid. Rupert flew right off the handle. They'd been invited six weeks before. How *dare* she do this at the last minute? Primrose's repeated humble apologies got her nowhere. He wound himself up more and more, until the spring wouldn't coil any further, so he slammed the phone violently down, and refused to answer it when she rang back.

An hour later, he was throwing a few things into his

overnight bag when a thought occurred to him. Was it worth a try? He hit a button on his mobile.

'Georgina? It's me, Rupert. What are you up to?'

'I'm off home. Daddy's invited some fearfully grand Austrian relatives for the weekend. I'm on parade.'

'Pity.'

'Why?'

'Prim's not still there, is she?'

'No, she left a while ago.'

'She backed out of something with me this weekend.'

'I know. I heard snatches of her end of the conversation. You *are* mean to her, Rupert.'

'Balls. She left me in the lurch . . . Anyway, this thing I'm going to could be rather fun. It's a bunch of my MBA classmates; we're getting together in the Cotswolds. Why don't you cry off sick to your parents, and come along?'

'I couldn't. Daddy would kill me, and I bet your friends are all bosom buddies of Prim. They'd hate me on sight.'

'They're my friends, not hers. She's only met most of them once. You really would enjoy them.'

'What would the sleeping arrangements be?'

'Obviously, Prim and I would have shared a room . . .'

'But if I came?'

'I'd have to see whether they have another room free. Or I could sleep on a sofa, or perhaps on the floor of your room, if you wouldn't mind.'

'I would.'

'Okay. Why don't I call and ask what the score is? Will you see if you can get out of yours?'

A spare room was created by one of the hosts' sons being redeployed to share his sister's room. It was an uproarious evening, and Rupert, who had a sideline in merciless mimicry, kept them in stitches. One of the other guys was a whiz on the ivories. Georgina was a definite success too. The men all did their best to flirt with her, and for all his protestations that they were just friends, Rupert had to endure much nudging.

By two o'clock the party began to wind down. Maddeningly, Rupert's kiddy room was in a different wing from Georgina's, so he was reduced to insisting on seeing her to hers. She opened the door and held it there while they both cried out good night to two other couples as they plodded wearily bedward. Then they were alone in the corridor.

'That was fun, Rupes. I enjoyed myself.'

'Glad you came?'

'Yes. It was interesting seeing you among your own friends. Don't take this the wrong way, but you seemed more at ease, more comfortable than when you're with Prim.'

'Maybe you're right. She and I *are* rather different species.'

'Anyway, time for bed.' She took his hand for a moment, then dropped it. 'Good night. Sweet dreams.' With that she blew him a kiss and closed the door.

Bugger. He stood stock still for a moment and then began to walk dejectedly away. He got as far as his bedroom, then retraced his steps and knocked gently on her door. It opened. Georgina looked wary.

'What?'

'I was wondering . . . I don't suppose there's any chance of a good-night kiss?'

She put an index finger to her lips and with the nail brushed it to and fro. Then she looked straight into his eyes and shook her head. Rupert pulled a face.

'Meanie.'

'I'm not a meanie, I'm your girlfriend's flatmate and dear chum, remember?'

'Maybe, but you're still a meanie. One tiny kiss wouldn't do any harm.'

'Oh yes, it would.'

Rupert shrugged. 'Okay . . . Good night.' He turned and began to walk off.

Georgina let him go a few paces, then stepped into the corridor, one arm still holding languidly onto the door handle and called out gently, 'Rupert.' He turned round. 'There is one thing you could do, if you like.'

'What?' By now he was watching out for a barb or a joke.

'Your car seats aren't very comfortable. They've made my back hurt. Do you do massage?'

'Do you have any oil?'

'I might have some in my bag.'

'Okay, you'd better get ready for action.'

She went into the bathroom, and emerged ten minutes later wearing loose Chinese silk trousers and top. She handed him the oil, turned the lights off apart from a bedside lamp, pulled the top off and lay down on her front. He moved over to the bed and poured some oil on her upper back. She tensed.

'That's cold.'

'Don't worry, I'll soon warm you up.' He smoothed the oil with big broad sweeps, then, lifting her lovely mane carefully out of the way, proceeded to knead her shoulders. 'This isn't too hard?'

'No, it feels wonderful. You've done this before.'

'Once or twice.' He stopped to administer more oil, and brushed it lower, pulling her bra strap first up, then down, before in one deft movement unfastening it.

'Hey, what are you doing?'

'Nothing. It was getting in the way, that's all.'

'I don't believe a word of it.'

He didn't reply and she let it rest. For two or three minutes he took care to work on the mainstream area, then stealthily began allowing his lateral movements to stretch further and further round her sides.

'That's not my back.'

'It's the side of your back.'

'Maybe. But it's the side of my front as well, you bad boy. I had nearly drifted off there. Now you've gone and woken me up again. You've got to keep completely away from there; it's very . . . sensitive.'

Rupert grinned and turned his attention to her lower back. When he judged the moment was right to chance his arm again, he slid the cerise trousers down a few inches until her black thong underwear hove into thrilling view.

'*And* there. That's even more off-limits.'

'Rubbish.'

He could tell from her voice that she was getting into this as much as he was. And he was getting very into it. There was no way he was leaving this room without exploring her further. Tonight he was taking no prisoners. With both hands he stroked the top of her bottom. The lack of further comment encouraged him enough to pull the trousers right down. Wow. Her bottom was *delicious*. He touched the base of her buttocks.

'Rupert, that's your last warning. Do my back.'

He opted for a brief tactical retreat, repositioning his hands as commanded. Soon, though, they were wandering again.

'Right, that's it. End.'

She reached behind her back trying to mate the ends of her bra straps. Before she could get them together, Rupert put one hand right under her midriff, and flipped her clean over on her back. She let out a yelp, and clasped her hands to her chest.

'What the hell do you think you're doing?'

'I'm going to take a proper look at you.'

'No, you're fucking well not.'

'Oh, yes I fucking well *am*, Georgina. And I'd say you haven't got a great negotiating position.'

He was right, sitting astride her as he was. Although no hunk, he was marginally stronger than her.

'I'll scream blue murder.'

He smirked. 'Go on, then.'

She let out a half-hearted squeal, not nearly powerful enough to pierce through the thick stone walls. That was his signal. He put his hands round her fingers and wrenched them, not without effort, away from her chest. He looked down in awe. The loosened bra had fallen completely away from her breasts. They were *humdingers*. He let go of her fingers and, with lightning speed, got his hands on her breasts before she could get

248

hers back there. For a second or two she tore vainly at his fingers, then gave up and sullenly turned her head to one side. In a sober, chilly voice she said, 'Why are you doing this, Rupert?'

'Because I fancy you rotten.'

'Will you let me go now, please?'

'Depends.'

She turned back and looked up at him. 'Depends on what?'

'I might let you go, if you let me look at the rest of you.'

'No way.'

'I'll just take a quick peek.'

'Don't you dare.'

'I do dare.' He levered himself down a bit, took hold of the black thong and eased it down to her thighs. He grinned. 'Mmmm . . . Lovely.'

'I can't believe you just did that.'

'*I* can.'

'Rupert . . .' Her voice was softer now, submissive. It meant she must love being subdued like this. 'Are you aroused?'

'What d'you think?'

'Prove it to me.'

Rupert grinned. 'I'll show you all right.' It was hard to get his zip down, sitting at that angle, and he had to step off her to do it. Gazing at her the whole time, he let his trousers fall down, then his shorts. He looked down at his weapon which, if not quite his finest feature, was looking convincingly enthusiastic.

Georgina looked at it too. Then, in a flash, she was off the bed, pulling her thong back up as she rolled, and running hell for leather towards the bathroom. Rupert, taken totally by surprise, tried to dash after her, but with trousers and shorts at half mast he was no swifter than a runner in a three-legged race. Two yards short of the bathroom door, he tripped and fell. As he crashed on the carpet, he heard Georgina turn the key.

Grumpily he got to his feet and pulled his clothing back up. 'What the hell did you do that for?'

'Because I didn't want you forcing yourself on me.'

'Balls. You wanted it just as much as I did.'

'Maybe, maybe not.' Inside the bathroom she was smiling and checking her hair in the mirror.

'What kind of game are you playing, you prick-teaser? Come on, George, open that door, and get that pretty little arse of yours back into this bed.'

'I'm glad you think it's a pretty little arse, but it's not going back to that bed, not while you're still there anyway. Whether or not I want it is beside the point. You're in a relationship with a close friend of mine. And even if Prim wasn't a friend, I still wouldn't. I don't two-time men, and I don't like two-timers.'

'Would it be different if I wasn't with her?'

'Who knows? If you were free, I might want you to throw me back on that bed and fuck me rigid. But you're not, and I'll never do anything to come between you and Primrose. Within a very short while, I'll belong to some lucky man – another reason for you to keep your groping hands off. Look but don't touch, understand? . . . Now, can I come out without being jumped on?'

He thought about it. He didn't have too much choice. 'Yes, I suppose so.'

She opened the door a couple of inches, saw that his smirk was gone, replaced by a mildly hang-dog look, and came out and stood beside him.

'Now, be a good boy, and run along to bed.'

'Okay.'

'D'you still want that good-night kiss?'

'Yeah.'

'Here then.' She reached up, pulled his neck down to hers and kissed him passionately. 'Go now.'

They walked over together to the door and she opened it. As he stepped past her, she reached out and put a hand on his groin. It didn't take long to spring back to life. Now he was regally confused.

'What *are* you doing now?'

'Just checking.'

Laughing the naughtiest laugh, Georgina pushed him out, and closed the door behind him. She clambered into bed, and put the lamp out. Through the small gaps in the curtains bright moonlight poured through. She closed her eyes and smiled. That had been highly amusing, highly enjoyable, and most satisfactory.

*

On Sunday evening, Primrose took a cab over to Rupert's. She felt heavy with trepidation. She had left a message saying she would bring some food over. He hadn't replied. Would he have forgiven her by now, or would he still be in a mood? She wasn't sure she could cope with one of his sulks or rants tonight. It had been an exhausting weekend, and not only because of nursing the kids half the night. Despite a growing cocktail of drugs, Maureen could hardly sleep these days, and

Primrose had spent hours doing her best to calm and reassure her. They were all very worried about what she might do if things went against Dan.

At least her dad had brought one piece of good news. It seemed that Weasel had made some progress on the witness front. Someone had given him a tip about Beckenham, and before long a thick wad of £50 notes found its way to a sergeant at the nick there. The sergeant didn't know very much himself, and hadn't been on duty at the time, but the word was that NCS had been called in one night a few weeks back. Odd thing was, the station record for that night had clearly been altered. He agreed to ask around discreetly and try to find out more. Weasel promised that if he succeeded, another wad would be his. After all, how was a forty-four-year-old with two teenage kids expected to live on a sergeant's salary?

Primrose's legal training had never touched on police procedure, so she had no idea what the rules were. Ronnie's understanding was sketchy too, but he'd picked up from Weasel some notion of the rules about disclosing the circumstances of witnesses. It seemed that the defence didn't have to be told of any special circumstances, like a grant of immunity, until much nearer the trial, but the Crown Prosecution Service had to be informed from the start. If the police at the Beckenham nick had tampered with the record, that might mean the NCS weren't planning to tell them. For the time being Weasel didn't have much to go on, but at least this scrap had brought a glimmer of hope to Maureen.

24

Ever since the Ted Stafford affair, Chris Owen had cursed his impetuosity. As Sally had seen right away, calling up Ronnie like that had been an own goal. It had made it less, not more likely that he could lock Lee Hill up. Of course, now that Dan was behind bars, Lee would inevitably be more centrally involved than before. But in the absence of another anonymous tip-off, nicking him was bound to be difficult. Owen had authorised an intensification of the surveillance on the gang. However, they couldn't follow them round all the time: that would be too costly, and too obvious. They'd done what else they could. A trip abroad by any of them would be a good sign that something was cooking, and the Immigration Service had been given the names of Ronnie, Lee, and Jack Price, and asked to watch out for them. But they'd seen nothing so far.

If he hadn't called Ronnie, they would have had a very good chance of being able to nail Lee sooner or later for GBH or some similar charge. However, the moment Chris had shot his mouth off, Ronnie, knowing that this wasn't a smart time to be provoking the police, must have given Lee the mother of all bollockings. You could see that Lee was now on the nearest he got to best behaviour, and the undercover officers who were shadowing him round the clubs, waiting and watching for incidents, got nothing to feed on.

Still, it wasn't the end of the world. This particular leopard wouldn't change his spots altogether, and over time he would forget the bollocking and revert to type. Perhaps they could help speed up that process. Be in his face, harry him, nark him. Maybe haul him in and question *him* about St Margaret's.

Sitting together over a beer, the team tried to come up with other ways to unsettle him. The first few, all relating to Lee's girlfriend, Michelle, were unrepeatable. Coming closer to family entertainment, one sergeant suggested doing something to his car. The black Porsche was clearly his pride and joy. Scratch it, maybe, or have a truck smash into it. That should get Lee's juices flowing. It would be great if they could find some reason to confiscate it. Unless it was being used on a job, that would be hard. How about clamping it then, or having it towed away? A minor irritation, obviously, but an irritation all the same.

They knew from watching him that he often parked illegally. They'd sometimes seen him tear a ticket from the windscreen, and chuck it contemptuously on the ground. Most likely when the summonses came through, he simply ignored them. Local councils were notorious for their lack of follow-through. If most citizens knew how lax the systems were, they'd do the same. Didn't some London boroughs operate a system that, once your car had been taken to the pound, it couldn't be released unless you'd stumped up for all unpaid fines? They could check it. Even if not, with a little preparation, it ought to be possible to invent such a system just for

Lee. Getting into the spirit of it, the sergeant offered to do some research, and amalgamate any outstanding fines registered against that Porsche. Owen joined in the joke. They all knew that the NCS had better things to do than worry about non-payment of parking fines, even for Lee Hill, but Chris was a smart enough manager to realise that, at light-hearted moments like this, it made no sense to dampen the mood by being too heavy-handed.

*

Fraser Morrison surveyed the bay and raised a glass of freshly squeezed orange juice to San Francisco. Paul O'Neill and Alistair Haslam joined him.

Things with Synapsis were proceeding most satisfactorily. The Americans had come over to London for detailed discussions. They lasted a week, and went well. Both sides had agreed on a very compressed timetable, and the due diligence checks on Orbia were already underway. However, the deal still needed the blessing of Synapsis's CEO, who was unable to get to Europe in time. And everyone felt that it was only appropriate for the Orbia top management to come over to the group's headquarters.

The Synapsis people had been courteous hosts. Over lunch their CEO had mapped out his strategy and vision of the synergies, convincing Paul O'Neill absolutely. The proposed reporting structure was fine, giving Orbia plenty of latitude, and the stock-option programme was generous to a fault. As further evidence of their hands-off approach, Synapsis had said that they would leave the individual allocations of options to Orbia's management, and, naturally, the carving up of the proceeds of the purchase was not something for them to interfere with.

It all seemed too good to be true. Even Alistair was coming round, in spite of himself. If it hadn't been for his on-going jockeying with Fraser, he too would by now have been an avid supporter. Privately, indeed, he was reviewing his own tactics. Back at West Point, there had been a hung jury on which of the alternatives to go for. Since then the sands had been shifting. The American visitors to London had made a uniformly good impression on all the partners they met. The sale to Synapsis looked overwhelmingly like happening, and he would lose out terminally to Fraser if he seemed dog-in-the-manger about it.

The main outstanding issue between the two companies was a final negotiation on price. They had agreed that it should not be necessary to meet physically for this. If everything else was settled, it could be handled in a conference call, and the contracts signed by fax. The due diligence would be completed by 20 November. Orbia were using their regular lawyers, Allen & Overy, and Synapsis had appointed Linklaters. Both sets of lawyers were now hard at work, and all the documentation should be ready by the end of the month.

Internally at Orbia, that left the question of announcements. The presence of the Americans had finally blown the lid on any serious attempt to keep the matter completely confidential, and they were besieged by enquiries from staff. It was getting harder to refuse to be drawn, but the three concluded that they had no choice but to brazen it out a little longer.

That still left the thorny issue of promotions. Both Fraser and Alistair knew that the two new partners they promoted might be important swing voters when it came to electing Paul's successor, and were anxious to pick candidates well disposed to themselves. As he listened to Fraser and Alistair wrangling over individuals' strengths and weakness, Paul saw that regretfully, affiliation was beginning to count more than talent. Heaven help people like Rupert Henley who were not clearly aligned, he reflected.

They finished their brunch and walked to their rental car. Since their flight home wasn't until late afternoon, the three men had decided to award themselves a day trip to Napa Valley.

*

'You'll definitely owe me that half million, Ronnie.'

'Oh? Why's that?'

They had gathered in a back room at *Spic and Span* to hear Rupert's proposal for the second job. Bottles of Dos Equis stood in front of them, plus nachos and a mound of unconvincing-looking guacamole.

Rupert had given much thought to how to handle this next one. Looking back on the *Timbookedtoo* job, he'd allowed himself to get too close to the firing line. Fortunately, he'd guessed right that the authorities wouldn't conceive of a connection between the burglaries and stock-market activity. However, if they had, sooner or later they might have tracked him down. He didn't want to take that sort of risk again. Ronnie's desire to re-engineer the bank robbery might be sentimental and unambitious financially, but the beauty of it was that it would place Rupert at zero personal risk. Pleasing Ronnie a little wasn't necessarily stupid, and it might be fun. Finally, he hadn't yet had another real brainwave, and he didn't want them to think that the Golden Goose had forgotten how to lay eggs.

Rupert smiled broadly at Ronnie. 'I think I'm going to make you a happy man. Let's recap what you all mentioned in the Oak Room. The reasons why going over the pavement, as you charmingly call it, doesn't work are, one, there's not enough cash in the average bank; two, there are cameras everywhere, so there's too much chance of being captured on video; and three, when the alarm goes off, the Old Bill has a nasty habit of turning up waving popguns. Correct?'

'Correct.'

'So to be lucrative enough and have a low enough risk quotient, we have to work round these problems. We have to find a way to up the take, to avoid getting caught on film, to be sure that no armed police will turn up to spoil the fun, and to have enough time to clean out the bank properly . . . Is that a reasonable summing-up?'

'Very fair. Very fair.' Ronnie had a swig of beer. 'Right – that's enough of diagnosis, what we want is 'ypothesis.'

'Starting with the armed police, it's simple really. The police have a limited number of armed response units. They're stationed all over the country, but only in major cities and towns. We have to identify somewhere that's large enough to have several banks, but at least thirty minutes away by road from an armed response unit, and preferably further.'

'What about choppers? They all got choppers or planes these days.'

'That I'll have to work on. However, even if we can keep away from armed police, there are still normal plods we have to worry about, and any town of the size we're talking about will have its own police presence. What we therefore have to do is find a way to ensure that they are taken out of the game during our raids.'

'When you say "raids", you're not talkin' about several robberies goin' on at the same time, are you?'

'Precisely. We clean out all the town's banks in one fell swoop. Essentially my plan is that we aim to have the free run of that place for half an hour . . .'

Three voices clamoured in dissent. Rupert was having none of it.

'Give me a chance, guys, let me explain how it works. Our town has, say, only three major roads leading into it, and like many towns these days, they all filter into a ring road round the centre, and probably the streets in the centre itself are all pedestrianised. All it would take is two or three crashes, or trucks shedding their loads at key spots, and within minutes the ring road would be paralysed, right? Shortly before these crashes occur, the police receive four or five emergency calls to areas a few miles out of town. Nothing too serious. Nothing to warrant back-up from elsewhere. An intruder here, a suicide attempt there, something like that. The few patrol cars the local force possesses are sent on their way, together with most of the policemen. By the time they realise that these calls are all hoaxes, they won't be able to get back in because, guess what, the traffic's at a standstill.'

'What about the coppers left on duty at the nick?'

'As far as I can work out, in a town of this size there would normally be no more than six or seven men on duty at any one time. Assuming that all the cars are all despatched, that leaves probably a couple of officers at the station. It might be that we need further distractions. A hysterical mother who's lost her baby, or a smoke bomb rolled inside. Think about it, though. If there are only a couple left, they can't leave the station unattended. One of them might run around the pedestrian precinct, blowing his whistle and waving his arms, but not both. And if we're there in force, what the hell can one copper do about it? Wave his truncheon at us?'

'What about the cameras?'

'Ah yes, the cameras. I'll have to check, but if we can cut the power supply, surely we can stop the cameras?'

Jack looked unconvinced. 'You got to be careful with power cuts. Them bank safes are wired to the mains. They all got electronic timers to stop anyone openin' them out of hours. I'm out of date, of course, but they might automatically lock shut if there's a cut.'

'Thanks, Jack, I hadn't thought of that. I'll look into that. Worst case, we might be able to do without power cuts, if you adopt my ideas on staffing.'

'What d'you mean?'

'An operation like this needs quite a big force. When we were talking about risk last time, you all said you didn't like using regular foot soldiers. They might grass us up in advance, or afterwards. If they are caught on camera, there's a very high chance that the police will track them down, because of all major crimes committed in the provinces, almost seventy per cent are done by London-based gangs. The police would check that immediately. Not only that, you mentioned that London staff are prohibitively expensive. Jack, how much did you say they would cost?'

'Thirty, forty grand each, minimum. Maybe more like fifty.'

'That's ridiculous. The reality is that here in London, we're in a very pricey location. The semi-skilled white male London villain is going to price himself out of his own market if he's not careful. Like any sensible company, we should look at importing from cheaper labour markets.'

'Like?'

'I don't know. Portugal? Spain?'

Ronnie shook his head. 'Spain's not cheap no more. Not for this sort of thing.'

'Okay, where's cheap? Turkey?'

Lee blackballed the heirs of the Ottomans. 'Don't trust them fuckers.'

'Poland, then? Romania? Or the Balkans?'

Suddenly, Ronnie's eyes lit up. 'When Jack and me were over in Rotterdam last time, Fat Boy said 'e'd got a whole bunch of refugees doin' regular stuff for them. Bosnian, I think they was. That right, Jack?'

'Yeah. Think so.'

'Do anythin' they will, Fat Boy was sayin', for a few thousand guilders. So, Rupert, are you suggestin' that we bring foreign boys in, and use 'em to do the legwork?'

'Exactly. If any of them get nicked, it's not our problem as long as they don't know who we are. It also means that it matters less if they're recorded on cameras. Hopefully they'll be in and out of the country in no time, and no one will recognise them anyway. Better still, they'll have funny foreign accents, so the Old Bill won't suspect London gangs.'

'So 'ow do we get them into the country? You can't normally get a work permit for bank robberies.'

'Our town will be very close to the coast. The squad will come in by boat, do the business, and leave immediately the same way.'

A grin was beginning to form on Ronnie's face. 'Rupert, the more you describe "our" town, the more I reckon you've chosen one already.'

Rupert smiled back. 'Maybe. What I did was design a simple computer programme. I downloaded maps from the AA site, and entered the locations of all the armed response units. Then I tapped in criteria like distance by road from those units, and distance to sea or estuary from the town, plus minimum population. That narrowed it down to around twenty towns, mainly in the North, East Anglia, Wales, Scotland and the West Country. Going on from there, I got hold of the branch networks of all the banks, which cut it back further. For example, the Welsh and the Scots have no money, so they have far fewer banks. After that, it was a question of looking at internet maps of town centres and nearby roads, and refining it by then looking at terrain, coastal access and so on. Little by little my list came down to four, to two, to . . .'

'Just like the Wine Cup.'

'Yes. Thank you, Lee.'

'Don't mention it, Rupes.'

Ronnie was waiting impatiently. 'So what's the one?'

'Barnstaple.'

'Where the fuck's Barnstaple, when it's at 'ome?'

'North Devon. Barnstaple's the sort of town that's famous for not being famous. Claims to be England's oldest borough, but it's been downhill all the way ever since, unless you count winning the odd floral competition. It looks perfect for us. The population's less than 25,000, it's on a river – two, in fact – and only seven miles from the coast. Did you know that of all police regions, Devon and Cornwall has the longest stretch of coastline? Two hundred and sixty-one miles, give or take the odd sandcastle. That would make getting in and out unobserved child's play.'

'And this Barnstaple – you sure it's got banks?'

'It's a prosperous area, with a large number of smaller businesses that still use cash heavily. All of the main high street banks are there. I suspect that they will be nice plump chickens. Between the four, we should easily get past the million mark.'

Jack was sceptical 'Not a lot, is it? One million, or even two. Less, if Fat Boy wants a slice. If we get nicked on a caper like this, you'll feel a right prat, Ron.'

'I know, Jack. But if Fat Boy supplies the troops and the boat, the old risk quotient should be low. Right, Rupert?'

'Acceptable, I'd say.'

Rupert avoided catching Lee's eye. Last night at the Pacific Bar, Lee had had a real go at him when he admitted that he planned to do what Ronnie wanted. Rupert promised Lee faithfully that he would make up any shortfall with a huge third job. In return, Lee had agreed to keep quiet and drop his objections to the bank robbery plan.

Ronnie looked round the room. 'Who's in favour then?'

Lee shrugged in grudging acceptance.

Jack nodded unenthusiastically. 'Okay, Ron, you and me'd better go and see Fat Boy.'

Rupert smiled. 'Good. Then let's do it soon. I'll go down to Barnstaple tomorrow to case the joint. Lee, feel like coming with me? I could do with a professional input. How about a short break near the sea? We could spend one night there and see what Devon belles have to offer.'

'We better go in the Porsche then.'

'Only if you let me drive too.'

'Fuck off. Get one of your own.' And Lee gave him a friendly, heavy punch on the shoulder.

25

Primrose came home from work and collapsed on the sofa in a heap. She'd no sooner finished the Italian job than she'd been asked to take on an equally complex German case. It would mean spending much time in Frankfurt, a persuasive contender for the title of Europe's most boring city.

She knew she couldn't cut corners at work, and since stinting on Dan and Maureen was just as impossible, it meant that there was a serious risk that Rupert was being neglected. Would it help, would it cut through the knot, if she came out and told him the whole family truth? About Dan, about why Maureen needed the help? She really wanted to now. The dreadful irony was that, however ready she might be, she couldn't do it. Rupert had, in the very best faith, persuaded Orbia to take her dad on as a client. If he heard the truth now, that those legitimate businesses were largely fronts for money-laundering, he would have to report it to his bosses immediately. They would be horrified. The reputational and possibly legal ramifications for Orbia would be incredible. They could be damaged enormously. Any prospect of him being made a partner in that or any other consultancy would vanish. In fairness to Rupert, she simply *couldn't* tell him. It was so frustrating.

'Oh, shit!' She shouted it out to the empty room.

'My, who's a happy camper?'

Primrose pivoted in surprise. Georgina must have been in the kitchen. In her bare feet, she had made no sound as she came into the sitting room.

'Oh, sorry, Georgina, I didn't know you were there.'

'What's getting you down? Work problems or man problems?'

'Both.'

'Work problems I'm not terribly good at. Man problems are more my scene. Is Rupert being horrid?'

'No, not really. He doesn't have the chance to be – doesn't see me enough. My fault as much as his, unfortunately.'

'How's bed life when you do meet?'

'Can't complain about lack of sleep when Rupes is around. Doesn't keep me awake like he used to. You know, I think I've forgotten what sex is.'

'Me too. Hang on, isn't it that aerobics thingie where the woman has to stretch her legs apart, and the man has to try to get his doodah in and out without her noticing?'

'Yes, that's the one.' Primrose giggled away. On her own, Georgina could be fun. It was a pity she changed for the worse the moment a man showed up.

'How's things apart from the bed zone?'

'He says the right things, says that he loves me.'

'How often? When did he say it last?'

'Today. Mind you, he was calling up to blow me out again, so it was probably obligatory.'

'Why did he do that?'

'Usual stuff. Work. Said he had to have dinner with some boring client.'

'Do you believe him? You don't think it could be . . .' she paused to pull a mock horrified face '. . . the other woman?'

'No, I don't think Rupert's *that* much of a shit. Anyway, I know he's not having dinner with one woman he's taken a fancy to.'

Georgina sat upright. 'How can you be sure?'

'Because it's you, and you're here.'

'*Me*? Surely Rupert doesn't fancy me?'

'Of course he does.'

'Rubbish. Does he say so?'

'No, but he's always asking about you.'

'Really? Don't worry about it. He's probably just being nosy, and I'm not at all sure he's my type. Think he'll marry you, Prim?'

'Hard to say. I'm not always sure I want to myself. For the time being I'm more worried about us making it through till Christmas . . . Fancy something to eat?'

'I'd love to, but I'm on my way out.'

'Where to? It's nearly nine.'

'The wretched man I'm seeing tonight couldn't get a table until nine forty-five.'

'Is he coming here to collect you? Want me to hold the fort while you change?'

'He's not even doing that. Says he hasn't got time to come all this way. I've got a cab booked for nine-thirty. See? Men really *are* bastards.'

'Is it a big secret who it is?'

'Absolutely. You never know – it could be Rupert.'

'Give him my love, then.'

'I will. Okay, now for a power shower.'

*

Despite a late and terribly tantalising night, Rupert rose
bright and early. Lee collected him at seven-thirty and
they drove straight to Devon. By lunchtime they were
in Barnstaple. They had something to eat, bought town
maps and guides, and started work on their recce. It
was a pleasant, unremarkable little place, its only dis-
tinguishing features a crooked church spire, a covered
market, and Butcher's Row, a powerful testimony to
the inhabitants' aversion to vegetarianism. The banks
all looked straightforward. Posing as a duo who were
thinking of starting a business, Lee and Rupert met one
or two managers and established that the branches did
plenty of business with local companies.

The police station was just beyond the inner ring
road, in the dreary low-rise 1960s Civic Centre, the
sort of eyesore that was built before architects were
invented. Rupert and Lee wandered into the station
for a look, and, pretending to be doing research for
a television documentary, managed to establish from
the chatty sergeant that all the video cameras in the
town centre fed through to the police station. That
might be important. The cameras were everywhere,
and had an uninterrupted view of three of the four
banks. Rupert would have to find out more about
how any emergency electricity supply worked. The
sergeant was also pleasantly forthcoming about their
radio systems. Before leaving, Rupert and Lee had a
good look at the police station itself. Apart from its front
entrance, it had six exits: three sets of fire doors along the
main road flanking the building, two back doors leading

to the car park, and one internal way into the main body of the Centre. It would be worth thinking whether they could do anything to incommode the police more.

They walked back into the town centre, and managed to get a window seat in a small hotel-cum-café called the Royal & Fortescue, which looked straight up the High Street. You could see one of the banks, HSBC, only a hundred yards up on the right side. This place might be a good vantage point on the day. They ordered a cafetière of coffee, spread the map out and began work on the roads. To the north of the town was the main North Devon link road from Exeter to the coast, with its twin exits to the east and the west of the town. Both of these eventually fed into the small inner ring, as did the only road from the south, which came across Longbridge, the old stone bridge spanning the River Taw.

It didn't take Rupert and Lee long to decide what to do. The patrol cars should all be sent on wild-goose chases to the north, and the town bottled up behind them to stop them getting back. Blocking the two exits from the link road wouldn't make sense: they were both about a mile from the centre, and you couldn't guarantee that the police cars wouldn't find a way back through one of the many rat-runs. No, it would be far more effective to create a giant tailback by paralysing the inner ring itself. The two small roundabouts on the north-west side, at the heads of the High Street and Boutport Street should be perfect. If they were both taken out, together with the bridge, the busy traffic would grind to a halt within minutes. Then they would use Longbridge to escape to the south. Comically,

269

although there was a video camera mounted high on a mast in the grass centre of one of the two roundabouts, it peered only up to the High Street. Neither it nor any other camera were there to monitor the traffic; it would take the police time to establish exactly what was going on.

They moved on to thinking about their escape plan. Naturally, if both the inner ring and the bridge were blocked, they wouldn't be able to use cars for the getaway. Motorbikes, maybe. And, although once the bikes were across the bridge, the road out should be clear, they would want to get off it as soon as possible. The last thing they needed was to run into some stray incoming police car. They would need to go cross country. Rupert had a sip of coffee and pulled out the ordnance survey map.

Ah, what was this? It was a dotted line, leading off to the west, parallel to the river, starting only a couple of hundred yards from the south side of Longbridge. The map marked it as the 'Tarka Trail'. Rupert checked in the guide. It was named after *Tarka the Otter*, whose author had hailed from nearby Braunton, and was a bicycle track built on the path of an old railway line. This could be perfect.

They walked it, Lee, booted and suited as ever, complaining the whole way that his mirror-polished black city shoes would be worn out. Two or three miles along the way they came to a jetty called Yelland Quay, which the guide said had once served an old power station. They took a good look. It might be the right spot for the Bosnians to embark after the job, being only three miles or so from the mouth of the river.

In inflatables they would be back on the mother ship within fifteen minutes. There were two snags, however. First, the quay was virtually opposite a Royal Marines base on the north bank at Chivenor. They would need to check that out. It could be a no-no, or it could be useful camouflage, if the locals were used to marines bombing up and down on the water. The second was the tide. It was low, and the receding water had left ugly mud flats. It would be vital to do it at high tide. That would need more checking.

Satisfied, they walked back to the start of the trail, and got in the Porsche to check out some beaches and coves to look for a landing site on the way in. Then they drove slowly round all the main roads in and around the town, and went on to look at areas on the north side which might be suitable decoy sites. To the north-west was the Pottington industrial estate. That should be good for a fire or a spill. The villages of Prixford and Shirwell further north looked prosperous enough to encourage intruders, and an old stone bridge nearby was just about high enough to qualify as a plausible suicide spot.

There were some more chores to be dealt with before they could relax, starting with driving a few miles to the south to inspect an electricity sub-station at Webbery, near Alverdiscott, which Rupert had located with some internet help. Then over to Exeter, both to see how long it would take to drive from Barnstaple, and to check out both the police headquarters and the little airport where their helicopter and plane were stationed. Finally, they looked for the regional police's VHF radio antenna which the sergeant had helpfully mentioned.

Right. Six o'clock. Time to head to their hotel in the outskirts of Exeter. They had dinner and drove back into the town to see what fun they could grow. There was no sign of much going on beyond pubs favoured by the students. Rupert and Lee tried to muscle in on some conversations and chat up the girls, but for once the karma was wrong. Even copious mentions of Porsches failed to work their usual magic. Partly it was Lee's mood. Rupert was expecting him to be jolly, whereas in fact he was rather withdrawn. By ten-thirty, they were slumped in the corner of a deserted night club, with no one for entertainment but themselves. Rupert decided to probe a little, raising this subject and that, hoping for a lucky strike.

'Has anything changed about Dan?'

'Maybe, maybe not.'

'What d'you mean, Lee? I thought it was likely he'd get sent down for quite a while. That's what you've always said.'

'Yeah, well, it's not so sure now. The old man told me last night that our brief's on to somethin' that might give Dan more of a chance of getting off.'

'That's great.'

'Yeah, course it is.'

Rupert thought Lee sounded less than wholeheartedly enthusiastic.

'So, what'll happen if he does get off? Will everything go back to being like it was before?'

'S'pose so.'

This was worrying news for Rupert. His carefully constructed alliance with Lee might be rendered worthless. The same thing happened often in consultancy if there was a management change at the client. It was always galling.

'Tell me, Lee, how close is Dan to Primrose?'

'Pretty close.'

'Closer than you are to her?'

'Rose and I never got on, even when we was kids. She's always been closer to Dan. And of course, she's the fuckin' apple of the old man's eye . . . Why d'you ask? Not thinkin' of dumpin' 'er, are you?' Lee smiled and thumped him in the ribs.

'No, no, course not. Hypothetically though, if she and I were to split up while our project was still underway, how would Ronnie react? Would he put business first?'

'Depends. If Rose gave *you* the push, it wouldn't make no difference. If it was the other way round, though, I wouldn't want to be in your shoes, mate.'

'So, that would be the end of our little arrangement?'

'Course it fuckin' well would. No way the old man would touch you after that. Except to give you a slap, p'raps.'

'How would you feel about it?'

'Wouldn't bother me either way. Not my business. The old man would be somethin' else, though, and Jack wouldn't be tickled pink neither . . .' Lee stopped for a moment to grin sadistically. 'Been linin' up somethin' on the substitutes' bench, 'ave you, Rupes? My advice is to shag the gel senseless, but don't let Rose find out about it. She'll be straight on to the old man.'

Rupert moved quickly to change the subject, and worked the conversation back to Lee's current favourite hobby horse – the second job. Before long, he had got Lee wound up again and all talk of Primrose was forgotten.

'The old man's lost it, that's all. This idea's a load of old bollocks from start to finish. Even Jack says so, and you know what Jack's like. I said it before, I know, but this is a total waste of your talents, as well as fuckin' risky.'

'I really don't think it's all that risky, Lee. And it could be quite a lark. I enjoyed today. And I *am* curious to see if it'll work – if it happens at all. Maybe Fat Boy Dutch won't play rent-a-refugee, or maybe the refugees will get lost at sea. What I'm trying to focus on myself is the one after that.'

'Good. What about givin' me a sneak preview?'

'Too soon. I'll let you know as soon as I've worked it out more. Could be a very big pay day. Only problem is, I doubt we'll be allowed to do it.'

'Why's that?'

'My idea involves a spot of freelance kidnapping, and Ronnie doesn't like kidnaps, does he? I think he'll block it. And what he says goes, right?'

'Makes me fuckin' sick, I tell you, specially after the way we're fartin' around on this one to please 'im.'

'D'you mind if I ask you something off the record?'

'Sure.'

'I'm interested to know how it works in a family like yours. If it were a company, there would be a retirement age for everyone, including the boss. Can Ronnie go on as long as he likes – sixty, seventy, eighty, whatever? Or is there a normal age when he hands over to the next generation?'

Lee considered. 'There ain't no 'ard and fast rules.'

'But does the guv'nor decide who succeeds him?'

'Usually, yeah.'

'So, that'll be Dan, will it? Is he the heir apparent?'

'If Dan cops ten years plus, it'll change things.'

'But what if he gets off? He'll resume his position as Ronnie's number two, and in due course become the next guv'nor?'

'Could be.'

'So what would happen to you then, Lee? You'd take orders from Dan until *his* son was ready to take over?'

Rupert could see Lee's face getting uglier with emotion.

'Dan don't want the boys in the business.'

'Well, that's something at least. Maybe when Dan's sixty and you're, what – mid-fifties? – you'll get a shot at emerging from a subordinate position.'

Lee cracked his knuckles.

'It's odd, because if I was in your place, I might think that this was close to the perfect moment to assert myself, to get control of the situation before Dan came back.'

'What you mean, Rupes? Become the guv'nor myself?'

'That hadn't occurred to me. But since you mention it, it would be one possibility, wouldn't it? Of course, it's not a plan you'd consider, and I certainly don't want you thinking that I'm trying to suggest it. All irrelevant, anyway, if we all stick to the strategy of three crimes then stop. And I'm sure that on your side, the proceeds are split equally between you, Ronnie, and Jack . . .'

Lee's face told a different story.

'Anyway, Lee, let's not harp on too much about this.

275

In many ways I find the family loyalty, the blind unquestioning obedience, very attractive in this day and age, when most people insist on thinking for themselves, and refuse to be pushed around by authority. It's old-fashioned in the best possible sense.'

Lee was staring hard at a far wall. He swung abruptly around. 'Can I ask you somethin', Rupes? If I challenged the old man, who'd you side with?'

'Well, like you I'm a simple obedient soul. All my years in the corporate world have given me an absolute acceptance of the established hierarchy. As long as Ronnie's the guv'nor, I follow him.'

'But if there was a new guv'nor?'

'Then it would be like at Orbia when a client changes its top management midway through a project. The Chief Executive is dead, long live the Chief Executive.'

'So you'd work with me?'

'Your word would be my command . . . Lee, I know this is all thoroughly hypothetical. However, if it did cross your mind to make a move . . .'

'Then what?'

'Then timing would be everything. And don't forget – any good revolutionary needs an excuse to send in the tanks.'

'Like what, in our case?'

'Well, we're all agreed on this second job. We may not all like it, but we've said yes. Opposing it now would look bad. And in a sense, letting Ronnie have his way weakens him. Together, we had three wishes, and he's wasted one on this nonsense. If after that, we come up with an idea for something that would make a shedload of money, and he has the effrontery to stop it . . . Wouldn't that be a better moment to strike?'

Lee rubbed his chin. Rupert slapped his back.

'Now come on, my friend, enough of this stuff. Let's drink up and see if we can find some girls with more interest in German sports cars.'

26

Glory of glories. Telesys came through.

The CEO called Fraser to pass the word on officially, and was courteous enough to put in a side call to Rupert. It was heart-warming stuff. The timing was perfect. The call came that Monday morning. His appraisal was on Thursday, the big decision day. Before then he was taking Tuesday and Wednesday off for his second visit to the West Country.

It looked like all was set. Fat Boy Dutch had gouged them on cut, demanding one third of the total. However, he was doing a lot for that, providing eight Bosnians, enough weapons to go round, and a ninety-foot pleasure yacht with trusted skipper and mate which could at a pinch accommodate nine passengers and two rigid inflatable tenders – one stowed, one towed. Neither side trusted the other enough to delegate money counting, so it was agreed that, before the job, Jack would be picked up by the yacht at some lonely spot on the South Coast, and would brief the only one of the eight Bosnians who was alleged to speak English. The yacht would then sail on round the coast until it reached Devon and, after the operation was over, would deposit Jack, plus two thirds of the loot, at the original rendezvous point.

Rupert had used the intervening days well. It was amazing what you could learn by ringing people and pretending to be a student on a project, a man from the ministry, a counsellor at an embassy, or whatever else sprang to mind. People just opened up and told you things.

The news on the power front was excellent. Rupert had feared that, in the event of a problem at the nearest sub-station, the national grid would automatically bypass it, and route the supply from elsewhere. Indeed, that *was* how the grid worked for its basic supply. However, when it got to local level, there had to be somewhere that stepped the power down from 20,000 volts to the domestic level, and his original information about Webbery had held good. Take it out and you took out the town, including the cameras.

As for the police station in Barnstaple, it did have an emergency generator, but it only covered lighting. Anything else needing power, including their telephone switchboard and their short-range UHF radio system for communicating with beat bobbies, would be lost. It was a bummer that the patrol cars were controlled from Exeter on this different, wider-range VHF system. That also meant that it would be harder to ensure that all the Barnstaple patrol cars would be sent in response to the decoy calls. As the sergeant in Barnstaple had told them, the Control Room Inspector in Exeter was just as likely to despatch cars from other neighbouring areas like South Molton, Torrington, or Braunton. They looked again at the map to make sure that the 'incidents' would always be nearer Barnstaple than any of these other towns. Maybe they wouldn't use Prixford after all; it was too near Braunton. Goodleigh would be safer. And maybe they wouldn't make all the calls through 999 either; it turned out they routed randomly to any of four or five Computer Aided Despatch call centres from Bristol to Plymouth and from Exeter to Taunton. By the time they had all got in touch with the Exeter Control Room, Lord knows what delays might be caused. Maybe it was better to do only one or two calls that way, and make the rest direct to the Barnstaple nick.

Rupert was heartened when one of his colleagues at Orbia, who had handled a series of retail banking projects, helped him understand how security worked at most bank branches. These days, most branches had their own emergency generators. In any case, whether or not the safes had an uninterrupted power supply didn't seem to matter: normal practice was to keep the safes' outer doors open during banking hours, leaving typically two inner doors which were opened manually by two key-holders. He picked another couple of nuggets from his colleague as well. Bank staff had standing orders to co-operate fully in case of any physical threat. And, astonishingly, at least in the case of smaller towns, any hidden alarm button pressed in a branch sent a signal not to the local police station but to the bank's head office. The delay and opportunity for confusion which that built into the system should contribute another few minutes' leeway. Some banks did have a basic alarm bell, too. However, all that did was to make a loud noise, and experience suggested that very few passing citizens paid any attention.

Rupert had a late-night session with the troops to run through the short strokes. Since it looked like Tommy would have a big role to play, he was invited along.

As soon as they got on to the power cut, Ronnie was set against using explosives until Rupert persuaded him that, although it was true that the plan would still work without it, a power cut would bring the risk quotient down substantially. Having looked at the photos that Lee had taken of the small, unmanned sub-station and its surroundings, they concluded that they needed help. Jack immediately proposed an old schoolmate called Sparky. He was one of the very few people who he and Ronnie relied on. A former Sapper, Sparky knew pretty much all there was to know about munitions and communications. His dual skill was even more critical when Ronnie flatly refused to countenance blowing up the VHF antenna as well. Jack was totally confident that Sparky would know of a cleverer way to deal with it.

The next thing they got on to was aircraft. Having established that there was only one service site in the county, Rupert had rung them, and lying furiously as ever, conned them into revealing the service schedule for both craft. Frustratingly, the helicopter had just been serviced, but the light plane would be coming in from Wednesday to Friday. So they had only one chopper to worry about. There was no way of predicting whether it would be on the ground in Exeter, or anywhere over the two counties. They looked at the maps. Barnstaple was an uncomfortably short flying time from Exeter, and a helicopter was the main thing – almost the only thing – which could jeopardise the whole mission. If the bloody thing came over the hills when the Bosnians were still on the Tarka Trail, or in the inflatables, they would be buggered. However, if the chopper was sent to, say, Plymouth, things would be different. Assuming a maximum flying speed of around a hundred and fifty knots, it would take upwards of forty minutes to get there. If they also counted on a delay of at least five to ten minutes from the start of the robberies to the pilot getting the signal, that should give them enough time to get everyone back on the boat, and down below. After that, from the sky it would look like any old yacht, even if it was a bit out of season.

It didn't take them all long to work out a plan for the helicopter. A few years ago one of Tommy's best mates had been one of the best drivers on the council estate circuit. The Law had only caught him once. For a few quid, he'd be happy to have an awayday. His flamboyant driving was sure to attract lots of police attention. They would send him down on the train, and give him enough cash for a nice overnighter in a fancy hotel. There would be no need to provide him with transport locally; he'd want to take care of that himself. And he wasn't the nosy sort, so Tommy wouldn't expect any questions.

Finally there was the question of tides. On the coming Wednesday, the only high tide in daylight would be at half past ten. That would determine the timing of the operation. They'd been lucky with the lunar cycle: even at high tide, the water was deep enough on only 260 days a year.

Rupert amazed them with his desire to witness everything personally. He was determined to have a grandstand seat in the Royal & Fortescue. They'd expected that he'd want to keep well away from the scene. When they talked it through, they accepted that it was true that there was no real risk for him. Even if the power cut didn't work and he was somehow captured on video, who would know who he was, or why he was there? However, Jack threw a right fit when Ronnie volunteered to join Rupert there. Even though he'd be taking no active part, if he was identified, their security would be blown wide open. Of course, Ronnie knew they were right. But to miss this glorious moment . . . With the greatest reluctance, he backed down.

*

The final battle on promotions took place in a partners' meeting on Tuesday. It was not a pretty sight. As candidate after candidate, each considered a winner by someone, was raised and dissected, tempers rose and then flared. There were stabbing references to past compromises, to the way some offices were treated more equally than others. Allegations of sexism, racism, and xenophobia filled the blue air. In the end every main proponent took his or her case to such extremes that they became ridiculous and cancelled each other out.

As the acrimonious session went on, it looked increasingly clear that the ruling triumvirate would not only have a casting vote, but would have virtually the sole prerogative in picking the two from the many. Fraser and Alistair had played it long, understanding the dynamic perfectly. Knowing how important this was for their own prospects, once the other forces were spent, the two began their own wary game, circling around each other like Graeco-Roman wrestlers probing for the first grip, each aiming to secure the promotion of two candidates likely to support them in a vote for the top job. None of this was referred to openly, of course, and the common currency of the bout was the individuals' strengths, weaknesses and potential. Try as they might, however, neither wrestler could manage to get a foot behind the other's ankle for that vital trip.

Finally, they relaxed their grip on each other and settled for an honourable draw, sanctioning one choice each from the two committed camps. Dominique from Paris and Martin from London got the nod. Paul O'Neill went along with it. For all the sore feelings round the room, the partners moved swiftly on to damage limitation with disappointed candidates. Fortunately, with everything looking good for the deal with Synapsis, they would have nice, sweet, consoling lollipops to offer to the losers.

*

Excitement was rising in Chris Owen's team. At last they'd got something. Ronnie Hill and Jack Price had been identified by Passport Control leaving the country for Rotterdam on a flight from Gatwick, returning later that day. Holland could only mean one thing. Another drugs run. And those preparatory trips usually took place very shortly before the operation.

Owen made sure that the switchboard operators were on red alert in case they got another anonymous tip-off. He spoke to his counterparts on the Customs investigative side, who were in complete agreement. If they could apprehend another of the Hill family members, they might smash the whole gang permanently.

So they spoke with the coastguards and asked them to watch out for any suspicious-looking vessels in the

Channel and the waters off Norfolk, another favourite drug-runners' area. Beyond that, it was largely a matter of keeping an eye on the Hills. It was a fair guess that Lee would take over the job of co-ordinating the boat and the beach parties. Being the lazy slob he was, he might well do that from a call box close to whatever club he was in. Their undercover officers should go to his regular haunts over the next few nights, and watch whether he slipped out to phone.

*

Primrose opened her e-mail and sighed. There were two hundred and four messages, and she'd only been out of the office two days. Down and down she scrolled. Most were complete garbage, and could be deleted unread. Lots more were internal junk which she knew she should read but never found time to. There was the monthly list of new business. She nearly deleted that too, then recalled her embarrassment with Peter a while ago. Better take a quick look.

Yeah, yeah, yeah. Forty-eight new clients in total across the Europe-wide Linklaters' Alliance. Hurrah for the firm. Banking, mining, pharmaceuticals . . . hold on. What was this? Management consultancy. The new client was Synapsis of San Francisco. Planned acquisition of a pan-European London-based consultancy. Primrose read on. The schedule never identified the targets by their real name; this one had a code-name *Orion*. There were precious few independent consultancies of this sort. It *had* to be Orbia. From the timing on the schedule, this project was well underway, and due to complete before year end. Did Rupert know about this? He certainly hadn't mentioned anything. Might he know that Linklaters were acting for the buyer, and be wanting to make sure he didn't put her in a tricky position by asking questions? If so, he was a paragon, because this was almost bound to affect him.

It might be very good news indeed. If he got that elusive partnership, he might cash in big time. Even if not, in these acquisitions of service businesses, they always bribed the staff with huge golden handcuffs. Just think of how much all those City bankers had landed over the years. It would be so nice for him to get a windfall like that.

She felt a huge impulse to call him right away, but managed to restrain it. She knew she couldn't. It would be a huge breach of the firm's rules. Couldn't she make one teeny exception? The good and bad angels perched on her shoulders debated it, and the good angel won. Damn. Anyway, even if Rupes was told, there probably wasn't much he could do with the information. He was already pulling out all the stops to get that promotion.

Interesting, though. Who was handling it? She made a mental note of the partner and junior lawyer, deleted the schedule and got on with the rest of the mail.

*

The team travelled down on Tuesday afternoon. Ronnie, Lee and Rupert went by train. They didn't want to run any risk that the registration numbers of their cars would be captured on video down there. Tommy had left earlier with the three toe-rags who were all going to act as drivers. They were in a nicked, but well disguised van, stuffed full with four motorbikes, eight nicked brand-new mountain bikes, and some rucksacks that they'd bought using clean money.

The team had decided it was too risky to use motorbikes for the Bosnians. Although at that time on a November weekday, there should be precious few walkers on the Tarka Trail, motorbikes would draw too much attention, and the noise would carry dangerously across the estuary. Anyway, Fat Boy had been less than sure that his troops could all ride them. Pushbikes were a different matter. Even in Bosnia small boys must learn to ride those. It would lengthen the escape time, of course. Not so much getting out of the town as on the trail. Over the three miles to Yelland Quay, he calculated that a mountain bike ought to be able to average twenty miles an hour, compared with fifty or sixty for motor bikes. That meant nine minutes versus three and a bit. If everything else went to plan, that extra six shouldn't be critical.

Tommy would later drop two of the toe-rags off at a motorway service station. Once it was dark, they would each steal a truck and, like Tommy and the third toe-rag, set off to find remote B & Bs to hole up in. Jack had already made his way down to the Solent. Pleasure craft were constantly moving to and fro in those waters, attracting little attention, even in winter. The big yacht cruised up close to Buckler's Hard, and when darkness came, an inflatable tender was quietly dispatched to pick him up. He climbed on board unobserved.

By seven, Ronnie, Lee and Rupert had checked into

their hotel a few miles outside Barnstaple. To be on the safe side, they used false names and indicated that they would pay cash. They had dinner together, but the conversation wasn't overly lively. All feeling the strain, they retired early and did their best to get a little sleep before the rigours of the next day.

27

When Wednesday's dawn finally came, it was a chilly, grey affair. The salt-laden, blustery wind in from the white-flecked sea was fast shooing away the traces of the night mist, and yapping at the scarves and turned-up collars of the good folk of North Devon as they made their way about their early business. Not a morning to bring cheery whistles to the lips or grins to the faces.

One hour before, two rigid inflatables had beached briefly in a cove round from Ilfracombe, allowing eight ghostly figures to stumble ashore. The patient sentinel flashed his torch from the top of the low, crumbly cliff and they scrambled up the thirty feet, cursing in their unfamiliar tongue. They were glad to be on terra firma. It had been a vile night aboard and, in spite of the pills the Dutch captain had given them, most had at some point leant over the side.

The men climbed into the back of the big green van, arranged themselves as best they could next to the mountain bikes, and cursed some more as Tommy bounced the vehicle like a bronco over the rough surface and back to the road. Tommy rolled his wrist. Six-thirty. Bang on.

Sparky had an early start too, leaving the comfort of his cosy farmhouse B&B before six to drive his van back to

Webbery. He'd taken care of his reconnaissance the day before, and decided that it didn't make sense to attack the sub-station itself. It wasn't that its tall fence was a serious deterrent: the problem was being certain that the station really *was* taken out. With the little warning he'd been given, it hadn't been possible to get hold of plastics, and anyway handling them was always more dangerous. He felt much safer working with good old-fashioned gelignite. With its lesser explosive force, he would be much happier targeting the pylons bringing the high-voltage electricity to the station from the grid. Any one of them would be enough. He had carefully calculated the angle of fall needed to rip the cables clear away. Two opposite legs of a pylon would take care of it. The only problem was that a cold, damp night could play merry hell with gelignite. That was what had stopped him using the wee small hours. However, this time of year, even in the morning, the dark was a welcome shroud. No sane farmer would go near a grazing meadow before dawn.

He reached the sub-station by six-thirty. Even though his van had false number plates, he didn't take any chances and parked it down a track, well out of sight of the road. Climbing out, he took a small haversack, walked a few hundred yards, hopped over the low fence into the field, and on over the soggy turf to the base of the pylon.

The first thing he pulled from the haversack was a pair of night sights. Using a torch would be madness out here. Soon both little bundles were tied with twine to the massive stanchions, the timers were rechecked, and he set off back towards the fence.

In the van he drew deeply on the cigarette he'd had to deny himself before, and took a look at the van's cheap digital clock. Six forty-three. He had plenty of time to kill before heading towards the elevated position near Exeter that he'd chosen for his broadcast. Better not stick around here, though. He flicked the butt out of the window, and started the engine.

The calls began to flood into the Plymouth police at around half past eight. This was a new one. Like every big town in Britain, they got their fair share of joyriders, but usually in summer, and always at night. You'd have thought that these kids would have hangovers to work off. The police put a call out on the radio, and the two nearest patrol cars responded.

By quarter to nine, more calls were coming in, with increasingly high estimates of the speeds the BMW M3 was doing. Parents were terrified. At least at night when joyriders strutted their stuff, little children were safely abed. At this time in the morning, with school runs and lollipop crossings, there could be carnage.

At eight fifty-five, the driver lost it on a bend, and was fishtailing, struggling to regain control, when he ran into the next junction. If the driver coming the other way hadn't swerved, it would have been head-on. His reaction saved both of their lives. As it was, the glancing blow hardly slowed down the renegade.

The officers in the leading pursuit car were thoroughly aware of the dangers at this scary hour. If they pressed the BMW too hard, they would only speed up the action, and convert tragedy from likely to inevitable. Their own vehicles, going at seventy or eighty down residential roads, were just as big a threat to life and limb as the pursued. They radioed in for instructions.

The senior duty officer was in no doubt by now. He grabbed the mike himself and instructed the two cars to pursue with caution, trying to keep visual contact, but hanging back at least a hundred yards, making no attempt to intercept the BMW. While he was doing that, the sergeant had dialled Exeter as he'd asked. He took over the handset.

'This is Inspector John Bligh, Plymouth Hoe. We have a joyrider situation here. Am requesting aerial assistance.'

'We have only one helicopter available, Inspector. Is the situation serious enough to warrant despatching it? Will the pursuit still be underway in forty minutes?'

'Frankly, we've got no idea, but these maniacs could have killed any number of schoolchildren by the time we finish speaking.'

'Okay, please hold, Plymouth.'

Bligh stood there impatiently, muttering away to himself.

'Thank you for waiting, Inspector. Okay, we have a go. The chopper is heading your way. It's now nine oh eight. ETA is nine fifty.'

'Thank you.'

In the police station in the Civic Centre at Barnstaple, Duty Sergeant Gordon McCallum felt hassled. He'd emigrated from Glasgow a few years ago for a quiet life. Three urgent calls between nine-thirty and nine-forty weren't his idea of peace. The incident at the plastic packaging works in Pottington sounded nasty. The man's arm had been completely severed. An ambulance had already been called, they said, but feelings were running high among the workforce, and the manager had to barricade himself in. Then there was an intruder in Goodleigh and a fatal road accident near Bratton Fleming.

The Control Room in Exeter seemed to be very stretched too, and he was having problems getting through to them. It was time to use his initiative. There was nothing for it but to run down to the room where a few patrol officers were hanging around the station, and send them straight off. By nine forty-five he was able to report to Exeter what he'd done, and was told that two more of their roaming cars had been sent to other incidents in the area. What a morning. It only left him and a young green constable at the nick. He fervently hoped that this was the only drama that Wednesday morning had to offer.

The lorry must have braked too late. It swerved violently before smashing into the roundabout across from Boutport Street, pushing a Ford Focus aside like a dodgem car. It was a miracle that no one was seriously injured. The burly young lorry driver jumped down, made a huge show of contrition, and offered to call for police and ambulances from his mobile. Several other drivers and pedestrians put theirs away and let him get on with it. Soon he was able to assure them that help was on the way. He sat down by the roadside, waving sympathetic enquirers away, insisting that the Ford driver's need for comfort was greater.

The onlookers watched as the traffic backed up. The

roundabout was blocked right across. How on earth would an ambulance get through? The driver said he knew where the police station was. Perhaps he would run over that way and make sure they knew the score. Despite the protestations of others, he jogged off.

Astonishingly, there was similar mayhem developing in two other places. As a knock-on effect from the first snarl-up, the driver of a huge red articulated truck failed to notice how bunged up the roundabout at the head of the High Street had become and back-ended an old Morris Marina. The Morris and two other cars were badly smashed, and the truck came to a rest with the cab halfway across the grass central section, its bumper resting neatly against the bent video mast. While most eyes were on the hurt occupant of the Morris, the youthful truck driver, suffering obvious shock, stumbled around, lit up a fag and wandered distractedly to and fro until, with nobody noticing, he slipped quietly round a corner.

Longbridge too was closed by a green van slewing sideways and stalling, blocking both carriageways, and defying the attempts of the driver to restart it. All around him horns sounded like angry insects. Covered in embarrassment, the culprit apologised profusely, abandoned his attempts to coax the motor back into life and, mumbling something about spark plugs, locked his cabin, and set off in search of a garage, leaving behind a growing crowd of mightily disgruntled motorists.

Rupert had settled down early in the café. He wanted to make sure he got a window seat, and took lots of newspapers to help pass the time. As zero hour neared, reading was an increasingly difficult task. He ordered his third cup of disgusting coffee. Not that he was planning on complaining.

He was thrilled to be able to taste the excitement for himself without being at any risk. And he wasn't only an observer. Whenever one of the pairs of Bosnians pedalled back past him, he'd give one ring on Jack's mobile to let him know.

Tommy had a more active part to play. The night before, he'd unloaded the four motorbikes in the station car park to the south of the town, and this morning, after collecting and delivering the Bosnians and their bicycles, he'd met up again with the third toe-rag out and handed over the van. Now, a few minutes before ten, Tommy had put on white overalls, thick glasses and a grey wig, and was walking along the long wall of the police station with his toolbox, languidly hammering small metal wedges under each of the fire doors. With traffic outside at a standstill, plenty of irritated drivers and passengers would see this workman going about his duties, and none would take particular notice of him.

Having firmly wedged six of the exits, Tommy stepped round to the double glass doors of the main entrance to the station. It was the only one with loop handles. No need for a wedge here. He fished something from his pocket, and deftly slipped it between them. With a cheery whistle, he ambled away. Within five minutes, he had crossed the jammed Longbridge, and made it as far as the railway station car park, where he smiled with satisfaction that only one of the motorbikes remained.

All three of the toe-rags must be safely away. Having checked that no one was watching, he pulled a leather jacket and helmet out of the pannier, replaced them with the overalls, glasses and wig, and started the engine. Then, describing a leisurely arc round the car park, he pulled out onto the main road to the south.

By a minute to ten, the officers had given up. They'd tried the address in the Pottington estate. The manager looked mystified. Definitely no severed arms, heads, or legs today, he had said with a chuckle. Jock, as everyone called McCallum, was known to have got things wrong before, so they drove up and down the dusty lanes of the estate, looking for other evidence of unrest. Nothing. Better radio in. The young constable picked up the car radio. Before he could speak, it burst into unusual life.

'What the hell is this?'

His more grizzled companion listened carefully, and opined in his West Country burr, 'I'd say that was Renée Fleming singing Strauss.'

'Well, it certainly ain't Sergeant McCallum. Better call in on the UHF and see what's going on.' The constable reached down to the radio clipped to his tunic.

'This is two three three, over . . .' He tried again. 'Odd. Jock's not answering. Hey, did you see that?'

'What?' The older man was enjoying the music.

'All the lights in those units over there just went out. Must be a power cut. What d'you reckon, Dave? Shall we get back and see what's going on?'

'What's the big rush? I like Classic FM.'

*　　*　　*

Rupert had almost worn out his cuff pulling it back. At last it was ten.

Ahhh, thank God for that. The lights went out in the café and all up the street. The other customers groaned. Rupert grimaced sympathetically at a biddy or two and turned back to peer out of the window. With no illumination reflecting from the shop windows, the heavily overcast weather created an eerie twilight. He could see lots of shopkeepers wandering out into the street to find out what was going on. It was good that it was so cold; they wouldn't tarry there long. Otherwise, the streets could have become too clogged for the bikes to get through in a hurry. He looked again at the sweep hand on his watch. Thirty seconds had passed. *Come on.*

Another full minute. Shit, had Tommy forgotten to check that the guys had the right time? Another ten, twenty, thirty seconds. Something must have gone wrong. It was nearly two minutes past. Where *were* the fuckers?

To his vast relief, a group of figures hove into view, pedalling effortfully up the hill. As they went past him, two continued right up Boutport Street towards Barclays, and the other six turned into the High Street. One duo would stop at HSBC, right ahead, one couple would peel off left into Cross Street to do Lloyds, and the last pair would keep right on till they got to NatWest. From now he would see nothing of them till they came back.

Inside Barclays, two of the tellers were on a coffee break, and the nineteen-year-old girl was out front on her own.

Within moments of the power cut, their generator had kicked in, and she was able to carry on business as usual. When the two strange mustachioed men came in with their big bags, she thought it was some sort of joke. One of them pushed an elderly woman customer aside, pulled what the girl thought was a toy gun, and screamed at her. *'All the money, safe, safe, all the money, fast, fast!'*

The girl giggled. She stopped when one of the men grabbed the old woman's hair and threw her down hard on the floor. Now the gun went to the girl's head.

'Fast, fast, all the money.'

Panicky now, the girl slipped off her stool, and went to the back in instant tears, unable to do more than babble to the manager and point to the front. The little bespectacled man, pate skilfully concealed beneath a lateral sweep of grey hair, rose wearily. What had happened now? Had someone been rude to the silly girl? Still, that was what he was paid for, to sort out life's little problems. He straightened his tie, and walked round the corner, ready to do battle with whatever the world had to throw at him.

And nearly shat himself.

One of the Bosnians hurdled the counter, and stuck the gun at the man's temple.

'Fast, fast, safe,'safe, all the money.'

The manager didn't hesitate. He walked back round the corner as quickly as his legs would take him, squealing to his deputy to come with him, and in a trembling trice had the safe open. While one robber started to stuff the two bags, the other was on guard by the door. As further customers came in, he gestured them with his pistol to join the frightened old woman squatting on the floor, well out of the line of sight of passers-by.

The rucksacks were soon filled, the manager helping as urgently as his shaking hands would allow. By ten past ten, the two had also scooped what cash there was in the counter drawers, and were on their way out of the door and back on their bikes, leaving behind customers too frightened to stand up, a teller girl crumpled in a sobbing heap, and a manager who was shuddering so uncontrollably he could hardly press the emergency button.

In the café, Rupert clenched one fist in satisfaction as he saw the two men flying back down Boutport Street and out of his view. He had already dialled the number on his mobile, and all he had to do was to hit the green button, listen carefully for one ring, and then press the red. So far so good, but too soon to relax.

He was right to be cautious. It was going less smoothly elsewhere. At HSBC one guy had tried to play hero, and had got pistol-whipped for his pains. If anyone else had followed suit, the Bosnians would have abandoned Jack's firm instruction not to shoot unless absolutely necessary. As it was, it slowed them down, and made them even more jumpy. By ten past ten they had only just got the safe open and, dressed in their heavy black gear, were sweating buckets as they pushed the cash into the rucksacks.

NatWest and Lloyds were okay for the first five or six minutes, until in each case, an unseen hand pressed an alarm button, triggering a deafening siren. Passers-by looked over without curiosity, guessing it was some sort of fault, and anyway not their problem. In Lloyds the one gathering the cash panicked and tried to bolt right away, leaving notes scattered all over the floor. He was shoved brusquely back by his cooler companion. All they were getting was a share of what they collected. And they'd been told not to worry about alarms.

It took Sergeant McCallum several minutes to get suspicious, and even then it was only the coincidences. First, the traffic outside was totally jammed in both directions. It often got busy at rush hour, but never like this. Then there was the power cut, which knocked out the phone, and the UHF system, plus that earlier spate of incidents. Suddenly, a ghastly thought dawned on him. Could there be a connection? Could there be something going on?

He looked out of the window. A young man was running on the grass verge outside. He went out of McCallum's view as he skipped past. When no one came in, McCallum assumed he had gone elsewhere in the Centre. Moments later, there was an infernal rattling. He sent the young constable out to take a look. The constable rushed back.

'Sarge, Sarge, the door's been handcuffed. The man's shouting something. I think he said there's been a bank robbery.'

'*Christ* . . .' Now the young man had come back round to the side of the building, and was gesticulating through the glass. McCallum pointed down the street towards the fire exits, and ran in that direction himself. He got to the first exit and shoved.

'What the hell . . . ?' He pushed again. And again,

harder. Never mind, try the next. On and on he ran, wheezing with the effort. He reached the last one. 'Och, *no*. For guidness sake.'

Crimson-faced now, he raced back, looking from window to window until he was face-to-to face with the young man. How could he speak to him? The big lower windows didn't open, only the postbox-shaped ones at the top. He clambered awkwardly up on a desk and pushed one open. He called out through it. 'Sorry. Can't get the bloody doors open.'

The young man was out of puff too. 'They've wedged them with something. I can't pull them out. Listen, there's been a robbery at Barclays.'

The man had shown commendable gumption. Seeing the two men in black run out of the bank with their bags and then hearing the alarm go off, he had chosen the direct approach and sprinted round to the station. He was still trying to recover from his exertions, sucking in great gulps of air.

'I think I heard an alarm going off in the High Street, too.'

'Okay, thanks, sonny.'

McCallum jumped stiffly down to the floor and ran back to his counter. In the drawer there was a mobile phone they used as a back-up. He looked up on the board to find the number. Finally someone at Headquarters answered. McCallum spoke gravely into the little handset.

'Exeter, we have a problem.'

Ten-fifteen. Two more black-clad figures appeared in the distant gloom and, veering this way and that past startled pedestrians, pedalled for all they were worth down the High Street, swung right in front of the café and were gone. Good, that was NatWest done. Before Rupert had a chance to ring Jack, the guys from Lloyds turned in from Cross Street and flew down the hill too. He rang the coded message through twice. Now there was only HSBC left. What had happened to them? They had the shortest distance to travel. What the hell was going on?

The BMW had left central Plymouth far behind, and was racing at speeds of over a hundred on the A388. Now that the chopper had arrived, the pursuit cars were hanging half a mile back, well out of sight, allowing the pilot to monitor it. At these sort of speeds, and in a high-powered BMW, the fuel consumption would be horrendous. Joyriders never filled up. Hopefully the tank had been less than full when he nicked it, and he'd run out any time. The moment the chopper saw him slow down, the pursuit cars would speed up. Though the boy would doubtless take to his heels, he wouldn't be able to stop his car in a place of his choosing, and with the chopper's assistance, they should be able to follow and grab him.

As they drove, the pilot was speaking constantly to them. This time the officers in the lead car couldn't believe their ears. They asked him to repeat what he'd said.

'Sorry. Breaking off pursuit. Repeat breaking off. Over.'

'What the hell d'you mean? We've almost got him. Over.'

'I've been ordered to Barnstaple. There's a major incident in progress there. Better luck next time. Over and out.'

They watched as the helicopter swung away. The lead pursuit car gave up there and then, and the other followed suit. Without the chopper they were blind. The lead driver got out of the car and wiped his forehead. As his two colleagues from the car behind joined him he grimaced.

'What a fucking joke, eh?'

Still no one had come out of HSBC. Rupert's eyes were stuck like glue to the High Street. What the hell was this? To his horror he saw in the distance a uniformed policeman running his way.

Feeling the need to do something, and keenly aware of the ignominy of being locked in his own nick, Sergeant McCallum had left the constable in charge, and had got on a chair, pulled a high window open, and levered his bulky frame through it, landing heavily on the grass outside. Without stopping to dust himself down, he had run as fast as his old legs would carry him up to NatWest. It took him only seconds to see he was too late. Statements could wait. Where next? Barclays was over, by the sound of it. Better try Lloyds. As he skidded to a halt at the corner of Cross Street, he could see a huddle of people standing outside. That was done too. It only left HSBC. It was another two hundred yards down the street. His heart wouldn't take much more of this.

As he saw the copper getting nearer, Rupert stood

up involuntarily, and had to struggle to suppress the instinct to flee. He forced himself to sit down again and watched in horror. It was too late, they were fucked. The man was only a hundred yards away. Less now, eighty, sixty.

The two Bosnians came rushing out in the street. The policeman was virtually on them.

They moved fast, though, and in those vital seconds they jumped on their bikes and swung them round so that they were pointing at him, like he was a stag at bay. In the street, a couple of elderly dears stopped, mesmerised. In the summer months, there were often street events. Was this one of those Arts Council things?

McCallum drew the old truncheon he'd grabbed from a drawer, and moved towards the cyclists. In response, one of the Bosnians pulled out a pistol. The old dears and the other onlookers staggered back. In a mad fit of courage, McCallum ignored the gun and came forward, but his prey wobbled out of his reach. In a last despairing dive, he tried to ram the stick through the spokes of one of the bikes. He missed and lay there panting, trying to work up enough lung capacity to call out, 'Stop thief!' and not making it.

The two old dears waited till the bikes were well out of sight before they came over to see if the policeman was all right.

Relieved for the moment, but still mightily fretful, Rupert tapped in the last call and looked again at his watch. If it had taken him till now to run all the way here, that old copper could have rumbled them around quarter past. He would have called Exeter right away. The police had a broad range of frequencies to call the helicopter, so these communications couldn't be jammed. The helicopter might have been turned round within seconds. It was now ten twenty-five. If they had calculated its flying time accurately, it would be overhead in around half an hour. They had agreed that the jamming of the VHF signal would stop at half past, to make sure that the Exeter police didn't have time to pinpoint the source. In five minutes police communications would be all but back to normal.

As they reached Longbridge, the HSBC duo mounted the pavement, where the throng of chatting motorists stepped smartly out of their way. On the bridge, the mood of ratty annoyance had subsided to resignation, and now a jocular atmosphere was developing. This was the fourth lot of cyclists who'd gone by wearing black, and they gave them an appreciative cheer. Probably some sort of charity thing.

The pair pedalled on past a broad roundabout, looking out for the small turning to the right which Tommy had shown them earlier. Hitting the start of the Tarka Trail, they headed west.

The two inflatables had cruised past Yelland Quay twice before the first team, from Barclays, arrived. They handed over the bags, and were shown where to sling the bikes so that they'd remain underwater for at least a few hours. No one had touched those bikes with ungloved hands, but they weren't taking chances. The men got into the first boat, crazed with desire to be out of there and back on the yacht. Hanging around was driving them mad. It was another five minutes before the NatWest team made it, did the same stuff with their bikes and joined their Barclays companions. The Dutch mate spun the boat round and it sped noisily off towards the river mouth.

Jack, at the tiller of the second boat, steered it alongside the quay just as the Lloyds pair turned up. Conscious of the delay, they were even more frantic to be gone. While he tried to placate them, Jack kept one hand on the gun in his jacket pocket. Where the hell were the last two? It was ages since Rupert had rung for the last time. What was happening in the town?

Rupert stayed on in the café, knowing that it was the safest place to be. He had agreed to send another coded signal by mobile to Ronnie and Lee to indicate that the four groups had got safely out of town, and then walk to the station and catch the ten fifty-eight to Exeter St David's. Ronnie and Lee had gone on ahead to Exeter by taxi after Lee had insisted that the last thing they needed was to get stopped in some roadblock.

Rupert looked back up the High Street. There were now hosts of policemen arriving on foot. They had probably abandoned their cars the other side of the traffic chaos and run here. Ten forty-two. The chopper would be getting near.

As the last Bosnians got to within one mile of the quay, one was lagging badly behind. The stress of the robbery had brought on asthma, and his breathing was getting very ragged. Pedalling this thing was exhausting. His mate stopped for a second to let him catch up, then hared off again, worried that he would be caught.

Each yard was an effort for the laggard now. It was all taking so much more time than they'd planned. And the more he panicked, the worse the attack got.

His mate had the quay in view now. Another minute and he'd be there. Seeing him, the second inflatable came back to the jetty. He slung his bike in the water, and got in with his bag.

Three Bosnians in a boat now, one to go. Jack looked at his watch. Ten forty-eight. Any moment now the chopper would be here. Should they leave the last man behind? No, that would be disastrous. He'd be caught and give the whole game away.

Finally he came into sight. Everyone in the boat could see him half-pedalling, half dragging his feet. *Come on, man, come on.*

Their collective effort of will seemed to work. He managed a spurt of a few more yards. One of the Bosnians yelled out encouragement. The man tried to raise a hand in acknowledgement, but the effort was too much, and the cycle wobbled and toppled.

Get up, *get up.*

Fuck it, thought Jack, I'm going to have to shoot him. Then he recalled who was in the boat with him. Maybe the cyclist wouldn't be the only one shot that day. He threw a rope round the old wooden post, gestured to one of the others to follow him, and they set off at a lick down the path. Though they managed to pull the exhausted man to his feet, there was no way he could walk on his own. Jack threw the bike deep in the bushes, and they put his arms round their shoulders to carry him. Shit, he was heavy. Jack grabbed a look at his watch. Eight minutes to.

The last few yards were excruciating as the man became a dead weight. Somehow they managed to tip him into the boat, the two other Bosnians catching him as he fell. As they cast off, and headed for the sea, Jack's eyes caught the most feared sight of all. A black speck in the sky. Soon he could hear its sound above the drone of the outboard. They needed another four or five minutes to reach the ship. If the chopper came right their way immediately, they were sitting ducks. Jack prayed that the pilot would first check the roads.

They were clear of the river now, and into the sea proper. Two more minutes. The chopper was very close, must almost be able to see them.

And then, Holy Mary, it veered to the east. Maybe the police were following some hunch. Jack kept an eye on it as they clambered aboard. The first bunch had stowed their inflatable and were hiding below. The Dutch skipper yelled at this lot to do the same, while the mate helped Jack attach the second boat to the stern. Jack looked back up. The helicopter had changed course again. Now there was no question. It was heading right their way.

Back on the bridge, the skipper pushed the throttle up and sent the boat surging forward. They had been moving less than three minutes when the chopper reached the water's edge, sweeping this way and that over the beaches and cliffs. Then it came out to sea, straight at them. This was it.

As it got near, his heart in his boots, Jack played his

last card and waved up to it. The pilot took a good look, gave him a thumbs-up, and banked back towards the land.

Jesus Christ, thought Jack. That's the last time I do something just to keep the guv'nor happy.

28

The Wednesday evening news had made for good viewing. All the signs were that the concerted attack on this normally quiet market town had left the police profoundly confused. In their official statement, the Devon and Cornwall Constabulary announced that, although the accomplices were definitely British, there was so far no information on the nationality of the main assailants, or on what had possessed them to select Barnstaple. The further comment that the attackers had fled 'across country or by boat' only served to underscore how much in the dark they were.

The team had all returned to their various bases without incident, including the intrepid BMW driver who, more than a little cheekily, had parked the car outside Plymouth station with the keys in the exhaust pipe before taking the train home. Even if the Law had found it quickly they had no idea what he looked like, so searching the express would have been an exercise in futility.

Once again, Jack had the harder job on the boat, having to deal with eight mutinous Bosnians, who were firmly of the view that this had not been the advertised cakewalk and demanded a renegotiation there and then. The weight of numbers encouraged a conciliatory approach, and after much haggling, Jack got off at the Solent with no more than seven hundred and forty-five grand, and a determination never to enter Balkan politics.

Lee was furious at the lowly proceeds, and even Ronnie was a little abashed. Rupert was prepared to get a bit shirty if Ronnie stuck to the letter of their agreement, but Ronnie waived the condition that the take had to be one million plus, and promised to transfer the bonus payment the next day. On that basis, Rupert was content. He was six hundred and forty thousand richer – not a bad little earner for a project that had taken less than ten man-days of his time. Quite some charge-out rate. Plus, he'd had a giant dose of excitement and adrenalin without putting himself at personal risk. It was like being on a battlefield but immune to bullets. And, above all, he'd won again. He had demonstrated to his own satisfaction that he had a brilliant criminal mind.

It would take time to come down from this high. He wished he had some sleeping tablets. He got up and poured himself a stiff whisky. That might do the trick. Otherwise, he'd never get a wink before the very different excitements of the next day.

It didn't work, and by two he was reduced to rereading an old copy of *Playboy*.

*

'Hi there, Rupert, come on in. Coffee?'

Fraser asked his assistant to get them a couple of cups, and then closed the door.

'Before we get onto the appraisal proper, that was fantastic news on Telesys. Really great. Brilliant job you've

311

done there. They were obviously terrifically pleased with our work in general, and yours in particular.'

'Thanks.' Rupert didn't want to dwell on this. There was only one thing he was interested in hearing.

'Okay, let's start with headlines of the appraisal, and then move on to the shorter strokes. Your focus, attention to detail, verbal and written presentations, and general communications skills both internally and externally are first class. No problems at all there. As far as client relations are concerned, we feel you've done well too. You admitted when you joined us that this was the area where McKinsey always marked you down, but clearly you've learnt to recognise the symptoms of potential difficulties and nip them in the bud. So, a good, solid performance . . .'

So far, so good. But Rupert was still waiting. He knew these games well enough, knew that if they were going to refuse him, they'd have to give a reason, find a hook to hang it on. Fraser hadn't fashioned one yet.

'Moving on to client acquisition, we've talked about this before. Basically, you haven't had much chance to develop those skills, or show what you can do. However, I do recognise that by bringing in Interleisure you've shown that, given the opportunity, there is no reason why you can't market the firm's services effectively.'

'I'm glad you think so.' Rupert was genuinely relieved. He thought that they might dismiss it as too small to count.

'The other thing that leaves is relations with members of your own team. If there's *any* area of concern which has flickered on our radar screen, this is it.'

Rupert felt his gut tightening. Was this the hook?

'Overall, you're quite highly rated. The main issue seems to be workload within the team. There is some feeling that you keep too much to yourself, and don't delegate as much as you might.'

'I delegate as much as makes sense. You know perfectly well, Fraser, that there have been moments on Telesys that we didn't have time for me to run a training seminar, and you wouldn't have wanted me to submit work that was second rate. The deadlines were very tight.'

'They often are. If junior staff are excluded at those key junctures, it can make them feel they're missing out on vital experience.'

Rupert remonstrated some more, but it wasn't getting him anywhere.

'The same could be said about your presentations. Think of the last two project review sessions we held. In both of those, you really monopolised, made very little attempt to involve the rest of the team actively.'

'Fraser, on both of those occasions you arrived late. I was trying to use the reduced time we had efficiently, for the project's sake, and for yours.'

'I know you were, Rupert, believe me. However, when we look at the reports from the team, they clearly were unhappy that they weren't seen to be contributing. Don't forget, they have their progress and promotions to worry about too, and they resented being denied the opportunity.'

'You can't have it both ways, Fraser.'

'All I mean is it's always a question of balance between the project itself and the development and morale of the staff . . . Let me ask you something. When you think how you tend to dominate those meetings is it *really* just a question of efficiency?'

'What are you talking about?'

'Is it possible that you're still not as secure as you might be? That you still feel you have a point to prove, and this stops you letting others share the limelight?'

Rupert felt his fuse crackling away, snaking towards the dynamite. 'No, Fraser, I simply don't think that's true.'

'Well, I think it may be.'

'Fraser, d'you mind if we, to use an expression, cut the crap? Am I being made partner or not?'

The other man paused for a second, trying to work out how to play it.

'I agree, let's get to the nitty-gritty. The bottom line for us, Rupert, is you're absolutely partnership quality. Indeed, many of the partners think you could go right to the top of the firm . . .'

'Great. So I get the promotion, right?' His sarcasm was already beginning to bite.

'Yes, of course.'

'I *do*?' For one moment Rupert was stopped dead in his tracks.

'. . . But not just yet.'

'Jesus Christ.' Rupert stared up at the ceiling.

'We debated this long and hard. Personally, I wanted to promote you. However, others felt that it was in your own best interests to have another twelve months working with teams as a project manager, to get over whatever this confidence issue is, and then move smoothly on. Otherwise, it could be a case of more haste, less speed.'

Rupert decided to opt for a sullen time-out. Detecting that, Fraser reached for the lollipop.

'Now, I know that may be disappointing, but it's not all gloomy news. You may be about to become rather more prosperous.'

'Oh yeah? How's that?' Rupert snarled rather than spoke the words.

'Although it's still secret, you may have heard rumours of some changes.'

'Obviously I have. Even the cleaners know about it.'

Fraser bit his lip. 'Well, I doubt that the cleaners know everything, and indeed I can't go into a lot of details myself at this stage. If what we're exploring comes to pass, it will give us far greater resources, make this a much more powerful firm, which as a future partner, I am sure means a lot to you.'

Frankly, Fraser, I don't give a fuck about the firm's future, Rupert was thinking, but he managed to stop himself saying it.

'Not only that, there would be some crystallisation of value in the firm. Although the final details are yet to be worked out, the partners feel very strongly that key staff – and top project managers in particular – should share substantially in it.'

'How much?'

'For the most important people it could be a sum equal to their annual salary. I hope that prospect brings a smile to your lips.'

Rupert shook his head aggressively. 'Why should it? Let me do a quick calculation. There are around seventy project managers in the firm. If I'm one of the top ones, that suggests that some others will receive less. Let's assume an average of a hundred grand a head. That's seven million. If more junior staff get a Christmas stocking too, that could add up to what? Another three million? I've no idea what Orbia is worth, but having worked in the City I'm not a complete dummy financially. I'd say it's got to be worth three hundred million minimum. Now, it depends on what deal you're thinking of, but most likely it's a merger with some other firm, a float or a sale. And, to use your own words, if there's a crystallisation of value going on here, that suggests that thirty odd partners are planning on sharing out at least two hundred and ninety big ones among themselves, and leaving scraps for the engine room of the business.'

This whole conversation was spinning badly off orbit. Fraser didn't know what to say, so he said nothing. Rupert filled in the blank.

'I have one question for you, Fraser. There are usually four or five people promoted. How many this year?'

'Only two, as it happens.'

'Is that because you'll have to cut them in on the real spoils?'

Fraser gulped like a goldfish. Rupert stood up. 'Now I understand. You *greedy* fuckers.'

He turned and walked out. As he did, Fraser finally recovered the power of speech. He called out after the retreating back: 'Rupert, we haven't finished your appraisal.'

Rupert was so cross he went back to his office, grabbed his jacket, coat and phone, and without a word to anyone, left the office.

He stormed for a while down Park Lane, but the weather was up to the same trick, so he marched back to Berkeley Square, turned right at the far corner, and went into a Starbucks café. He got himself a double espresso and sat down on a stool by the window. Could you believe it, that they'd pull a stunt like that? He should have quit there and then. Better still, he should call the CEO of Telesys, let him know he was leaving, and tell him the reason why. What a bunch of . . . Ugh, it made him so *mad*.

His mobile rang. He fished it out and checked the incoming number. Prim. She knew that it was today and would be wanting to check whether he'd heard yet. Well, bugger that. He couldn't cope with her sympathy at the moment. He waited till it flipped over to message. It rang again. Bloody woman.

No, this time it wasn't Prim, it was Georgina. He pressed the little green symbol.

'Hi, George, what's up?'

'Where are you right now?'

There was no particular reason to lie. 'Near Berkeley Square. I'm having a coffee in Starbucks.'

'I know the one. Mind if I join you? There's something I need your advice on. I'll be there in ten minutes. Bye.'

What on earth could she want his advice on? Some half-baked business venture? For all that they'd now met a few more times, he wasn't finding it any easier to read her. She wore bedroom eyes all the time, but regularly exhorted him to do the decent thing by Prim, and constantly reminded him of her own search for a mate. Was she no more than a divine prick teaser, or was she secretly hoping he'd ditch Prim? He couldn't work it out at all.

She shimmered in, dressed in a gorgeously tailored camel-hair coat, offset with a sable hat. She looked ravishing. He trotted off to get her a tall skinny latte.

'So? What's the big problem? All my consulting experience is at your disposal.'

'Thanks, Rupert. It's financial, really.'

'What kind of financial?'

'Tell me, what's your opinion of pre-nuptial agreements?'

'Never thought about it. Not terribly romantic, are they?'

'Practical, though. And maybe realistic in this day and age.'

'I suppose so. Why?'

She smiled conspiratorially. 'It's still a huge secret, so you mustn't tell anyone, but I think I've found my man.'

It hit Rupert like a thump in the solar plexus. He had to struggle to stop his feelings showing.

'What d'you mean, *think*? Hasn't he asked you yet?'

She pulled back her head and gave him a distinctly old-fashioned look. 'Of course he has. He's been begging me all week.'

'So you haven't answered?'

'No, but I'm just about to. He's German. On the plus side he's terribly good-looking and has a pedigree that goes back to Charlemagne. The minus is that he doesn't actually *do* anything, which is fine if you have vast stacks of money, but not if, like Wilhelm, your stacks are a teeny bit smaller than they might be. That's why

318

I need your advice. If I include what I'll inherit one day, I'm worth ten, twenty times what he is, and it would be very boring if some nasty court took half of it away from me, don't you see?'

'Definitely have a pre-nuptial then.'

'That's where I need your advice. The subject hasn't come up yet. If I call him now and say the good news is the answer is "yes"; the bad news is "hard luck about the lolly", do you think he'll run a mile?'

As she was speaking, Rupert had a vision of this lovely creature drifting irrecoverably out of his reach and being locked away in some dreadful Bavarian *Schloss*. This might be the last time he got to meet her alone. His senses were writhing with her perfume, her voice, her hair, her legs. God, this was a *truly* lousy day. He forced himself to reply.

'No, he won't run a mile. Not if he loves you.'

Georgina smiled. 'Good, that's what I think. I just needed a second opinion from a man. Thanks, Rupes, I'd better run and put the poor Hun out of his misery.' She slipped off the stool, held her cheek out for him to kiss, and made to go. He caught hold of her hand.

'Georgina.'

'What?'

'Sit down again a sec.'

'I really must be off.' But she sat down and looked into his eyes.

Rupert ran a hand through his hair. 'This is ridiculous. I feel like Trevor Howard in *Brief Encounter*.'

'What on earth do you mean?'

'Look, George, I don't know how to say this, but I want to be with you.'

'How can you say that? You're with Prim and I'm on the verge of being married.'

'The Prim bit I can fix.'

'By doing what? Dumping her unceremoniously, when she's been so good to you?'

'No, she hasn't. Prim's not the angel you think. There's a lot of shit I've put up with, which has eaten away at my feelings for her.'

'Like what?'

'Like her lies.'

'*Lies*? Prim? Rubbish!'

'It's not rubbish. She lies to everyone. To you, too.'

Georgina tried to look horrified, but couldn't keep the delighted fascination entirely from her eyes. 'Prim lies to *moi*?'

'At least she used to, and she's never told you the real truth.'

'Give me an example.'

'Do you remember her father?'

'Vaguely. Drove an Aston Martin, I think. Rather good-looking.'

'Well, he's not her father.'

'You're *kidding*. Then who is he?'

'Some sort of friend of her father.'

'Then what was the matter with her real father? Why didn't *he* come to school?'

'Because he was in prison . . . That's why Prim was sent to boarding school in the first place.'

'How utterly extraordinary! And what had he done, her father? Not murdered the mother, I hope.'

'He was a gangster. Still is, apparently.'

'I can hardly believe this. It explains a lot, though.

320

What decent parents would have saddled her with a name like that? . . . And you suspected nothing, you poor dear?'

'Nothing at all. I met her father, of course. The gangster bit I only found out by chance.'

'How?'

'Out of fairness to Prim, I think I'd better draw a veil over that. Ever since, I've been waiting for her to level with me. If she'd done that, I could have forgiven her, got over it. But month after month she's passed up the chance, till now I feel cheated, tricked – above all, used.'

'Well, I have to admit that does put a new complexion on things. The scheming little . . .'

'George, what I've just told you was in the strictest confidence. Yes, my relationship with Prim has been falling apart, and I would have ended it any day now. However, I wouldn't want her to think that I was running around behind her back passing on her dark secrets.'

Georgina put her hand on his. 'I won't breathe a word.'

'Thanks.'

'And you really are going to finish it, regardless of any feelings you may have for me?'

'I give you my word. So, what do you say? Will you give me a chance?'

'A chance to do what?'

'A chance for us to be together – as an item, I mean – and see where it leads?'

'And where might that be?'

'Who knows? A passionate love affair certainly. More

perhaps.' He wasn't receiving a lot of encouragement here. 'Getting a place together. Marriage one day, maybe.'

Georgina squeezed his hand. 'Thanks for the offer, Rupert, but it's not at all tempting. I've always levelled with you. You know what I want – and now I've got it. I really must run. I've got a call to make. Thanks for the advice.' She got off the stool and, without looking back, walked straight to the door, pausing only to take her phone out of her Chanel handbag. Rupert watched as she disappeared round a corner.

Ten seconds later, scarcely knowing what he was doing, he flew out of Starbucks, round the corner, and hared up the street after her. He could see the phone clamped to her ear. He sprinted the last few yards, grabbed it clean out of her hand, pressed the button to end the call, and thrust the machine in his own pocket.

Georgina looked crossly at him. 'What the hell are you doing?'

'Please marry me. I want you to marry me. I mean it.'

She half laughed. 'Come on, Rupert, stop fooling around. This isn't funny.'

'I'm deadly serious.'

'I don't believe you.'

'Maybe you'll believe this, then.' Damp as the pavement was, he threw himself straight down on his knees. 'Marry me. I love you.'

'Don't be silly. Get up. People are looking.'

'Not till you say yes.'

'I can't. I need time to think.'

'No, you don't. You're always saying trust your instinct. Come on, George. You don't want to live in Germany, do you? Will you, will you marry me?'

'I really have to decide now?'

'Yes, you do. Otherwise I know you'll say yes to that Kraut.'

'Okay then.'

'Okay what?'

'Okay, I'll marry you, you silly boy.'

'You *will*?' He stood up and kissed her passionately. 'Let's go to the Ritz and have a glass of champagne.'

'Why stop there? Hotels have rooms, don't they?'

Grinning from ear to ear, Rupert took her by the hand towards Piccadilly.

'Rupes, can I have my phone back now, please?'

'Why?'

'I need to finish that call.'

'What, right now? Can't it wait?'

'No, I'd rather get it over with.' She took the phone and pressed redial. 'Hi, Mummy, sorry you were cut off. The most amazing thing just happened. You'll never believe what.'

29

The worst part for Chris Owen's team was not knowing whether the drug-run they were waiting for had already happened. For a couple of days they had lost track of Lee Hill altogether. He hadn't hung out in any of his usual spots. That was consistent with running a big operation, especially if he was taking it seriously. But there had been no anonymous tip-off this time, not a word of any sort.

If it was over, there might be nothing else for months. They might have to think more seriously about goading Lee. Maybe having his car towed wasn't such a bad idea after all. All they'd have to do was wait for him to park it illegally again. It was worth having the vehicle removal people alerted so they could turn up fast if Hill gave them their chance.

The Dan Hill case itself had reached a state of stasis as preparations for trial went on. Unless any of the five changed their tune, the key was going to be the black lad. His testimony, and the calls made from that phone to the Mitsubishi and Ronnie's house should be enough to pin it on him. The CPS were unhappy that more supporting evidence hadn't materialised, but went along with the view that this should be enough.

In the office, there were jokes going round about Devon, mainly along the lines that illegal immigrants were finally getting on their bikes. A few MPs from the West Country were putting pressure on the NCS to make solving this crime a high priority. As far as Owen was concerned, there was nothing to get worked up about. No one had been badly hurt, and the gang had got away with less than a million and a half. They had got lucky hitting a sleepy little joint like Barnstaple. If they ever tried somewhere bigger, they'd get bullets up their backsides as they pedalled away.

Owen caught the lunchtime news in his car. The bikes had all now been found. The Devon police expressed their view that one had deliberately been left near the track in order to encourage the police to search that area, find the others in the water, and draw the obvious conclusion that the robbers had escaped down the river. In fact, they did not believe this had happened, and they were supported by the failure of a police helicopter at the time to detect any small craft. The police's conclusion was that this was all a ruse, and that the robbers had hidden while the helicopter was circling, and then continued either on foot or in some other form of land transport. They were probably still holed up in the area, and should on no account be approached if encountered.

Owen switched off before the end of the bulletin. He had bigger fish to fry than a ragtag army of thieves.

*

At three-thirty, Rupert stepped out of the luxurious suite he'd taken in the Ritz, having told Georgina that he needed an hour to take care of some things. He was still fairly sure he'd done the right thing proposing to her, even if it had all been a bit impetuous. Seen in the semi-daylight, Georgina's body had been all he'd remembered it from that first thrilling encounter. As soon as the man bringing the champagne had left, they'd flung off their clothes and had wild, abandoned sex. That was how it felt to him, anyway, and she seemed to enjoy it too. A little later they'd gone a second time, which was less wild and abandoned maybe, but still pretty wild by most people's standards, and had lasted a lot longer.

Now, however, he was going to have to move fast. Since Georgina had already told her mother, word could start hitting the bush telegraph fast. He'd made her swear to tell no one else until he'd done the deed with Prim, but he didn't yet know her well enough to be sure he could trust her. And before he dealt with Prim, he needed badly to get himself a large insurance policy. As soon as he got back to the office he called Lee.

'Lee, things have become more urgent. We need to move fast on the next . . . you know what.'

'Got it, Rupes. What you want me to do?'

'Get hold of Ronnie and Jack. Tell them we need to discuss it tonight. And Lee . . .'

'What, mate?'

'If they won't go along with my plan, will you show them you've got balls?'

'Count on it.'

'And if you have to strike, have you thought about how?'

'Don't reckon there's much to think about. If me, Tommy, and my fellas leave, there ain't much left there, only the old man and Jack. We'd get on with the business and ignore 'em.'

'They would be greatly weakened, yes – but they could keep the business ticking over till they see what happens to Dan, couldn't they? They would still have the restaurants and so on. For operations, they could rent ground troops like before. Ronnie could set up the deals, Jack could do the marshalling. And then you wouldn't really be the guv'nor at all, would you? You'd be just a tiny off-shoot . . . Lee, isn't it time you took charge properly, and made them accept it?'

'The old man never will.'

'Then it all turns on Jack, doesn't it? Ronnie's not much of a force on his own, and with Dan inside, Jack's all he's got. Couldn't you persuade Jack to side with you?'

'Jack's pissed off at the old man 'cause of the way things turned out on that last caper, but basically that don't change nothin'. Jack's the loyal type, like a dumb dog.'

'Then you've got a straight choice, haven't you? Either you leave things as they are with Ronnie in charge, or you have to take Jack out of the equation.'

'Top Jack? Nah, I don't particularly like the fella, but Jack's family.'

'I didn't mean *that*. I meant, couldn't he have a little accident?'

'I'm still not with you. What does it matter what Jack and the old man get up to, as long as you and me do our stuff together?'

'Sorry, Lee, I can't take that chance. If I ditch them and go with you, they might come after me.'

'I doubt it.'

'And I tell you, I'm not taking the chance . . . Prim

and I are on the verge of breaking up, so he'll have another reason to get mad at me too.'

Lee chortled away. 'Ooh. Naughty boy. You started shaggin' that other number?'

'No, of course not, Lee, but there *are* reasons why I need to tell Prim very soon. If you really are going to take over, it would help me a lot if you'd get on with it.'

'Okay, I'll give it a think. And I'll get them all along to *The Legless Frog* for, what, eight?'

'Make it seven.'

*

The session started amiably, with further plaudits to Rupert and further good-natured complaints from Jack. Lee was silent. Ronnie got business moving.

'So, what's the big rush, Rupert?'

'We all agreed to try to do the second and third jobs in quick succession, right?'

'Right.'

'Well, what I have in mind will take a bit of advance planning, so I thought we shouldn't waste any time.'

'Okay, hit us with it.'

Jack joined in: 'And make sure there's no Bosnians involved.'

Rupert smiled. 'Don't worry, Jack. What we did yesterday in Barnstaple was re-engineering bank robbery. Now I want to redesign the kidnap.'

Ronnie's body language was clear; he switched from an open, hands on the table pose to sitting way back in the chair, arms folded. Rupert was unabashed.

'I know what you think of kidnaps, Ronnie, but I

think you'll like this. What we do is identify five or six top entrepreneurs – men who've made a shitload of money over the last few years – and invite them to fly by private jet to an isolated luxury villa in the Caribbean.'

'For fuck's sake, why would they agree to go?' Jack couldn't resist sticking pins in already. He hated the first sound of this.

'Because of who was doing the inviting. It would be Prince Charles, or the Prime Minister, or Richard Branson, maybe . . . At any rate, it would appear to be. They'd get a personally signed letter of invitation, and the telephone number on the letterhead would be properly manned. It would be for the ultimate top-level get-together, the most prestigious invite these guys would ever receive. Imagine, Prince Charles wants to confer with a handful of people, confidentially, in complete seclusion. Who could resist?'

Ronnie was very untaken. 'Let's just assume for the moment that these geezers are big enough dipsticks to cancel all their plans and accept. What do we do next?'

'They get the red-carpet treatment all the way from England to the villa, of course, and when they arrive, guess what? No heir to the throne.'

'And what instead?'

'The kind of people I'm thinking of all have huge assets. With a phone call or two they could transfer serious amounts of loot from their accounts to ours.'

'How much would the ransom be?'

'We'd let *them* set it.'

'What you on about?' Ronnie's voice had lost all trace of affability.

'Since they wouldn't be likely to tell us how much cash they've got in liquid form, we'd make them compete to give us the most. It would be a cross between a blind auction and a game. A game with several rounds. In each one, they'd be asked to write down a number. That number would be a sum of money. Once they'd written it, they'd have to get on the phone – under our supervision, of course – and arrange its transfer from their bank accounts to ours. After all the transfers were complete, we'd draw up a list of the numbers, and whoever had bid the lowest would be taken out and shot. Then the next round would begin, and so on, until the winner was freed.'

Ronnie was shaking his head. 'Jesus, you're a bad bastard. Worse than us, I reckon.'

'Not really. Don't forget that you wouldn't actually have to shoot them. As long as the losers were dragged off kicking and screaming, pissing themselves as they went, and a few seconds later there was the sound of a gunshot, that would be enough. It's the *fear* of execution we'd need, not the actuality. We could lock up all the losers somewhere else till the game was over. Obviously, we *could* kill them all, including the winner, if you thought it was better.'

'And if we don't, the idea is that we let 'em go? You don't think it might cross their tiny minds to go to the Old Bill afterwards?'

'I think we could dissuade them. We would tell them we know where they live, the names of their wives, which schools their kids are at, and that if any one of them went to the police, we'd kill all their families. Plus I think we could cover our tracks well enough.

And as for proceeds, I think we're looking at twenty million plus.'

'Maybe, Rupert, maybe, but if they've got that kind of loot, they'd try to track us down and sort us out, Law or no fuckin' Law. We're not the only firm that works for the right price, you know. This is off the scale on your famous risk quotient.'

'No, it's not. About the same as Barnstaple.'

It was a barb aimed straight at Ronnie. He didn't care for it.

'Like all your ideas, Rupert, it's smart. It's like *Big Brother* from hell. But you're wrong – it's risky as fuck. It would give us all coronaries. *And* there's no guarantee we could keep the money away from the Law. Even places like Panama ain't what they used to be. The buggers can track it down anywhere if they know what they're lookin' for. I feel bad sayin' this, 'cause I'm sure you put a lot of effort into it, but we ain't goin' for it. Right, Jack?'

'I agree. Too risky. Sorry, Rupert. Don't worry about it; you'll come up with another idea.'

Rupert stared coolly back at Jack, then at Ronnie. The tense silence was broken by another voice.

'I disagree.'

Ronnie turned very slowly to his left, looked at Lee for a second, thought about saying something sharp, then decided against it. He would sort this out later.

'Sorry to 'ear that, Lee, but I've decided.'

Lee leant in further. 'I don't think you 'eard me right. I said I disagree. I think we should do it.'

Ronnie's dander was rising. 'There ain't nothin' wrong with my ears, but there *is* somethin' wrong with your brain. In case you can't work it out for yourself, I don't give a fuck what you think. *Geddit*?'

Lee stood up, backheeled his chair away from him and barged out, slamming the door of the private room behind him. Ronnie shrugged his shoulders and grinned.

'Sorry about that, Rupert. All families 'ave their little differences once in a while. Now, let's order, eh, and put that behind us. We ain't celebrated Barnstaple yet. Champagne?'

'I'd love to, Ron. Tell the truth, there's something for Orbia I have to take care of tonight. I wanted to meet in case there was anything on the kidnap front we needed to organise in the next few days. However, as there's not, I should get on.'

'Okay. Off you run. Let's talk again when you got your next brainwave.'

Ronnie stayed on and dined with Jack and then shared a ride back to Kent, dropping Jack off on the way to Chislehurst. It was around eleven when Ronnie got home. Susie was engrossed in a film and made the most token effort at conversation as Ronnie sat there, a large brandy in hand. He was still fuming.

'I'm gonna 'ave a right word with that little bastard, I tell you.'

'You do that.'

'Lee's been askin' for it for ages.'

'Mmm.'

The conversation was interrupted by the doorbell ringing. Susie looked at the clock.

'Who can that be, at this time?'

'You won't know if you don't find out.'

'I'm watchin' TV . . . You're so selfish, sometimes I don't know why I put up with . . .' Her voice trailed off as she went out into the corridor. She came back a few seconds later. 'It's Lee and Tommy.'

'What they want?'

'No idea. I don't want to miss any more of this film. I opened the gates and the front door: they can see themselves in. If you got somethin' to talk about, can you do it somewhere else?'

Thirty seconds later Lee walked into the lounge, followed by Tommy. From his chair, Ronnie glared up at his son.

'What you want?'

'A word with you.'

'Good. 'Cause I fuckin' well want one with you. Susie – switch that thing off.'

'Ron, you know what I—'

'Piss off and watch it in the bedroom.' She threw a fierce look at him, but did as she was told.

Ronnie didn't invite them to sit down. He jabbed a finger towards Lee's face. 'I don't wanna 'ave to tell you again. Don't ever, *ever* fuckin' try to mug me off in front of anyone.'

'I weren't tryin' to mug you off. You're fuckin' well capable of doin' that yourself.'

'You saucy little bastard. You need a fuckin' clump.'

'Oh yeah? You and Jack goin' to give me one then, are you?'

'I don't need Jack to 'elp me give you a whack.'

'Just as well then, innit?'

'What the fuck you mean by that?'

333

'You'll find out. You're getting too old for this game. And that's what you think it is – a fuckin' game. All that bollocks for a poxy seven 'undred and fifty grand, just so you can prove to yourself you're still one of the chaps.'

'What about you, you arrogant little ponce? Givin' a soppy little office boy a few stitches, and for what? Fuckin' nothin'. That's what mugs do, not the chaps.'

'I'm gettin' bored with this conversation, old man. You're past it, *gone*. It's time for new blood to take over the firm.'

'What? *You*?'

'Too fuckin' right.'

'Over my dead body.'

'If that's 'ow you want it.'

Ronnie got out of his chair. Tommy stepped forward alongside Lee. Even in the red mist of his rage, Ronnie knew he couldn't take both of them.

'Piss off out of 'ere, both of you, right now.'

Lee didn't budge. It was his turn to jab his finger. 'Now you understand this. You're retired, *out*. I'm runnin' the firm now – clubs, restaurants, drugs, the fuckin' lot. I'll 'ave the nod on what jobs we do or don't do.'

'Think you're smart enough, do you?'

'Well, at least I'm smart enough to work out that this next twenty-mill job is better than your bank bollocks.'

'You're forgettin' one thing, boy. Rupert works for me.'

'Oh yeah? Give 'im a ring. Ask 'im. After that, try callin' Jack. You'll find the poor fella's 'ad a bit of an accident. Ambulance should've got 'im to the Infirmary by now . . . Go on, speak to Rupes.'

'I don't need to. Rose would never let Rupert do a thing like that.'

'Better check that too. I'll call for you.' Lee picked up the phone and dialled Rupert's mobile. 'There you are.'

In the Berkeley suite at the Ritz, Rupert tore himself from the sleepy embrace of his succulent beauty and strode lankily through to the bathroom to take the call. He was shitting himself over this, but there was no turning back now.

Ronnie was still so much in denial, he started out polite.

'Rupert, sorry to bother you late. Lee and Tommy are takin' your name in vain, and they say you'll work with them, not me. That's bullshit, right?'

Rupert took a deep breath to keep the tremor from his voice. 'Look, Ronnie, I'm just a simple consultant. If I work for a firm, that means working for whoever is the boss at the time. I've very much enjoyed working with you, but frankly I'm a little confused. I'm not sure who's running the show. If you can assure me that the whole team remains under your command, naturally I'll keep working with you. But if that's no longer the case, then I'll have to continue with whoever *is* in charge.'

'You mean Lee?'

'Well, tell me, Ronnie – who *does* report to you at present? Jack, I presume.'

'The fuckers worked Jack over.'

'Oh dear. I don't think I'll ever get used to the way you fellows settle your disputes. But otherwise, that's it, is it? You're only in charge of yourself? In that case, I have no choice. I only hope you can accept the new management structure with a good grace and stay on as part of the team.'

Rupert had been terrified that it would all go horribly wrong, that they might bottle out when confronted with Ronnie's temper, or that he might turn the tables on them. In the worst case, they could have crumbled and blamed him for putting them up to this. But it sounded like Lee had actually done it. Ronnie had been taken so much by surprise that it was *him* who was crumbling.

Ronnie played his last card. 'When I tell Rose about this . . .'

'I'm afraid I have some rather sad news on that front. Prim and I haven't been getting on so well for a while now, and it's come to a natural end.'

'*What*? You dumped my gel?' The words came out like an explosion.

'As you may know, she's abroad at the moment, and unfortunately her mobile's switched off. I've been trying to get through. I'll tell her as soon as I can.'

'I get it, you scum. You didn't 'ave the balls to do it before and face up to me. Now you've got your new friends, you think you're all right. Well I tell you, sonny, you fuckin' well—'

'Sorry, Ron, I'm busy. I have to go now. Good night.'

Ronnie stared at the receiver, incredulous that anyone – *anyone* – would hang up on him. When he got his hands on that tall streak of piss, he'd . . .

Lee was waiting with his arms crossed, his face a vast smirk. 'Satisfied?'

Ronnie couldn't think what to say. He knew that any more threats would be empty, pathetic, impotent.

'Get the fuck out of 'ere, and never come back.'

'I ain't plannin' to. And by the way, Rupert's one of us, don't forget. When you was guv'nor, if anyone did anythin' to one of the firm, 'e was dead meat. Same applies now. You lay one finger on Rupes, and we'll come for you . . . *and* 'er upstairs.'

Lee jerked a thumb in the direction of the master bedroom. He and Ronnie glared at each other with looks of limitless mutual contempt. Then with a parting sneer, Lee wheeled round and marched out. Tommy bowled along behind him.

Ronnie stood there, listening to the sound of car doors closing and the Porsche moving off. He dialled Jack's number. There was no answer. He got the number of the hospital and called it. Eventually a nurse told him that Jack had just been admitted with a smashed leg and jaw. He'd lost a lot of teeth. He wouldn't be walking or talking for a while.

Ronnie put the phone down, poured himself another brandy, slumped back in his chair, and buried his head in his hands.

'Oh Dan, *Dan*.'

30

Primrose woke with a start. She couldn't think where she was. Oh yes, the wretched Frankfurterhof Hotel. She looked to the side of the bed where the digits glowed green from the clock. One-fifteen. Was that all it was? God, her throat hurt.

She had got back to the hotel at eight-thirty feeling grim. It was only an early winter cold, but bad enough for any man to call it flu. All day she'd been leaving messages for Rupert asking him if he'd got the partnership and, as the day progressed, laced those messages with increasing doses of sympathy as the likelihood grew that the news was bad. However, as the day gave way to evening, her mood changed from concern to mild resentment, and she switched her mobile off before going to sleep.

After a gargle, she thought she would check again. It was past midnight UK time. He must have left the result by now. She switched it on. Two new messages. She pressed another button and waited. It *was* Rupert, but just saying it was important they speak and could she call him first thing in the morning? If it was that urgent, maybe she could call right away. Hold on, was the second from him too?

No. It was from her best friend Emily, also saying that there was something very important, and that she should call whenever she got this, even in the middle of the night. She dialled her number.

'Em, it's me. I'm so sorry to call you so late. I just got your message. What is it?'

Emily had been fast asleep, and was still struggling to wake up. 'Wow, um . . . Prim, I don't know quite how to put this . . . Have you and Rupert talked today?'

'No.'

'Shit . . . Prim, I'm sorry to be the bearer of bad tidings. Jemma Freeman called me this evening. Remember Jemma? Big friend of Georgina's.'

'Yes.'

'Jemma got a call from Georgina. It was supposed to be a huge secret, but that didn't stop Jemma passing it on. Georgina told her she was in a suite at the Ritz.'

Primrose was shaking her head as she held the phone. 'With Rupert?'

'I'm afraid so.'

'Oh, fuck.' She started sobbing.

'Prim, it gets worse.'

Primrose's reply came out through the convulsions of sobs. 'How can it . . . get worse? I don't . . . understand.'

'Jemma says that Georgina told her they were engaged.'

Primrose dropped the phone.

'Prim, *Prim* – are you all right? Prim, please speak to me . . . *Prim* . . .'

It was useless. Primrose was on the floor, writhing with the stabbing pain of those words.

Rupert was sleeping more than a little fitfully in the broad ornate bed. By any standards he had his fair share of worries. Doubts had begun to creep back on the Ronnie front. Lee had put Jack out of the picture, and mounted a successful palace coup. Would it stick though, or would Ronnie be scheming a counter-revolution? And how long would it take him to put one together? Presumably at least until Jack recovered from the beating. It would be awful going through life worrying that Ronnie would come after him. When he'd made the last crock of gold, should he and Georgina emigrate for a while? Maybe live somewhere like California until Ronnie and Prim had got over their initial soreness.

Orbia was another headache. Missing that partnership was a serious bummer. Handling it so that he didn't look a total loser would need careful thought. And then there was Prim herself. Poor Prim, asleep in some Frankfurt hotel. However much he rehearsed his justifications, he couldn't get away from the feeling that this wasn't his finest hour.

Out in the hallway of the suite, he heard the rustling sound of something being pushed under the door. He glanced to his side. It hadn't disturbed George. As softly as he could, he got up to look.

It was an envelope. He tore it open. The note inside had evidently been dictated over the telephone.

> *Dear Rupert,*
>   *You are a real class act. Tell the scheming bitch that anything of hers that's still in my flat at seven p.m. Friday evening gets burned. Repent at leisure.*
>   *Primrose*

Fuck. He sat for a minute or two, head in hands.

George must have called someone while he was out. The stupid bitch. He stomped into the bedroom and angrily switched the main light on. She sat up and blinked.

'What the hell did you put that on for? I was fast asleep.'

'You'd better read that.' He chucked the message roughly on top of her.

'Shit . . .' She turned on him accusingly. 'Did you tell someone?'

Rupert felt his hackles rise. 'No. But you told your parents.'

'Are you blaming Mummy and Daddy for doing this? You haven't even met them yet and already you're running them down. I can't believe this.' She started to cry. 'I've done nothing wrong, and you're being so horrible to me.' She turned away, pulled the sheets up, and sobbed into her pillow. Rupert watched her for a while, then lay on the bed beside her and put an arm round her. She elbowed it crossly away.

'George, George, I'm not blaming you for anything. I am so sorry if it came across that way. I was upset because I don't want to hurt Prim any more than necessary.'

A lamenting voice emerged from the direction of the pillow. 'All you care about is Prim. What about the feelings of your fiancée?'

'I know, I know. I'm so sorry. Please forgive me.'

'No.'

'Please, George, please.' He began stroking her hair. 'Please, I beg you.'

'Only if you promise never to be so mean to me again.'

341

'I promise.'

'Swear.'

'I swear.'

'All right then, I forgive you.'

'Thank you.' She turned back, nuzzled his chest, then reached up and began kissing him. He felt himself getting aroused.

'George, d'you feel like . . . ?'

'Of course. But I think this time we should resist the temptation. It's four o'clock, and I have to be up early to move my things out of the vixen's earth.'

*

Ronnie got to the hospital by seven in the morning and asked directions to the ward.

Jack's head was a mass of bandages, the lower part jutting out to protect the wiring for the jaw. Only his eyes, one swollen and closed, and some of his hair protruded. His leg was encased in plaster to the hip. He was asleep. Ronnie sat down and waited. A weary nurse came by and changed one of the drips. She took a look at Ronnie. The patient hadn't been able to tell them how he'd got injured, other than mouthing the word 'stairs' through his shattered gums.

Half an hour later, Jack woke. Ronnie reached and touched his hand. 'Jesus, Jack. What went on? They came and asked you to join 'em?'

Jack moved his one good eye.

'And I guess from the way you look you didn't say yes.'

Another tiny flicker.

'You wouldn't 'ave 'ad a chance, not with your arm. A

342

few years ago, you'd 'ave taken 'em both, no problem . . .
Jack, it's all my fault. You was always warnin' me that
Lee'd turn against me. I'll get them for you, though,
Jackie boy, don't fuckin' worry.'

Slowly, painfully, Jack shook his head. Ronnie couldn't
get his meaning.

'What? You *don't* want me to go after 'em?'

Again, a painful shake.

'Why, for fuck's sake?'

Jack tried to mumble something. Ronnie strained to
make it out. It was useless.

'Sorry, mate, can't catch a word. Tell you what, you
should get some more rest. I'll come back tomorrow.
Maybe you'll be able to talk better then.'

He got up, patted Jack on the arm, and walked out.

Ronnie drove home, deeply depressed, and totally
uncertain what to make of that. Susie was there and
made him a fresh cup of instant. He described how
Jack looked and was still shaking his head when he
recounted what had passed for a conversation.

'It must be the morphine makin' 'im think that way.
Jack's a born fighter.'

'Yeah, Ron, you're right. Jack's a fighter, and a lovely
fella. And clever with it. Clever enough to know that
enough is enough. What you gonna do? Maim Lee and
Tommy? What good'll that do, eh? There still won't
be a firm left. It's over, Ron. There's a time the old
generation's got to give way to the new. I know it
was Dan you wanted to take over, but Dan's behind
the door. If Dan gets off, it might be a different story.
For now you ain't got no other option but to let Lee run

with it – not unless you want to get yourself killed. Jack can see that, clearer than you.'

'I ain't gonna let them bits of kids get away with murder.'

Susie was getting cross too. 'Lee ain't a bit of a kid, Ron, 'e's thirty-two and as much of a man as 'e'll ever be. You may not like 'im, and you know I detest the little bastard – specially now 'e's done this to Jack. But face it, Ron, at thirty-two you was running your own show.'

'Only 'cause my dad kicked the bucket before that.'

'Don't matter. At that age, you wouldn't've stood for bein' treated like a child. You've brought this on yourself, you know that, don't you?'

'Balls. I'm the guv'nor. Lee and Tommy should—'

'I don't want to listen to any more of this guv'nor rubbish. You're not the guv'nor no more. Let it go.'

'Susie, lay off, will you? I can't take this lyin' down.'

'Oh, you can't, can't you? Well then, Ron, you can take it without me.'

'What you on about, woman?'

'Unless you promise right now that you won't go after Lee, I'm off. I mean it.'

'Susie, I ain't in the mood to get fucked around. You know you don't mean it.'

'Try me.'

'Fuck off, then. See if I care.'

'Right, I will.'

She went out, slamming the kitchen door. Ronnie heard her heavy steps as she stomped fiercely upstairs. He didn't go after her. She often behaved like this. She'd cool down in a few minutes, and come back. He made himself another coffee, and tried to think straight. Lack of sleep plus a thumping great hangover made him feel like *he'd* been the one slapped around.

Soon there was the clackety-clack of high heels on the marble hall floor. That would be her coming to make up. He waited. The front door banged. What was she doing? He walked through and took a look outside. She'd got one of the garage doors up and was getting in her MGF. Cup still in hand, he went outside in the cold, and walked over towards her. She had the engine started by now, and as he approached her, she drove right past him without so much as a look. Fuck. She really knew how to pick her day, didn't she?

He went back into the kitchen. Up till now he'd hardly had a chance to start worrying about Rose. If Rupert had really ditched her, she'd be in a bad way. He would do whatever he could to be a loving dad. Maybe there was a silver lining to the cloud. At least he wouldn't have to keep fretting about Rose finding out that Rupert knew.

*

Primrose woke from the little sleep she'd managed, and dragged herself through to the bathroom to check the damage. It was dire. Her eyes were shot through with scarlet and surrounded by dark Saturn rings. Her nose, already red yesterday from the cold, now looked like a clown's. She felt like she'd aged ten years overnight.

She couldn't face the thought of those dour German bankers. She got the concierge to change her flight and called the bank to say her cold was worse. Having given that bitch Georgina the deadline, she'd have to stay away from the flat till the evening. It would be a strange sensation to come back to a suddenly half-empty place, more as if her lover had moved out, rather than her lover's woman. Would Rupert go there with her to help Georgina pack? More than likely. She would probably find his set of keys next to hers. Seeing them together would be a hard moment.

More than anything she wanted to see Uncle Frank, but it would worry him so much to see her in that state. She'd have to pull herself together a bit first. Maybe Ems would be free for a late lunch. She'd have wise advice too, and it would be all right to cry in front of her.

*

Emily thoughtfully booked the darkest basement restaurant in London, a grotty old place with candles and half-burnt red lampshades on the tables. They ordered some nursery food with thick gravy. Emily started by making the right soothing noises, but her heart was heavy with knowing that for Primrose there was still worse to come.

'Prim, there's something else I've got to tell you.'

'Please, no, Em. I don't think I can stand any more.'

'I know, but you've *got* to hear this.'

'Okay, what is it?'

'Georgina's saying that you tricked Rupert. That you lied to him.'

'I don't believe this. Lied to him about what?'

'About your father. I feel silly saying this now, Prim. She's telling everyone that your lovely dad isn't your father at all . . .'

346

Emily paused. She wasn't getting the incredulous dismissal of this she expected.

'She says he was just a family friend, who played the part of your father because your real father wasn't able to come.'

'Did she say why my father couldn't come?'

'She said it was because he was in jail. Is it true, Prim?'

Primrose nodded and bowed her head. 'And what's Rupert claiming I lied to *him* about?'

Emily reddened, visibly even in that dark place. 'Well, the same thing basically.'

'What? That my father was once sent to prison?'

'Yes.'

'Anything else?'

'She's sort of implying that he's still, you know . . . breaking the law.'

Primrose could stand the airlessness no more. 'Sorry, Em, I've got to go outside for a minute. I must get some air.'

She stood up, staggered a few feet, and crashed to the floor.

31

Having been telephoned by her father, Primrose met him at eight and fled at ten past. The nightmare of her discovery about Georgina and Rupert had already been magnified beyond belief by what Emily had told her. Now, with the discovery that his knowledge came not through guesswork by Rupert, but from a pact between him and her family, her world exploded with the fury and force of a Big Bang.

She ran from the Meridien into the teeming rain, bumping into walkers, getting yelled at, not caring. Anything to get away from her dad, from his terrible words about *Timbookedtoo* and bank robberies, and lies, lies, lies. Ronnie had thrown a £50 note on the table and tried to go after her, but he was taken by surprise by her sudden bolt.

Where should she go, what should she do? She'd left her overnight bag and briefcase at the Meridien cloakroom. To hell with it, she couldn't face going back there right away. Nor could she face going back to her flat with its emptiness, its taunting reminder of a brave new life that now lay in pieces.

She stormed on through the rain. Oh, how very clever Rupert had been. If she told anyone, Rupert would go to jail, but so would her father, and for all his wretched betrayal of her, she did not want her dad ending his life behind bars.

She had walked as far as Knightsbridge now, her coat half undone, dripping wet, and trembling with cold. Uncle Frank. Please be in. She'd left her mobile in her briefcase, so she had to keep walking till she found a phone box.

Thank God, he was in. He told her to hurry there, to get a cab the whole way, and not to worry, he would pay for it at the far end.

*

They both gave her great big hugs, and Molly took her up and ordered her into the steaming bath she'd prepared. After that, Molly served thick tomato soup and lamb cutlets with mashed potatoes and peas, and insisted that she concentrate on eating, not talking. It all tasted good, and for one moment at least, the world felt fractionally less miserable a place.

When Primrose had finished, Molly abruptly announced that she was going to bed, and Frank asked her to join him for a nightcap in front of the fire. They went through, poured some drinks, and settled down. Frank smiled at her in that way only he knew.

'Why don't you start at the beginning, my dear, and tell me the whole story. Take your time.'

Frank listened carefully, nodding occasionally, asking only the odd question. He topped up her drink and sat down.

'What a sad, sorry tale it is. There's one thing I don't quite understand. After Rupert found out that your dad is what he is, why did Ronnie keep working with him?'

'For the money, of course.'

349

'That, certainly. But there was no other reason?'

'What d'you mean?'

'Although Ronnie's behaviour sounds inexcusable, he may not have had much alternative. Without Ronnie expecting it, Rupert discovered the truth. Even if they'd stopped there and then, the cat was out of the bag. Being the kind of person he is, Rupert would have dropped you and blabbed to others. Ronnie probably felt that continuing was the lesser of two evils.'

'Whatever. I'll still never be able to forgive him. Can't you see that?'

'My dear, I would be *very* upset if you forgave him right away. He has been a very wicked father, and I'll tell him so to his face. I think it behoves you to be very, very cross with him for an impressively long time. But never is . . . so very long. Even prisoners on life sentences get out one day. Rupert, however, is a different matter, and I think he needs to be brought to justice. The same applies in spades to Lee. I hope you won't mind me being rude about your own flesh and blood, but I doubt that Lee has the intellect to have conceived this coup on his own. Even from this distance, I think I detect the influence of this ex of yours, so his hands have blood on them too. What they did to your father was outrageous. And what they did to Jack Price is genuinely unforgivable. Yes, yes. We must certainly do something about this.'

'Like what, Uncle Frank? All I can think about doing is crawling into a hole in the ground.'

'Let me think about it. As for holes to crawl into, the only thing you're going to crawl into, my girl, is a nice warm bed. It's good that it's Saturday tomorrow. You'll stay the weekend here, and you won't go near work on Monday unless Molly is convinced that you're over that cold. I'm sure she can find some new clothes for you in our local shops. And while you're resting up, I think you should look on the bright side.'

'The bright side?'

'Yes. In other circumstances you might have married that monster. And for better or worse the truth is now out. That is a weight off your shoulders. Of course, some so-called friends may drop you on hearing where you originally came from. Let them. And there may be others who will take a hard line about the importance of honesty, and won't even try to understand why a shy, frightened thirteen-year-old, uprooted from all that was familiar, and without even one parent to guide her, took refuge in a white lie, and then didn't know how to escape it. Let them go, too. The friends who stay with you may be smaller in number, but you will know that they're real. Primrose, for the first time for fifteen years you are free of those old clanking chains of untruths. Seize the chance. You will never – that big word of ours – *never* again have to fear being unmasked as an imposter . . . Now, off to bed with you.'

She gave him the biggest kiss she could muster, and went upstairs. Frank looked at the clock, and picked up the phone.

'Ronnie? Good evening. In case you were worried, I thought I should let you know that Rose is staying with us . . . There's one other thing. I want to see you. How

351

about lunch on Monday? In the circumstances, I won't suggest the Ritz. Claridges, one o'clock. Good night.'

*

Rupert's parents were ecstatic about his news, and desperate to meet Georgina at the earliest possible moment. Hers felt the same, so Rupert suggested that they jump in the car and do a whistle-stop tour on Sunday, having lunch with his parents in Hampshire and taking tea with hers in Gloucestershire, before heading back late to the capital.

Rupert had decided to surprise George. Earlier in the week she'd made more than one disparaging comment about what she called his girlie car. On the quiet he'd found a car broker, paid a hefty premium over list price, and arranged to get delivery by late on Saturday. Insurance was a nightmare, of course – imagine what it would have cost if he'd put George on it too – but it would be fun, it was a statement and, hell, he could afford it. So Sunday's outing was in a brand new, gleaming Ferrari 360, just like Peter Nicholl's. Except that Rupert had chosen a proper red one. His mother and father were amazed by it, although his father asked impertinently how he could possibly afford it. Georgina's parents said nothing, but he could see her father taking it in, and he was sure it projected the right first impression.

Car apart, the day was successful. His mother gushed endlessly, and George gushed right back. Her parents were an odd couple, whose main occupation seemed to be bickering. The new battleground was the engagement party. Her mother had thrown herself into this with a vengeance, and was determined to hold it at Spencer House in St James's. Unfortunately, the one free date before Christmas was the Tuesday only eight days hence. Her father thought that absurdly rushed, but her mother was clearly used to her invitations trumping earlier ones, and disagreed about the virtue of longer notice. Although Georgina affected indifference on the timing, Rupert got the distinct impression that she was far from unhappy that her mother would obviously carry the day.

The only slightly jarring moment came when they were stuck in slow-moving traffic on the admittedly tedious drive back. Georgina had suddenly attacked the car for being noisy, and announced that she hoped he was getting a 'proper' car too.

On Monday morning he thought he'd better go into Orbia. He hadn't yet made up his mind whether to quit right away or stay long enough to collect the hundred grand. His mind was almost instantly made up when he heard who'd been made partner. Some third-rate woman from Paris he could cope with. But Martin King! The man was a half-wit, a crafty, conniving, devious, Machiavellian moron, so far up Fraser Morrison's arse that he could probably see out of his navel. The idea that this odious little creep would collect a cheque for one or more million, while he was thrown loose change, was more than flesh and blood could bear.

He was on his way to Paul O'Neill's office to do the deed when like a bolt of lightning it hit him. The big idea. The home run ball.

The kidnap idea had appealed vastly to his sense

of humour: the vision of those high-profile big shots crapping themselves, competing to give away their fortunes, and squealing like pigs when they were dragged out to be shot. What a hoot. But he had deliberately understated the risk, and it would be even higher now that the experience and cunning of Ronnie and Jack were no longer available. Lee couldn't run more than a train set, and Tommy's mind was fully taxed trying to pee straight.

No, the only reason he'd proposed that idea was to make perfectly sure that Ronnie rejected it. That being achieved, he knew that he'd have to come up with an alternative which was safer, simpler, involved only muscle work for Lee and his merry men, and yet was highly lucrative. A tall order, or so he had thought. Now he had it. God, he was a genius. This he would have to act on. He called Fraser's assistant and demanded to see him. By ten he was in there.

Fraser looked mighty wary. He was assuming that this was either the resignation speech, which would be a bloody nuisance for Telesys, or a straight financial demand. They had a bit more latitude for bribery – maybe up to two hundred thousand – but definitely no more than that.

Rupert smiled. 'Fraser, I'd like to apologise for my behaviour a couple of days ago.'

'You would?' Fraser was very taken aback.

'Yes. I reacted intemperately and rudely. I let my disappointment get the better of me, which was very unprofessional.'

'It was understandable in the circumstances.'

'I was so upset, in fact, that I went right to a headhunter to ask about other opportunities . . .'

Fraser's guard, which had only dropped a fraction, went back up. This sounded like the usual blackmail.

'They put me in touch with one of the smaller consultancies who offered me a partnership immediately. My first response, as you can imagine, was to grab it. However, I slept on it again, and now I'm not so sure.'

'Why's that?'

'I thought a lot more about what you said about my hogging the limelight, and I've come to the conclusion you're right. I *am* insecure, and until I can conquer that, I'll make a lousy partner anywhere. What I've come to see is that it might be in my own best interests to do exactly as you suggested and spend another year working on it.'

'I'm glad to hear it.' Fraser was impressed. He'd clearly done a better job of softening up Rupert than he'd imagined.

'There is a however, though. In making the comparison with this other opportunity, I can only assess the Orbia I know. From what you've hinted at, we're about to go through some corporate sea change, and I've no idea what we'll look like after that.'

'Don't worry, Rupert, it can only make things better.'

'Fraser, don't take this the wrong way, but I'm going to have to form my own view on that. Ideally, I'd like to be able to wait for the official announcement, but my situation is that I've got to say yes or no to these other people this week. Unless I have a much clearer picture, sadly I'll have no option but to say yes.'

'I think that would be very rash.'

'Perhaps, but it's what I'm going to have to do all the same.'

Fraser considered. It didn't seem to be blackmail, after all. He hadn't asked for more money – not yet, anyway – and seemed genuinely disposed to stay. It would be a pity if they lost him, with all that would mean on the Telesys front. And if he heard what the plan was, surely it would clinch things. He decided to chance it.

'Okay, Rupert, I'll let you into the inner circle. Before I do, though, you must understand that, apart from the partners, of course, no one is privy to this information, so I need your word that you will tell no living soul until it's announced. Is that agreed?'

'Of course.'

'Very well. The plan is for us to be acquired by Synapsis, the San Francisco software giant.'

'For cash?'

'Yes. Those who prefer can elect to take shares in Synapsis, but basically it's a cash deal.'

'What's the price?'

'Not agreed yet. They'll table an offer on Thursday. We expect it to be around four hundred million.'

'And the timing?'

'The partners will meet here next Friday to consider the proposal. If there is a positive decision in principle, it will be left to Paul, Alistair and me to hold the final negotiation on Saturday.'

'The Americans will come over here for that, presumably?'

'No. They've been here and we've been there, so there's been plenty of face-to-face contact. We're not expecting the negotiation to be a particularly complex affair, so to save either side having to travel again, we've agreed to do it in a conference call.'

'Here in the office?'

'Is that relevant, Rupert?'

'Just curious. Is it a state secret?'

'If you must know, Paul hates to be in town at weekends, so we're doing it at his house down in Dorset. Assuming all goes well, the plan is we'll sign right away using fax. Now I'm sure what you really want to hear about is the strategy and the stock option plan.'

Rupert shook his head. 'No, that won't be necessary. This sounds a great idea. Count me in. Thanks for your time.'

And he got up and left, leaving Fraser relieved and profoundly surprised how well that had gone. Letting him into the secret had been a very good move.

32

As soon as he was no longer absolutely needed, the board of *Timbookedtoo* had terminated Peter Nicholl's contract. It had upset people seeing him around and it was best for all concerned if he moved on.

Peter was at a very loose end, somehow not keen to accept the solace of a few weeks back up in Sunderland, but with nothing much to do in London either. Unable to break old habits, he rose early and went to the gym. That only got him to nine o'clock, and there was little to fill the next hour other than to go to a café and read *The Times* from cover to cover, including the announcements of forthcoming weddings.

That Monday morning he couldn't believe what he saw. There must surely be some mistake. Could there really be two Rupert Henleys? He called a friend who confirmed it. He said it was the talk of the town. The background was that Rupert had unearthed some shattering piece of dirt on Prim and, while still reeling from this discovery, had flung himself headlong into the arms of this Georgina girl. None of them had met her yet, but the word was filthy stinking, drop dead.

Peter was deeply shocked. Poor Prim. Whatever she had done, she patently loved Rupert to distraction. She must be devastated. What could he do? Was it the wrong thing to intrude on her grief? Should he leave well alone for a few weeks at least?

He thought of his own case. She had been right there for him, hadn't she, leaving the note on that terrible Sunday. She hadn't made herself scarce, hadn't kept a safe distance away when he faced his humiliation. It was up to her whether she felt like speaking, but he owed it to her to try. He dug out his mobile and called.

'Hi, Peter. How are you?'

'I'm fine. How are *you*? Are you surviving?'

'Hanging by a thread. No, I'm okay. I'll get through.'

'Prim. You were there when I needed a shoulder to cry on. Literally. I'm sure you've got hundreds of friends rallying round, and I know we hardly know each other, but . . .'

'It's very kind of you, Peter. I think it's maybe best if I keep myself to myself for a while.'

'I understand that feeling, Prim, after what I've been through recently. But people need people. Can't we meet, even for a quick coffee?'

'Not possible. I'm not in London anyway.'

'Where are you?'

'Gerrards Cross.'

'Oh, I see. Prim, forgive me, something just came up. If I call you back at exactly twelve-thirty, will you promise to answer?'

'I'm not sure.'

'Please promise.'

'Okay, I promise.'

As she lay, as she had done all weekend, cocooned in the safety of that bed, Prim lamented. Of all her friends, she would be more comfortable meeting Peter than most of the others. And the tragedy was that, after what her dad had told her about *Timbookedtoo*, she would probably have to keep away from him permanently. How could she face him when it was her own family that had brought him to his knees?

She lay there another half hour, then got up, showered, dressed and came downstairs, to howls of disapproval from Molly, who'd made her call in sick, and prescribed a full day in bed. Frank had long gone out to work, so the two of them sat in the nice sunny kitchen, and Primrose ate up her porridge, washed down with gallons of orange juice.

Her phone rang again. She looked at her watch. Right on time. 'Hi, Peter.'

'Hi. Okay, where are you? I'm in the centre of Gerrards Cross.'

'You're *where*?'

'You heard. I want to have lunch with you.'

'I totally can't. I've got a cold. I look like something that the cat was too scared to drag in.'

'I don't care. Where can I come and pick you up?'

'You can't.'

Molly whispered, 'Who is it?'

'Hold on a minute, Peter . . .' She covered the mouthpiece with her hand. 'It's a friend. He's come all the way to Gerrards Cross. He wants to have lunch.'

'D'you want to invite him here?'

'Definitely not. Peter, I'm sorry you've come all this way, but I can't. I'm not well, honestly.'

'Then I'll stay here until you're better. I'll camp in the car. You know how much I like being in it.'

'That's ridiculous. Please go home. I'll call you some other time.'

'No dice. I'm staying here and I'll call you on the hour, every hour.'

'I'll switch it off.'

'I'll leave messages.'

'Oh Peter, *please*.'

'Just let me see you for five minutes. Then I'll leave you in peace and drive back to London a happier man.'

'I don't know what to do . . .'

Molly, no bad reader of body language, interceded for this mystery man. 'Better ask him to come here. Pass it to me, and I'll give him directions.'

*

Chris Owen had spent the last couple of days ruminating on the news that Jack Price had taken a beating. He wasn't surprised to hear from the local police that Jack was saying nothing. Indeed, it sounded like he could hardly speak at all. They were assuming it was some unfathomable gangland thing, a pay-off for an insult or an unsettled bill. Chris had told the undercover officers to see if they could find out any more, but there was nothing so far.

A knock came on his door, and the sergeant put his head round it. Owen had a mouthful of cheese and pickle sandwich, but gestured him in.

'Excuse me, sir. Found an odd thing.'

'What's that?'

'The plan to have Lee Hill's car towed away . . . I was checking up on his outstanding tickets and—'

'I wasn't serious about doing that,' Owen interrupted.

'If my boss gets to hear that this is how we're spending his precious resource, he'll . . .'

'Give me a chance, sir. There were fifteen or sixteen tickets. One of them's a bit peculiar.'

'What d'you mean? Is it green with pink spots?'

'Not the ticket itself, sir, the circumstances. It was issued for a parking violation on a double yellow line at five forty-five p.m. on August the tenth.'

'So?'

'That was the evening before St Margaret's Bay.'

'I know that. What's the significance?'

'The ticket was issued in Wapping High Street – only fifty yards from the Nelson pub, sir. Where our anonymous informant made his call.'

'Jesus Christ. You sure?'

'I have the details here.'

'That's amazing. So Lee Hill could have made the call?'

'Or one of his group, sir, if they were with him.'

'But why should any of them do a thing like that?'

'I've been thinking about that, sir. I don't suppose that Lee could have wanted to get rid of Dan Hill?'

'No way. I've heard that Lee resented how much his old man depended on Dan, but even Lee wouldn't do *that*. Not to his own flesh and blood.'

'Even if it was him, sir, I'm not sure what we could do with the information. Obviously Lee would never admit it or testify.'

Owen swung round on his swivel chair, stuck the rubber end of a pencil between his teeth and looked out of the window. The sergeant began to feel awkward.

'Shall I go, sir?'

Owen turned back to him. 'I agree it won't directly help the case. And I still don't believe he did it. But if it were true, imagine how Ronnie and Dan would react. If Lee knew what he had coming, he'd be desperate. He might be willing to do *anything* to stop Dan being released, even if that meant testifying against him. If he were offered protection and a new identity, he might turn Q.E. big time and shop Ronnie and the whole lot. This could be the thing which breaks the entire gang. We've got to prove that Lee was in that pub. Go over there with a photograph and see if the barmen recognise him. If they remember him being there, was he on his own, or in a group? And let's get Lee Hill in for questioning. It would be perfect if we can hang him with his own words.'

*

Ronnie and Frank nodded to each other, shook hands, and settled down for lunch at Claridges. Ronnie's mood was sombre. He hadn't slept for nights. He was distraught at what he'd done to Primrose, guilt-ridden about Jack, and uncomforted by Susie, who was at her sister's in Ongar and was refusing to talk to him. Yesterday he'd driven over there, and her sister had kept the door half closed, shooing him away. In any other circumstances, he would have ignored her, pushed his way in and looked around till he found Susie. His instinct had told him that wouldn't be a good move yet.

They ordered some food, then Ronnie filled in the gaps. Frank was shocked by how Ronnie was. It wasn't only that he was drowning in a sea of shame; he looked hunched, humbled, diminished.

'Rose didn't tell me that you were only planning to do one last job.'

'She don't know. She ran off before we got to that bit.'

'And what do you think, Ron? Will they really do that, then stop?'

'Not Lee. It won't be enough to be rich. Now 'e's the guv'nor, 'e'll want to enjoy it, strut around like a peacock.'

'It won't last, though, will it? He'll soon fall out with the people he has to deal with. And all the clever new stuff depends entirely on this Rupert character, doesn't it?'

'Totally. And the last thing Rupert wants is to get caught. Think what'd 'appen to 'im in the boob. No, Rupert'll stop after this next one, I reckon.'

'Will they really do this madcap scheme?'

'I ain't sure, to tell the truth. The more I think about it, the more that kidnap plan wasn't like Rupert. Too risky by far.'

'D'you think he set you up to say no, to give Lee his opening?'

'Could be. There's nothin' I wouldn't put past the fella now.'

'Apart from the kidnaps, were there any other ideas he mentioned?'

Ronnie shook his head. Frank decided to get onto other, more difficult, territory.

'Ronnie, I've got to ask you. What *are* you going to do about Lee?'

'I dunno, Frank. I brought a lot of this on my own 'ead, I can see that now.'

'Yes, you made mistakes, Ronnie, but you can't let this go. Not what they did to Jack, and not the way Rupert humiliated Rose. They're well out of order, both of them.'

'No doubt about it, but there ain't nothin' I can do to make it better. I can't force Rupert to take Rose back, and I won't kill my own son, even after all this. Susie's right. Maybe for once I got to let it go.'

'Susie's not right. She doesn't understand. There are some things you can't let go.'

Ronnie shook his head mournfully. 'I know you're right. But, to be honest, Frank, I'm tired.'

'So you're going to let it go?'

'What you want me to do? Beat Lee up? Yeah, I could do that. But what about the rest of them? I might take one, two, but they'd get me. If not then, later. They might do Susie too. Without Dan or Jack, I'm on me own, Frank, and it feels a lonely place.'

'Is that your last word on it?'

'Maybe it is.'

'I'm disappointed in you. I never thought the day would come when I'd see Ronnie Hill run away from a fight. When we were kids, even if it was us against lots of them, you never backed down . . .'

Ronnie looked down and twisted his napkin. He said nothing.

'And I tell you another thing, Ronnie. You may think it's all right to let it go. I don't. And I *won't*, believe me. If you change your mind, let me know.'

*

An hour or so before, Peter had steered the Ferrari into

the drive, and was welcomed by Molly. Having had breakfast such a short while before, Primrose wasn't hungry, but Molly threw together a snack lunch for Peter. The three of them chatted about nothing in particular.

Around two Peter proposed a walk, which Molly rapidly vetoed on account of the cold, suggesting instead that he take Primrose out for a spin in his nice-looking car. Much as she'd enjoyed his company over lunch, Primrose was horrified at the thought of being alone with Peter, and had been sending a rapid series of distress signals at Molly. Unfortunately, Molly's antennae seemed to go on the blink at the wrong moment, and Primrose was bundled, protesting, into her coat, and into the passenger seat of the shapely beauty.

In an effort to keep on safe ground, Primrose egged him on to put the car through its paces. Peter indulged her with a few token spurts, but to her alarm coasted to a halt in a quiet leafy lane.

'What's the matter? Has it broken down?'

Peter smiled. 'Not yet.'

'So what are you doing?'

'I thought it would be nice to have a chat. Molly's adorable, but it's not easy in front of her.'

'A chat about what?'

'Why are you looking so nervous? Don't worry. I only want to check you're okay.'

'I'm okay-ish.'

'D'you want to tell me what happened?'

'Not really.'

They lapsed into silence. Primrose knew she was being rude. He was trying to be kind, to help. He couldn't know how difficult it was. Perhaps it wouldn't hurt to give him the bare bones.

'Okay, there were two things. One is that he met my flatmate and fell for her. The other is that I'm not quite sure what Rupert bargained for. He thought he was getting a twin set and pearls number from a nice Queen Anne house in the country . . .'

'But that's what you are, isn't it?'

'No, that's what I've always pretended to be. The truth is different. I'm the daughter of a criminal. My family's business is organised crime.'

Peter's eyes opened wide with surprise, reinforcing Primrose's fears of how everyone would react.

'Please drive me home now. I won't ever bother you again.'

Peter looked out the windscreen, then back at her. 'Prim, that must've been a terrible burden to bear, and whatever you did, whatever lies you told, anyone else in your position would probably have done the same . . . Rupert only discovered this in the last few days, did he?'

'That's what he seems to be telling people.'

'And it's not true?'

She had to be careful here. 'He's known for a while. Not very long, admittedly, but it wasn't in the last few days.'

'And did he tell you that's why he was leaving you?'

'He didn't give me any reason. We haven't spoken. He did try to reach me – I imagine to tell me. I'll never know what he would've said. I heard from a friend that he was in a suite in the Ritz with *her*.'

'What a callous bastard.'

'It's probably all my fault. Everything seems to be.'

'Crap. Rupert was always sly.'

'Anyway, I don't think I'll be bothering with relationships again for a long time.'

'That's crazy.'

'No, it's not. I honestly think I should keep away from them. I'm a bad person.'

'Prim, remember what you said to me, that I'd lost my baby, that I had my grieving to do . . . Well, you've lost Rupert, and maybe more, but time will heal things for you too.'

'That's not what you thought that Friday night.'

'True. Sometimes winter's so cold, you don't believe it can ever get warm again, can't remember what summer feels like. But the seasons *do* keep on changing. I'm still in pain. Horrible pain, to be honest. But the sense of despair is ebbing. I know life will eventually go on.'

'It doesn't matter if over time I recover, Peter, because no one will want to be with me.'

'Forgive me, Prim, but that's bollocks. Any man – apart from an idiot like Rupert – would adore to be with you, and wouldn't give a damn who your father is or isn't.'

'It's sweet of you, Peter, but you only say it because you don't know it all.'

'Don't know *what*? I thought I'd been through the shock horror revelation. Is there more? I'm all ears, but I guarantee it won't make any difference.'

'I can't. You're the last person I could tell this to.'

'Why? It's not anything to do with me, surely?'

'Please, *please* take me back now. I can't discuss this any more. I've already said too much.'

Peter's computer of a mind was whirring. 'My God, was your family involved in those burglaries?'

He took the silence as assent. His voice became a little cooler, more business-like. 'Prim, there's one thing I need to ask, and I need your word of honour that you'll tell me the truth . . . Did *you* know it was happening?'

She shook her head.

'When did you find out?'

'Last night.'

'And you had no knowledge of it, and you didn't in any way put them up to it?'

'No.'

'And that's the God-honest truth?'

'I swear it.'

'Then, Prim, it's got nothing to do with you. Whether the burglars were from your family or somebody else's family makes bugger-all difference, and catching them won't change anything. If you're worried that I'll shop them, you can stop right now. I promise I won't. There, does that make things better? See, problems aren't as bad as they seem.'

'Yes, they are. It's worse than you think.'

Peter laughed incredulously. 'This is like one of those Russian dolls. Each time you think you've got to the last one, there's another inside.'

'Yes, but in my case they get bigger, not smaller.'

'Tell me then.'

Primrose was at the end of her tether. 'If I were to tell you the whole story, I'd have to make you swear never to tell another soul, including the police. And if you agreed, once you'd heard, it would drive you *insane* with fury . . . Do you really want that?'

'I'll take my chances. I swear never to tell anyone and, in particular, never to go to the police.'

She told him. He listened far more calmly than she had expected and showed no emotion at all. At the end, he thanked her, reiterated his promise and started the engine. They drove back to the house, in silence apart from the thrum of the big V8. It was four-thirty, and pitch dark already. Frank was back by then. Molly quietly filled him in on who Peter was.

Tea came and went, and soon it was six. Peter's attempts to make the right noises about leaving were drowned by a gin and tonic brought unsolicited by Frank. At seven he tried for a second time, and was machine-gunned by Molly, outraged that he would bypass the fish pie she had in the oven. Molly and Frank both liked this young man, and were both reflecting that if Primrose had picked someone like him in the first place, she would be much happier now.

Conscious of the drink-drive limits, Peter protested every time his wine glass was filled. Frank, who had seemed so careless on that issue, abruptly switched to extreme caution, pointing out that a car like that would be a magnet for unwelcome attention. It would be irresponsible for them to let him drive. Whether he liked it or not, he was staying.

Slightly to her surprise, Primrose was ordered to bed at the same time as Molly, leaving Peter to be offered a nightcap with Frank. As she tucked Primrose in, Molly asked her how the afternoon had gone. Primrose shyly admitted what she'd told Peter, what he'd promised, and the surprising way he'd reacted. Molly kissed her good night, and slipped back downstairs for a moment to collect something from beside the fire, managing to whisper to Frank before going back on up. What she said made Frank even keener to have a word with this young man.

33

That same evening, Rupert got together with Lee and Tommy in the bar at the fashionable Sanderson Hotel. He told them of his engagement and champagne was duly ordered. Lee looked crestfallen when he was told that the Caribbean kidnap idea would be dropped. It was the sort of thing he could really get into, and a burst of winter sun would have done them a power of good too. Rupert promised that they would all go on holiday together after the next job was done, hire a big villa, a yacht, or whatever.

Explaining the new plan took three or four attempts, and strained the powers of comprehension of Lee and Tommy. Rupert had to persevere, though, because it was vital to demonstrate that this time, he was bringing far more to the party than anyone else, and there would need to be a substantial renegotiation of the profit split.

When Lee had, after a fashion, understood it, he freely agreed that they could look again at the share-out, especially as there were now fewer mouths to feed on his side. Rupert was so heartened by this that he struck while the iron was hot, then quickly sensed that he'd pushed his luck too far when, having suggested that they reverse the arrangements, with him keeping eighty per cent, he saw the colour rising in

Lee's cheeks. He backed off fast, and they settled at fifty-fifty.

Lee also told Rupert that he'd been asked by the police to come in for questioning the next morning. Rupert was worried that it might be connected with Barnstaple, but Lee reassured him that it was only about St Margaret's Bay. Both he and Weasel had thought it was ridiculous. They couldn't possibly have anything on him. He'd been tempted to tell them to go to hell, and dare them to arrest him, but Weasel had advised him that he had nothing to lose except a lie-in by going along with it.

Both Tommy and Lee asked lots of questions about Rupert's fiancée and he enjoyed boasting of her father's acres, assets, and connections. He made no mention, though, of the engagement party at Spencer House.

*

As so often, the English climate had ensured that what it gave with the left hand it took away with the right, and the memory of those endless warm, hazy days had been washed away by one of the wettest autumns on record. Tuesday was the first bright morning for weeks, and Primrose was given a dispensation by Molly to go for a walk. Off she and Peter went, both wearing wellies from their hostess's ample collection.

'Do you miss Rupert dreadfully?'

'Of course I do, in spite of it all. I can't stop myself. I loved him a lot, you know.'

'I know. Do you hate him now?'

'For what he did to me? Yeah, a bit. I recognise that it was partly self-inflicted, but the way he did it, and the way he betrayed my secret, wasn't kind. For the way

373

he ditched my dad, and connived at having Jack beaten up, I hate him quite a lot more. Then there's what he did to you, a close friend.'

'We weren't really all that close. Much less than we used to be.'

'Does that make it okay?'

Peter smiled. 'No, I don't mean that.'

'For what he did to you, I *detest* him. Truly, madly, deeply. I'd like to get him back for that, I tell you.' He looked at her. Her eyes were ablaze. 'Frankly, Peter, I'm amazed you've taken it so well. I know I made you promise not to tell anyone, but didn't you spend the whole night dreaming about doing nasty things to him?'

'No.'

'Not at all?'

'Not dreaming about it, *thinking* about it.'

'Meaning?'

'All I promised was not to speak about it; you didn't make me promise not to *do* anything about it. I'm not going to let him get away with it either. Between ourselves, Frank feels the same way, both about Rupert and your brother.'

Primrose laughed. 'I know – he said the same to me. It's so sweet. Just imagine dear old Frank mixing it with Lee. It'd be like something from *Dad's Army*. Still, he means well.'

'I know it seems like a joke, but he was sounding quite serious to me last night. Perhaps it was the wine and the whisky, but I thought his eye had a pretty flinty glint to it. Anyway, he tried to recruit me to the cause.'

'And what did you reply?'

'I joined up there and then. Why not? I like him. And you never know, he might have something to contribute.'

'And what's your experience of combat, Peter?'

'A few tussles in the playground of St Bede's Primary School, usually on the losing side. Apart from that, not a lot. At *Timbookedtoo* we had a company outing to an army tank training range in Dorset. We all had a go at driving one.'

'How were you?'

'Terrible. I got the hang of it by the end, but for the first few minutes I'd have been quite a liability in a supermarket car park.'

'So to sum up, our hit squad consists of one elderly property developer who wouldn't hurt a fly, one unemployed geek who's a liability driving tanks, and one woman lawyer who doesn't get on too well with the truth. If they only knew, Rupert and Lee would be quaking in their boots.'

Peter looked slightly miffed. 'Are you saying we give up without a fight?'

'No way. I made up my mind late last night. I'm going to get them.'

'Good. Well, we'd better turn back, or we'll be late.'

'Late for what?'

'The first council of war. Frank's in the chair. He instructed me to make sure I recruited you too.'

*

Lee and Weasel rolled in, deliberately late, at eleven-thirty. Owen in turn made them wait fifteen minutes before showing up with his sergeant. It wasn't through pique however. Just before he went into the interview room, one of the undercover boys reported that Lee was thought to be going around claiming to have taken over from Ronnie as the head of the clan. It seemed incredible. He had no time to digest it properly; if it was true, there might well be a connection with what had happened to Jack Price. It all made the interview he was about to conduct even more tantalising. However tempting it might be, he had to take care to show no sign of knowing about this. All that would do was to put Lee even more on his guard, and Owen needed him to be as relaxed as possible.

He walked along the corridor with his sergeant and paused outside the room to take a deep breath and put on his most friendly, welcoming expression.

'Good morning, gentlemen. Thank you for agreeing to come in. This shouldn't take long. Mr Hill, as you know from Mr Weizler, we would like to ask you some questions in relation to events which took place at St Margaret's Bay in the early hours of the eleventh of August this year.'

Lee was impatient already. 'Get on with it, Owen, I got things to do.'

'Very well. Where were you on the previous evening, Saturday the tenth?'

'In Parmigiano's restaurant in Bromley. With the old man, my brother Dan, and our women. After that I was in a club, and if you want, there's plenty of witnesses to say I stayed there until four, so . . .'

'That won't be necessary. We're not interested in the later part of the evening.'

Both Lee and Weasel looked surprised. They had both

assumed that the police would try to accuse him of being in on the telephone marshalling as well as Dan.

'No, it's the earlier part before you were in Parmigiano's that we're interested in – say, between five o'clock and eight. Where were you then?'

Weasel intervened. 'Before my client answers, why are you asking? Are you suggesting that this is connected to what happened the next morning?'

'Possibly. As you are aware, Mr Weizler, two of the accused were in a Mitsubishi Shogun. We have been trying to track the movements of that vehicle earlier in the day. We believe that they may have had a meeting in London that afternoon, and we want to know whom they met. All we wish to do is to eliminate Mr Hill from our enquiries. If we cannot, obviously we will have to . . .'

Owen was busking it, playing fast and loose with the truth, and the sergeant knew it. It was as well that this bit wouldn't come to court.

Weasel was concerned that Lee would dig himself in deeper. 'Excuse me, Mr Owen. Can I have one minute alone with my client?'

The police duo dutifully trooped out. Lee didn't see why he should say anything. Weasel replied that if he hadn't met the beach-party men and had nothing to hide, he'd be better to knock this on the head, rather than be obstructive for the sake of it. Lee told him he'd been having an early evening drink at one of their clubs in Shepherd's Market, and that the manager could confirm that. Weasel made a note and went to the door to bring the officers back in. When they were all seated, he relayed that truth on behalf of his client.

Owen kept a poker face. 'If I recall, Mr Weizler, that establishment is owned by the Hill family. It's not for me to judge, of course, but I'm not sure that anyone will attach a great deal of credibility to the unsupported testimony of someone in Mr Hill's direct employ. Especially as it's contradicted by black and white evidence that Mr Hill was in fact elsewhere in London at that time.'

Weasel was narked. Ronnie and Dan he trusted. They might not tell their brief the whole truth, but they never lied and never made him look foolish. Lee was a different matter. If Lee was in charge now, as he claimed, and Ronnie had grudgingly confirmed, dealing with the Hills would be a much less satisfactory business. Weasel had already decided to restrict his contact with Lee to the absolute minimum. For now, though, he had no choice but to do his best for the little scumbag.

'What evidence did you have in mind, Mr Owen?'

'A parking ticket, issued at five forty-five on August the tenth in Wapping High Street.'

Lee shifted uncomfortably. Weasel looked at him. Owen quickly rattled off another tale.

'We have reason to believe that the suspects in the Mitsubishi could have parked the other side of the river, near Butler's Wharf, and then crossed Tower Bridge on foot for a meeting in the Tower Hotel. As you know, that hotel is part of the St Katharine's Dock complex, a comfortable walk from Wapping High Street.'

Lee was getting increasingly agitated. This was all news to him, and bollocks as far as he was concerned, but if those two geezers *had* gone to the Tower Hotel for some reason, and some witness claimed to have seen him with them, he would soon wind up with Dan in the dock. He reached for the ejector button.

'Oh, yeah, comes back now. I was in Wapping, but I didn't go near St Katharine's.'

'What were you doing there? A summer stroll, was it?'

He should have said yes. Probably would have said yes if he'd taken another time-out with Weasel, but he was embarrassed about the last lie, irritated that his first contact with Weasel since he'd become guv'nor had gone this way, and a little flustered all round.

'No, I was in a boozer.'

'Called what?'

'Can't remember.'

Owen looked suitably sceptical, and nodded to the sergeant knowingly.

Oh bugger it, thought Lee. In for a penny, in for a pound. 'The Nelson, I think.'

'The Nelson? . . . Sergeant, please make a note of that. Are you sure? Your memory isn't hazy on that?'

'No, that was it. Warm it was, that Saturday. Felt like a beer by the river, that's all. No law against that, is there?'

'Were you there with anyone?'

'I was on me tod.'

'And you didn't run into anyone you knew in there? No pals, no business associates, no long-lost lovers?'

'No.'

'So there's no one to corroborate your story?'

'Not unless one of the barmen's got a photographic memory. Not a regular for me, that place. And on a summer Saturday, even in the afternoons, them river pubs are all wall to wall.'

'Let's move on to timing. If the ticket was issued at five forty-five, approximately when did you enter there?'

Lee was trying hard to calculate. If they had a time fix on when this Tower Hotel caper happened, the smartest thing would be for him to stretch the time he was in the pub, to try to make sure he had an alibi.

'Must've been a good bit before five. Don't recall exactly.'

'And when did you leave?'

'Oooh, well past six. Nearer seven, maybe.'

'Sounds like you drank a fair bit?'

'What you goin' to do about it, Owen? Breathalyse me?' Lee thought he'd got himself out of the choppiest waters now, and the cockiness was flowing back. Owen let it go.

'So would you be prepared to make a statement that you didn't go to the Tower Hotel, that you drank on your own at the Nelson, and that you were in there from before five till well after six?'

Lawyer and client conferred in a whisper. Weasel nodded, and Lee turned back to face Owen.

'Yeah, don't see why not.'

*

On the stroke of noon, Frank called the meeting to order.

'We should start by considering how they'll be seeing things. Are they expecting a counter-attack from Ronnie, or do they think he's given up? Even if Ronnie doesn't come after them, what happens if Dan gets out? Then there's you, Rose. They probably believe you are isolated, estranged from your dad, and in a crumpled heap emotionally, too weak and alone to threaten them. Are they worried that you might tell Peter about what happened on *Timbookedtoo*? I doubt it; they'll suspect that, even now, you'll do nothing that might harm your dad. If so, they'll expect you, Peter, to be still in the dark, licking your wounds. The conclusion has to be that, although they won't drop their guard, they will see no reason not to carry on as usual, planning that last job, and executing it as soon as possible.'

'If it's this kidnap thing, the preparation could take ages.' As soon as she'd said it, Primrose remembered that Peter didn't know about the Caribbean notion. She filled him in.

Frank commented, 'I didn't tell you last night, but yesterday I had lunch with your dad.'

'How is he?'

'Contrite. Unhappy. Alone. Susie seems to have left him.'

'Why?'

'He didn't say, and I didn't want to pry.'

'Poor old Dad. I hate what he did to me, but it can't be much fun for him at the moment, to have lost the firm, Susie and me all in one week.'

'No, I don't think it's been his best-ever few days. Ronnie and I discussed this kidnap plan and we both thought that the whole thing could've been a ruse to give Lee an excuse to take over. If it's true, it means we have no idea what the last crime will be or when it will happen, other than probably fairly soon.'

Primrose and Peter nodded.

'Let's see if we can narrow it down at all. If we look at the track record so far, the crime in Devon was a one-off, because it was done to please Ronnie. It wasn't a true Rupert creation: all he did was to make the best of what professional criminals would normally consider a bad job. I think it's fair to assume that for the last one, Lee won't be contributing much of the thinking. Agreed?'

They agreed.

'So, if we exclude crime number two, that leaves us number one and a plan for number three which, even if a ruse, may give clues to the way his mind works. If we take those two together, the targets are people in the world he inhabits, the world of big business. What they have in common is that they are rich and successful, and there also seems to be a thread running through this of wanting to humiliate people who have done better than him. From what you told me last night, Peter, about you turning down Rupert's plea for finance, I suspect there was a vindictive element there. This was a way to get even with you too.'

Primrose nodded. 'I'm sure that's right. He never forgave Peter for that.'

'This suggests to me that, if we're to identify the next likely target, we need to find a person or group of people who are very wealthy, and who might conceivably have slighted Rupert in some way. Rose, I recall you telling me how upset he was at being given the heave-ho by his old company, McKinsey. From what you said, they must be a very wealthy firm.'

'Oh, yes.'

'And his former bosses there, will they be hugely rich personally?'

'Not mega, perhaps, but certainly very well-heeled. I think Rupert said the top ones earned two or three million each.'

'But they haven't made really big money in a flotation, or whatever?'

'No, they're a private partnership . . . Hang on a minute.' A strange look came over her face.

Peter turned in concern. 'What is it, Prim?'

'Some of my colleagues at Linklaters are working for an American company called Synapsis on a project to buy a medium-sized consultancy. If it's on track, it must almost be done by now. The schedule I saw didn't name the seller, but from the description, it looked very like Orbia. If it is, the partners there might get serious wedges.'

Peter looked impressed, Frank merely confused.

'But, Rose, surely you told me that Rupert was about to be made one of these partners any day. Surely he wouldn't want to rob himself?'

'Last Thursday – the day Rupert was in the sack with that woman – was the day he was supposed to be told. I left half a dozen messages but, not surprisingly as it turned out, he didn't get back to me, so I never heard whether he made it. It's the last thing I'd have thought about since.'

Peter was now perched on the very edge of the seat. 'Wow, d'you think he would have been made partner?'

'He certainly thought he deserved it. He'd worked very hard for it. And, especially after all that McKinsey stuff, if he was turned down again, he would be very, very bitter.'

'Especially if he narrowly missed out on a big windfall.'

'I hadn't made the connection before today, but that would have raised the stakes immensely. He wouldn't just be bitter; he would be livid.'

Frank smiled. 'That's very good progress. I think we've got a possible target. Time for lunch. Afterwards we'll try to work out how he might use that situation.'

34

Chris Owen's elation at the interview with Lee was short-lived. When he got back to his office there was a fax from the Crown Prosecution Service.

They had received representations, the letter said, from Dan Hill's solicitor, asking for clarification of the circumstances surrounding a recent identity parade. He wanted confirmation from them that this witness had come forward voluntarily, and had not been arrested or otherwise interviewed by police in connection with any offence he might have been suspected of perpetrating. It added that, if there was any doubt on this matter, they would not only cross-examine the witness in this regard, but also subpoena all officers who were on duty in the area at the time.

The CPS were not only demanding Owen's refutation of this, but chapter and verse of how the police encountered the witness, with supporting documentation from the relevant officers or police station.

Shit. It was clearly an inside job. Weizler was widely thought to bribe police officers for information, and it looked like he'd done a very good job here. It had looked perfect; now Owen deeply regretted cutting those corners. It was okay to agree a plea bargain or other trade, provided it was declared to everyone. In fact, they didn't have to declare it to the defendant's lawyer until closer to the trial. However, procedure required that the CPS be informed fully from the outset. And that he hadn't done. He couldn't, because he hadn't told his own boss. And he hadn't told his own boss because it had been the middle of the night, and by the next day it was too late. Then what was done was done, and if he'd spilt the beans, his boss might have disapproved and told him he'd made the witness unusable. Sally had told him the next morning that he was a fool, and, like bloody always, she was right.

What the hell was he to do now? He could feel Dan Hill slipping through his fingers. There was only one last hope, to see if he could use the Nelson information with Ronnie.

He called him up and drove there alone.

Chris was shocked by the man's appearance. Ronnie was pale, hadn't shaved, and, instead of his usual highly-polished shoes, big bare feet protruded from the crumpled trousers. It looked like he'd slept in both those and his shirt. His normal air of calm defiance was gone too. Without a word, Ronnie made him a coffee and they walked through together to the lounge.

'What's up, Ronnie? Where's Susie?'

'Left me.'

'For good?'

'No idea.'

'Sorry to hear that.'

'Thanks . . . So – what is it, Chris?'

'I hear Jack Price took a beating.'

Ronnie nodded.

'Accident, I suppose?'

'Yeah.'

'Word is that Lee's going round saying he's the new guv'nor.'

Ronnie made no comment, just looked out the window at the leafless trees. His own wintry look matched the view.

'Putting two and two together, I'd say that those events were connected.'

'I never was good at sums, Chris. Is this just a social call, then?'

'Not quite. Lee came and saw me this morning.'

'I know. Weasel told me.'

'Made a statement, he did. Always a pleasure when the younger generation wants to co-operate with the law. Want to read it?'

'Not particularly.'

'I think you should, Ronnie. You'll find it interesting. Go on, take a gander.'

He tossed it casually on the gold-rimmed coffee-table. Ronnie hesitated, then, with an air which suggested that he was soiling his hands, picked it up and glanced through it. He chucked it back down contemptuously.

'What's so interestin' about that?'

'Nothing in itself. But take a look at *this* piece of paper.' He passed a slip across with something hand-written on it.

'So? It's a number.'

'A telephone number. Try dialling it.'

'Why?'

'Just do it.'

Docilely, Ronnie picked up the cordless phone, and

squinting to read the number, dialled. They both waited a few seconds.

'No one's answerin'.'

'Give them a chance.'

He hung on another minute. Finally someone did. Without saying anything, Ronnie put down the phone.

'It's that pub. I still don't get it.'

'As you may have gathered, Ronnie, our boys didn't turn up at St Margaret's on the off-chance. Sometimes we need a little help to be able to keep up with bad people like you. In this case some little dickie bird sang a song to us the afternoon before that. Made us look very clever on the television news, which we're always grateful for.'

'Get *on* with it.'

'I know I shouldn't be telling you this, Ronnie, but what I have here is a transcript of that incoming call, together with the log of the date, time, and number it was made from. Take a look.'

Ronnie only looked for confirmation. He'd worked it out for himself. The colour was back in his face, a fierce blend of scarlets and purples. And already he looked bigger, less hunched. It was as if an out-size balloon had been pumped back up to its full size.

'What you want?'

'I want Lee. So must you. He's fitted up Dan, beaten Jack, and humiliated you.'

'What's that to you?'

'With your help I can put him away for a long, long time. I'm not asking you to testify. Just tell me where to look for evidence. I'd lay even money that it was

Lee behind the murder of Jimmy Smith. If I can nail him for that, I'd die happy.'

Chris looked at Ronnie. He could see nothing there now but barely controlled fury. He had to get on with the deal now.

'However, I know that unless I offer something in return, you won't play ball. So I want to offer you something remarkable.'

'Oh yeah? Like what?'

'If you help me get Lee, I'll use all my influence with the CPS to drop the charges against Dan.'

Ronnie stared coolly at him, his lip curling in something close to a cruel smile. Owen sensed that he wasn't going for it, but couldn't stop himself flailing on.

'In fact, I've already had a word, and it looks very good indeed.'

'Chris, what d'you take me for? You're so full of shit you've stopped noticin' your own smell. You think I don't understand the law? I know you can't get charges dropped on your say-so. If Dan's case don't go to trial, it's because the fuckin' case's collapsed. Because *you've* failed. And I tell you another thing. If I ever wanted to deal with any member of my own family, as long as I draw breath, I'd *never* ask the Law for 'elp. So fuck off, Chris, and don't come back.'

Owen tried to think of something else to say. There was nothing. He stood up. Ronnie didn't even see him out.

He got into his car, drove out of Ronnie's drive and parked again a few yards down the lane. He couldn't face going back to the office right away, not to deal with that miserable fax, not to have to go on his hands and knees to his boss. He would go home to Sally, he decided. She'd be good to him, would know what to do. Why hadn't they agreed that she would stay in the force, and he would look after the children? Trouble was, she was better at both. He permitted himself a wry smile. He would get no big promotion now, no return in glory to the Kent police. He might even get into serious trouble over what happened at Beckenham. But the sun would still rise, the kids would still squabble, there would still be fish fingers for tea, and there would still be nothing on TV on Saturday nights. Life would go on.

Back at *The Gables*, Ronnie dialled another number.

'Frank, it's me. I changed my mind. I *want* the little bastard.'

'Okay, Ronnie, you'd better come here this evening. Our house has become mission control. Pack a bag for a few days.'

'Is Rose still with you?'

'Yes. And a friend of hers.'

'Who?'

'Never mind. Someone you'll like.'

'What if Rose won't speak to me?'

'You'll have to run that risk.'

*

Ronnie's monumental anger with Lee had not subsided one inch by the time he reached Frank's house at half seven, but the prospect of seeing Primrose wiped it from his countenance. Frank let him in, grabbed his bag from him, and took him aside. His plan was to put Ronnie alone in the sitting room and send Primrose in there to see him. He told Ronnie that they had agreed with her that if, after that, she didn't want to be under the same roof with him, they would ask him to leave. Everyone, including Ronnie, recognised that she was owed priority.

The others had been waiting, drinking tea in the kitchen. Primrose got up and gave Molly and Frank a hug. Peter looked at her with the warmest, kindest eyes. She leant down and gave him a hug too. Then she went through and closed the door behind her.

It was nine o'clock when she walked back into the kitchen, alone, which was not a good sign. She had clearly been crying, which meant little either way. They stood up, and she looked from one of them to the other. The tension was killing them.

She took a big breath, trying to stop her voice breaking as she said, 'My dad is a thoughtless, selfish, inconsiderate monster.' They were all disappointed, but tried to look understanding. Then Primrose's face broke into a broad smile. 'But I'm daft enough to love him, so I suppose he'd better stay.'

Peter whooped. Molly beamed. Frank hugged her. They all trooped through to greet Ronnie. He looked dreadfully sheepish as they came in.

'Jesus. Biggest bollockin' I ever 'ad in me life.'

Over supper Ronnie told them his discovery about Lee, which did nothing to dampen their ardour, and Primrose responded by filling him in on her hunch about Orbia. Peter had tracked down a friend of a friend who knew someone there. Although nothing had yet been formally announced, the word was that

Rupert Henley had missed out. That intelligence apart, they had passed a highly frustrating afternoon, unable to conceive of what Rupert might spring on the partners beyond a straight kidnap. If he did anything to block the sale going through, the partners would have no money for them to steal. And once it was completed, yes, they'd be wealthy and ransomable, but all the usual risks and difficulties of a kidnap would apply. They felt like they were in a maze with no exit.

Having heard all the circumstances, Ronnie agreed that Orbia was a natural target, but was unable to throw any more light on Rupert's likely methodology so, rather than flog a comatose horse, they agreed to try to pinpoint the likely timing of any attack. Primrose volunteered to see if there was anything on that front she could discover from the Synapsis team at Linklaters. That would also give her the opportunity to confirm that the acquisition target really *was* Orbia, since otherwise they could be barking up a totally wrong tree. Fortunately, the junior lawyer on the team, Margaret Wheeler, had been on the same induction course as Primrose, and had no reason to know about her Rupert connection. She ought to be able to wheedle something out of her.

Molly was still mildly disapproving of her going back to work, but was unable to deny that Primrose's cold was much better. As Primrose had been told in more than one phone call in the last two days, the colleagues covering for her on the Frankfurt project were being horribly hassled by the client. They would be mightily relieved to see her back.

*　　*　　*

On Wednesday morning all five of them left the house: Molly to lay in provisions, Peter to pick up clean clothes, Ronnie and Frank to visit Jack Price, and Primrose to go to the office. Frustratingly, Margaret was tied up all day, so Primrose had to shelve her enquiries and get on with some real work.

Thursday was better, and they managed a quick sandwich lunch together. Margaret apologised for being so pushed for time. Primrose took care to do no more than murmur sympathetically, and bemoaned her own recent fate at the hands of the Italians and the Germans, providing plenty of factual snippets about those trans-actions to set the right open tone. Then she switched to the social.

'I've been meaning to get you round for supper for ages, Margaret. I'm sure it'll be hard for you while this acquisition is on the go. Can we pencil something in?'

Primrose hopefully pulled out her organiser. Margaret smiled.

'I needn't bother checking. As from next week I'm wide open. I've had to block out everything, pending this. I'm working on an acquisition, and my client, Synapsis, is in San Francisco. It's such a nuisance dealing with Californians. They don't get in until four o'clock our time, and then expect me to be available until *their* five p.m. at least. They think I'm a machine. It's pretty much done now, thank goodness. The contracts are all put to bed. It's mainly just a matter of price, and the carve-up on their side.'

'What d'you mean, "carve-up"?'

'For God's sake don't tell anyone, because both sides in this deal are manic about confidentiality, but what they're buying is a partnership called Orbia. The ownership is less clear-cut than shares in a regular company. We suspect the Orbia partners can't agree who gets what, and are still gouging each other's eyes out. We've been asking for a schedule for days and their lawyers, Allen & Overy, have been stalling us.'

'Wonderful thing, human nature . . . So if it's going to be done and dusted this week, can you come over at the weekend?'

'Sadly not. Our side will bung in their offer later today. Then there's a final negotiation on Saturday.'

'Couldn't we meet after that, if you're not too tired?'

'Wish I could. No, it's going to be done in a conference call. And, again because of the time difference, it won't start till late afternoon, and could go on half the evening.'

'At least you'll be there at the kill though. That can be fun.'

Margaret shook her head. 'Not this time. I won't be within a hundred miles of it.'

'What are you talking about? Surely it's happening somewhere in London?'

'No. The managing partner of Orbia can't stand to be in London at weekends, apparently. So, believe it or not, he's making the other top two people on their side go all the way to his country house. I'll be round at Allen & Overy mopping up after them.'

'Sounds to me like this Orbia man's got his priorities right. I rather admire him. Where does he live?'

'Dorset, I think it was. Now, come on, Prim, are you just going to sit there with that organiser open, or are you going to invite me to something? And if there aren't some interesting, available men there, I'll never talk to you again.'

Primrose went back to her desk and rang Peter, who'd gone to his flat to check the mail and get clean clothes. She apologised that she hadn't found out more. He told her she was crazy. A date, approximate time, and county were a very good start. She told him not to bother with telephone enquiries – she'd already tried and the only P. O'Neill in Dorset was ex-directory. He promised that, come hell or high water, he'd have the address by the end of Friday. If he couldn't somehow trick it out of the fellow's secretary at Orbia, he'd drive all round Dorset asking until he found some pub or shop who'd heard of him. The man was rich, wasn't he? So it would be a big house. That would narrow it down, as well as make him better known locally.

In fact it took Peter less than an hour. The secretary was protective, and despite his invention about a delivery, refused point-blank to give an address or a phone number, offering only to inform Mrs O'Neill. Pam O'Neill rang back in five minutes. No, she hadn't ordered three sides of Scottish smoked salmon. Oh, a gift was it, from one of Paul's clients? And they'd thought he might prefer to have it delivered to the country rather than town? Pam O'Neill considered and decided to take one in town and two in the country. That would be very nice with Christmas coming. Peter carefully read back both addresses and post codes to her. Then he got on the Internet, and downloaded detailed maps and an aerial photograph of the vicinity, which he printed off to take with him. What he would also take, but wasn't sure he should show Prim, was a grand-looking invitation which had arrived that morning, inscribed to Mr Peter Nicholl and guest, for an engagement party next Tuesday evening. Amazing. Rupert Henley's brass neck was truly amazing.

*

Friday's meeting of partners was grimly tense. Everyone was disappointed by the offer from Synapsis. While knowing that it would be around £400 million, Paul and the others had hoped to push them nearer to £450, and had never stopped mentioning their flotation alternative to keep their feet to the fire.

This tactic had failed dismally. At £375 million, their offer was at the very low end of the partners' expectations. David from Goldman was there to advise them. He said that it was a pity that the public markets had been so weak in recent weeks. Synapsis's own share price had fallen by fifteen per cent. The prospects for a float in February by Orbia were less rosy than before. If they went ahead, they would both have to cut back the size of the offering and be less ambitious on the pricing. And, in any case, it looked very unlikely that the market capitalisation would be any higher than the price Synapsis were offering. After much fractious debate, it was decided that Paul, Fraser and Alistair should be instructed to press for £400 million but, if they made no headway, they were, very grudgingly, given authorisation to accept the offer as it stood.

The low price hugely exacerbated the other open

issue. It seemed that every partner had now developed a hard and fast view of the minimum he or she should receive. The problem was that, totting up their demands, you got to over five hundred million. The quart simply wouldn't fit into a pint pot. At £450 million, it would have been possible to accommodate everyone to a fair degree, whereas at £400 it was tricky, and at £375 million the pips started squeaking very loudly. This time the triumvirate weren't standing loftily above the debate. Even Paul O'Neill found he'd come round to the view that knighthoods weren't the only thing that mattered and, if the worst came to the worst, he could buy one. Neither Alistair nor Fraser had needed to come round. The three of them had proposed a formula which not only had various sliding scales to reflect seniority and business-winning, but contentiously also included an element with a heavy weighting for management responsibility. It meant that, even at the miserly £375 million level, they were looking to take between £20 and £25 million each, compared with an average of less than three million, and a low for the two newly elected partners of barely one million.

And the three of them were determined to fight tooth and nail for it. If necessary they would slug it out through the night until no one was left standing. As long as they stood firm, they should be able to keep all or at least most of what they wanted.

*

During supper at Frank's that evening they pored over the maps and photographs, and discussed the whole thing endlessly. Their mood wasn't overly positive. Frank summed up.

'Basically, we're still in the dark. An attack on Orbia makes sense. However, it's a hunch, that's all. If it's right, then, yes, Rose and Peter have probably found the right time and place. As we're all agreed, though, if it's a kidnap, Rupert and Lee aren't going to risk being recognised, and they won't trust the toe-rags to do it alone. I suspect it's far cleverer than that – more like the attack on Peter's company – and might be executed from a safe distance. Unless it gets in the papers, we may never even know it's happened. I don't see any point in just turning up on spec at this house in Dorset. If we're to counter them, somehow or other we need to know more.'

There was a silence. Peter was the only one with an idea.

'Isn't it worth alerting the Orbia bosses?'

Frank shook his head. 'They wouldn't take us seriously, not unless we could tell them why we knew, and doing that would take us straight back to problems for Ronnie.'

Primrose wasn't giving up easily. 'Of course it's unlikely that they'll turn up there in person, but you never know. What's the harm in us going and watching? Worst case, we waste a Saturday. And we may be giving Rupert too much credit. What if he couldn't think up another really original idea? Imagine how we'll feel if it was just some variation on the kidnap theme and we missed our one chance.'

Frank was unconvinced. He turned to Ronnie. 'I still reckon we need more information. Isn't there any way we can get something from Lee? Or, more likely, his girlfriend? Will he be boasting to her?'

'Nah, even Lee knows better than to tell Michelle anythin'. And the toe-rags know that if they blab to their women, Lee'll cut their tongues out. I've racked my brain, Frank, but I can't see what we can do to find out.'

Frank looked across the table at Primrose. Tears were welling up in her eyes. He sighed.

'Well, maybe Rose is right. If we don't have any better ideas, perhaps we should just take our chances there. What d'you think, Ronnie?'

'Yeah, it's better than sittin' around on our arses. We ain't all goin', though. If it is a kidnap, they'll all be carryin'. I don't want Rose anywhere near the place if there's a risk of shooters goin' off.'

Rose screwed her face up in exasperation. 'Dad!'

'Sorry, darlin', I've decided.'

'Dad, you aren't my guv'nor. I'm twenty-eight, and I'll make up my own mind. Anyway, why shouldn't I go if Peter's allowed?'

'Peter shouldn't be there either. Nothin' personal, but I don't imagine a nice fella like you wants to get mixed up with argy bargy like this. Could be very dangerous.'

Primrose's temper was rising. 'You underestimate Peter, Dad. He's a tank driver.'

'A what?'

Peter smiled shyly. 'Prim's exaggerating, I'm afraid. I once had a stab at driving one, that's all. As to your question, Ronnie – no, I'm not a hero. I'd run a mile from any sort of violence. If bullets started flying, I'd be *wetting* myself, you can be sure of it. But Rupert Henley did some bad things to me and he did some more to Prim. Even if I have to wear nappies, I want to be there.'

Primrose clapped him on the back. 'Well said, Peter. That's exactly how I feel too. And that's why I'm going to be there, whether you like it or not.'

Ronnie shook his head mournfully. 'No bugger listens to me any more.'

Primrose ploughed on. 'However, while we're on the subject of participation, there's one person I do feel strongly about.'

'Who's that, Rose?'

'You, Uncle Frank.'

Frank looked completely taken aback. 'And why is that?'

'Please don't take this the wrong way. You've been amazing. You've organised us, galvanised us, given us focus, leadership, and above all, you've given us the *will* to fight. But, Frank, you're the only one among us who hasn't been damaged by them personally. Ultimately it's not your quarrel. And, don't forget, you aren't as young as you used to be. You'll be sixty next year, and I know you're thinking about retirement. You and Molly have so much to look forward to. What if you got injured or killed? It's different for Dad because he's been chancing his arm all his life. Frank, if you find a spider in the bathroom, you take it out to the garden rather than washing it down the plughole. Just *think* how you'd feel if you walked into that house in Dorset and found Lee pointing a gun at you.'

Peter kept quiet. Privately he was inclined to agree that Frank should be kept well out of the firing line: if anything actually happened, the old boy might be quite a liability. But Prim should have sorted that out privately, though, and not waded in like this. Getting no reaction, Primrose broke the embarrassed silence herself.

'Come on, support me . . . Molly? Dad?'

Ronnie exchanged glances with Molly and Frank, and coughed. 'Rose, could I 'ave a word with you in the kitchen?'

Primrose looked puzzled. 'Why? What about?'

'Never mind. Can we?'

Ronnie stood up. Primrose followed him through to the kitchen.

Primrose refused Ronnie's suggestion that they sit down. She stood leaning against the fridge, arms crossed.

'So? What is it?'

'Rose, you know the way that, until a while back, Rupert didn't know everythin' about you?'

'Yes. So what?'

'Well, there's a thing or two about your Uncle Frank that you don't know either. You often said to me yourself that if you was out at lunch together, and you ran across someone who was in the business before, they always showed Frank a lot of respect.'

'Yes.'

'And you thought that was on account of Frank's success in property, bein' a real gent, and 'avin' a bit more education than most of us? Well, let me tell you, love, them chaps don't get respectful that easy.'

Primrose was becoming more confused by the minute. 'I don't get this at all. So why was it then?'

'In our business, once in a while, evil bastards do somethin' bad and they 'ave to be sorted out. You can't go in mob-'anded, though, like in the Wild West, with shooters goin' off all over the place. That's only in films. What you need is someone who'll go in alone, track the geezers down, and solve the problem for you.'

'I still don't get it, Dad. What's this got to do with Uncle Frank?'

'That's what 'e used to do, way back. Frank was the pro's pro.'

'Hang on – when you say he was a pro, you don't mean a pro at *killing people*?'

'Frank always 'ad business interests, of course, and this other stuff was once in a blue moon. Only ever took a job on if 'e reckoned the geezer in question 'ad it comin' to 'im. It was never just for the money. Frank was the nearest there was to a sheriff in our world. If bad people got the word that Frank was after 'em, they got the kind of diarrhoea that Imodium don't stop.'

Primrose turned and put her head against the fridge door. 'I can't believe it. My Uncle Frank? *Jesus!*' Ronnie went over to try to comfort her. She spun round and fixed him with a fierce stare. 'Does Molly know?'

'Course.'

'What about Dan and Lee?'

'Yeah, they know too. But I put them on notice that if they ever told you, I'd knock them black and blue from their arses to their elbows. I tell you another thing, Rose. In there, you asked what would Frank do if he faced up to Lee? It's the other way round. If Lee catches sight of Frank on Saturday, 'e'll *crap* 'imself. We don't want any killin' if we can avoid it, but if I got to go in there, I need 'im with me, Rose.'

Primrose looked out the window at the dark empty night. 'Dad, I just don't know what I'm meant to think or say any more. How on earth am I supposed to handle what you just told me?'

'All I can say, love, is that every cloud's got a silver linin', and if ever there was a good time to find this out, it's got to be now, when we need a bit of experience. Why not let it ride until after Saturday, and worry about it later, eh?'

'You said it was a long time ago. Isn't he too old and out of practice to be any use?'

'Frank still goes to a gun club every week. Best shot there. Could've made the Olympics years ago, but 'e didn't want to draw attention to 'isself . . . Rose, it's dead simple. Without Frank, we can't do this. We'll 'ave to drop the Dorset idea and try to get at them bastards some other way.'

'I don't want to do that. It'll take me time to get used to this, that's all. I don't know what I think about it.'

'Thanks, princess. So, can we go back in then?'

'Not yet. I'm going to tell Peter first. It's only fair that he knows. You go back first and send him in here.'

Primrose was taken aback by Peter's reaction. He was gobsmacked, but recovered fast, and not only declared it welcome news in the circumstances, but had the cheek to add that if the girls at St Mary's had known that he was a hitman, they'd have found him even more glamorous. Primrose thought it was a very odd thing

403

to say, but agreed to keep her feelings to herself when they returned to the dining room. As they walked back along the hall, he heard her muttering under her breath something about spiders.

When they went in and settled down at the table, lots of awkward looks were exchanged, but no words. Frank, too, was possessed by embarrassment and worry about how Primrose would take this. For now, though, he decided there was nothing for it but to go on with the planning as positively as possible.

'Right. Let's just proceed on the assumption that this really is going to happen, and, whether or not Lee and Rupert are there in person, their foot soldiers *will* be. Now, what are our options? It's not realistic to think that we could get any of us hidden inside in advance without running a huge risk of being found by the owners. We could try to conceal ourselves in a garage or outhouse, but if they're at all professional, Lee's men will check those. No, I think our only real option is to watch discreetly from a distance, and move in after them. Of course, we'll have to take care not to be seen. If the enemy think that anyone's keeping an eye on them, they might scarper, and we don't want that.'

'Why don't I do the watching, and let the rest of you keep well out of sight? Nobody pays any attention to old women.'

Frank looked aghast. '*Old*? Molly, you could pass for forty-five. But you can't get involved. It's too dangerous, and if Lee's there, he'll recognise you.'

'Away with you, Frank. Lee hasn't seen me for five or six years. If I wear a headscarf and overcoat, he won't have a clue. And I'm not taking orders from you any more than Rose is from Ronnie.'

Her husband sighed. 'I'm sure you're not, but just keep out of harm's way. Okay, we won't know when the enemy will get there. I doubt that they'll want to go in before the two guests have safely arrived. Assuming that's right, Lee's lot will probably enter sometime from lunchtime onwards. If Molly insists on being our look-out, she'll let us know by mobile phone if she sees anyone coming. We'll let them get on with the kidnap or whatever it is. They'll be nervous, edgy, and watching like hawks in case anyone else appears at the house. It won't be easy to get close without being seen. We'll have to approach from the back or the side and try to sneak in.'

'Won't they have locked all the doors?'

'Definitely, Peter, but that's the least of our worries. It's more a question of making sure we're not observed when we do it. Ronnie, I think we need to create some sort of diversion. Something that will draw their complete attention for a few minutes.'

Primrose, still a great welter of emotions, decided to be flippant.

'You could always ask the Red Arrows to buzz the house, or if that's too expensive, Peter could turn up in his tank.'

Peter and Ronnie guffawed. Molly smiled. They were all relieved to hear Primrose saying something light-hearted. Frank didn't join in the laughter. He looked at Peter.

'That could be a brilliant idea. Peter, can you really drive one?'

'I only did it for an hour or so. I suppose I did get the hang of it, after a fashion. You control it with two tillers, one for each track. The one I drove, the Challenger II, had six forward gears and two reverse, and a twelve-hundred horse-power engine. It was enormous – about ten yards long and ten feet wide. The turret and gun barrel can swivel all the way round in ten seconds. Fantastic, it was.'

'How many crew d'you need to man it?'

'Four. The commander, gunner, and loader, who all sit under the turret, and the driver, who has his own little cockpit right at the front.'

'But can the driver manoeuvre the tank on his own?'

'He can't move the gun. The gunner controls that. It would be locked in the straight ahead position. Otherwise, yes.'

'Where did you do this training?'

'An army training camp at Lulworth. That's in Dorset, too, come to think of it.'

'D'you remember what security was like there?'

'It looked pretty tight to me but don't forget, I'm no expert.'

'Very interesting. We might need to borrow a tank and a transporter for a few hours. I'm not sure whether it would be better to pinch one or pay a little backhander to somebody there. Army types can be more open-minded than you might imagine. I have an old pal called Brendan who knows one or two useful people. I'll get on to him.'

Peter smiled and shook his head. 'Unless you really need a new one, you don't have to do this illegally. To the untrained eye, one tank looks much like another.

The officers at Lulworth told me there's a dealer in Portsmouth who supplies old Chieftain tanks for about five thousand pounds. They're decommissioned, of course, so they won't fire.'

'That doesn't matter. Getting hold of tank ammunition wouldn't be easy anyway. All that matters is that the opposition think it *might* fire. Okay, tomorrow's our last day to prepare. Peter, would you try to track down this dealer? Ronnie, you and I need to visit a certain mutual acquaintance to get some other equipment, and you also need to be doing some forward planning on what to do with prisoners of war if we are successful. Rose and Peter should keep their thinking caps on for any last-minute brainwaves about what the enemy's plan might be.'

'*Fuck!*' Primrose's hands flew to her mouth.

'*Language*, Rose.'

'Sorry, Dad . . . Why didn't I think of it before? It was staring me in the face. Any lawyer should have seen it.'

'What?' Everyone round the table said it in unison.

'It's just occurred to me what Rupert's plan must be. It's so simple – using his own misdeeds against them. It's the perfect revenge and the perfect crime. And, yes, he'll be there. He'll *have* to be.'

35

On Saturday London was cold. Dorset was bitter.

Since they were planning to go in by the front door, Lee and Rupert saw no reason not to use their respective steeds, so they set off mid-morning in convoy. Tommy had never been in a Ferrari, so he bagged a ride. One of the toe-rags went as a passenger in the Porsche, and the other two followed in a big white Mercedes.

Everything had been planned and discussed. The toe-rags had been sent to do a little recce in midweek, so they knew the general lay-out, and there was little else to be said. They all stopped for lunch in a pub near Dorchester, and paced themselves to get there on schedule for two. Rupert had calculated that, given the time difference with California, the earliest they might start the negotiation was four, and they wanted to be in there long – but not too long – before that.

The convoy pulled into the verge half a mile from the house. The plan was that Rupert would go in first, and Lee and the others would wait for his signal.

As he turned into the long drive, and cruised up between the elegant poplars, Rupert felt on a true high. This time he wasn't hiding in the wings, he was right up front, putting his balls on the line. Not that the risk was high. He knew his bosses' mentality well enough to be confident how they would react. Even if he guessed wrong, he had a safety net in the cover story he'd manufactured. All the same, there had to be some residual risk of something going wrong, which would add a thrilling whiff of danger to the delicious anticipation of what he was going to put those three men through. After the way they had treated him, they would richly deserve every last bit of it.

As he passed the last trees and crunched onto the gravel semi-circle, he swung the Ferrari to the left of the main door of the house and switched the engine off. He was amused to see the symbolism of Fraser's Audi and Alistair's Saab parked on opposite sides, as far from each other as they could manage. Rupert walked over and pressed the old brass bell. He could hear it clanging inside. After a few seconds, the tall door was opened by a thick-hipped middle-aged woman.

'Can I help you?'

'Mrs O'Neill?'

'Yes.'

'I'm Rupert Henley, from Orbia. I'm so sorry to trouble you, but I need an urgent word with your husband.'

'Well, you'd better come in out of the cold. He's in a meeting with one or two other people from the company. I'll see if I can interrupt. Why don't you come through to the study and I'll get Paul?' She put him in a small, book-lined room, and disappeared.

The news of this uninvited guest caused surprise and annoyance in the drawing room at the rear of the house.

They hadn't yet finalised the exact tactics for trying to push the price up, and couldn't afford to waste time. However, they all agreed that Paul would have no option but to go and find out what this was about. He walked through to the study. Rupert stood up as Paul entered.

'Hello, Rupert, this *is* a surprise. I'm afraid that Alistair, Fraser and I are in the middle of a very important discussion, preparing for a conference call. Unless it's something that can't wait, may I suggest we meet on Monday instead?'

'This absolutely can't wait.'

'What is it?'

'I think it would waste less of your precious time if I told all three of you together. I assure you, it's of vital importance for your conversation with Synapsis.'

Paul was shocked that Rupert knew anything about Synapsis, but there was no time to dwell on that now. They'd better get this over with.

'Very well, come through then. But please do keep it short.'

Fraser looked ill at ease as Rupert was shown into the drawing room. Naturally, he hadn't told the others about taking Rupert into his confidence, and he had a horrible feeling that it might now come out. If Rupert was going to use this occasion to beg for a bigger payment, he was mad. His prospects in the firm would plummet.

Paul invited Rupert to sit down. 'Now, please tell us. What is it?'

'Thank you all for seeing me. Could I begin by

asking a question, Paul? Have Synapsis done a lot of due diligence on Orbia?'

'Naturally.'

'And I imagine you've tried to be as co-operative and open as possible.'

'Of course we have. There are no skeletons in our cupboard. We have nothing to hide.'

'So if there had been any skeletons, you would have disclosed them?'

'Of course.' Paul was getting irritated.

'Good, that's a relief. I'm glad I got here in time.'

'Why on *earth* . . . ?'

'Because I've found one. A skeleton.'

Paul turned pale. 'What have you found?'

'It's one of Fraser's clients.' Fraser began to redden.

'*Which* of my clients?'

'Interleisure. You know, that restaurants project you put me on.'

'Put *you* on? That was—' Fraser just caught himself in time. Taking on clients in the slapdash way he'd done was strictly against the firm's policy. It was always the partner's responsibility to make the choice and do the checks.

Rupert saw Fraser's dilemma and smiled. It was as he'd predicted.

'It's very bad news, I'm afraid. I've been truly horrified to discover last night that Interleisure's restaurants, bars and so on are, in fact, fronts for something quite different.'

Fraser looked like he might vomit. 'For what?'

'For serious organised crime. They are gangsters, members of the underworld.'

411

Paul ran a hand through his white hair. 'And when you say a front, you mean what, exactly?'

'They're mainly used to launder money generated from distributing Class A drugs.'

'Holy shit.' Alistair looked horrified. Fraser was speechless. Paul was desperate to establish more facts.

'And, until last night, you were unaware of this?'

'Absolutely. I had some suspicions, of course, because of the unusual cash nature of the businesses, but the penny hadn't dropped. Frankly, I've been so tied up with Telesys that I haven't concentrated on Interleisure very much. Naturally, in my absence Fraser will have held the regular project review sessions with our team, so perhaps with his greater experience he picked this up.'

Fraser glared at him. The bugger of it was that he couldn't admit to having had only one such meeting on the subject after the clients first came in, and a cursory run-through at that. He decided it was wiser to leave the enquiries to Paul.

'So what happened last night, Rupert?'

'I was with one of them, Lee Hill – Fraser knows him – and he came right out and told me.'

'*What*? He said, in so many words, that they were criminals?'

'Yes. I was shocked, as you can imagine, but for him it wasn't such a big deal. He said the police know all about their gang, and they have a pretty good idea what the restaurants are used for, they just can't prove it. Sounds like we're dealing with the big time here. Lee also told me his brother's in prison on remand after getting caught in a multi-million-pound drug bust.

412

Might get twenty years, apparently. It really does look like we are consultants by appointment to the mob. Sorry, Paul. Did you have another question?'

'Who have you told? The Interleisure team?'

'No one. I thought I had better come here and see you three first. Fortunately, Fraser had told me where you were meeting.'

Fraser wanted the ground to swallow him as Rupert went on.

'I was sure you'd want to alert the buyers straight away. I know Americans are usually cautious souls who worry themselves silly about anything to do with the law. It'll be all right though, won't it? They'll still go ahead with the purchase, won't they?'

Paul stood up, walked over to the window and looked out. He replied without turning round, 'They'll run a mile.'

Rupert was still enjoying his noble fool act. 'But that's all right, isn't it? You can always sell the company to someone else or float on the stock market.'

Paul was still staring out, trying to decide what to do. He shook his head sadly as he replied. 'After disclosing something like that? It would be impossible for at least ten years. Our reputation would be in ruins. Frankly, I'd be surprised if we still had any clients.'

Alistair wasn't giving up his millions that easily.

'Look, Rupert, I'm sure both Fraser and you took this Interleisure client on in good faith. If they'd never told you that they're criminals, neither of you might ever have found out, right? We'd have all been in blissful ignorance. How long did the project have left to run?'

'It's nearly over.'

'There you are. We would have been paid our fees, closed the chapter, and that would have been that. Right?'

'Yes, Alistair, I suppose you're right.'

'And, therefore, the only fly in the ointment is this unfortunate conversation last night, which I'm sure was off the record, anyway.'

'Certainly.'

'Could have been a joke, if you think about it. Perhaps he was pulling your leg. You don't have any proof, do you? So it's only an interpretation. You *thought* at the time he was being serious, but if later on you concluded that it was a joke, we could leave it there, couldn't we?'

Paul turned back to face them. He wasn't sure whether he could go along with this. Alistair read his mood and, while Paul was still vacillating, he went for the kill.

'And if you saw things our way, Rupert, I'm sure we could take another look at the one-off payment we've pencilled in for you. Paul, Fraser, don't you think we could stretch to two hundred thousand?'

Fraser nodded. Paul didn't demur. Rupert smiled warmly. 'That's very generous of you, Alistair, but I'm afraid there's a snag.'

'What sort of snag?' Now that they were nearly home and dry, Alistair wasn't going to let go. Rupert's expression became even graver.

'Lee Hill didn't tell me who they are by mistake. He did it for a reason.'

Alistair's right eye suddenly developed a tic. 'Which is what?'

'They'd somehow found out that Orbia was about to

414

be sold. Not from me, I assure you. And I don't suppose Fraser told them either . . .' He paused sadistically, forcing Fraser to deny it. 'It was probably one of the Interleisure team in an unguarded moment, or even one of the secretaries or receptionists. As you'll be aware, the attempts by the partners to keep this process confidential have been risible.'

That narked all three as much as intended, but Paul was still focused on getting to the bottom of this.

'Yes, yes, yes. You haven't said *why* he told you.'

'The gang aren't stupid, that's why. They've worked out that, if we're about to sell the firm, the information that we work for the mob could be worth a lot of money to a newspaper, or maybe to Orbia itself. They threatened to beat me up if I didn't agree to pass the word on to you.'

Now that he understood, Paul's eyes went steely. 'So they think they can blackmail us, do they? Well, I for one am having nothing to do with it.'

Alistair wasn't so sure. 'Hold on a minute, Paul. Of course it's outrageous, but shouldn't we ask what they want? Have they told you, Rupert?'

'Yes, and they say it's non-negotiable. They want thirty million.'

'*Thirty million*?' All three said it in unison.

'I'm afraid so. It *is* rather a lot, isn't it?'

Fraser had been harbouring a suspicion, and decided to go for broke.

'Paul, we asked Rupert if he could've had his leg pulled. Have you considered that this is exactly what might be happening to *us*. What proof do we have that this is true? It could be a huge practical joke. I think we should set this aside, proceed as planned with Synapsis, and look into this later.'

All three looked at Rupert. Would he admit it was a joke and burst into laughter? His face still looked distressingly serious.

'Yes, Fraser, I anticipated that one of you might think that. So did Lee Hill. He thought you might demand proof. If you can be patient for a few minutes, I'll get it for you.'

He took out his mobile, pressed the button, and said a few words into it.

As soon as he heard the crunch of the two cars arriving, Rupert rose and went to the front door, returning moments later with Lee and Tommy. Rupert announced who they were. Handshakes were not exchanged. Paul, Fraser, and Alistair were horrified. Paul felt that his beloved house was being raped. Men like these were the living nightmare of the civilised classes.

Suddenly he remembered his wife.

'Where's Pam?'

Rupert tried to look solicitous. 'There are three other gentlemen in the house, and one of them is with Mrs O'Neill. Mr Hill has promised that she'll come to no harm . . . Now, Fraser, in case you think this is also part of a practical joke, would you like to see their guns?'

Without further bidding, Tommy and Lee took weapons out from shoulder holsters. Tommy had a small Czech automatic pistol; Lee's was a Magnum. Alistair's tic went into overdrive. Rupert carried on.

'And I'm afraid their colleagues have Uzi sub-machine guns. Anyone want to verify that? Fraser? No? Okay.

416

Lee, I've told the gentlemen what you have requested, but perhaps you would like to confirm it.'

'Before I do that, any of you geezers got mobiles on you? Cough 'em up.'

Fraser and Alistair produced theirs. Paul, being at home, didn't have one to hand. Lee pocketed the two.

'That's better. Yeah, we want thirty million. You're floggin' your company, right? So you got to tell the buyer who the loot goes to. Right?'

Paul nodded.

'Then it's as easy as pie. You change the list to put us down for thirty. We're bein' generous. You still get the lion's share, don't you?'

Paul's practical sense overrode his fear. 'We can't do that. The money will go direct to the personal bank accounts of the partners. We have no outside shareholders. If we send the buyers a list with some other name on it, they'll smell a rat immediately.'

'Yeah, we thought that might be the case. So we came up with an answer. If you can persuade Rupert to co-operate, you can use 'is name and bank account, and we'll get the money back later. Rupert won't dare cross us.'

Paul was getting ever more exasperated. 'That's absurd. Rupert isn't even a partner.'

'Then make 'im one.'

'What? Just like that? We don't have the authority.'

'Well, get it then. Ring round, if you want.'

'That is absolutely impossible. It's not just a question of making Rupert a partner. I agree, there are ways we could do that if necessary. The real problem is that the figures have all been agreed among the partners after long agonising discussions. If we cut them across the board by nearly ten per cent, they'll all be up in arms.'

'Then don't. Give us our cut from your own shares. I bet the three of you 'ave taken big fat slices. Own up. 'ow much?'

Rupert looked at Lee, impressed. He hadn't muffed one line yet.

'Come on, let's see the list.'

Paul hesitated. Lee pulled the Magnum back out. It worked its potent magic. Alistair scurried across the room to fetch it. Rupert prayed he'd guessed right that they'd help themselves to around fifteen each.

Lee took a look at the paper and whistled. 'Says if the price is three 'undred and seventy-five million, O'Neill gets twenty mill and the other two fifteen apiece. You all get more if you can push it up to four 'undred. Nice work if you can get it, eh? Frankly, Mr O'Neill, I don't give a fuck who pays up. That's for you to work out. What I do want to know is whether we're going to do business together or not.'

Paul tried one last line of defiance. 'What if we say no? We might lose our deal, but you'd lose out too. We'd be right on the phone to the police, and you'd go to jail for attempted extortion. Have you thought about *that*?'

It was obvious from Lee's expression that he didn't take kindly to being threatened. Both Fraser and Alistair could cheerfully have strangled Paul for provoking him. The Magnum came out again and he walked over to Paul and pointed it right at his forehead. The poor man began shaking. Fraser and Alistair were trembling too. They looked like three oversized jellies. Rupert had to fight back a fit of the giggles.

Lee lowered the gun a few inches until it was aimed at Paul's chest.

'Yes, Mr O'Neill, I fuckin' *'ave* thought about that. And 'ave *you* thought about the fact that we know where the three of you live, where your wives like to shop, where your kids go to school or, in your case, where your grandchildren go? You go anywhere near the Old Bill, my friend, and we'll roast every one of the fuckers alive. Understand?'

A vision of his darling granddaughter flashed through Paul's mind as Lee's voice rasped on.

'So, what's it to be? Will you cancel the deal or go ahead with it and get rich? Pay us our slice and you'll never see us again. And before, Mr O-fuckin'-Neill, you ask if you can be sure we won't come back for seconds, the answer is you *can't*. Except that I believe in fair play, and I reckon thirty mill's about the right number. You'll 'ave to take that on trust. We'll even pay your invoice on time for the Interleisure work. So, what's it to be?'

Paul looked up meekly. 'Can you give us five minutes to decide?'

'Course – as long as you keep well away from that phone, eh?'

*

Half an hour before, after walking up and down for hours in the cold country lane, a woman in an overcoat and a headscarf had pulled out a mobile phone and reported that three cars had stopped close to the house, and a red one had gone into the drive, leaving the other two parked by the verge.

Frank, Ronnie and Primrose left Molly holding on

while they decided what to do. Gratified as they were that it *was* happening, they hadn't reckoned on the enemy's forces being split in this way. What a dilemma. Wait on and they might miss all the action; go in now and they would lose the chance to take the whole group by surprise. They hummed and hawed, then opted to stay put a little longer, hidden behind bushes a few hundred yards to the east of the house.

The second phone call from Molly was the signal to get ready for action. The other cars had gone in too. Frank checked all of their weapons one more time. Primrose was given one as well. Having decided that, if she was coming, she'd better not be unarmed, Frank had taken her to the gun club on Friday evening and made her practise until her arms ached so badly she thought they might fall off.

It wouldn't be long now before they would make their move. Ten minutes at most.

*

Peter got the call as he sat, all nerves, beside one of Brendan's most trusted drivers in the cab of the transporter which, after the first input from Molly, had moved up to within two miles of the house. The driver started the engine and got the massive vehicle moving. It would take them around five minutes to get near the mouth of the drive and another five to decant it down onto the road.

*

Paul and his colleagues took more like ten minutes than five, whispering urgently to each other. Lee didn't rush them. He could see all three were crapping themselves, and anyway, Rupert was convinced that, come what may, the younger two would opt for half a loaf rather than no bread at all, and would carry the older geezer with them in the end.

Rupert's assessment was spot-on. Alistair and Fraser were desperately trying to persuade Paul to accept. They all shared the physical fear, present and future, if they didn't co-operate, and Alistair was arguing persuasively that once they'd got their money, it wasn't in the interests of these thugs to make this affair public. The skeleton really could be reburied.

Paul felt horribly uncomfortable deceiving Synapsis. If this ever came out, he'd be ruined financially and his reputation would be in tatters. He wrestled with his conscience while his increasingly frantic colleagues wore him down. Finally, he gave way, and with a sense of dreadful foreboding got up and walked over to Lee.

'We've decided that you leave us no choice but to accept your demands, and to give it all from our own share. However, we can't pay all that to Rupert's account – we'd never be able to explain it internally. We suggest instead that we claim it's some sort of donation to good causes by the three of us. Both Synapsis and our own people may find that odd, but as it's our own money, they've no right to challenge it. God knows what the tax implications will be; I can't get my head around that now.'

Wrongfooted as he was, Lee improvised beautifully. He barked at Rupert that he wanted a word in private, and the two chatted quietly in the corridor. Reluctant as Rupert was to abandon this elegant backdoor way to a partnership, he quickly conceded that it made no sense to place the main sting in jeopardy. It was lucky that the offshore account was numbered, not named, so they wouldn't know he controlled it. They took care to wipe the smug smiles from their faces before they opened the door. Lee added the theatrical touch of shoving Rupert roughly back into the room, before nodding to Paul.

'Okay, I agree. This is our account number.' Lee handed over a slip of paper from his pocket with the Bermuda bank details on it. Paul took it.

'Very well, we'll amend the list and fax it through to the other side's lawyers, Allen & Overy, as soon as we've agreed the basic price.' He looked at his watch. It was quarter past three. 'The Americans will be ringing in five or ten minutes. I presume we take the call as planned. God alone knows how I'm supposed to negotiate in this state.'

*

Wretchedly, there had been a glitch getting the tank off the transporter. The driver was unfamiliar with the mechanism and twice it got stuck. Peter was beside himself as he kept calling through to the trio waiting impatiently behind the bushes. If they didn't get the tank off soon, it might be too late.

It really was stuck halfway down. There was nothing for it but to winch it fully back up and try again. That took more fretful minutes as Peter paced, alternating between biting his nails and running his hands agitatedly through his hair. Come on, come *on*.

At last the tank began cranking smoothly down, and the rear of its tracks clattered hard onto the tarmac.

Okay, time to get in. He clambered up the front plate and hauled himself into the cockpit. Before pulling the hatch down, he made one last call.

Frank slipped the phone in his pocket. It was hard to get at it with his bullet-proof jacket on. He told Primrose to check once again that hers was on tight enough. They ran through it again. As soon as the tank came clear of the poplars, they would begin crawling forward.

*

Inside the house, there was a peaceful calm as they waited for the phone call. Paul had been allowed to go, escorted, through to the kitchen to check on his wife. Her nerves shot to pieces, and her face streaked with tears, Pam had been pressed into service making tea. Paul volunteered to carry the tray through to the others. They stood around in the drawing room.

One of the toe-rags knocked on the door. Tommy opened it. The man pushed past him and dashed over to where Lee stood nursing his mug.

'Boss, boss, there's somethin' comin' down the drive.'

'What?'

'Can't see yet. Thought I should let you know.'

'Tommy, go take a butcher's.'

'Sure, Lee.'

Tommy put down his mug and shot off to the dining room, which from its broad window commanded the best view to the front. He stared out, then grabbed the binoculars from the toe-rag's hands. He looked through them once, then fiddled with the knurled controls, trying to get them to focus better, or to make more sense of what his eyes were trying to tell his brain. *Well, fuck me rigid.*

All of a lather, he thrust the glasses back into the other man's hands, and hared back to the drawing room.

'Lee, *Lee* . . . There's a tank comin' down the drive.'

Lee laughed and took another sip of tea. 'What you on about, Tom? What you mean, a *tank*? What kind of tank?'

'A fuckin' big one.'

'Let me see.' Lee let the mug drop from his hand and onto the carpet and went to look for himself. Seconds later he was back, his gun drawn, all smugness vanished from his face. He yelled angrily at the three consultants.

'You three, come 'ere!' He frog-marched them through to the dining room. Rupert followed. They all stared out, with matched looks of incredulity.

A Chieftain tank was moving slowly down the drive. Less than two hundred yards from the house, it was veering slightly to left and to right. But it was unquestionably heading their way. Lee used his Magnum to gesture at it.

'What's this, O'Neill? What the fuck's goin' on?'

Paul was shaking his head. 'I haven't the faintest idea. I *swear*.'

Lee could see that he meant it. He turned to scream orders at Tommy.

'Okay, we'll keep these three in this room. We might need them as a 'uman shield. Make sure the old bag's tied up in the kitchen and rip out the phone in there.

Then get everyone in 'ere with their shooters. Who the fuck can be in that thing? The Filth? The fuckin' army?'

He got no answer from Tommy, who was mesmerised watching the tank continuing its wayward advance. They could hear its warlike rumble now. A hundred yards, eighty, sixty. Lee pushed the consultants forward to the window, hitting Fraser hard with his gun when he tried to slink away from it. Behind them, Lee's men were all in position, guns at the ready. Fifty yards, forty, thirty . . . It was clear of the trees now and into the gravel apron in front of the house. The white Mercedes was right in its path.

Not any more it wasn't. The tank reared momentarily and flashed its dark, oily underbelly, then plunged heavily down again, flattening the car and coming remorselessly on. Twenty yards, eighteen, fifteen . . . The noise of its motor was getting deafening, and they could now see right into the dark barrel of its fearsome gun. Ten yards. Christ, wasn't the bloody thing going to stop? Lee barged Paul aside and opened fire through the window. Tommy did the same. Their bullets pinged off the tank's turret as it came on towards the elegant portico. Five, four, three, two . . . *shit*.

With the force of an explosion, the tank's tracks smashed through the pillars of the portico, bringing the masonry of the lead-covered canopy toppling down on its turret, and the muzzle crashed through the door, sending it flying off its hinges.

Just when it seemed the entire tank must smash right through the house, it came to a roaring halt, like some fearsome bellowing monster pausing cruelly before ripping its prey from their lair and hungrily devouring them.

Lee and Tommy went to the hallway to fire through the gaping door. Rupert flung himself on the carpet beneath the Georgian dining table. Fraser, Alistair and Paul did the same, and lay curled up with their hands over their heads. The hideous vibrations from the tank's rumbling engine were shaking the house to its severely threatened foundations, masking altogether the sound of the phone that had started ringing on the sideboard.

The tank began moving again, backwards this time. Reversing wildly, it first crunched the black Porsche, then swatted the Ferrari sideways, banging it against the Saab. The panicking gunmen moved back to the dining room. There was no glass left at all in that window now, only the fragile bare white bones of the wooden framework. Through the great gaping hole they were still firing with everything they had.

The tank had swerved twenty yards back before it stopped. The engine began to roar even louder. Amid the continuing hail of bullets, it lurched forward again.

It was heading straight for the dining room. Jesus Christ, they'd all be killed. Lee had used up the few spare bullets he'd brought, and chucked his gun on the floor. Tommy loosed off the last from his spare clip. The same was happening to the three with Uzis. They threw themselves back as the monster came forward and forward and . . . *crasssh*. The mighty barrel smashed through the shattered window frames and flew right into the room, scraping the ceiling and bringing down a cascade of plaster fragments. Too scared even to flee, Lee and the toe-rags stood transfixed, waiting in

426

paralysed horror for the shell that would send them all to kingdom come.

Seconds passed. It didn't fire. Was whoever was inside it going to let them surrender? Lee raised his hands, and was instantly copied by Tommy and the toe-rags. Rupert and the other three consultants didn't budge from their foetal position on the floor.

At that moment the tank cut its engine. There was an astonishing silence. Lee and the others still stared at it. Who would get out of it? Lee was calculating whether they could do a runner out the back before that. No, if they had a tank, there were probably hundreds of Filth or soldiers out there too. They'd run right into them. They had a better chance of survival inside. Slowly he began to drop his hands to see what would happen.

A voice came from the doorway. 'No, Lee. Keep them up.'

Lee swung round. He gulped audibly and went as white as if he had seen a terrible ghost.

'Oh, Jesus. No . . . No, Frank, please. I can explain . . .'

Frank was standing there alone, holding a small Browning automatic in his right hand. He said nothing.

'Believe me, Frank, this is all a misunderstandin'. We was goin' to go round tonight to make it up with the guv'nor.'

Still he got no reply.

'And Jack, too. That was all Rupert's idea. I wanted nothin' to do with it.'

Frank moved the gun into firing position, both arms slightly extended. Lee fell to his knees.

'Frank, I'm beggin'.'

Frank stepped forward into the room. Behind him,

Ronnie and Primrose came into view, guns in hand. Primrose tossed sets of plastic slip handcuffs onto the carpet beside Lee.

'Put those on Tommy, and those three toe-rags. And on *him*.' She gestured with her gun at the huddled, horizontal Rupert.

Lee did as he was told, while Frank kept a cold eye on his movements. When it was all done, he ordered Lee back to his knees, and stepped aside. Ronnie marched over to where he knelt, swung his powerful arm sharply to one side, and brought the back of his hand crashing across Lee's cheekbone.

'Grass up your own brother, would you? You're fuckin' *finished*.'

*

By the time Peter had backed the tank out and jumped to the ground to join the others, they had handcuffed Lee too, and had ordered all the miscreants, including Rupert, to lie face down. Frank invited the three consultants to get up. They were all covered in a fine coating of dust.

'Good afternoon, gentlemen. I know you're pressed for time, so I won't waste any more of it on introductions or explanations. We know these individuals were trying to extort money from you.'

Paul O'Neill found a voice. 'Who *are* you, for God's sake? Are you some sort of police?'

'No, we are not. Mr Morrison may recognise this man on my right.' Ronnie nodded faintly to a terminally muddled Fraser. Frank continued. 'Don't worry, Mr O'Neill, we are not here to steal from you. The only other thing you need to know is that we are your cavalry. Now listen to me carefully. We know where things stand with your planned transaction. Although this attempt at extortion has been thwarted, you may feel that you have to tell your Americans what has happened. Alternatively, you may prefer to draw a veil across it. Personally, I think it remains in your own interests to keep this affair a private one, but that is for you to decide.'

Paul was still too dazed to respond properly. 'Look what you've done to my house.'

Frank didn't feel overly sympathetic. 'Yes, it's a pity it was damaged. However, if you keep your wits about you for the next hour you should have plenty of money to pay for the repairs.'

'I don't understand. Surely these men and Henley – who I now see was up to his neck in this – must go to jail. The whole thing will have to come out.'

'Not unless you wish it to. *We* will deal with these six. Apart from that, you may have to field a few questions from your neighbours about the house and the tank. I'm confident that three clever men like you can concoct some suitable story. A practical joke that went wrong, perhaps.'

From somewhere under the debris on the sideboard the phone rang again. The sound galvanised Paul, who swept wood and plaster away to unearth it. He picked up the receiver.

'Oh hello, Dale. Oh, did you? . . . We didn't hear it. Tell you what, could you possibly give us another ten minutes? . . . We'll call you right back . . . Thank you.'

Paul turned round again. 'I really don't know what to say.'

Frank smiled. 'In that case, say nothing. We will be on our way. We'd better get the tank out of your drive before the noise of the engine ruins your call. We have a van nearby to take away these men, and we'll send someone round later to collect what remains of their cars. Oh, and Mr O'Neill, before your call to California, I think you'd better go and check on your wife.'

'Oh *Christ*, I'd forgotten. Is she all right?'

'She's fine. I think we may have surprised her, the way we came into the kitchen, and we thought it best to leave her tied up as she was till things settled down. We'll release her now, but she may need a touch of reassurance from you.'

'Of course. I'll do it right away.'

'Then we'll get moving. Have a nice day.'

36

The prisoners were driven in the van to *The Gables*. When they got there, Ronnie drove out his cars to make room in the garage. He bound their legs too, and gave them water and a bucket to piss in.

They left them alone there on Saturday night and all Sunday to soften them up. Inside the warm house, the time was largely devoted to a debate on what their fate should be. They started with Rupert. Although Primrose knew he had to be punished, she argued in favour of leniency. Peter supported her. Frank was more unforgiving, and Ronnie was only willing to be swayed to a degree. By at least condoning and more likely suggesting the attack on Jack, Rupert had crossed a line. He had behaved like one of their kind. Now he would have to be dealt with like one.

Lee's case was worse. He should be made to understand how it felt to get stitched up, but would also have to face the wrath of Dan – preferably after a long drawn-out bout of anticipation. There was no question of grassing either of them up to Owen. Not only would that stick in Ronnie's craw: if Lee or Rupert were going to go down for a long stretch, they would undoubtedly try to drag the others down too, to get something off. No, if official justice was to play any part, it would have to be somewhere abroad where no

431

one cared what the culprits had got up to elsewhere. The length of any sentence needed fine-tuning too. It should be long enough to be uncomfortable, but short enough to discourage them from making things worse by prompting additional trouble back home.

The cases of Tommy and the toe-rags were quickly disposed of. They agreed that Tommy wasn't a bad lad at heart, just stupid. Lee had clearly put him up to everything. However, he'd earned a slap for what he'd done to Jack, one he wouldn't forget for a long time. As for the toe-rags, they would simply be cast into the outer darkness with the direst warnings of what would happen to them if they ever uttered a word to anybody about anything.

In the garage, Lee squatted in miserable silence. Any hope that blood might be thicker than water had been dashed by those words that his old man had said. How the guv'nor had worked out that he'd fitted up Dan was beyond him.

The presence of Frank made the threat even more hideous. Rupert, who was living through his own nightmare, had seen how Lee had reacted to this odd, avuncular-looking man. In the lightless garage on Saturday night he'd asked about him. Lee said the old geezer was a pal of his dad and like a godfather to Rose. Yes, the one who had visited her at school. With words that made Rupert's blood run even colder, Lee told him that Frank was like a bogeyman. It was well known that he'd always kept himself to himself and only showed up in their world when there was one job to be done. Although this was all before Lee's own time, the man was still a legend. He had never backed off and never failed. It was probably their death warrant. Rupert asked if they should try to escape. Lee shook his head. Even if they got the garage open, imagine if, manacled as they were, they tottered a few steps and ran slap bang into this avenging angel. It didn't bear thinking about.

If they slept little on Saturday, Sunday night was even worse. The garage floor was too cold to lie down on and they huddled together for warmth. And before long the garage was smelling like a cesspit inside.

On Monday morning around nine, the electric garage doors whirred open and the prisoners blinked away the unfamiliar light. Ronnie ordered Rupert and Lee to stand, and made them hobble round the back to the sun lounge. An unsmiling bench of magistrates were sitting waiting – Frank, Primrose and Peter. Lee and Rupert were shoved roughly into wicker chairs several feet apart. Rupert tried his best to look full of pathos and remorse. If he had any hope, it was that underneath it all, Primrose still loved him and would want to save him. It was less than two weeks since they'd split up. Her feelings couldn't have died yet. This was no time to forget the tactics which had always worked with her before. His little-boy-lost act might yet get him off the hook. He tried to catch Primrose's eye.

She looked right back at him. There was no softness there. To his surprise, it was she who led off the conversation.

'Rupert, I'm sure you believe that imitation is the sincerest form of flattery, so you'll be delighted to hear that we're going to imitate you. We plan to play the clever game you invented. Peter, can we pass them both the paper and pencil? Thank you.'

Their hands were cuffed in front of them, so they would just about be able to write.

'Our version of the game is much simpler than the original. There is only one round. As you'll recall, you have to write down a figure which represents a sum of money that you wish to donate. Whoever writes the higher figure is the lucky winner, and exactly as Rupert proposed, we will help facilitate your transfer of that money. As for the loser, he will be taken from here to the garden and shot through the head. Now, is everything clear? No colluding, please. Okay, you have two minutes. Begin.'

Both men were so horrified, so unprepared for this that they spent the first half minute fighting to overcome the shock. When Lee's head cleared, he knew right away he had an impossible task. His share of the first two jobs had been less than Rupert's, and he didn't have much of the ready before that. Had he told Rupert that? He couldn't remember. He looked over at him. Shit, this was tricky.

Rupert was trembling and sweating; his throat was dry. What would have been Lee's cut of the first two crimes? Had they been paid out yet, or were they still in some family account beyond his reach? And how much did he have before that? Maybe not very much. He totally, absolutely, did not want to lose this, but if it turned out he'd handed over most of his loot unnecessarily, that would be incredibly galling. He glanced over at Lee. Shit, this was tricky.

434

Primrose was watching the clock. 'You have thirty seconds left.'

They looked at each other again.

'Fifteen seconds. Ten . . . Five . . .'

Frantically, they both scribbled something.

'. . . Time. Pencils down. Peter, would you mind . . . ?'

As Peter stepped forward to collect the papers, Rupert had a panic attack and grabbed the pencil again. Handcuffed as he was, his movements were awkward, and the sheet was whisked away before he could change it.

Peter passed the papers over to Primrose, who took a look, handed them to Frank, and on to Ronnie. Lee and Rupert were both leaning right forward in the chairs, half mad with fear and anxiety. Milking the moment for all it was worth, Primrose took the papers back and re-examined them in a leisurely manner, before addressing the two wretched victims.

'Well, gentlemen, you'll be pleased to hear we have a clear result. No messy draw, or spoiled papers, or anything like that. Would you like to hear it? Rupert has gone for a round million. Lee for one point two five.'

Lee looked mightily relieved. Rupert looked up at the roof.

'Why didn't I go higher, for fuck's sake? I *knew* it. That's why I wanted to change it.' He looked imploringly at Primrose. 'Please, Prim, I *beg* you. Can't we have another round? What about best of three?'

Lee wasn't having any of it. 'Balls to that, mate. You lost fair and square.'

Primrose nodded. 'Lee's right.'

Rupert hadn't given up yet. 'Prim, Prim . . . for the sake of the love we shared, have mercy, please.'

'Sorry, Rupert. This time it's impersonal. Well, there we are. I'm afraid we haven't got all day: I should be getting to work. Peter, can you get a phone for Lee, please, so he can get on with the transfer? He'll need to have one hand free, so let's cuff the other one to that rubber plant. Thank you. Frank, Dad, would you be good enough to take Rupert out into the garden? Try not to make too much of a mess.'

Rupert couldn't believe that they were going to do it right there and then. As they came over to get him, he reached new depths of terror.

'Oh no, no. Please don't. *Please*. My family's got money too. Great pots of it. You can have that.'

Ronnie shook his head. 'We don't want it. Now, come on, Rupes, take your medicine like a man.'

'No, I *shan't*. You can't do this – it's against the law!'

'Okay, we'll do it the 'ard way.' As they moved to grab him, Rupert threw himself on the floor and tried to curl his legs under a wicker sofa chair.

Ronnie sighed. 'What a pathetic little prat.' He lifted the sofa clear away. 'Grab 'is left leg, Frank, I'll get the right.'

Rupert started kicking furiously. It took twenty seconds to catch the flailing limbs and subdue him. Ronnie was already out of breath.

'Come on, Frank, let's drag the fucker. On the count of three . . . one, two, three.' Off they went, out of the sun lounge, banging Rupert's head hard several times on the crazy paving, then over the grass to a tree where they'd prepared a rope.

The whole way he was yelling hysterically. When he

saw the rope and a gun with a silencer next to it, he switched to sobbing. As they went to pull him to his feet, he strained every sinew clinging to mother earth. Ronnie couldn't be bothered.

'Never mind, Frank, I'll tie 'im to the bottom of the trunk. You can shoot 'im there.'

Ronnie did the tying, while Frank reached in his pocket for an ammunition clip; he clicked it in place, and then screwed on the silencer.

Rupert was still wailing. '*Please* don't. I'm so sorry, Ronnie. I'll do whatever you want. Marry Primrose, anything.'

Ronnie cuffed him. 'You cheeky little fucker. You think my gel would marry you now?'

'Okay, I'm sorry, I'm sorry. But I'll do anything else. And you can have all my money. Only please, *please*, don't kill me.'

Ronnie crossed his arms. 'Anything, you say?'

'Anything. I promise.'

'And you'll wire all of your share of them two jobs, plus the bonus I gave you?'

'Yes, yes.'

Ronnie scratched the back of his pate and looked at Frank. 'Tell you what, why don't we give 'im a reprieve of an hour while we see if there's anything particular we want 'im to do? In the meantime Rupert can get on with the wire transfer. What you say, Frank?'

Frank looked unimpressed. 'Ron, you know me. Once I've started a job I like to finish it.'

The desperate hope in Rupert's eyes gave way again to total terror. Frank checked the gun again and aimed it straight at Rupert's temple. Then he lowered it again.

'But you're the guv'nor, so maybe I can make an exception just this once.'

He began unscrewing the silencer. Rupert threw himself forward and hugged Ronnie's ankles.

'Oh, thank you, thank you.'

'Don't thank me too much. You ain't out of the woods yet.'

Rupert stumbled to his feet and they led him inside.

It took two hours, and by the end of it Rupert, like Lee, was cleaned out. Ronnie came back in to see him.

'Okay, Rupert, there's an errand I need run. I owe a business associate in Marbella some cash. You'll take it down tomorrow.'

'And that's all?' Rupert couldn't believe his luck. He'd assumed that as a minimum he'd have to run the gauntlet of a drugs run. 'How much?'

'Not a lot. Three, four 'undred thousand dollars. But it's important. I need someone I can trust.'

'Would I go on my own?' Rupert was already wondering about bolting once he was away from them.

'I might send Lee down with you. That little fucker's got to earn some brownie points too.'

'And after we get back from Spain . . . is that it? Do I have to do anything else?'

'As soon as you're out of Spain, you're a free man.'

Rupert breathed a huge sigh of relief. If this wasn't a hoax, it seemed that there *was* light at the end of the tunnel. Yes, he'd lost all his money and, presumably, his job, but basically everything else was intact. Orbia would have to handle his departure discreetly, so his reputation wouldn't be totally trashed. And he was going to marry an heiress. *Oh Christ*, he'd forgotten the party. If he missed that, she'd never forgive him. She might even break the engagement. He *had* to be there.

'Er, Ronnie. Is there any flexibility on the timing of this run? It's just that I've got a vital meeting tomorrow evening.'

'What time is it?'

'Seven o'clock.' Rupert was amazed that Ronnie had become so calm and reasonable so quickly.

'Shouldn't be a problem. You can be there and back in one day. There's a flight that gets into Gatwick around five.'

'Great. Ronnie, I don't suppose I could make one quick call to confirm that I'll make the meeting?'

'Be my guest.' Ronnie fetched a phone.

'I don't suppose you could take the cuffs off while I do it?'

'You can manage as you are. I'll dial for you. Say you'll be there, that's all. Then I'll cut you off. What's the number?'

When Georgina answered, she erupted. Rupert shut her up long enough to utter the vital words, and the call was cut off before her full lava flow engulfed him. It was lucky that she'd spent the weekend at her parents' place, and wouldn't have got back to Methley Street until yesterday evening. Methley Street triggered a basic practical thought.

'Ronnie, I'll need my passport, won't I? Shall I pop round to my house this evening?'

'Don't worry, we'll get it for you. You gave Rose a key, remember. As long as you ain't changed the locks,

439

we'll manage. And don't worry, we'll make sure we don't bump into that new gel of yours. Right, I better go and 'ave a word with Lee. Frank'll put you back in the garage.'

'Do I have to go back there? It's so cold.'

'Sorry, Rupert, security.'

'What about something to eat? I'm *starving*.'

'Peter's fed the others while you was out, but there might be a few scraps left.'

As Rupert was being led back, Ronnie went into the sun lounge, where Lee was poorer, but beginning to relax. He could always make more money. If this was his only punishment, it was no more than a slap on the wrist. He'd get his own back in due course, when they weren't expecting it. On the old man, Prim, Frank even, if he could catch him unawares. Ronnie came in, nodded to Peter and Prim, and sat down.

'Guess what, Lee? Good news.'

'What's that?'

'Got a call from Weasel. Case against Dan's collapsed. They're lettin' 'im out tomorrow.'

Shit. Lee felt his gut tighten. 'Good.'

'Yeah, thought you'd be pleased. We'll 'ave to go and get the fella, welcome 'im back. You up for that?'

Lee looked very unsure.

'Unless you're busy tomorrow, of course. Dan don't yet know what I know. Whether I tell 'im or not depends on whether you're back in my good books. Not sure you ever will be, tell the truth, but if you try 'ard enough, you never know. There's an errand you could run for me tomorrow. With Rupert.'

440

'*Rupert*? I thought 'e was fuckin' dead.'

'We changed our minds. Decided to show the lad some mercy, like I might do with you. So? Want to do it?'

'Depends, don't it. What is it?'

'Takin' some money to a man called Mendoza.'

Lee was suspicious. 'Who's 'e?'

'Old drinkin' pal of mine in Marbella. The money's a down payment on some charlie. I'm back on the old game, and I need a new source.'

'I ain't bringin' any gear in, if that's what you mean.'

'You give the man the cash and fly back, that's all. Frank and I'll come out to the airport to see you off and meet you.'

'This ain't a fit-up, is it?'

'Don't go if you're that worried about it. Stay and see Dan.'

'No, I'll do it.'

Despite his noisy objections, Lee was also put back in the garage. Over coffee in the kitchen, Ronnie casually related Rupert's keenness to get back for some meeting. Peter blurted out something about the engagement party, and immediately regretted it. Primrose's lips trembled slightly. Despite everything, that news clearly still stung. She tried to sound cool.

'Where is it?'

'Spencer House. Believe it or not, Rupert had the cheek to invite me and a guest. Sorry, Prim, I should've kept quiet about it.'

'No, you did the right thing. I would've heard sooner or later.'

Around noon on Tuesday, Rupert and Lee stepped off the Iberia flight. The weather was beautiful. They went through Immigration and Customs without any problem, Rupert carrying the big briefcase with the money. As they'd been told, there was a driver to meet them, and they were whisked away in a black Mercedes.

The drive was short and uneventful. At the restaurant two bulky men in light suits and sunglasses were waiting for them. After handshakes, a huge pan of paella was put in front of them, washed down with Rioja.

Rupert kept looking at his watch. He hadn't been allowed to speak again to Georgina, and had a pretty good idea of the mood she would be working up. He wanted to get back a long time before the party got underway. And these men made him twitchy, the way they said so little, just ate and stared. The sooner this was over and they were back on the plane, the better. As the plates were being cleared away Rupert nudged Lee, who slid the briefcase to the opposite side of the table.

One of the men shoved it back. No, their boss, Mr Mendoza, wanted to thank them in person. He'd been busy at lunchtime, but soon he should be back at his house. They would meet him there. Rupert and Lee glanced at each other. They had no choice. From the bulges in their jackets, it was obvious these men were carrying.

The second ride was taking longer, and time was ticking

by. They needed to be back at the airport by three-thirty, and it was already a quarter past two. They asked how much further it was and were told 'not far'. The road curled on and on. Soon after Rupert's fourth and most frantic enquiry, they drove through the gates of an imposing villa.

An old peasant woman opened the door. She muttered something to the men, who explained that Señor Mendoza had called to say he would be another few minutes. Since Señor Mendoza preferred to drive his guests to the airport in person, they would be on their way.

When they left, Rupert and Lee sat down. Within minutes they were both fidgeting. This was ridiculous. It was twenty to three, and they had no idea how long it would take to get from this place to the airport. If Mendoza didn't turn up soon, they would have no choice but to get the old woman to call for a taxi, and leave the money in her care. Maybe they should order one right away as a fallback. Since Lee knew no Spanish, and Rupert had a rudimentary knowledge, he was deputed to go and ask her.

He went through to the kitchen. She wasn't there. Beyond it, the door to the terrace was open. Very open, in fact. Someone had made a right old mess of the lock. There was no one on the terrace either, or by the pool. Same story at the tennis court and in the garden. She must be somewhere inside.

He called out as he looked around in the utility room, the gym, the bedrooms and the dining room. No sign. What was this little room? Some sort of study, maybe. He put his head round the door. His eye caught a half-open wall safe, and his curiosity was too strong to resist the temptation to peek inside. He pulled it open. How disappointing. He went back to find Lee.

Lee was pacing round agitatedly. This didn't feel right, and hearing from Rupert that the servant seemed to have vanished did nothing to help his peace of mind. He wanted to get out of there. As Rupert started to say something, Lee held up a hand.

'Ssh . . . There's a car comin'. Must be Mendoza. Okay, let's get the bag, jump right in the car, and tell 'im to take us to the airport straight away.'

Rupert grabbed it, and they made for the front door. Lee was right. If they went now, they should just make it, but there was no time to waste on politeness. Through the coloured glass door, they could hear the sound and see the shape of the car pulling up. Quick, quick, before he got out. Lee threw open the door and they rushed out.

What the *hell* was this? What was a patrol car doing here, and why were these police officers pointing guns?

*

By one o'clock, everything was ready for Dan's welcome-home lunch. The kids had come over earlier, and were running round the house like rabid rabbits. The chef from Parmigiano had prepared a grand buffet. Sadly it would be another week before Jack was discharged, so he wouldn't be able to join them. Maybe they would all go and visit him later on.

Maureen had decided that she wanted to go alone to the prison to collect him, so Ronnie had arranged a limo and left it at that. By now they were just hanging around, and it was time for a much-delayed conversation. Primrose and Peter sat him down.

'Okay, Dad, you know what this is about. We're all glad that Rupert and Lee lost their ill-gotten gains. That still leaves the fact that most of the money effectively came from *Timbookedtoo* shareholders.'

Ronnie nodded. 'Yeah, I know, Peter. I owe you a cut. What about 'alf of what we got back from them two?'

Primrose answered for him. 'Half of *that*? You've got a nerve, Dad. It's over ten million you made from his company.'

Ronnie pulled a face. That money was his retirement plan. 'Okay, a third of the lot. Call it a round three million.'

Primrose yelled at his mathematics, but Peter intervened.

'Thanks, Prim, but I can answer for myself. I know what I want.'

Ronnie looked wary. 'What?'

'All of it. All ten point seven million.'

'You're a right greedy bastard, Peter. No way. I'll give you 'alf, tops.'

'Sorry, Ronnie, that won't do it for me.'

Ronnie flicked a glance at Primrose, hoping for a measure of support. She was looking very beadily back at him.

'Okay, two thirds. That's my absolute best offer. I ain't budgin'. Come on now, Dan'll be 'ere any minute. Let's shake on it, eh?'

'Dad, if you don't agree right now to what Peter wants, you'll have not so much gained a son as lost a daughter.'

'Come on, Prim, I know we done wrong by Peter, and if I'd known what a smashin' fella 'e is, we'd've picked on some other company. But for 'im to want the full ten mill, it's too much. Come on, share and share alike.'

Peter smiled. 'It's not for me, Ronnie.'

'What? You said that—'

'Yes, I want you to hand over all that money. If we're to be friends, I can't tolerate the fact that you got rich at the expense of my shareholders. But I don't want a penny of it for myself.'

'So what you wanna do with it? Give it back to the shareholders? 'ow can you do that, without givin' the whole game away?'

'I can't, more's the pity.'

'So what do you want to do with it?'

'Give it to charity.'

'To *charity*? Who d'you think I am? Robin bleedin' 'ood? Charity begins at 'ome, remember.'

'Not in this case.'

'If I give that lot to a charity, it'll stick out like a sore thumb.'

'I'm sure they're used to coping with large contributions from donors who want to remain anonymous. Or you could spread it round a whole range of charities. You can pick what they are. I don't care who gets it, as long as they're worthy causes and *you* don't keep any.'

Ronnie knew he was beaten. A wry smile flickered on his lips. 'Do political parties count as worthy?'

'Definitely not. Why? Are you interested in politics?'

'Not as such. I quite fancy a peerage though.'

Primrose chuckled. 'Lord Hill of the Scrubs? It's got

a ring to it, all right. Come on, Dad, what's it to be? I'll help you pick. How about Battersea Dogs' Home, Save the Children, or Cancer Research?'

'Okay then.' Might as well take it with a good grace. 'A mill to the dogs, two mill to the kids, and the rest to the old Cancer Research. That satisfy you, Peter?'

'Perfect. Oh, one more thing . . .'

'What now?'

'About the money you stole from those banks in Barnstaple . . .'

'Fuck me, you're not after that too, are you? Come on, a fella's got to be allowed to earn an honest living.'

'That was what I was going to say. I've always hated banks, the whole stinking lot of them. They wouldn't lend me a penny when I was getting the company started. Bugger them. You can keep it, with my blessing.'

'Well, I s'pose I got to be grateful for small mercies.' The doorbell sounded, and the two children in a nearby room started whooping excitedly. 'That sounds like Dan. Let's go and give the boy a welcome, eh?'

They went out to the drive. As the gates opened, a limo swept in, followed a few seconds later by an MGF. What was Susie doing here? How did she know? Had Frank or Molly tipped her off?

*

By six, Georgina Parham was a very unhappy bunny. By six-thirty, having gone over to the gaudy magnificence of Spencer House, she was livid. By ten to seven, she was homicidal. For the fiftieth time she tried his mobile. *Off.* Right, that was it. She stomped over to Rupert's parents, who had turned up early and were deeply regretting it.

'Where the hell is he? This is *outrageous*. Are *all* your children so ill-mannered?'

Rupert's father wasn't sure he liked the girl's tone. This was very different from the charming visitor of the other day. Okay, so their son was a bit late. Georgina had better get used to it. Management consultants always lived life on the run. His wife tried to strike a friendlier note.

'I'm afraid punctuality has never been a strong point with Rupert. I remember when he was fourteen, he . . .'

Georgina glared at her. 'Mrs Henley, I don't give a damn what he did when he was fourteen. Unless he's here in . . .' she checked her gold Cartier watch '. . . five minutes, I'm washing my hands of him, I tell you.' She stalked off back to her parents, and berated them too.

At seven on the hour the first guests started arriving. Georgina was overcome with panicky embarrassment. Should she hide in the loo, or stick it out? Better stick it out. Rupert probably *would* turn up at any minute. After the party was over, she'd give him a level of hell he'd never experienced before. For now, though, there were appearances to be kept up. She smiled radiantly and went over to join her parents in the receiving line, telling everyone that Rupert was delayed by some terribly important assignment and proferring for their inspection the sparkling rock he'd bought her.

Over the next half hour, she got a lot of practice with that story. At seven forty-five she abandoned the receiving line, and was passing through the room, putting on the bravest of faces, and ignoring the whispers that she

448

caught here and there. Her father came over. The plan had been to make speeches at seven-thirty. He was worried that if they didn't do it soon, some people might drift away. His conversation with his daughter was difficult, to say the least. They compromised on doing it at eight.

As eight struck, there was nothing else for it. Her father took her arm and propelled her across the room, to where a microphone had been placed. They stood side by side. Her father held up a hand and around the room, conversations drained away.

'Thank you all very much for coming tonight to celebrate the engagement of our darling daughter, Georgina, to Rupert. We hope you are all having a wonderful time. As some of you may have noticed, sadly Rupert isn't with us yet. He must be stuck in traffic or, more likely, stuck in some meeting. That's the problem with management consultants – they're chained to their desks. Perhaps I should offer a reward to anyone who offers to free him, or can confirm his whereabouts.'

As the sound of the sympathetic laughter died away, a woman's voice called out from the back. 'How much is the reward? I claim it.'

Everyone turned in astonishment. It was a pretty, dark-haired girl standing next to a stocky young man. Georgina, her face screwed tight with rage, pointed imperiously at Primrose.

'That person is a gate crasher. Could someone please ask her to leave?'

Primrose held her ground. 'Oh no, I'm not. I'm the guest of this gentleman. And I know where your fiancé is.'

Georgina gulped. Everyone in the room was consumed with curiosity. Some of them knew Primrose and were aware that this could lead to fireworks. The crowd parted spontaneously, and Primrose marched forward through the gap, heading straight for the microphone. To the visible fury of Georgina, her father stepped back to make way. Primrose adjusted the height.

'Ladies and gentlemen, I'm afraid that the news I bring is not very good. Rupert probably *is* chained as I speak, but not to his desk. I have just heard that he has been detained in Marbella on suspicion of burglary. It's unlikely that for the next couple of years any of us will see him, except Georgina, who I'm sure will move to Spain so she can be near him . . . Well, that's it. Thank you. Enjoy the party.'

As Primrose tried to step back through the stunned crowd, Georgina barred her way and hissed under her breath, 'You utter, fucking cow.'

Primrose smiled sweetly back. 'The moral for you, Georgina, is don't mess with the criminal classes. Good night.'

She pushed her aside, and swept back to Peter. He didn't need a cue and they went out together to collect their coats.

Outside it was freezing. Primrose put her arm through Peter's as they walked up St James's Street. He looked at her.

'D'you have to go into work tomorrow?'

''Fraid so. I've taken so much time off recently, I'll lose my job if I don't.'

'You couldn't go in a bit late?'

'Why?'

'I'd like to take you for a walk somewhere special. In the last few months I've often spent time wandering around there.'

'Where?'

'Can't you guess?'

'Not a clue. Where is it?'

'Primrose Hill.'

'Never heard of it.'

They both laughed. Primrose shuddered and squeezed closer to him. 'God, it's freezing. Fancy a drink?'

'Sounds good. Where shall we go? The Ritz is the nearest, but I don't suppose you feel like going there.'

'Oh, why the hell not? They say when you've fallen off a horse, you should get back in the saddle. In fact, I hear the Ritz has very nice suites. I wonder if there's one free tonight?'

POCKET
BOOKS

BLACK CABS

JOHN McLAREN

Three London cabbies take on the might of
international investment and banking companies as
they attempt to make a killing on the stock market.
Using information that they overhear from indiscreet
clients they have already amassed a tidy sum, but
this could be the big one. . .

Unfortunately, it seems that things are getting out of
hand when a top financial executive is found
murdered in the back of a black cab.

Against their will the cabbies are drawn into
revealing the cover-up which is being perpetrated at
the very top of the banking world.

ISBN 0 7434 4946 0

PRICE £6.99

POCKET
BOOKS

PRESS SEND

JOHN McLAREN

Hilton Kask is a whizz-kid systems inventor on the
brink of a breakthrough with a highly sophisticated
Artificial Intelligence package. The great American
dream is finally within his grasp. Then the
unthinkable happens . . .

A team of venture capitalists unite to blow the dream
out of the water. Then the unthinkable happens . . .
Again.

Hilton dies. *Or does he?*

For his enemies, Hilton has some ambitious plans.
And revenge has never been sweeter than when it
reaches from beyond the grave.

ISBN 0 7434 1493 4

PRICE £6.99

POCKET BOOKS

7TH SENSE

JOHN McLAREN

Calum Buchanan has one driving ambition - to win back the love of the beautiful Marianna. But Marianna has something else on her mind: money. And money is what Calum doesn't have. Yet. Disillusioned, Calum leaves America for the wilds of the Hebrides where he discovers a relative - Morag Buchanan - an eccentric, penniless old witch who possesses a power that, incredibly, could change Calum's fortunes:

7th Sense

But when Calum eagerly exploits this extraordinary power, he attracts the attention of people with very different agendas. He is soon made aware that there are many other, less altruistic, uses for his telepathic powers: the Military, for example, are very interested. And before long, he is plunged into a global whirlpool of intrigue, deception and lethal covert operations with just a fading link to Morag his last chance to save his life . . .

ISBN 0 7434 1494 2

PRICE £6.99

**POCKET
BOOKS**

This book and other **Pocket** titles are available from your book shop or can be ordered direct from the publisher.

☐ 0 7434 4946 0	**Black Cabs**	£6.99
☐ 0 7434 1493 4	**Press Send**	£6.99
☐ 0 7434 1524 8	**Running Rings**	£6.99
☐ 0 7434 1494 2	**7th Sense**	£6.99

Please send cheque or postal order for the value of the book, free postage and packing within the UK; OVERSEAS including Republic of Ireland £1 per book.

OR: Please debit this amount from my:

VISA/ACCESS/MASTERCARD ....

CARD NO ....

EXPIRY DATE...

AMOUNT £ ....

NAME..

ADDRESS..

....

SIGNATURE..

www.simonsays.co.uk

Send orders to: SIMON & SCHUSTER CASH SALES
PO Box 29, Douglas, Isle of Man, IM99 1BQ
Tel: 01624 83600, Fax 01624 670923
www.bookpost.co.uk
Please allow 14 days for delivery.
Prices and availability subject to change without notice.